OF BONES AND SKULLS

SAMANTHA ZIEGLER

For my mother.
It's always been for you.

Content Warnings

This book contains content that may not be suitable for all readers, including:

-Blood and Gore
-Violence and Murder
-Attempted Sexual Assault
-Abuse of Sex Worker
-Suicide
-Loss of a Parent/Sibling
-Substance Abuse

For more details regarding the content, please visit the trigger warnings page on my website:

samanthaziegler.com/trigger-warnings

PLAYLIST

My wonderful friend, Karina Mancillas (AKA Kiza Reads), created a Spotify playlist for *Of Bones and Skulls*. There are far too many songs to list them all, but you can listen to the playlist by following the QR code below.

Trust me, it's phenomenal.

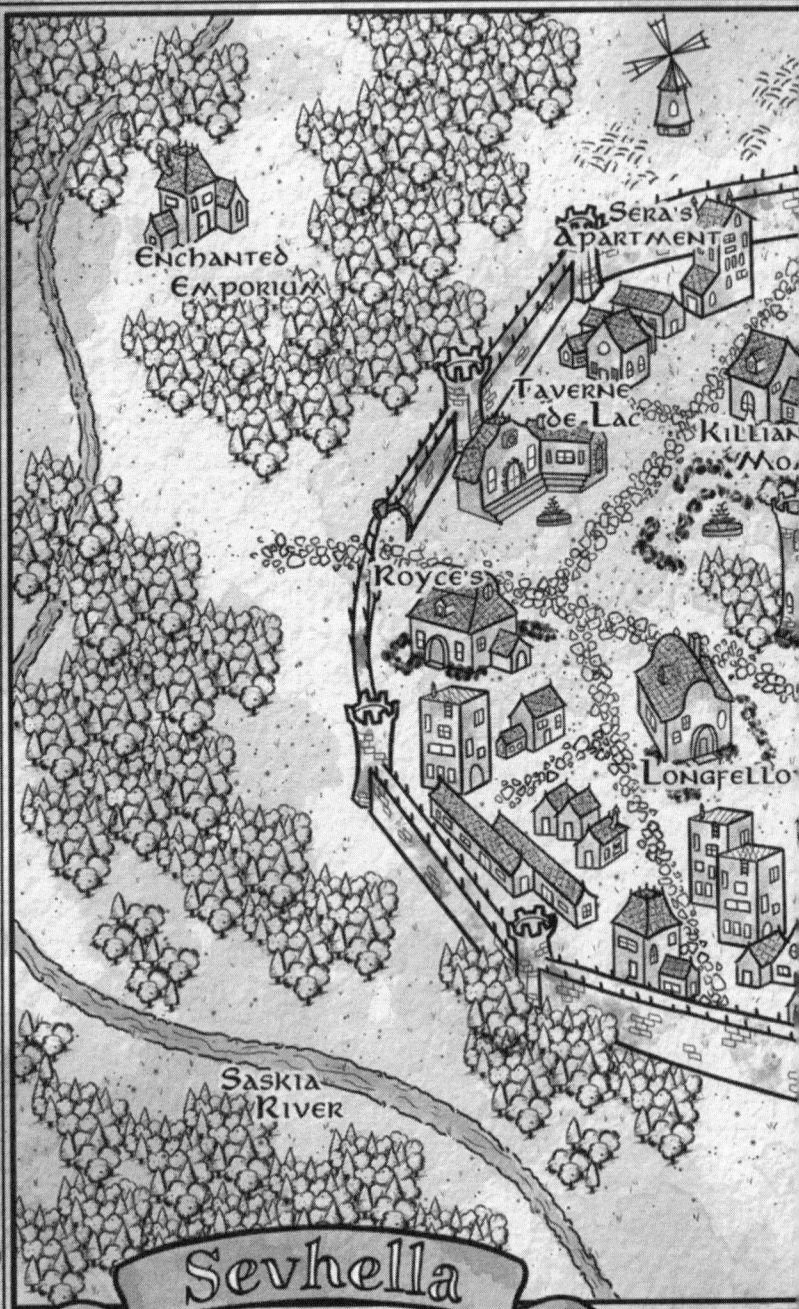

Sevhella

Enchanted Emporium

Sera's Apartment

Taverne de Lac

Killian Mo.

Royce's

Longfello

Saskia River

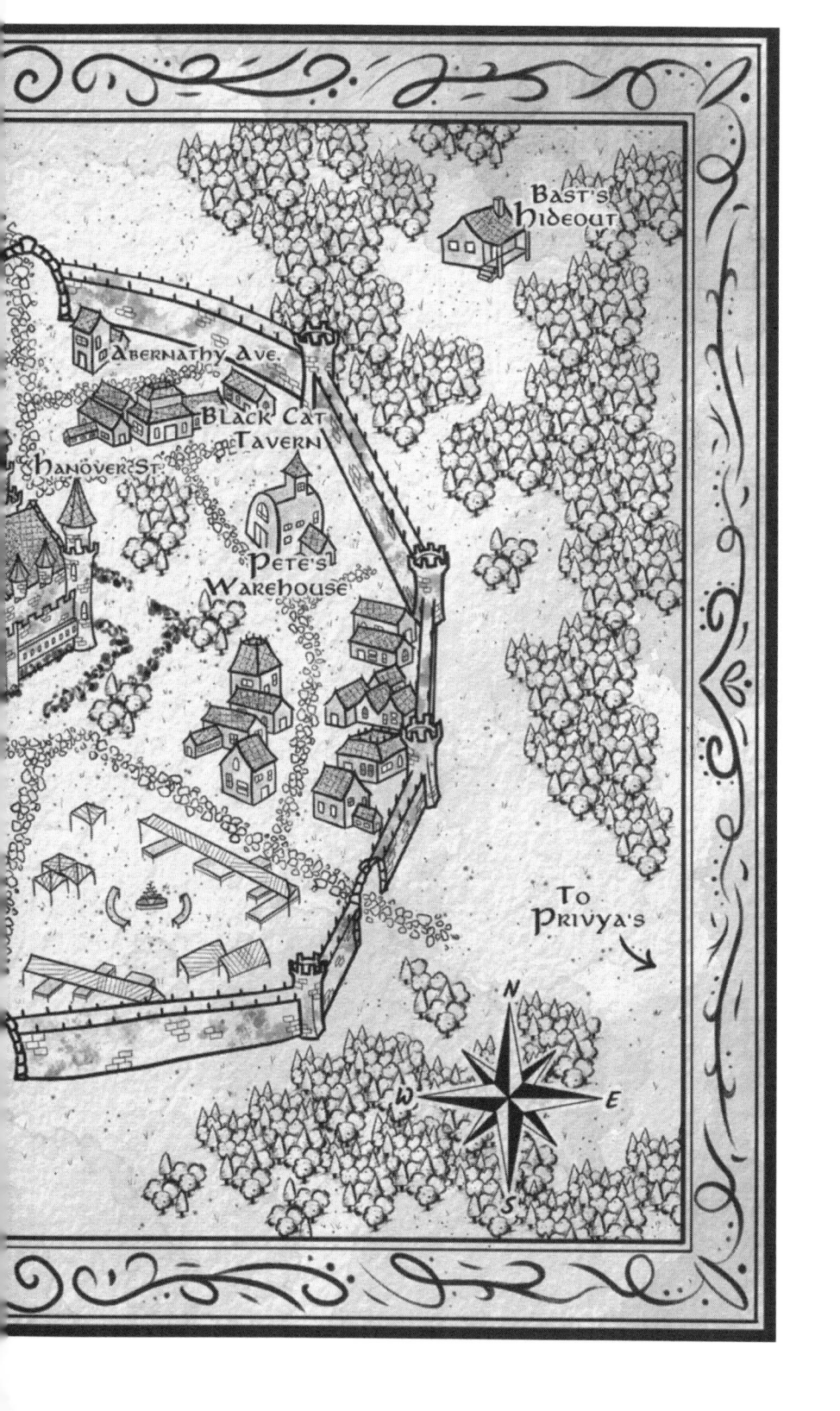

PROLOGUE

K ing Cyril Vandever III was killed in early spring, on a night when the full moon shone brazenly across the sky.

It had been an ordinary day, full of boring meetings discussing the kingdom's economy, military, et cetera, et cetera. In the evening King Cyril dined with his wife, Queen Andrielle, and his son and daughter, the Prince and Princess of Rhodan. After dinner, the royal family played a game of cards while enjoying a vintage mead. After all, it was a time of peace and had been for decades; there was nothing to keep them from taking their leisure.

It was nearly midnight when the king and queen retired to their bedchamber. As always, two guards flanked the doorway to their rooms, and as always, the king merrily wished them goodnight. A lady-in-waiting helped Andrielle undress and brushed her hair while King Cyril readied himself for bed. The servant blew out the candles in the room before leaving the happy couple to their slumber. She was the last person seen exiting the room.

The guards kept their watch as servants and courtiers retired for the evening, and the palace quieted. The candle wax that dripped lazily down the dwindling tapers was the only movement, silent and placid.

A sinister feeling crept through the corridor, sending shivers up the spines of both guards who stood watch outside the royal bedchamber. They met each other's stares, eyes wide and faces pale. Slowly, one of the guards let his gaze slip to the floor. Through the dim candlelight, he could see something oozing out from under the door. A puddle of something—a dark red liquid.

The other guard noticed it too. They exchanged frantic glances before bursting into the room, their swords drawn.

Nothing but darkness and stillness greeted them.

Their footsteps splashed along the floor as they ran to the canopy bed where the king and queen lay sleeping.

"Your Highness!" they shouted. One of the men put a hand on the king to shake him awake, only to draw it back quickly. The king was soaked in the same liquid that covered the floor.

The other guard ran to the curtains and threw them open, letting the moonlight illuminate the room.

The king lay on his back, every inch of his body drenched in blood. There were no cuts, no wounds, only blood bubbling from his lips, seeping from his eyes, nose, and ears—so much blood it had flooded the bed, spilling onto the floor and spreading across the room.

"Dear gods," the guard breathed, while the other moved to inspect the queen.

She was breathing—the calm, slow breaths that accompanied sleep. The guard tried to rouse her, shaking her violently, sending blood sloshing across the bed, but she hardly stirred, a dreamy smile tugging at her lips.

The first guard tore from the room, calling for help as he rushed down the corridor. He returned moments later with a bucket of water and a dozen more guards, all of them ashen and wide-eyed. A few of the men carried candles, and the flickering light only made the scene more horrifying. Someone vomited in the corner of the room.

"Stand back!" ordered the guard holding the bucket. He splashed the water across the queen, waking her in a dreadful panic.

She opened her mouth to curse whoever had just doused her, but the sight of so many men in her bedchamber made her pause. Yet no one, not one single guard, knew what to say to her.

"Cyril?" she whispered, her voice quivering. She reached a hand toward him—and it was then that she noticed the bedding was soaked with more than just water.

She turned to face her husband, the king, and a scream erupted from her lips.

CHAPTER 1

— · —

ELYSE

E lyse glared at the paunchy man who had spent the last ten minutes trying to decide if he should buy a rabbit's foot or a crystal pendant. As she used her mortar and pestle to grind up herbs for a potion, she imagined it was the man's head she was smashing.

He had been so rude to her from the moment he walked into her shoppe. She didn't appreciate the judgmental way his eyes had lingered on the shelves full of potions and hex bags, nor the way they had lingered on her. Still, she'd politely asked him what he was looking for and pointed him toward a table of good luck charms. She'd held back her grimace when he asked, "Is this it?" And when he balked at her prices, she'd even refrained from telling him where he could shove his money. Instead, she reminded him that she was the only reputable vendor of magic paraphernalia in the capital city of Sevhella, but that he was more than welcome to make the twenty-mile trek to Foxboro. That was when she'd excused herself and returned to her workstation.

The stocky man finally made his way over to Elyse and held up the rabbit's foot as evidence of his selection.

"That'll be six and twenty gold pieces," she told him.

"Six and twenty?" the man groused, his pock-marked face contorted into a snarl. "You said it was only two earlier."

Elyse set the mortar and pestle aside and laid her hands flat on the haggard old worktable.

"It is," she explained coolly. "But the vial of poison in your pocket is worth much more."

To his credit, the man hardly blanched at her accusation. With a grumble, he reached his hand into his tattered cloak and pulled out the vial. He set it on the table and slid it toward Elyse, followed by two gold pieces.

"Thank you for your business," she crooned. She even managed a smile.

The man rolled his eyes and waddled toward the exit. As he reached for the doorknob, Elyse gave a delicate flick of her fingers. The latch slid shut, locking the door.

The man cursed and tugged at the latch, but no matter how hard he tried, it didn't budge. Watching him struggle gave Elyse a flutter of satisfaction. She rounded the worktable and slowly, silently on her bare feet, strolled toward the door while the man continued to yank fruitlessly at the handle. She stopped just behind him and let out a quiet, sinister laugh.

"You didn't think you could get off that easy, did you?"

The man leapt at the sound of her voice. He spun around, and his bloodshot eyes widened, frantically taking her in.

"Let me out, you witch," he spat, his voice trembling slightly.

"Unfortunately, I can't let you wander off just yet. No one tries to pull a five-finger discount on me and walks away in one piece." She crossed her arms and tilted her head, pretending to be contemplating her next move.

"It won't happen again," the man sputtered. His back was against the door now, and Elyse watched with delight as his throat bobbed.

"What's a fitting punishment?" she wondered aloud, drumming her fingers along her chin. "Ah, I know. How about I take one of your fingers?"

The man whimpered.

"But not just any finger," she taunted, savoring every word. "A thumb."

"No, please," he cried, spinning back and trying once again to work the latch. The clank of the metal, his blubbering, it was all so terribly pathetic.

"Enough!" Elyse demanded. "*Pollexes aut remotatem.*"

She knew she didn't have to speak the spell aloud for it to work, but she enjoyed the way the words struck horror in her victims.

The man started shouting, flailing like an injured animal and crashing against a nearby shelf. The skin on his thumb swelled and puckered, like a string had been tied around it and was being pulled tighter, tighter, tighter—until the thumb was cut off completely, quick and bloodless, leaving a stump of shriveled skin.

The severed thumb fell to the wood floor with a quiet *thump*—though it was hardly audible over the man's screaming.

"Don't be so dramatic, the spell doesn't hurt that much." Elyse stooped and picked up the thumb. "I'm keeping this," she added as she pocketed it.

The man was holding his wrist, staring at the hand that now only had four fingers. "You *bitch*! I thought the rabbit's foot was supposed to be lucky," he screamed at her.

Elyse couldn't help but laugh. "It is," she called over her shoulder as she sauntered back to her workstation. "You still have one thumb, don't you?"

The man took a step toward her, his good hand balled into a raised fist. "You cu—"

"I suggest you think carefully about what you say, or your tongue will be next," Elyse warned.

The man's nostrils flared as he leveled her with his gaze, but he lowered his fist. He took several heaving breaths before he finally pivoted back to the door. Elyse opened the latch with another flick of her fingers, and the man stormed out of the shoppe, slamming the door behind him.

"What a piece of work," she muttered to herself before returning to her work. The thick, leather-bound ledger already lay open on the table, and Elyse confirmed that the sale had been magically recorded, as all her transactions were. Then she scooped up the gold pieces and deposited them into her black velveteen coin purse, the one her mother had given her so many years ago.

As she so often did, Elyse found herself missing her mother. The Enchanted Emporium had been her pride and joy. Her mother had made it seem so easy—doting on customers, always smiling and telling people to come back and let her know how the love potion or lucky pendant worked out. No one ever haggled with her mother or complained that the spells were too complicated—a grievance Elyse had already heard twice that week. But Elyse didn't have the patience to grovel over customers, to make them feel good about themselves as they bought another vial of tonic that kept them looking young. If they wanted to buy her wares, they'd have to do it on her terms.

Even with all the headaches of running the Emporium, she couldn't imagine her life any other way. Selling potions and relics during the day, practicing magic in the evenings, and retiring to her bedroom above the shoppe each night—it was all she'd ever known. There was too much tying her here, too many memories and responsibilities, to ever dream of anything else.

It was another twenty minutes or so before the chime of the bell hanging over the shoppe door signaled the arrival of another customer.

"How can I help you?" Elyse asked, trying her best to sound friendly toward the man who strolled inside.

This new customer, he was too much. Too tall, too clean, too well dressed. His dark hair was curled in short ringlets with a crisp part along the side, and his face was clean-shaven, revealing smooth mahogany skin. When he smiled at her, he had a dimple on one cheek.

He looked like a do-gooder, and in her line of business, that always meant trouble.

CHAPTER 2

— . —

KILLIAN

K illian hated magic.

Of course, of all the lieutenants in the Royal Guard, he was the one assigned to investigate the mysterious assassination of King Cyril Vandever. He knew it was an honor to be chosen for such a prestigious task, and having known King Cyril well, Killian was determined to avenge his beloved monarch.

He just wished that finding the king's murderer didn't involve dealing with magic wielders. Although most forms of magic were legal as long as taxes were paid and regulations followed, there was still a taboo around it. Normal, everyday people didn't usually indulge in such things as potions and spells. They left those sorts of perversions to the occultists, who preferred to conduct their business in back alleys and seedy taverns.

Of course, witches and sorcerers and the like were human beings—they were just humans who chose to dabble in unnatural pursuits. They were all wicked at their core, a lesson Killian had learned early in life and was only reiterated by King Cyril's murder.

Over the past two days, he'd interviewed four warlocks, two fortune tellers, and one medium. They had all told him that if he wanted to know about the ins and outs of spell work, he needed to travel an hour's ride north of the capital to a little shoppe that sold every magical item imaginable. Apparently the shoppe's owner was a very powerful and resourceful witch—the last sort of person Killian ever wanted to meet.

So there he was in the middle of the forest, hoping to get answers so that he could avenge his beloved king.

The shoppe wasn't as desolate as he'd expected. Flowers lined the stone walkway leading to the entrance, and a wooden sign declared "The Enchanted Emporium" in a quaint scrawl. Still, Killian shuddered at the eerie feeling that seemed to emanate from the property.

He glanced over his shoulder and drew comfort from what he saw: a dozen soldiers on horses were gathered fifty yards off, partially hidden by foliage, ready to spring to action if he didn't come out of the shoppe. This witch he was about to meet was not a suspect—at least, not yet—but one could never be too careful around occultists. He had ordered his men to raid the shoppe if he didn't come out unharmed within twenty minutes, though he hoped it wouldn't come to that.

Killian closed his eyes and let out a long, slow exhale before turning the knob and opening the wooden door.

The inside of the Emporium was a myriad of mismatched tables and shelves, every inch of which was covered in elixirs, jars of teeth and hair, worn leather books, and antique jewelry, among countless other items. The odor of burning incense assaulted him, and he heard the crackling of a fire. He looked to the hearth at the back of the room and found a cauldron that boiled with some sort of putrid green liquid.

It was all so much worse than he'd thought it would be.

He just needed information. Five minutes, maybe ten at the most, and then he could be back outside riding far, far away from this place.

"How can I help you?" called a woman's voice.

Killian turned his gaze to the corner and saw the shopkeeper for the first time. No wonder he hadn't noticed her. She was a petite woman, and her oversized jacquard tunic practically blended in with the disarray of the whole place.

"Just browsing," he said. He pretended to be inspecting whatever was on the table before him—an assortment of jars holding bones of various sizes and shapes—but he continued to watch her from the corner of his eye.

She didn't look like a witch, or at least not like what he'd imagined she'd look like. Her hair was silky and silvery blonde, not coarse and black like he'd expected. She had no warts, no cleft chin, no wayward eye that followed him around the room.

"Nobody travels all the way out here to browse," the shopkeeper said. Though she was a good foot shorter than him, she carried herself in such a way that made her seem much taller. She wore an arrogant smile as she asked, "What is it? Wife caught you cheating again? Need a memory charm to make her forget?"

"No," Killian replied sternly. "I need some information on a spell."

"Ah," the shopkeeper answered as she crossed her arms and leaned against the wall beside her. "Let me guess. You need something to protect your stash of gold. No—" she said with a glance toward his trousers, "something to help below the belt."

So that was how this was going to play out.

The witch's near-black irises glimmered with amusement, and Killian felt the heat of anger burning in his chest. He glared at her, but that only seemed to enthrall her more. *Fucking witches.*

"Are you always this impudent?" he snapped.

"Are you always this prudish?" she snapped right back.

He steeled his expression into an apathetic facade. Don't let her get a rise out of you, he scolded himself. Just get the information you need and go.

That was easier said than done, though. Just being in this shoppe had him on edge.

The shopkeeper hadn't moved from where she leaned against the wall, her gaze still sizing him up, still calculating just how far she could push him.

Finally, he raised his chin and said, "I'm looking for information on a particular spell. One that causes a very nasty, agonizing death."

The shopkeeper raised one eyebrow. "I'm sorry I ever doubted your manhood."

Killian sighed, already tired of her games. "I'm not looking to use it," he explained. "I'm looking for information about how it's conducted, maybe the ingredients used or a list of individuals capable of such magic."

The shopkeeper seemed to consider this request, then asked, "Who was murdered?"

Gods above, he was never going to get his answers.

"That's confidential," he said flatly.

The woman stood straight and sauntered through the shop, wending her way past a tattered armchair and a bookcase that held various household items along with a sign that read "CURSED OBJECTS—BUYER BEWARE." She stopped when she reached the hearth and stirred the simmering liquid, which was now a deep shade of purple.

"Word travels, even all the way out here," she said, condescension coating her tone. "Would this have anything to do with King Cyril's death?"

It was an effort not to flinch at her words. Killian wanted to tell her that confidential meant none of her damn business. He wanted to tell her to keep that man's name out of her wicked mouth. But he needed her to cooperate, so he ceded a single, cool nod.

"I should've known you were in the Guard," she said as she tapped the spoon on the side of the cauldron then set it atop the mantle. She returned to her slackened posture, crossing her arms across her breasts in what appeared to be her usual stance. "Sergeant?"

"Lieutenant," Killian corrected.

The shopkeeper looked him up and down again, no doubt trying to discern his age and how a man so young had risen to the rank of lieutenant.

"How'd the king die?" she asked casually.

"Suffocated by his own blood."

The witch cocked her head to the side. "Like a slit throat? That doesn't exactly sound supernatural."

"No." Killian cleared his throat. "The amount of blood in his body multiplied until it filled every organ and he drowned, all while his wife slept peacefully next to him. There was no one in or out of the room, no sounds, nothing unusual at all until the guards standing watch in the corridor noticed the blood spilling out from under the door."

The shopkeeper shuddered—actually shuddered. Killian couldn't help but furrow his brows. Who was this witch who paled at the mention of blood?

"I know of a spell like that," she said, strolling to a nearby bookshelf. Her fingers traced the spines down a row of books until she found the one she was looking for and plucked it from its place on the shelf. She thumbed through the pages as she walked back to her workstation, then grabbed a piece of blank parchment, scrawled four lines on the paper, and handed it to him. "It doesn't take many ingredients, but they're incredibly rare. And you have to be in close proximity to conduct the spell. So the killer would have been in the room."

"Thanks," Killian said, a bit shocked that he was actually getting some answers. He took the parchment from her and looked it over, reading the ingredients aloud.

Blood of an ogre
Fae dust
Molten rock
Bones of a virgin

"And not just any bones," the shopkeeper clarified. "Her ring finger bones."

Killian held back a sigh. "Do you sell these things?"

"Of course," she scoffed.

"Have you sold any . . . fae dust lately?" Gods, this whole thing was ridiculous.

The shopkeeper bit her lip as she thought. "I haven't sold any of those things lately." She tapped her fingers on a book that lay open on her worktable. The book was enormous, nearly as big as her. "I could check my ledger, though. It goes back six months."

"Actually, Miss . . ."

"Elyse," she said curtly. "I don't have a family name."

"Okay, Elyse," Killian said, curbing his annoyance. She was being helpful, he reminded himself. "I'll be needing to take that ledger into evidence."

She laughed, a cocky sort of chuckle, and slid the book across the worn table toward him. "You're more than welcome to, but it's all written in code. Witch's tradition."

Killian peered down at the massive book. Sure enough, the letters were scrambled, making it completely indecipherable.

This time, he did sigh. "Well, I'm going to have to insist that you review the transactions and let me know of any individuals who have purchased any of those items."

"Do I have a choice?" Elyse asked coolly.

"No," he said with a smile. He relished telling her no.

She folded her arms again, but her face conveyed resignation. "Is that all?"

"Have you heard anything suspicious lately?"

She scoffed and shook her head indignantly. "My whole business is suspicious. But no, nothing treasonous."

"What about two nights ago? Did you see or hear anything treasonous?"

"No, nothing at all."

He could tell by the acid in her tone that she was growing tired of his company. He didn't care.

"And where were you two nights ago?" he asked, his eyes pinning her down.

She was an obvious suspect. She certainly had the means to commit the murder. For a moment he let himself fantasize about arresting her, and wiping that damn smirk off her lips. But truly, he could think of no motive she would have for killing the king. And the way she had shuddered at the details of his death . . .

"Why don't you just come out and ask me if I did it?" Elyse spat. "I was at the same place I go every full moon, in the woods outside the city with my friend, Madam Sera."

"Doing what?" Killian pressed without missing a beat.

"A ritual if you must know." Her dark eyes never left his as she spoke.

"Very well," he said. "Write down her address and I'll verify your alibi."

Elyse obliged, though she huffed as she scribbled down the address on a piece of parchment.

"Anything else?" she asked in a fake simper.

He hated what he was about to ask, hated that he would have to crawl further into this grimy world of magic wielders.

"Yes, actually. If you were investigating a supernatural murder, where would you go to learn more information? Perhaps a pub, or a meeting?"

Elyse rolled her eyes, then gave him a look as if to say he couldn't be serious. When Killian didn't change his expression, she said, "Black Cat Tavern. All the loose-lipped scumbags go there."

Killian was about to say thank you when she added, "But they'd never let *you* in."

Her gaze told him that he irritated her just as much as she irritated him—which was very, very much. If he was going to have to suffer, then maybe he could at least find joy in her suffering. Misery does love company.

"What if I was escorted there by an esteemed member of the occultist community?" he asked.

"No" was her immediate response.

Killian took a step toward her and stood tall, letting himself tower over her. His fingers grazed the pages of her ledger.

"This is quite thorough record keeping," he drawled. "And it looks like business has been good."

"What's your point?" she grumbled back.

"Well, Ms. Elyse *Crenshaw.*" She shivered at the mention of her surname, and Killian let a smile grace his lips. "Before I came here, I checked the auditor's records. It appears you've paid a mere forty gold pieces in taxes over the last five years."

"Ten percent, just like everyone else," she said calmly, though her eyes drifted toward the ledger.

"I'm sure," he purred. "Let's say you accompany me to the tavern tomorrow, and I won't drag you and this monster of a book down to the dungeons for tax evasion and let you suffer in a cell until the auditor is able to decipher this code of yours and confirm what you say is true."

A long, tense silence passed. Elyse's nose wrinkled as she glowered at him, and Killian swore he could hear her teeth grinding. He was certain she was imagining ways to torment him, trying to decide which of the hundreds of potions and cursed objects she owned would cause him the most anguish. He couldn't help but delight in her blatant frustration.

"Fine," she eventually growled. "Now buy something and get out."

He had won their little pissing match, and she knew it. Her insistence that he buy something, that he compensate her for her time, was a petty demand. But he had won, so he didn't mind indulging.

He picked up the nearest bottle—a vial of black liquid labeled "ANTI-HEX POTION." As much as he loathed the idea, the potion might actually come in handy someday. Maybe even someday soon.

"How much?" he asked, holding the bottle for her to see.

"Four silvers."

Killian let out a low whistle as he fished a gold piece out of his pocket. He tossed it to her, and she caught it, then quickly set it on the worktable as if it carried a disease.

"Keep the change," he mumbled over his shoulder. He was almost at the door when Elyse called out.

"Lieutenant?"

He stopped, taking his time as he turned back to face her.

She looked every bit like the witch she was as she shot him a cunning glare. "Next time, leave the cavalry at home." Her voice was gruff, her annoyance visceral.

How had she known? He did indeed have a small cavalry of soldiers waiting outside, but they were far off, scattered behind trees and brush.

He realized the futility of his wonder. Of course she would know. She had probably known who he was the entire time but played along, letting him think he had the upper hand.

"I'll meet you tomorrow outside the tavern at sundown," he said, no longer bothering to mask his disgust.

Then he strode to the door and flung it open, all too eager to leave.

CHAPTER 3

— · —

ELYSE

The door slammed shut behind the lieutenant.

"Bat-brained twat," Elyse muttered under her breath.

She flipped through the pages of the ledger. It would take hours to go through it all, and she was almost positive no one had bought any of the ingredients needed for the spell in the last six months. No, she certainly would have remembered that.

She scratched absentmindedly at her forearm, and when the itch didn't subside, she stomped across the shoppe to the door at the back that concealed a staircase. Up the wooden stairs she went, grumbling and scratching until she reached her small bedroom. She trudged to the bedside table where she kept a jar of ointment, and rolled up her sleeve, revealing an angry patch of red, festering skin. The ointment soothed and cooled the nasty papules, but she knew it was only a temporary relief. The itch would return, a constant reminder of her disease.

It was spreading more and more quickly. A few months ago, the rash was nothing but a spot of dry skin. She hadn't given it much thought until her skin had begun to swell and discolor, and she realized the gravity of the situation. Every day she checked her forearm, studying it to see if the disease had spread overnight. And every few days, she was disheartened to find that it had.

She knew how it would progress. Eventually the disease, known as widow's decay, would make its way to her internal organs, eating away at them, until she would die, just as her mother had several years ago.

Her mother had given her everything–life, companionship, the shoppe. It was only fitting that she passed along her cause of death as well.

When her mother had first noticed the rash, she and Elyse sought out every healer in the Sevhella. They'd all said the same thing, that there was no cure for widow's decay. Even her mother's vast collection of spell books couldn't offer any help, and eventually she succumbed to the disease, leaving Elyse alone.

And now, it seemed Elyse would suffer the same fate. The fear of the unknown hung over her every day, as much as she wanted to ignore it. She tried to take comfort in the fact that her troubled soul might finally be at peace, or that she might be reunited with her mother. But most of the time she was in denial, rejecting the notion that her life would soon end.

When the ointment was completely absorbed into her skin, she put the lid back on the jar and walked to the window. Pushing back the mossy green curtains, she peered outside to the surrounding forest. There was a whole world out there, and she had experienced only a tiny part of it. Yet if the customers that tramped into her store day in and day out were any indication of how the rest of the population carried themselves, she wanted nothing to do with it. If people had half the arrogance of that lieutenant, barging in with his accusations, she would stay right there in her cozy cottage.

Her mind wandered back to the conversation with the lieutenant, replaying every quip and jab. How dare that man bring a dozen soldiers onto her property. And when he'd blackmailed her for tax evasion, she'd had to stop herself from throwing every hex in the book at him. But she knew it would only cause more trouble. Those soldiers outside would have retaliated, and though she probably could have taken them easily enough, she would have had to flee, to leave her shoppe behind . . . It was easier just to spend one evening with him at the tavern. One wretched evening.

Besides, the look on his face when she'd revealed she knew about the soldiers, that she'd known who he was all along, was worth more than the most expensive spell book in the whole shoppe.

CHAPTER 4

—·—

KILLIAN

Killian checked the address of the building in front of him against the address Elyse had written down. They were the same.

Calling it a "building" was generous. The exterior wood was rotting away, and the entire two-story structure had a lean to it. None of the other housing complexes on the shabby dirt road were any better, and there was not a soul to be found. Just a gentle stirring of wind that fluttered the laundry that lay drying in the windows.

"Freaky," said the man standing next to Killian. Manny was Killian's second in command. They both wore the uniform of the Royal Guard—black boots, black trousers, black jerkin—but otherwise they looked nothing alike. Where Killian was tall and lean, Manny was several inches shorter, and his muscles were more pronounced. His blond hair was pulled into a hastily tied bun while Killian's dark curls were parted and neatly combed. Manny's green eyes held a sense of whimsy, whereas Killian's held nothing but disdain.

"Let's get this over with," Killian growled as he marched toward the entrance. His meeting with the witch had left him in a bitter mood, and if the building's tattered appearance was any indication, this next meeting wouldn't likely be much better.

Inside, the building was at least somewhat nicer. Sconces lit the walls, casting flickering shadows in every direction, and an oversized damask rug welcomed their footsteps. Directly across from the entrance was an oak door with a metal number "1" affixed to its front.

"We need apartment thirteen," Killian groaned, glancing at the rickety staircase to the left.

"There are thirteen apartments in this place?" Manny asked. He sounded more intrigued than skeptical.

They made their way up the wooden stairs, each step creaking louder than the last. When they reached the second floor, the landing held another damask rug and a single door labeled "2". Across the landing was another wooden staircase ascending to another floor.

The men exchanged a look.

"Didn't this place look like it only had two stories from the outside?" Manny wondered aloud.

Killian didn't bother responding as he trudged across the landing and up the stairs.

Eleven stories later, the men arrived at the top floor. They breathed heavily, resting their palms on their thighs as they took in the landing.

There was no number labeling the apartment. There wasn't even a door. Instead, iridescent beads dangled across the threshold. Killian could smell incense wafting into the hallway.

Great.

He knocked awkwardly on the door frame, unsure what the protocol was. "Madam Sera?" he called. When no reply came, he passed through the jangling beads and into the apartment.

The room was . . . spacious. And bright. The walls were intact, every surface immaculate and delicately decorated with stylish trinkets. Rich cerulean curtains framed a window on the far wall, where colorful potted flowers stretched toward the sunlight.

A woman emerged from a door on the right—or rather, from a threshold decorated with more beads. She was slender and tall, with silky, straight black hair that hung to her waist. Her features were soft and kind, and so different from the shrewd witch he'd just endured. If Killian had to guess, her family hailed from Otsuk, a lesser kingdom known for its beautiful women with dark hair and hooded eyes.

"Hello, gentlemen," she called almost dreamily.

"Madam Sera?" Killian asked.

She smiled, and he interpreted it as affirmation.

"I'm Lieutenant Southwick and this is my second in command. We'd like to ask you a few questions about the other night."

Madam Sera padded to the round table that served as the centerpiece to the room, her long pink dress trailing behind her. She seated herself in a velvet tufted chair with tasseled trim, all the while gazing at Killian through her black lashes. Every movement she made had a sense of both drama and leisure.

"Please, be seated," she offered with a wave of her alabaster hand.

Killian turned to Manny with a look of irritation at the woman's flamboyance, but Manny was already pushing past him to sit at the table. Killian sank into the chair across from Madam Sera, and begrudgingly admitted to himself that the upholstered cushion was actually quite comfortable.

"Madam Sera, where were you—" he began, but she interjected.

"I will tell you everything you wish to know," she said, "*after* your reading."

She produced a deck of tarot cards from somewhere within the many layers of fabric that enveloped her frail figure.

She can't be serious, Killian thought. What was it with these people? First the witch had made him buy something, and now the clairvoyant was making him sit through . . . whatever this was.

"Let me guess," he said with a sigh. "This reading isn't free."

She tilted her head to the side and looked at him the way an adult might look at a child when they've said something ridiculous yet endearing.

"Why would I give such valuable information away for free? It will be three silver pieces," she told them. "Each."

24

Every person in this gods-damned city was going to drive him mad. But he needed her cooperation, and his encounter with Elyse had drained him of any fight. At least Madam Sera was pleasant. She hadn't challenged his manhood.

"I've got this one, boss," Manny said as he pulled a handful of silver coins from his purse. He slid them across the smooth table to Madam Sera, who winked at him in return.

She spread the cards across the table, her fingers lovingly caressing each one. The cards were a gradient of lavender and baby blue, and though they were worn, they radiated with the same beauty as the rest of the apartment. Manny lifted his hand to select a card, but Madam Sera tsked at him.

"The lieutenant first," she demanded, giving no further explanation.

Killian rolled his eyes and selected the card directly in front of him. He flipped it over and tossed it across the table where it slid, bumping into its siblings. Depicted on its face was a man clad in leggings and a puffy jerkin, his leg kicked back and arms spread wide, like he was dancing. Beneath the illustration, "The Fool" was scrawled in swirling letters.

Manny snorted a laugh.

"Oooh, the Fool!" Madam Sera cried, sounding all too delighted.

Killian frowned. There was nothing *foolish* about him. He had been top of his recruitment class when he joined the Royal Guard, though that didn't say much considering the brawny buffoons that usually joined the Guard. Still, he was a lieutenant, a capable man, a man who saved his money and handled his ale and occasionally even read books.

"Wait 'til I tell the guys about this," Manny laughed.

"The Fool is nothing to joke about," Madam Sera urged him. "It signifies the start of a journey, the naïveté of what is ahead. We are all Fools many times in our lives."

Killian was grateful he didn't believe in such things. The only "journey" he wanted to take was a promotion to Captain, but that wouldn't come for another few years at least.

"My turn," Manny said. His hand hovered above the cards, his fingers dancing with anticipation. He slid his hand to the left, to the right, back to the left—

"Just pick one," Killian barked.

Manny closed his eyes and blindly felt the cards until he selected the perfect one. Slowly, he turned it over.

"The Queen of Swords," he announced.

Killian looked at the picture. A beautiful and dignified-looking woman sat on a throne, a crown atop her head and a long sword across her lap.

"And a very pretty queen you are," Killian said with a smile.

"Thank you, Fool," Manny replied in a sophisticated lilt.

"This speaks volumes about your maturity," Madam Sera explained.

Killian started to laugh but stifled it with a cough. He didn't think anyone had ever applauded Manny's maturity before. Having grown up on the streets of Sevhella, Manny had been forced at a young age to steal for survival, conning anyone who would listen to him. He was only caught stealing once, when he was eighteen. Killian's own father, a captain in the Royal Guard at the time, told Manny he could either go to prison, or put his wits and covert skills to use by joining the Guard.

Manny had happily joined. He'd said he'd always loved conning the wicked, tricking them and taking that which they didn't deserve. He'd told Captain Southwick that being in the Guard would be the same, just with a sword and a uniform. And while he was damn good at his job, he'd never conducted himself with any sort of dignity. Killian often told him he'd missed his calling as a court jester.

Sera ignored Killian's snide laughter and continued explaining with enthusiasm. "The Queen of Swords signifies someone who acts rationally while acknowledging the desires of their heart. Someone who has severed ties with things that bring them pain. Someone or one who is progressing forward."

"Well," Manny said. He leaned back in his chair and crossed his arms, a smug grin meeting his lips. "I can't argue with that."

Killian shook his head at his friend, then turned his focus on Sera. "Will you answer our questions now?" he asked.

Madam Sera gathered the cards and shuffled them idly in her hands.

"You wish to know about my evening two nights ago? On the full moon?"

Was she merely putting the pieces together? After all, two members of the Royal Guard had shown up at her apartment two days after the death of the king. Or was this a display of her talents?

"Yes," Killian answered. "How did you know?"

Sera continued shuffling the cards. "It's obvious, isn't it? Everyone knows the king was murdered that night. Anyway, I was doing the same thing I do every full moon—performing a ritual with my blessed sister, the one you called on earlier today."

Blessed sister? There was nothing blessed about Elyse. And Killian certainly didn't like the way she spoke knowingly of his own whereabouts.

"What is this ritual?" Manny chimed in.

Madam Sera smiled from one side of her mouth. "It is a beautiful ceremony. A ritual of gratitude to the divine mother, the one who grants us our powers. We cover ourselves in lamb's blood and dance naked."

Manny's mouth hung slack while Killian rolled his eyes. He knew his friend was calculating the number of days until the next full moon.

"So, Elyse was with you for the whole night?" Killian asked.

"Of course," Madam Sera replied. "The ritual lasts from dusk until dawn."

Killian kept his face neutral as he contemplated her words. There was, of course, the possibility the fortune teller was lying, that she was covering for her friend, but Killian doubted it. For all his worth, he couldn't think of any way these two women would benefit from the death of the king.

Manny leaned forward, resting his forearms on the table. "Have you heard anything unusual lately? Anything that might be related to the king's death?"

"I hear things of an unusual nature nearly every hour of the day," Madam Sera said. Her eyes glazed over, as if she was visualizing the strange encounters. "I hear souls calling to their loved ones. I see futures segmenting into infinite possibilities. But I do not see anything that will assist you."

What a load of shit.

"I think we're done here," Killian said, standing from his chair.

Manny cleared his throat and stood as well. "It was a pleasure to meet you, Madam," he said with a bow.

"Don't be strangers, boys," Madam Sera called as they led themselves back through the curtain of beads and into the rundown hallway.

Killian gave Manny a look that told him not to say a word until they were outside the building, so down, down, down the twelve flights of stairs they went.

"You don't think it was that witch—Elyse—do you?" Manny asked once they were back on the street. It was still as empty as before, but now thunder rumbled overhead.

"No, I don't." Killian answered as he flipped up the collar of his jerkin and headed down the street. "She has no reason to kill the king. That alibi was enough to confirm her innocence in my mind."

Manny didn't say anything. The two men rounded a street corner and found themselves back among decent society, with children running through the dirt road and mothers bustling after them.

"Is she blonde?" Manny asked, skepticism in his voice.

Killian leveled his gaze on his friend. "Who?" he asked, though he already knew the answer.

"Elyse," Manny obliged him. "Is she blonde?"

Elyse's silvery-blonde hair and the way it framed her haughty face flashed in Killian's mind. "What are you getting at, brother?"

Their eyes met but Manny quickly looked away. Killian didn't appreciate the insinuation. Her hair color meant nothing. Yes, he may have a soft spot for blondes, a soft spot that Manny had picked up on after many nights spent at the tavern together chasing maidens. But he hadn't made it to lieutenant by letting pretty girls—no matter their hair color—distract him from his job. And never, ever a witch.

"Nothing," Manny said, staring straight ahead. "Nothing at all."

CHAPTER 5

— • —

ELYSE

D usk captivated the sky, painting the horizon a glowing ripple of coral and indigo. The air was warm and humid from the early spring showers that had drizzled on and off that day. Elyse walked through the forest surrounding her cottage, toward the perimeter of the wards that prevented anyone from magicking themselves in or out of the property. As she walked, the birds stopped their twittering to fly away, and the squirrels scurried into their hiding places.

A tingle passed over Elyse as she stepped through the wards, and with a gloved hand, she pulled a small vial of bright blue liquid from the pocket of her cloak. She toyed with the vial for a moment, contemplating if she wanted to do this—if she truly wanted to spend an evening at a seedy tavern surrounded by arrogant, untalented warlocks and a lieutenant who irritated her. The answer, of course, was no. She would rather slave over a cauldron or memorize spells. But what choice did she really have? Going to the tavern tonight was the best solution—far easier than evading the lieutenant, fleeing the capital, and setting up shop in some unknown city. With a scowl, she threw the vial on the ground, and it exploded into a vibrant blue smoke.

Hanover Street, she said in her mind over and over, picturing an alleyway near the Black Cat Tavern.

The blue smoke faded into wispy tendrils that floated upward, revealing a small, dingy space between two brick buildings. Elyse straightened her cloak and traipsed down the alley toward the busy street.

Vendors of all manner were closing up their shops, stowing away their goods in their wagons. An old woman stood in the doorway of an inn, leaning on her broom while talking with another old crone. A quartet of young men exited a pub, moving together in a stumbling group, bellowing some drinking shanty.

As she ambled down the street, Elyse scratched absentmindedly at the rash on her arm, which was covered by her elbow-length gloves. She searched for the lieutenant among the many busy citizens, but she didn't see him. The sun hadn't set fully yet, so she was a few minutes early, but she had no doubt that the lieutenant would be waiting for her, tapping his foot and checking his timepiece. He seemed like the overly punctual type.

Then she spotted his curly, dark hair. It was no wonder she hadn't spotted him sooner—he was hardly recognizable. He wore a black tunic with a ragged brown vest over top. His leggings were torn, and his black boots were muddy and well worn, not the shined and polished ones he'd donned before. His hair was somewhat disheveled and he'd even let his stubble grow out.

He scanned the crowd, no doubt looking for troublemakers that he could throw to the gallows. When he spotted her, his eyes narrowed, then his lips pursed. Elyse imagined he was taking in her appearance the same way she'd taken in his—with surprised amusement.

"Lieutenant," she greeted him brusquely.

"Ms. Crenshaw," he replied in the same fashion.

"It's Elyse," she corrected, enunciating each syllable for him.

He smirked in a way that told her he'd been looking forward to calling her by her hated surname all day.

"And what's your name? You never told me," she said.

There was a pause, a long pause where the lieutenant stared at her, likely determining how much he could trust her.

Finally, he said, "Killian."

"Killian," Elyse repeated. She'd expected something much plainer, like John or Lucas. "Well not tonight, you're not. Tonight, you're Lou."

"Lou?" he asked. "Is that short for—"

"—lieutenant? Yes. Brilliant, isn't it?"

It may have been her imagination, but she thought she saw a flicker of a smile on his lips.

"How does it feel to be one of us tonight, Lou?" she asked, her eyes roaming over him once again. "You certainly look the part."

"Horrid," he replied, his expression grim. "Let's just get this over with, shall we?"

"Agreed. But there's one thing we need to do first." She fished a vial of clear liquid from her cloak, unstopped the vial, and drained half of it, shuddering slightly at the bitter taste. Then she held the tiny bottle out to Killian.

He didn't budge.

Elyse sighed. "If you want to get information out of people, you'll need to fit in. And that means drinking."

"I know how to get information out of people," he retorted.

"And drinking leads to memory loss and poor decisions," she added, putting her hand on her hip.

"I know how to hold my liquor, if that's what you're insinuating," he drawled, arrogance practically oozing out of him.

Elyse rolled her eyes. Did everything with him have to be so damn difficult? "This tavern doesn't serve normal ale and wine. It's considerably stronger than what you *regular folk* drink." She spat the words *regular folk*.

Killian let out a huff and then crossed his arms. "I'm not drinking anything a witch gives me."

Elyse shook her head. Was he dense?

"Who do you think will be serving your drinks tonight?" she asked, her tone full of incredulity.

But Killian didn't concede an inch. "I'm not drinking that potion." He glared down at her, and she was acutely aware of just how tall he was, how much physical power was hidden away beneath that tunic.

"Fine," she spouted, tucking the remainder of the potion back into her cloak. "There's no weapons allowed in the tavern, but I always keep a knife in my boot as a precaution."

"As do I," Killian said with a hint of a smirk.

Elyse gave him an appreciative look. Finally, something they could agree on.

They said no more as they disappeared down a shadowed alley and back behind a brick building. A rusty metal staircase led down into a grimy, puddle-filled space with an iron door at the bottom. Elyse could practically feel Killian's judgment, and she was certain if she turned back to look at him, his nose would be wrinkled in disgust.

She gathered up her long skirt and stepped carefully down each slippery step. When they reached the bottom, she lifted a hand and knocked once, then twice, then four times.

An eye-level slot in the door slid open, and a grizzled face peered out. The man behind the door scowled, but then his haggard eyes lit up.

"Elyse! It's been months. If it wasn't for folks bringing in your products night after night, I'd've thought you were dead."

Elyse put on a fake smile. Well, half fake. She did somewhat enjoy the notoriety.

"Charming as ever, Camus," she replied. "Now are you going to let us in?"

"Maybe," Camus answered, his eyes shifting to Killian. "Who's your friend?"

Elyse turned toward the lieutenant, and this time her smile was entirely fake. She slipped one hand around his waist and used the other to slide a gloved finger down his jawline, all the way from his ear to his chin. Even as exquisite as he was, touching him felt revolting, but she forced herself to pretend to enjoy it. Besides, there was added benefit of knowing the gesture probably made Killian even more uncomfortable.

"Oh him?" she purred. "I wouldn't say friend. He's more like . . . a pet."

To her surprise, Killian leaned into her touch. His breath even caught—ever so slightly. He was a better actor than she'd pinned him to be.

"Of course." Camus sounded flustered on the other side of the door. The slot shut abruptly and the door creaked open.

Elyse let go of the lieutenant and paraded through the doorway. Killian followed closely behind—closer than she would have liked.

The cramped breezeway was dank, and their footsteps echoed off the brick walls. At the end of the long hallway was another iron door, and Elyse stopped just before it, shooting Killian an expectant look.

"It's polite for a gentleman to hold the door for a lady," she explained in a low voice so Camus couldn't hear.

Killian stood rigidly in place.

"It would be *strange*," she urged through gritted teeth, "for me to be seen opening the door for myself when you're here, my pet. And you don't want to seem *strange*, do you?" She cocked her head to the side and narrowed her eyes on him. Could he not put his pride away for one hour?

Killian made a noise somewhere between a sigh and a groan before he grasped the knob and pulled the door open. Elyse grinned in her triumph, and at the last moment she slipped her hand into Killian's. Together, they entered the tavern.

CHAPTER 6

─ ⋅ ─

KILLIAN

At first glance, the tavern appeared to be a normal underground pub where lowlifes gathered for celebrations, black market dealings, and bar fights. Patrons were seated at a bar along the far wall, sipping their ale from pewter mugs, and various other customers littered the tables, grumbling to one another about this or that.

But then Killian looked more closely.

The man at the nearest table had elongated incisors, and he sipped a red liquid that was far too thick to be wine. Another table held three men who looked identical, down to the scars that marked their faces from their eyes to the corner of their lips. And in the corner, an upright piano trilled a jolly tune—though no one sat before it.

Elyse squeezed Killian's hand as she leaned toward him. Years of training kept him from backing away or cringing. "Find us a table," she murmured in his ear. "I'll get us drinks."

Before he could tell her that he didn't take orders from her, she sauntered away. As Killian made his way to a table, he noticed how everyone in the tavern seemed to watch Elyse. Some smiled and waved at her, greeting her with a sort of zealous enthusiasm, while others seemed to shrink into themselves, hiding away from her.

Apparently, she had quite the reputation. Camus was happy to see her, and he hadn't even batted an eye when she introduced Killian as her "pet"—as if that weren't completely despicable. What did that even mean? That he was under some spell, forced to grovel for her in exchange for affection? Or was he supposed to be some sort of follower of hers, enthralled by her power? Whatever it meant, he wanted no part of it.

Killian picked one of the three empty tables and sat down. The chair wobbled. The table wobbled more. Killian held in his sigh. All he could do was hope the ale would at least be decent, and that one of these miscreants would give him useful information.

He watched as Elyse chatted with the bartender, an older man with an eye patch. She seemed at ease, and if he weren't so certain that it was impossible, he would have guessed she was actually being friendly. The bartender said something, and Elyse threw her head back and laughed, her silvery hair dangling behind her.

He wondered if her laughter was genuine. She'd already proven herself to be quite the actress—first when she pretended she didn't know he was in the Royal Guard, and then again tonight when she sidled up close to him and caressed his cheek. She had done it as if it was nothing, as if it was a game and she was trying to see if he would recoil.

Truthfully, it was hard not to flinch at her touch, but he was a trained soldier, practiced at deception. Nothing about this night would be easy, but there was no doubt in his mind that he would be able to convince them all just how comfortable he was around magic.

Alcohol would help. What was taking Elyse so long? She had just picked up two steins and was turning to head to the table. As she walked, her black velvet cloak flowed behind her, exposing the pale skin of her upper arms. Her black velvet gloves, which ran from her fingertips to just above her elbows, contrasted starkly with her ivory coloring.

As a reflex, Killian stood and pulled the chair out for her as she plunked the two steins down on the table.

"I hope you like ale," she said, then plopped herself into her seat, not bothering to thank him for pulling out her chair.

Killian took his seat again. "Was something funny?" he asked.

Elyse looked at him curiously as she took a sip from her mug, then realization gleamed in her eyes.

"Oh, yeah. Thomas, the bartender—he called you a pretty boy," she said casually.

He looked back to the bar to see Thomas watching him. When their eyes met, Thomas puckered his lips, sending a kiss in Killian's direction.

Killian shuddered and quickly looked away. "I can't tell if he's into me or if he's mocking me."

"That's kind of his thing," she explained. "Hopefully the former. He hears a lot of gossip, maybe the two of you can discuss it over dinner," she said with a wink.

Killian shot her a nasty look. She was right about one thing, though. He was on a mission to get information, and the sooner he got it, the sooner he could leave.

"Drink," Elyse urged him, nodding at his mug. "You're too tense."

He thought he was being rather cool given the situation, but then he noticed his leg bouncing wildly beneath the table. He abruptly stopped the bouncing and reached for the ale.

"You'd be tense too if Old One-Eye was blowing you kisses," he quipped.

And then she laughed again, her chest rising and falling with each chuckle.

"Old One-Eye. I like that." She took another sip, a smile still tugging at her lips.

"Well, hello there," called a voice from behind Killian. A soft, breathy voice. One he knew.

Madam Sera rounded the table and came into view. She must have just entered because there was no way he would have missed her before. She wore a white gown with pale blue accents and a yellow scarf tied around her head, her outfit so at odds with all the black and leather in the room.

"Sera!" Elyse smiled genuinely as she stood and embraced her friend. "Please join us. I don't think I can handle him alone," she added with a snide glance at Killian.

Sera turned to Killian and offered him her hand, and he promptly stood, took her hand in his, and planted a brief kiss on the back of it.

"I didn't know you visited this establishment, Lieu—" she began, but Elyse cut her off.

"Lou," she said, perhaps a bit too loudly. "Yes, *Lou* here has never actually been to the Black Cat before. I brought him here as a treat."

"How lovely," Sera replied, her eyes darting between the two of them. Then she faced Elyse. "Don't worry, darling, I'll be back as soon as I fetch myself a drink."

She waltzed away toward the bar, and Elyse and Killian resumed their places at the table.

"Did you tell her to come tonight?" Killian asked in an agitated whisper. It seemed like something she would do—ganging up on him by inviting her friend.

"No," Elyse whispered back. "But this is probably a good thing for you. She's better with people than both of us combined."

"Speak for yourself," Killian said. He leaned back in his chair and surveyed the room. When he caught the eye of a woman with curly red hair, he smiled at her casually, lifting his mug in greeting.

The woman wrinkled her nose, stood from her seat, and walked promptly toward the exit.

Killian gritted his teeth as he watched her go. In a *normal* pub with *normal* people, that would have been more than enough to send a girl into a fit of giggles. This place was foreign to him.

He looked to Elyse to see if she'd noticed the exchange, and the way she pursed her lips to keep from laughing told him she had, indeed, witnessed it.

Sera returned with a chalice of wine and seated herself with the elegance of a dancer.

"Well," she asked in a low voice as she leaned in toward the center of the table. "What *are* you doing here?"

Elyse smiled and batted her eyelashes at her friend. "Lou here said that he'll throw me in the dungeon for tax evasion if I don't help him get into the tavern tonight. He needs my help to get information on the king's murder." Her voice had a forced sweetness to it. She took several long swigs from her ale before setting it back on the table and adding, "So here we are."

Sera gasped and held a manicured hand to her lips. "Lou, I never would have thought you capable of blackmail!"

Killian rolled his eyes. It wasn't blackmail, not really. He was just doing his job.

"Isn't that what you do for a living? You know things?" Killian asked, not bothering to mask his bitterness.

"I *interpret* things," she corrected.

"Whatever," Killian mumbled as he took another swig of ale.

"Be nice to my friend," Elyse growled, her brows furrowed. "Especially since you need her help."

"I don't need—"

But Sera was already clapping her hands together excitedly.

"I'd be delighted to help! Ooh—does this make me an honorary member of the Royal Guard?" she chimed.

Elyse made a noise that sounded like a retch.

Killian took a deep breath. Perhaps getting Sera involved wasn't the best idea. "No, you would not be an honorary member of the Guard. I just . . . We need to make friends," he said as calmly as he could.

"He already sent one woman running," Elyse snorted.

Sera giggled. "I'm more than happy to oblige you, dear Lou," she said. Her purple eyes flitted around the tavern. "I'll be right back," she said, before promptly standing and sauntering away, leaving Killian and Elyse alone again.

He had nothing to say to Elyse, and apparently she felt similarly. They sat in silence for several long moments, Elyse staring at her mug and scratching her arm. He took another sip of his ale—which was much more delicious than it had any business being—and eyed the room.

"How old are you?" Elyse abruptly asked.

Killian wiped his upper lip with the back of his hand. "Nine and twenty. Why?"

Elyse shrugged and fiddled with her mug. "You just seemed young for a lieutenant."

Killian cleared his throat, but he relaxed a bit in his seat. "Anyone with half a brain can move through the ranks pretty quickly," he confessed.

With one brow raised, she asked, "Do you always downplay your accomplishments?" She held his gaze as she sipped from her mug, her dark eyes drilling him.

Killian scoffed. "What, should I strut around like you? Act as if I'm the greatest thing that's graced this earth?"

"Oh please," she replied, narrowing her eyes. "It's just for show. It's good for business," she added with a shrug.

"Please, enlighten me—how is it good for business?"

Elyse sighed and leaned her elbow on the table. "First of all, I'm a female shoppe-owner who lives alone in the middle of the woods," she explained, sounding annoyed that she even had to do so. "I don't exactly want to be seen as easy prey."

Killian took a swig of his ale. That seemed like a fair statement.

"Second," she continued, "who wants to buy powerful magical objects from a meek little kitten? My reputation is just as much a factor in attracting customers as my product is."

"Really?" Killian drawled, letting the disbelief seep into his voice.

"Really," Elyse affirmed. "Take your soldiers, for example. Are you kind to them? Do you hold their hand?" She didn't wait for an answer before continuing. "No, you show them you care about them by being hard on them, by preparing them for whatever dangers they might face.

40

You *do* care about them, but you have to play your part. You have to be the leader they expect you to be."

Killian took another sip of ale as he considered her words. She had a point. It was such a strange conversation, though. Most women touched his arm and asked if he'd ever killed a man. But Elyse . . . She acknowledged his success but didn't fawn over it. She spoke to him more like an equal.

"How old are you?" he asked, suddenly curious.

"Eight and twenty."

He studied her, trying to decide if she seemed older or younger than her true age. Her petite frame made her seem younger, but her cynicism aged her a good amount. Elyse seemed to notice his staring and glared at him.

Across the bar, a high-pitched laugh sounded, and Killian looked up to see Sera, her arms linked with a wiry man with a tattoo over his brow.

"Oh, you have to tell my friends your joke," she insisted as she guided him to the table where Killian and Elyse sat. "Friends, this is . . ."

But Killian didn't catch the man's name. Sera and the man sat, and he was vaguely aware that the man was telling a joke. He even laughed loudly at the punchline, though he couldn't remember what the joke actually was.

Killian looked down at his drink. Elyse was right. This was not normal ale. There was no way he should be feeling so out of it after half an ale. And there was no way Tattoo Face was actually that funny.

Yet it was delicious—addictingly so. Despite himself, Killian chugged some more.

Tattoo Face yammered on about something or another, and Killian looked to Elyse. She was laughing. Was it fake? Or real? Was she laughing with him, or at him?

Another round was poured, and Killian found himself drinking more. And more. Tattoo Face's friends arrived and joined their growing party. Killian couldn't remember their names either, so he deemed them

Brawny, Tawny, and Tiny, based on their appearances. He giggled to himself at his own cleverness.

"Doing okay there, Lou?" Elyse asked as she leaned in close. "I tried to warn you about the drinks."

"Pshaww," Killian replied with a wave of his hand. This was fun. He was having fun—in a black magic tavern of all places. Damn, did he love this ale.

But he did have a job to do—one that had somehow slipped his mind. He cleared his throat and addressed the group, coming up with the best segue he could think of.

"So how about that king, huh? Murdered, eh?"

"Subtle," Elyse muttered under her breath.

Brawny threw back a shot of a brown liquid and slammed the empty glass on the table. "I heard it was a spell. Made him go crazy and slit his own throat."

"You got it all wrong," Tawny interjected. "It was a ghost. Everyone knows the palace is haunted."

"I heard it was the queen. She slipped poison into his tea," came Tiny's voice.

At any other time, Killian would have told these men what idiots they were being, even Brawny with his biceps that were probably thicker than Killian's legs. Instead, he was amazed by their answers, their sheer confidence despite their lack of knowledge.

"No," he said in a voice so quiet that everyone at the table leaned toward him to hear better. "It was dark magic. They bled him from the inside out." He sat back in his chair, shaking his head as he lifted his ale to his lips. "It had to have been someone powerful," he uttered.

The table sat in silence for a moment. Tiny scratched at his goatee pensively, then said, "I don't know about powerful, but Bast was in here last night braggin' about killin' someone important. Someone very high up."

Elyse scoffed. "Bast is nothing but a two-bit magician. He's only good for parlor tricks."

"I'm just relaying what I heard," Tiny answered with a shrug.

Bast. Bast. Bast. Killian repeated the name over and over in his mind, willing his drunken self to remember it later. Elyse didn't seem to think this Bast fellow was capable of assassinating the King of Rhodan, but it was worth looking into. Stranger things have happened—like him, sitting at this tavern, chumming it up with . . . whoever these people were.

"Another round?" Elyse offered as she stood from the table.

"I'll come with you," Killian said. "There's a bartender whose intentions need clarifying."

He could tell Elyse wasn't thrilled about his accompanying her to the bar, but she didn't say anything. She walked in her usual cool saunter while he stumbled until they reached the bar, which Killian immediately grabbed hold of to steady himself.

"Is it too late to have a sip of that cocktail of yours?" he asked quietly.

"Unfortunately, yes. You have to take it before consuming any alcohol," she explained.

Bullocks.

Thomas approached them with a "What'll it be?" and before Killian could say anything, Elyse answered.

"A round of ales for the table, and put a kettle on for Lou here."

When Thomas turned away to pour the drinks, Killian leaned toward Elyse.

"You don't have to order for me, you know," he grumbled.

Elyse sent him a look of annoyance and rolled her eyes. "Calm down. It's just for appearances."

Killian was certain that it had nothing to do with appearances—that she was, in fact, just a bossy witch with control issues—but he didn't press the matter.

"I don't think these guys know much," he whispered. "We should talk to some others."

"*We*," she began, "don't have to do anything. This is your evening, not mine. I've already held up my end of the bargain."

Killian leaned in even closer, until his lips were practically brushing her ear. "And just how much money did you make last year, Ms. Crenshaw?"

"Don't," she growled.

Killian gave her his most menacing glare, though he knew his swaying undermined his threat.

But Elyse sighed, defeated. She glanced around the bar, then turned her attention to Killian. "Look, if you want information, then . . . Just follow my lead." She took a deep breath, and shouted, "No! No more ale for you. I told you, you're far too drunk for gambling."

Killian stared at her dumbly. What was she on about? Then, over her shoulder, he caught a glimpse of a table where five men sat playing cards. Two of the men had turned in their chairs and were watching their conversation with wide, eager eyes.

He cleared his throat and said, "Nonsense! You know I play best when I've had a few."

Elyse turned away from him, holding up her hand in dismissal. "Oh please. Remember last time? You lost all your rent money and had to come begging me to pay your bills."

Killian was not a fan of the picture this conversation painted of him, but it was working. The entire table of card players was now looking in their direction.

"I don't need your permission," he grumbled, just as Thomas returned carrying two mugs. He set them on the bar, and Killian immediately swiped one and started chugging it.

"You worthless idiot!" Elyse sounded thoroughly fed up as Killian continued to slurp from the mug. "You'd gamble your whole life away if it wasn't—"

"All due respect ma'am," called a low voice from behind her. "The man said he wants to gamble." Though he was speaking to Elyse, the man was looking at Killian, watching him, practically salivating over the easy target.

A well-timed belch escaped Killian's mouth.

"There's always room for one more at the table," the man said as he gestured a scarred hand toward his friends.

Killian gave Elyse a scathing, defiant glare, and she winked at him in return.

"I wash my hands of you!" she said before swiping her mug and sulking back to the table, leaving Killian alone with the stranger.

"Right this way," the man offered with a menacing smile.

So Killian followed him, concealing his own smile.

CHAPTER 7

— • —

ELYSE

E lyse hoped the men drained Killian for all he was worth.

She traipsed back to the table, wondering just how long Killian would last with his new friends. When she reached Sera and the others, they were in a heated debate over which of the men would win in a fight.

"C'mon, Sera. You know it'd be me!" said the tattooed one. "I'm quicker'n all of 'em."

"Speed is important," Sera confirmed.

"But I'm the strongest," said the big man.

"It's a fight, not an arm-wrestling match," the shorter one said.

Elyse tuned them out. She didn't give a damn which one of them would win in a fight. One look at them was enough to know that she could wipe the floor with any of them—with one hand tied behind her back.

She peered over Sera's shoulder and watched the men playing cards as they dealt Killian in. She recognized a few of them. Nearly everyone in the Black Cat had been to the Emporium at some time or another. Her mother would have remembered all of their names, but Elyse practically forgot them as soon as they walked out the door. That was another reason for her tough exterior. If everyone was too afraid to talk to her, then she didn't have to bother trying to remember them.

Killian quickly lost the round, and Elyse hid her smile behind her mug.

"I think I get the game now," she heard him say as he shook his head vigorously. The dealer passed out new cards, and Killian studied his hand. When it came to his turn, he hesitated before tossing a copper piece into the pile. One by one the other plays backed out, and Killian grinned as he swept his small winnings toward him.

Lucky bastard.

The tattooed man and the others continued pleading for Sera's validation, but all of Elyse's attention was trained on Killian. He won the next round, and then the next, acquiring a decent little pile of coin. One of the men called for another round of drinks, smirking when Thomas plunked a mug of ale before Killian.

But the ale didn't slow down his winnings. Elyse watched with more amusement than she cared to admit as the pile before Killian started to grow, and the men at the table began shifting in their seats.

Maybe "lucky bastard" was inaccurate—"cunning bastard" seemed more fitting. As much as the lieutenant annoyed her with his propriety, she could at least respect his ability to hustle.

"Excuse me," Elyse said to her group, but they hardly took notice as she stood and strolled away from them.

"Read 'em and weep, gentlemen!" Killian shouted as Elyse neared the table. The men all griped under their breath while Killian collected his coin. He was getting reckless.

"Looks like you might be able to pay me back," Elyse said. She stood next to Killian, a hand on her hip.

"Game's not over yet, lady," said the man who invited Killian to play. Apparently "all respect" was no longer due.

Killian beamed up at her and winked before downing more ale.

Another hand was dealt, and Killian lost, but only a few coins. He more than made up for it the next round.

Elyse watched him with a curiosity she hadn't felt in years. It was rare that anything astonished her, but Killian's swaggering was a sight to behold. He was truly drunk, but to be honest, with the amount of ale he'd consumed already, she was surprised he was even functioning. She was torn between wanting to see just how much he could win, and worrying how the men might retaliate if Killian cleaned them out. They gave each other sideways glances every time Killian won a hand, silently communicating their discord to one another.

Not my problem, Elyse reminded herself.

"Well, if the king had my luck, he'd still be alive!" Killian joked as he stacked his winnings.

Elyse rolled her eyes at the forced change in conversation. Was that really the best he could come up with?

"Luck's got nothing to do with the king's death," said the man to Killian's left. "Was dark magic that did him in."

"No," Killian gasped, his eyes wide. "Was it really?"

Another man nodded. "Aye. It was voodoo. Someone made one of his guards do it."

Elyse noticed the slight drop in Killian's shoulders. These men knew no more than the last group.

"All I know is," said another man, "Bast came in here yesterday with a full coin purse, and he kept goin' on about how someone paid him to take care of somebody. Somebody important."

Bast again. True or not, the man needed to learn to keep his trap shut.

"You think if Bast did it, he'd come in here and brag about it?" shouted another man as he gave his friend an indignant look.

"WellWell, who do you finger for it?"

"The queen did it. Killed him in his sleep."

Elyse had heard enough. She remembered why she hardly ever left her cottage—the capital was full of idiots. She was about to walk away when a loud *bang* erupted from behind her.

In an instant, Killian pulled the knife from his boot, stood, and whirled toward the commotion.

Elyse turned and saw two men—the tattooed one and the short one—facing each other as they stood in fighting stances. Apparently, just debating about who would win in a brawl wasn't good enough.

The whole tavern froze as everyone stared at the men, waiting for them to attack one another. Sera still sat at the table, sipping at her wine and regarding the men as if she were at the theater.

"Hey!" Thomas called from behind the bar. "No fighting in here!"

The men's friends moved to de-escalate the situation, but the tattooed man ignored them.

"*Omaniti*," he shouted as blue sparks flew from his hand toward the short man, who went flying into the table behind him.

The large man grabbed the tattooed one around the shoulders and began dragging him out of the bar, while the tan one ran to his short friend to see if he was okay.

Elyse turned back around, disappointed that the fight had been broken up so quickly. Killian still stood, wielding his knife, his eyes wild with—was that fear?

"It's just a bar brawl, mate," one of the gamblers said, condescension clear in his gruff voice. They all sniggered, and Elyse laughed too.

But when she looked at Killian's face again, her smile faded. This wasn't just an ordinary fear that marred his expression. No, something deeply troubled him. She felt the smallest tinge of compassion.

"Sorry boys, he was in the war. Gets skittish around loud noises," she explained lightly. The men's brows furrowed—there hadn't been a war in over a decade—but she ignored them and pulled Killian aside.

"You can put that away," she whispered, gently touching his hand. "It's all over."

He seemed to snap from whatever nightmare he was living in as he shook his head and lowered the knife. The horror didn't leave his eyes, though.

"Do you want to leave?" she asked, keeping her voice soft, and he nodded.

Elyse glanced at the table and vast pile of coins he'd collected. She sighed.

"Okay," she said in a low voice, her lips nearly touching his ears. "Lose this hand and we'll leave. Bet it all."

He didn't say anything, but she felt him tense.

"You think these men are going to let you walk out of here with their money? I don't feel like saving your ass. So lose, and then we'll go."

Killian swallowed, then nodded almost imperceptibly.

He sat back down, and Elyse took her place, standing just behind him.

"One last round for me, lads," he said with a mischievous grin. "The missus is getting . . . restless."

Elyse frowned at the insinuation, but whatever he had to say to get out of here alive would do.

The dealer passed out the cards, and Killian held them close to his chest, but Elyse still got a good look at them. Two mages and a crow. She knew enough about the game to know that this was a damned good hand. She just hoped that he wouldn't be stupid.

The bet went around three times, and each time the men tossed a gold piece toward the center of the table. The fourth time around, Killian pushed his entire stack of coins to the middle.

"All in," he said with uncertainty.

Three of the men folded immediately, but one man, the one who had invited Killian, pushed his own stack to the middle as well.

"Ladies first," Killian said with a grin.

The man returned his grin as he flipped his cards over on the table. A mage and two wolves. A good hand, but not as good as Killian's.

Elyse's heart pounded in her chest as her eyes lingered on Killian. He stared at his cards . . .

And tossed them face down into the pile of discarded cards.

"You win," Killian said softly.

The man whooped and reached for the hoard of coins. Relief flooded Elyse before she realized she should say something.

"You idiot!" she shouted. "You blew it all!"

Killian turned to her. "Front me some money! Just a few coppers!" he pleaded.

Oh, he was selling this.

She ignored the urge to smile, instead schooling her expression into one of anger as she grabbed him by the sleeve and yanked him out of the chair.

"Just one more hand! I can win it back!" he insisted.

But Elyse just tightened her grip and kept on walking, only flashing him a small smile once they'd passed through the iron door.

CHAPTER 8

— • —

ELYSE

When they emerged from the alley, the street was nearly empty. A lone panhandler sat against a nearby building, mumbling to himself beneath a starry sky.

Killian immediately headed east down the street, and Elyse watched him take a few steps before she said, "The palace is the other way."

He looked left, right, then shrugged his shoulders and turned around.

Finally, Elyse would get to return home. The rash on her arm was practically burning, and she longed to slather it with ointment. The night wasn't as bad as she'd dreaded, but interacting with strangers was still taxing. She vowed not to leave her shoppe for a whole month as she pulled one of the vials of blue transportation potion from her pocket. She was just about to throw it on the ground when Killian called from the end of the block.

"Hey! Aren't you going to walk me home?"

He sounded like a whining child.

Elyse didn't move. He was joking, right? "This is as far as I go."

Even from twenty yards away she could see the sappy grin on his face.

"I told my unit that if I didn't make it home tonight, they should show up at the Emporium and arrest you."

Elyse's shoulders sank. She was getting tired of this cat and mouse shit. With gritted teeth, she trudged toward him.

Killian stumbled as they took off together down the street, and she grabbed his wrist to steady him. She debated magicking them to just outside the palace gates but decided against it. Transportation wasn't exactly pleasant. In his state, Killian would likely vomit, and that was the last thing she wanted to deal with.

"Can I ask you something?" he said in a too-loud voice.

"I imagine telling you no won't stop you?" she groused.

"Did you kill the king?" His tone was light, but that didn't stop irritation from smoldering in her chest.

"If I told you I did, would you even remember it tomorrow?"

Killian didn't bother responding to her question. "My friend thinks I believe you're innocent because you're pretty," he slurred instead.

Heat flooded Elyse's cheeks. She held her gaze forward, toward the empty street ahead of her, not daring a glimpse at Killian. When was the last time anyone had told her she was pretty? Certainly not in a long time. Her most recent lover, Jaime, had left town over a year ago.

Elyse was glad when Killian broke into song, fumbling through the lyrics to some brash military cadence, even if he did sing off key. He stumbled again, and when she pulled him upright, he broke loose from her grip and wrapped his arm around her shoulder.

They ambled along the last few blocks, Killian still bellowing out the crude lyrics. An elderly woman stuck her head out the window of her apartment and hollered for him to shut up, but he didn't listen. Part of Elyse was annoyed by him, ready to dump him at the palace gates. But another part of her preferred the drunken version of the lieutenant, loud as he may be, to the uptight, prudish version.

They arrived at the stone wall that surrounded the palace, where two guards bearing halberds stood flanking an iron gate. The guards gawked at them as they approached, and Elyse wondered if they were more intrigued by her presence or Killian's drunken state.

"Good evening, Lieutenant," called one of the guards in an official-sounding voice.

"Hidy ho!" Killian called in response.

Elyse pointedly removed Killian's arm from her shoulder and pushed him toward the guards.

"There. Make sure his unit knows he got back in one piece," she drawled. "He's your problem now."

The iron gate slid open to accept Killian, and Elyse turned to leave. She'd only made it a few steps when he hollered, "The Royal Guard thanks you, Ms. Crenshaw!"

She didn't break stride, just continued to saunter down the dark street. She turned into an alley, and her body rejoiced at being alone again, back in the shadows. As she reached into the pocket of her cloak, her fingers wrapping around the vial of blue liquid, she contemplated if she would ever see the lieutenant again.

CHAPTER 9

—·—

KILLIAN

K illian stumbled into the mess hall in the late morning. His head was splitting. It had taken him twenty minutes to change out of the clothes he'd worn the night before, which he had carelessly slept in, and into a crisp, clean uniform. He'd hoped the change of clothes and a splash of water on his face would help, but as he moped between the long wooden tables toward the kitchen, he thought he might vomit.

What in the gods' names was in that ale last night? He hadn't been sick like this after a night of drinking since he was a young soldier with money burning a hole in his pocket.

Cook mumbled something about breakfast being hours ago, but he still warmed a bowl of porridge for Killian in the hearth. Killian trudged back into the mess hall and plunked down at the nearest table. He stooped over his bowl, forcing down the porridge, each bite more nauseating than the last.

As he ate, he tried to remember the events of the night before, but everything was murky. He remembered arriving, remembered the haggard bouncer and the one-eyed bartender, but he didn't recall much after that. His stomach lurched as he realized what he had to do.

"There he is!" called a voice from behind him. Killian winced at the loud sound. Manny plopped down on the bench across from him with a grin on his face. "Are you just now getting up?"

Killian rubbed at his temples. "Can you lower your voice?"

Manny chuckled. "Well, I hope whatever information you got was worth feeling like shit today."

When Killian didn't reply, instead still rubbing his temples, Manny added, "You *did* get information, right?"

Killian dropped his hand and sighed. "No. Or at least, I don't remember if I did."

"Oh, brother," Manny breathed. "What happened?"

Now that was an excellent question.

"There was something off about the ale," Killian said vaguely.

Manny tensed. "Did the witch drug you?"

"No," Killian said as he tried to recall the night. He had been careful to watch his drink, at least at the start of the night. "No, I don't think so. She tried to warn me that the ale was stronger than what we drink. She even offered me a potion to help combat the effects before we went into the tavern."

Manny seemed to relax at that. "But you didn't take it because . . . ?"

Killian shot Manny a deadpan look. "Would you have taken a potion from a witch? Even if she drank some herself?" He returned to rubbing his temples. Even this simple conversation was taking everything out of him.

Manny shrugged. "So what are you going to do?"

Killian dropped his elbows onto the table and smothered his face with both hands. "I'm going to go ask Elyse what happened," he groaned through his palms.

Though Killian's eyes were closed, he could hear the smile in his friend's voice. "Now this I have to see."

CHAPTER 10

— · —

KILLIAN

K illian and Manny entered the clearing in the forest where Elyse's cottage sat nestled in a small garden. Despite the fresh air, the hour-long ride atop a horse hadn't eased Killian's nausea, and he pushed ahead of Manny toward the shoppe, eager to escape the too-bright sunlight. Once again, he just wanted to get this interaction over with. He had no doubt that the witch would gloat about his hangover, rubbing it in his face that he "should have listened to her" and that he said he could "handle his liquor." If she did, he would strongly reconsider his promise not to bring her in for tax evasion.

The bell jingled as he trudged inside, Manny a few steps behind him, and a silvery blonde head of hair lifted to greet them.

"Hello, Lieutenant." Elyse stood behind her worktable, her arms crossed over her chest. Her smirk told Killian she knew exactly how much his head was pounding at that moment.

When her eyes drifted toward Manny, Killian said, "This is Manny, my second in command."

"Pleased to meet you," Manny offered, extending his hand.

"I'd say pleased to meet you as well, but I detest lying," she said curtly.

Manny's eyes widened as he retracted his hand, and he stared at Elyse with something like fascination.

Elyse gestured to the enormous book spread before her on the table. "I was just finishing up going over the ledger. It doesn't look like any of the ingredients were purchased here in the last six months."

Great. So no leads there—if she was telling the truth.

"That's good to know, but that's not what I'm here for." Killian stumbled over his words. "Can you . . . Can you tell me what happened last night?"

He could see the muscles of her mouth working to contain her grin. She arched an eyebrow and said, "I tried to get you to take that potion, but you refused me."

"I know," he said, taking an earnest step toward her. "I know, and I'm almost certain that if it wasn't for you, I wouldn't have made it back to the barracks last night. But I just need you to do this one last thing. Tell me what happened last night—please?"

He tried to look sympathetic, but another wave of nausea hit him as the word "please" fumbled from his lips.

"Is this more blackmail? Or simply asking a favor?" she asked, cocking her head to the side.

Killian swallowed—or at least attempted to. His mouth was still dry, his voice hoarse. "I'd prefer to think of it as a favor, but if blackmail is necessary—"

Elyse sighed and held up her hand, stopping him.

"Look, you didn't get much of anything last night. The two big contenders that everyone seemed to point fingers at were the queen and a lowlife named Bast."

Killian shifted his weight from one foot to the other. The queen? Surely he would have remembered anyone accusing Queen Andrielle. He had interviewed her himself, had seen the grief in her eyes, a grief he recognized well. No one could fake that kind of sorrow.

"So, you know this Bast fellow?" he asked, praying that it was a solid lead. Thinking about the queen's anguish reminded him just how badly he needed to find and punish this murderer.

"I do," Elyse said as she strolled around the table and leaned against it. "He's middle of the food chain—on a good day. I wouldn't pin something this big on him, especially if he's stupid enough to brag about it."

Damn. It was worse than he'd thought. Still, Bast was the only name that had come up so far. Killian turned to Manny to gauge his thoughts, but Manny seemed to be more intrigued by the potions on the shelf next to him than the conversation.

With a sigh, Killian asked, "Do you know where we can find him?"

Elyse chewed her bottom lip, seemingly debating how helpful she would be.

"Please?" Killian pressed. The witch likely knew exactly how difficult it was for him to ask for help.

"That wasn't so hard, was it?" Elyse replied with a simpering smile. "He lives in a ramshackle house northwest of the city. You'll take Pilcrow out of town, then head west along the creek. Should lead you straight to him."

"Thanks," Killian said. He turned to leave, eager to pursue the only lead he had, but Manny spoke up.

"Is that a—" He cut himself off abruptly, his eyes wide and mouth ajar. "I never thought I'd see one."

Both Killian and Elyse followed his gaze up to the top of a bookshelf propped against a wall. Perched on the highest shelf, its wings splayed and its beak open, was a phoenix. Or at least, a replica of one.

"Yes," Elyse confirmed as she scratched absentmindedly at her arm. "It's a phoenix."

"Wow!" Manny just stared at the beast. "Is it real?"

Elyse made a sound that was a mixture of flattered laughter and a contemptuous scoff. She pointed her finger at the creature, and Killian watched, with some contempt, as it levitated off the shelf and floated down toward them, following the path of Elyse's pointer finger. With her magic, she set it gently down on the worktable, and Manny rushed to see it.

"It's real," she mused as Manny gently brushed the phoenix's crimson wings.

"It's beautiful," Manny praised.

Killian had to admit, the creature was stunning. The plumage seemed to transfigure in the light, shifting from scarlet to burgundy to gold.

"How much does something like this go for?" Manny asked.

Elyse shrugged. "It's one of a kind, so it's hard to put a price tag on it," she admitted.

Manny's face was so close to the bird, his nose practically touched it. "Is it a spell? Or is it like traditional taxidermy?"

"Both," Elyse said. "It's a grueling process."

Killian groaned. Since when did Manny care so much about birds and preserving their remains? He could have smacked him for dragging this interaction out if the effort wouldn't threaten to make his breakfast come up.

"So, you knew the person who did this?" Manny asked. "Was it you? Your father?"

Elyse's eyes narrowed immediately, and Killian caught a slight twitch of her lips. He wasn't sure if he wanted to smack his friend, or applaud him. He did know that the grave expression on Elyse's face meant Manny had struck a nerve far closer to home than any of Killian's petty jests had.

"I'm sorry," Manny backtracked. "I shouldn't have asked something so personal."

"No, it's fine," Elyse said with a weak smile. "I didn't know the taxidermist well. He was just traveling through."

She raised her hand again to levitate the bird back onto its shelf, and as she did so, the sleeve of her tunic slipped down her forearm. Red, blistering skin peeked out. Killian shuddered as he recognized the rash, and was about to say something when Manny blurted out, "I didn't know my dad either."

Killian froze. Why in hell had Manny just said that? It was true—his mother never told him who his father was—but there was no need to bring it up now.

Without moving, Killian shifted his gaze to Elyse. She stared at Manny, seething, her nostrils flared and her chest rising and falling.

"What did you say?" she growled. Before Manny could answer, she took a step toward him and snapped, "What makes you think I don't know my father?"

It was likely true. When Killian researched Elyse before coming to the Emporium, he'd noted that no man had been attached to the property in over three decades. He didn't know if Manny knew that as well, if he'd picked up on something else, or if he'd just taken a wild guess.

Regardless, it had been the wrong move.

"I . . . I just . . ." Manny sputtered. It was rare for him to be at a loss for words, but he seemed to have no explanation.

"Get. Out." Elyse snarled each word as she lifted a trembling hand and pointed toward the door.

"I'm sorry—" Manny started.

A breeze stirred from somewhere in the room, blowing Elyse's hair. She looked absolutely wicked as she glared at Manny, and a shiver went down Killian's spine.

"If you weren't in the Guard, I'd flay you both alive," she spat. "*Get out!*"

Killian didn't need to be told a third time. He grabbed Manny by the wrist and ignored the jolt of his stomach as he pulled his friend out the door.

Back outside, in the still-too-bright sun, Manny freed himself from Killian's grip. Killian expected Manny to apologize or to spew out some excuse, but instead, he gave the lieutenant a mischievous smile.

"What the hell?" Killian asked, dumbfounded.

Manny shot him a look, one that Killian knew meant that he would tell him later, before he stalked off for his horse. Killian stared after him for a few moments, stunned, until he stumbled after him.

It wasn't until they'd made it about a mile down the road that Manny finally broke the silence.

"Do you want to head straight to Bast's now or regroup at the barracks first?" he asked, looking at Killian as if nothing had happened.

Killian pulled his piebald stallion to a stop. "Are you going to explain what all that was about?" he demanded. "Since when do you care about taxidermy? And why in the gods' names are you bringing up your father?"

Manny smiled, and he looked almost as wicked as Elyse had—almost. He reined his mare to a stop and reached into his pocket, fetching out a small vial of clear liquid. He held it proudly, as if it explained everything perfectly.

Killian just stared at him. "Please tell me you didn't steal that."

Manny tossed the vial into the air and caught it, grinning the whole time. "I did indeed." He leveled his gaze on Killian, and explained with a knowing sort of air, "First you flatter them by feigning interest in something, and then you make them uncomfortable, so they just want to be rid of you." He winked and added, "It's one of my oldest tricks."

Killian didn't know whether to roll his eyes or yell or punch his friend in the arm. "You're bloody stupid, you know that?" He didn't want to think about how Elyse might retaliate if she found out.

"Impulsive and stupid are not the same thing," Manny corrected.

Killian just shook his head. Of all the dumb tricks Manny had pulled, this might be the dumbest.

"But *why?*" he stressed. "Why steal it in the first place?"

Manny just shrugged and tucked the vial back into his pocket. "It's truth serum. I thought it might come in handy."

Killian's headache seemed to double. He rubbed at his temples again as he asked, "But why not just pay for it?"

62

Manny smirked, and Killian knew the answer wouldn't be good. "All she had to do was say, 'Pleased to meet you as well.'"

CHAPTER 11

— · —

ELYSE

Elyse sent a blast of magic to slam the door shut after Killian and his idiot friend ran out.

The phantom wind still stirred within the shoppe, rattling the antiques and flipping the pages of the ledger. She closed her eyes and took a deep breath, forcing herself and her magic to calm.

It shouldn't have bothered her, but every time she thought of her father—or lack thereof—it unsettled her. And worse than the visceral despair in her stomach had been the look in that imbecile's eyes.

Pity—that's what it had been. As if he was better than her. Good for him that he'd come to terms with his absent father, but that gave him no right to *pity* her.

Elyse still felt her anger flowing through her veins, so she did what she always did when she was restless: she cleaned.

She picked up a feather duster and started combing through the shelves one by one, all the while trying to get that stupid, stupid, stupid man out of her head.

He didn't know her. He didn't know her situation, or how much it ate at her that she didn't know who—or what—her father was. He didn't understand what it was like to be more afraid of the truth than being in the dark.

Elyse moved on to a table full of glass vials and began meticulously dusting them off. She felt her heartbeat start to settle along with her slow, careful movements.

Perhaps Manny did understand her pain, at least somewhat. That didn't give him the right to try and force her to talk about it. What sort of madman did that?

She finished with the dusting and picked up the broom, hoping to work off the rest of her frustration. By the time she had swept the entire shoppe, she realized that maybe—just maybe—Manny had been trying to be kind. And, perhaps, she had overreacted.

Elyse leaned the broom back against the wall and stared up at the preserved phoenix for a long moment. She had forgotten about it up there. It had become a fixture of the Emporium, no more significant than a door hinge or a floorboard. But now she saw it again with fresh eyes, saw its marvelous colors and sharp talons and fierce pose. How could she have gone so long without acknowledging its beauty?

It was curious how intrigued Manny had been. She'd assumed he would be just like Killian, skeptical and rigid, but his eyes had lit up with genuine intrigue at the creature. Even before that, she had seen the way he took in the shoppe, how he studied the books and the talismans, the wands and the potions. He'd stared at it all in awe, not contempt.

She might have felt bad for her actions if she actually gave a damn. But she would never see Manny or Killian again, so it would be easy to forget that she ever let either one of them get under her skin.

As she strolled through the main aisle, the widest one that ran from the entrance to her worktable, a chill caressed her spine. Something was off.

She peered around at the trinkets scattered throughout the shoppe. Yes, something was certainly missing. Her eyes roved over every book, every object, every potion—

A potion was missing. Every morning Elyse restocked the potions, grouping them into sets of five. Yet one group, the group of vials containing a clear liquid, held only four, and she had not sold any potions today. She knew instantly which potion it was. Truth serum. And she knew exactly who had taken it.

Killian and Manny.

Had it been an act then? Feigning interest in the phoenix to distract her? Bringing up her father to get in her head? He hadn't been trying to be kind at all—he'd been riling her up as a distraction. And worst of all, it had worked.

Fury burned inside Elyse, heating her skin and stoking her magic.

Oh, they were dead. Worse than dead—she would curse them, curse their children, curse their children's children . . .

Fortunately for her, she knew exactly where they'd be.

Chapter 12

Killian

The sound of Killian's fist banging against the heavy oak door reverberated through the clearing. The door was the only thing about the shabby lean-to that seemed substantial. There was no walkway, only a path of dead grass that had been trampled by feet coming and going, and the exterior walls were stripped of any lacquer or luster. One of the upstairs windows had a broken pane, and the scent of stale air wafted from the house. But peculiarly, the oak door stood strong.

Killian knocked again.

He and Manny had followed Elyse's instructions exactly as she told them, and a few hours later they found the lone, dilapidated house. With each passing minute, Killian hoped the endeavor wasn't a giant waste of time, but as they stood before the seemingly abandoned house, waiting for a reply that wouldn't come, he knew in his heart it was a dead end.

"He's not home," Manny said, confirming Killian's own suspicions aloud. "I don't think anyone's been here in some time."

Manny's face reflected Killian's emotions—though, no doubt Manny was more upset about not being able to use the newly acquired truth serum than about having to figure out a different way to track down Bast. He never lost sleep over such things the way Killian did. He always insisted things would find a way to work themselves out. And maybe that was true for Manny, having been plucked from a life of deceit and hunger—but Killian knew better than to believe that same fortune applied to him. No, if there were any gods, they were not keen on giving him a break.

Killian pivoted and was about to leave when he heard a noise—not from inside the house but behind it. He shot Manny a look, and Manny's narrowed eyes confirmed he had heard it too.

With his hand on the hilt of his sword, Killian strode to the side of the house, trying to step as quickly and quietly as he could through the tall grass. Manny followed inches behind him.

Despite his training, unease settled into Killian's stomach. It was the same unease he'd felt as he'd entered Elyse's shoppe, or when he'd gone into the Black Cat, an eerie sort of tension that nagged at him. He tried to ignore it as he slithered along the side of the house, his grip steady on his sword. Elyse seemed to think Bast was harmless, but if he had killed King Cyril, then Killian needed to keep his wits about him. He didn't trust any warlocks to fight fair.

Before they even reached the back of the house, a man darted through the clearing behind the house and disappeared into the thicket of trees. His heart pounding, Killian sprinted after him.

"I am Lieutenant Southwick of the Royal Guard of Rhodan!" he shouted after the man. "I demand that you stop!"

But the man didn't even slow down. He glanced frantically back at Killian and Manny, then ducked his head and veered left, lunging through the air over a fallen tree.

Sweat was already pouring down Killian's brow as he raced after the man. Normally he would have enjoyed a dangerous pursuit through the forest, welcoming the challenge, but his head still pounded and his stomach still churned. It was an effort to keep his legs pushing forward, dashing between trees, but he mustered every bit of strength he had and kept going.

Manny kept pace beside him as they closed the distance between themselves and the man. They were both nearly an arm's length away from him. Killian could see the streaks of gray in his wild hair, could smell the lingering odor of alcohol on him—

Then the man looked over his shoulder and flicked his hand at something on the ground, sending red sparks from his fingertips.

Before Killian realized what was happening, he felt his feet leaving the ground. Manny's body smacked into him, but he could barely move to push him away. His arms and legs were tangled in a net that hoisted them up, high into the branches of the trees.

The man only sent them one final glance to make sure he'd succeeded in thwarting them before he sprinted away, disappearing among the trees.

Shit, shit, *shit.* They had to get down, had to find Bast or whoever that was before he got away.

Killian groaned. Manny's knee was digging into his ribs, and he tried to reposition himself but failed.

"Mate," Manny called, his voice far too jovial for Killian's liking. "This is a first, even for me."

"I'm glad you're enjoying this," Killian grumbled back. He maneuvered his hand to his right hip, straining to reach his dagger, and finally his fingers grasped the hilt. He pulled it free from its sheath.

A plan. He needed a plan. He closed his eyes, ignoring the swaying motion and the wind that whipped through the branches, and tried to figure out what to do.

He felt the air stir as something flew by, cawing loudly, and Killian flinched, releasing his hold on his dagger. He watched it fall all the way to the forest floor, more than forty feet below them, and let out a slew of curses. Manny just laughed.

"Instead of laughing, why don't you try helping me?" Killian shouted. He wanted to shoot him a scathing look, but the way their bodies were tangled in the net didn't allow for that. It didn't allow for much of anything as the rough fibers of the rope dug into their skin.

Manny shifted and groaned, then sighed. "I can't reach anything, my arms are stuck. Can you fish my knife from my baldric?" he asked.

Killian groped around Manny's chest and hip, fighting against the restraints of the net. Finally, his hand grasped the knife.

"Normally I make a lady buy me a drink before we get this close," Manny chuckled.

"Shut up," Killian replied. He was trying to form a plan, and Manny's jokes only made his head hurt worse. It would do no good to cut the main rope that was holding the net up—they'd surely break something or worse if they fell from this height. But if he cut a hole from the bottom of the net, he could try and lower himself to the closest branch. He craned his head to look down below him. No, the closest branch was too far down and didn't look very sturdy. Perhaps they could swing the net toward the trunk of the tree, then cut themselves loose . . .

"Do you hear something?" Manny asked, his tone no longer light.

Killian held his breath and listened. He heard a twig snap, then the sound of slow footsteps shuffling through the grass.

"He's coming back," Manny said. There was no fear in his voice, only a statement of fact.

Killian squirmed, trying to get a better look at the forest floor. The footsteps continued, and then finally he caught sight of a silvery blonde head of hair.

"Elyse!" he called. "Thank the gods you're here."

But even from so high up, he could see her fury, the sinister look that dazzled in her dark eyes. She was not there to help.

Chapter 13

Killian

"Oh *shit*," Manny muttered to no one in particular. Killian agreed with the sentiment.

Elyse stood far, far beneath them, peering up with an amused expression at their predicament.

"Elyse, let us down please," Killian called to her. He didn't choke over the word "please" this time, not as a breeze sent him and Manny swaying again.

"And why would I help a couple of thieves such as you lot?" Her voice was cold, mocking.

Dammit, Killian thought. She knew. She knew and she was there to punish them. A lump the size of an apple formed in his throat, preventing him from saying anything more.

"Why'd you do it?" she called up to them. "Was that your plan all along? Get on my good side and then rob me?" Beneath the sincere and overwhelming anger in her voice, Killian detected a hint of pain.

"It wasn't him," Manny shouted down to her, sounding sincerely apologetic. "He didn't even know I took it until after we were long gone." A lie, but a small one. "And I'm sorry about it. I shouldn't have done it, but I saw the truth serum, and I knew it would come in handy. And you were such a b—" He stopped abruptly and cleared his throat. "You weren't very welcoming, so I didn't think you'd sell it to us."

Elyse crossed her arms. Killian could feel her gaze scouring him, terrorizing him. The net spun in a slow yet agonizing circle, and he could feel his breakfast fighting him.

When she finally spoke, it was with an unexpected curiosity. "Did you even get to use the potion on Bast?" she asked.

"No," Killian groaned. He hated that they failed, and hated even more to admit it to her. "We don't even know if it was him that did this to us. He ran off and we chased him right into this trap."

Elyse grinned but no laugh escaped her lips. "What did he look like?"

Killian thought for a moment. He hadn't gotten a good look at the man's face. "He was short—about Manny's height."

"Hey!" Manny dug his knee deeper into Killian's ribs.

Killian elbowed him back before continuing. "He had pale skin and gray streaks in his hair," he hollered down to Elyse.

"That's him," she said, sounding almost bored.

The men continued to twirl in languid circles inside the net, and Killian held his breath, waiting for Elyse to exact her revenge. His left arm was starting to go numb from where the net dug into it, and his ankle was twisted in a painful direction. Beside him—and above and beneath him—he felt Manny tense.

Killian couldn't remember a time when he'd been so helpless. Surely Elyse could have them safely back on the ground in no time, but she simply stared at her nails, looking disinterested. He hoped she was just taunting them before letting them down, but he wasn't sure how much longer he could stand being contorted in this damned net.

Then Elyse twirled her wrist and pointed her finger. She looked up to Killian, smiling earnestly, urging him to decipher what exactly she was up to. He followed her slender index finger down to the ground, down to his knife, which had plunged into the forest floor.

The knife wiggled, then emerged from the ground, floating upward, gaining speed as Elyse pointed her finger up, up, and up toward the net.

"What are you doing?" Killian shouted as Manny squirmed. "Come on, Elyse!" He tried to keep his voice calm, tried to sound like one friend reasoning with another, but the sight of the knife whizzing through the air toward them made his heart race.

"You stole from me," she replied coolly. "I've castrated men for less."

Killian didn't doubt for one second the truth of that statement.

The knife hovered before him, dancing around in a sick, tantalizing sort of way. Then it levitated higher, toward the rope that held the net.

"Don't!" Killian yelled.

"Too late," Elyse purred as the knife rose higher.

"Dammit, Elyse!" he cried out, but she didn't bother responding. She grinned as the knife came within an inch of the rope.

"I have a date with your friend!"

It was Manny who shouted these words, much to Killian's—and Elyse's—surprise.

Killian looked down at Elyse. She looked tiny, like an ant. A very angry ant.

The knife slowly lowered down toward Manny, angling itself at his face. Killian held his breath, unsure what to say or do.

"My friend?" Elyse roared. The knife moved lower, toward Manny's trousers.

"Please don't cut off my manhood! I don't think Sera would like that," he moaned.

"Manny, if this is a joke—" Killian began.

"It's not a joke!" Manny cried, his voice more frantic than Killian had ever heard it. "I might have . . . gone back to her apartment yesterday and asked if I could take her out," he confessed.

Despite the situation, Killian let out a laugh. Manny never ceased to astonish him.

"You walked back up all twelve flights of stairs?" he asked, twisting his head to try and get a look at his friend.

"Yes," Manny groaned. "I was very sweaty."

"Shut up, both of you!" Elyse growled. The knife lifted again toward the rope. "You just sealed your fate. I don't want my friend going out with a petty thief."

Killian felt Manny recoil at her words. It may have been years since he lived on the street, stealing for survival, but Killian knew that a small part of him was still haunted by it, by being nothing more than a "petty thief."

The knife began to saw back and forth at the taut rope.

"I'm sorry!" Manny shouted down to her. "I couldn't help myself. I love a good challenge. It's what attracted me to Sera in the first place. She's so pretty—she's way out of my league."

"You're right about that," Elyse called back to him.

The knife was a quarter of the way through the rope now, and Killian was sweating profusely, soaking the fabric of the net.

"I think she really likes me!" Manny persisted. "Don't you want your friend to be happy?"

"Happy? Yes. Hoodwinked? No."

The knife was halfway through the rope. The broken pieces were unraveling, fraying. Killian tried to remain calm, but Manny's panicked breathing only rattled him more.

"Can you at least let me out of here?" Killian bellowed at Elyse, which earned him another elbow in the ribs from Manny.

"Absolutely not," she replied coolly. "You both have five seconds to think of your last words."

Only a few strands held the rope together, and Killian and Manny both squirmed frantically in the net.

"Five . . . Four . . ." Elyse called. Killian could hear the grin she wore, even over the groaning of the thin rope that strained to hold them up.

"Elyse!" Killian yelled.

The knife kept cutting.

He had to think of something, some way to convince her to let them live.

"Three . . . Two . . ."

He closed his eyes, took a deep breath, and prepared for disaster.

"I know your secret!" he screamed.

The knife stopped cutting, and Killian exhaled. Manny went completely still.

But it was too late.

The few remaining threads couldn't bear their weight, and the rope snapped with a loud *crack*, sending them hurtling toward the forest floor.

This time, Killian didn't try to mask his fear as he screamed.

Branches whacked and scratched at them relentlessly, sending them tumbling this way and that, but not enough to slow their descent. They cleared the lowest branch, and there was nothing but air between them and the hard ground.

Killian cursed the gods for letting him die this way.

And then it stopped. The ground stopped moving closer, the air stopped whooshing by. The screaming didn't stop, though. It took both Killian and Manny a moment to realize they were no longer falling.

Elyse stood, one hand on her hip, the other pointing at the net, at *them*. She glowered at them, her nostrils flared and her eyes narrowed, as she flicked her finger upward, sending the men higher into the air.

She was levitating *them*. Blimey, she was powerful.

They hovered in the air a few feet above the ground, making them eye level with Elyse—with her dark, sadistic eyes.

"What did you say?" She spat each word at him through gritted teeth.

"I know your secret," Killian repeated, nearly out of breath. "I know you're dying."

The forest was completely still. The only movement was Manny's eyes as they darted between Killian and Elyse.

When Elyse didn't speak, Killian continued. "I saw the rash on your arm. It's widow's decay, isn't it? You've searched and searched, but not even magic can help you find a cure."

She looked away from him, and in that moment, she wasn't a fierce witch holding them captive. She was a scared and lonely girl. Something quieted in her dark eyes, like resignation. Killian felt his chest tighten. He could relate to the pain he saw in her tight-lipped expression.

"It's what killed your mum, isn't it?" he asked in a quiet voice.

And just like that, the scared girl was replaced by the brutal witch. Her nostrils flared, and Killian and Manny plunged toward the ground again, only to be yanked back up as Elyse shouted, "You shut your mouth!"

"I'm sorry," Killian said, and he meant it. He didn't know why he had felt so bold as to bring up her mother. He tried to lift his hands defensively, but he was too tangled in the net. "I just—I had it too," he explained. "The disease."

She studied his face, her eyes narrowed as she searched his features for some clue as to whether or not he could be trusted.

"Then how are you still alive?" she asked flatly.

"Because," he breathed. He steadied his voice, pouring sincerity into every word. "I know someone who has a cure."

Elyse took a step toward him, nearly quivering with rage. "Tell me—now!"

Killian willed his voice to stay calm. "Let us out of here and I will."

He knew by the way she glared at him that he'd gotten her where it counted, that he had the upper hand. She waited, though, as if clinging to her power for as long as she could before conceding. She let the net fall to the ground, and Killian and Manny landed atop one another with an *oomph*.

Elyse handed Killian the knife, and he began cutting away the net as she stalked off to lean against a nearby tree. She propped her foot up, her knee bent and her arms crossed, staring off at something in the distance. A pretty picture of casual calm, but Killian knew she was smoldering.

When the men had liberated themselves from the net, she finally spoke.

"Tell me about the cure," she demanded.

Killian stretched his arm over his head, rotating his torso. His muscles rejoiced at their new freedom. He refused to look at Elyse as he stretched out his sore limbs, but he knew she was growing more irritated with every moment he made her wait.

"I can't tell you—not exactly," he began. Elyse let out a low growl, and he quickly added. "I was too young to remember, but my mum will know. She can tell you."

Elyse raised her chin and coolly ordered, "Take me to her."

Killian forced a stony expression on his face. "No," he said, then smiled. "I want to make a deal."

Elyse bounded toward him at the same time Manny muttered, "What are you thinking, mate?" But Killian calmly raised his hands.

"Just hear me out," he said calmly. "Help us with the case, and I'll ask my mum about the woman who cured me."

He knew it was bold. He knew Elyse could tear him to shreds and put him together piece by piece just to get her way, but something deep down told him she wouldn't. Or at least, he prayed his intuition was right.

Manny seemed to be holding his breath, waiting for Elyse to either agree or sic the knife on them again. She finally parted her pursed lips and said, "How do I know there's actually a cure? You could be lying to me."

Killian was expecting this. He smiled slightly as he said, "We may have just met, but I think you know me to be a man of my word. However, I'd be willing to take a more direct measure if needed."

He turned his gaze toward Manny, who stood staring at him dumbly. When Killian held out his hand, it took Manny a moment to realize what he was getting at before he reached into his pocket and pulled out the truth serum. He glanced at Elyse, and she nodded curtly.

Killian took the vial from Manny and uncorked it. He sniffed it, but the liquid was odorless. With a raise of his hand and a tilt of his head, he knocked back a generous gulp of the potion.

It was tasteless, too, but he felt its presence in his body, a minty cool sensation that spread from his throat to his lungs and out toward his extremities, a tingling that lingered on his lips and tongue. He had expected to feel nothing—or to feel vulnerable—but instead he felt . . . tranquil. Even as Elyse's onyx eyes gleamed at him nefariously, he calmly faced her with a blank expression.

"What's your name?" she barked at him.

So she was starting with something simple.

"Killian James Southwick," he replied.

"Did you tell your friend you think I'm pretty?" she asked next.

Killian studied her face, but no rouge graced her cheeks at the question.

"I did not tell him that," Killian said in a flat voice, "but he knows me well and surmised my attraction to you, even though I myself was unaware of it at the time." Somewhere deep inside himself he knew he should be fighting this, but the serenity of the potion made it impossible to even care.

"I knew it," Manny said with a grin. "It's always the blondes."

"How many women have you been with?" Elyse snapped.

"Manfried thinks the answer is eight women, but the truth is four," Killian said.

"You don't have to use my full name, mate," Manny grumbled.

Elyse ignored him. "What do you *really* think of magic?" Her eyes narrowed in on Killian.

He took a deep breath. "It's repugnant. People who use magic are selfish and reckless and cannot be trusted. Nothing good comes of it."

He'd expected her to blanch, to snarl at him or hex him, but the only movement she made was a tiny bob of her throat.

"Where's the cure?" she asked.

"I don't know, but my mother will. She would never forget the woman who saved her only remaining child's life."

Elyse shifted slightly on her feet. "And why shouldn't I just demand your mother's whereabouts and go ask her myself?" she quipped.

"You could," Killian said, "but you won't. You've been lonely since your mother died, and helping with the case is the most excitement you've had in a longer time than you can remember."

Manny stared at Killian, but Elyse looked away. Killian may have been the one who took the truth serum, but the veracity of Elyse's feelings was plain on her face.

Killian shuddered as the serum released its hold on him, leaving him feeling hot and tired again. And hoping beyond hope that he hadn't completely offended the witch.

"Do we have a deal then?" he asked, willing his voice not to betray his uncertainty.

Elyse returned her gaze to him. She was already back to her usual cold demeanor.

"Deal," she said, extending a small pale hand toward him. "I'll help for one week."

Relief was a tidal wave that nearly knocked Killian off his feet, but he didn't dare show it.

"A month," he countered.

"A week," she repeated.

"Two weeks."

"One."

"Fine."

Killian reached to grasp her hand—then paused.

"One more condition," he said, slowly, carefully. He knew he was pressing his luck, had already pressed it too far, but there was one more thing he needed. "You have to drink the truth serum first."

Elyse's fingers coiled back into her palm, and her lip twitched. Out of fear, anger, or both, Killian wasn't sure.

"Clear your name, once and for all," he said.

Killian swore he heard her growl, as if insulted that he demanded such a thing. But she held her hand out flat, and Killian placed the vial in it. She quickly snatched it up. Instead of a girlish sip, she tilted her head back and poured the remainder of the contents straight down her throat.

Killian watched as her eyes seemed to glaze over, their usual fire diminished.

"What is your full name?" he asked her.

"Elyse Crenshaw," she answered dryly, without cringing at the surname she apparently despised.

Killian tried to think of more questions to ask to test the power of the serum, maybe to even have a little fun. She had asked him the number of women he'd bedded, and though he was a tiny bit curious about the sexual habits of witches, he was far too much of a gentleman to ask.

"What do you think of the name Manfried?" Manny asked, head held high.

Elyse turned toward him, no hint of emotion on her face.

"It's a terrible name," she droned, and Manny slouched.

"That's an awful question, Manny," Killian said, rolling his eyes. "It's not like she would refrain from telling you that without the serum."

Manny shrugged. They needed to ask her something she would never admit in a century, in a millennium.

"Are you afraid to die?" Killian asked, his voice a mixture of hesitation and intrigue.

"Yes," Elyse replied immediately. "I am not only afraid of dying, but of dying alone."

Her expression remained neutral, her eyes locked on his.

So the fearless bitch-witch was actually afraid *and* lonely. That was enough confirmation for him.

"Did you kill the king?" he asked.

"No. And I don't know who did."

No one spoke for a second as they let her words wash over them. She was innocent. Killian didn't realize how much he had been hoping to confirm that—until it was, indeed, confirmed.

Elyse shuddered and her eyes narrowed again as disgust filled them once more. She spat at the ground as if ridding her system of the vulnerability she'd allowed herself to show.

Killian held out his hand to her.

"Let's get started, comrade," he said with a smile.

Elyse ground her teeth, but she didn't extend her hand. "Let's get on with it," she drawled, and she stalked off toward Bast's cabin.

CHAPTER 14

— • —

ELYSE

The bastard had made her drink truth serum.

To be fair, he hadn't *made* her do anything. She could have easily pried off his finger nails one by one until he agreed to take her to his mother, but she didn't love the idea of spending the rest of her life glancing over her shoulder, looking out for a vengeful lieutenant. It was one week of her life. She would survive.

In truth, she would more than survive. She still couldn't believe that Killian knew someone who could cure widow's decay. The idea of being rid of the terrible rash thrilled her, and yet . . . She couldn't shake the feeling that she didn't deserve a cure. Why should she, of all people, be spared when so many others had succumbed to the disease? Would Killian still have offered the cure if he knew her secret—her *real* secret? Suppressing the guilt that churned her stomach, she forced herself to walk with her usual swagger. She wasn't willing to let Killian and Manny see any more vulnerability than they already had.

"Were you really going to kill us?" Manny asked as they waded through the forest.

Elyse sent him her most cunning smile but didn't answer.

She had never intended to kill them, or even maim them. She planned on scaring the wits out of both of them, though, and finding them suspended in the net was the perfect opportunity to do so. Watching Manny squirm as she levitated the knife had been exceptionally gratifying, and she had immensely enjoyed hearing Killian beg.

As angry as she'd been at Manny, she knew that killing two guards would be reckless. And, as much as she hated to admit it, there was some truth to Killian's words. He'd guessed that she was lonely, which was true. She didn't particularly like most people, and Killian and Manny certainly weren't an exception, but helping them gave her some sort of purpose.

Besides, it might work in her favor to have two esteemed members of the Royal Guard in her pocket.

They arrived back at the rundown shack that Bast called home. The men seemed apprehensive to go in, probably worried there were more booby traps, but Elyse just rolled her eyes and pushed the back door open. Apparently Bast had been in too much of a hurry to lock it.

The place reeked of spilled ale, and flies buzzed around happily, feasting on tidbits of leftover food that was strewn throughout the house. As they crept from room to room, the men carried their knives and Elyse readied her hands for casting spells, but the house was empty. There was hardly any furniture—just a wobbly table with two chairs and a pallet bed on the floor upstairs.

Elyse watched as Killian strode to the fire and knelt down. He sifted through the ashes, likely searching for remnants of evidence that may have been burned.

"Anything?" Manny asked.

Killian shook his head.

"Let's get out of here then," Manny said. "The smell is making me dizzy."

Elyse was more than eager to comply.

Back outside and taking deep, purifying breaths of warm spring air, the trio stood together, planning their next move.

"Should we go somewhere and regroup?" Killian asked.

"Aye," Manny agreed.

Both men glanced at Elyse.

She raised an eyebrow. "We're not going to my shoppe," she stated plainly. "You two are never welcome there again."

If they thought she would actually let them step foot inside the Emporium, they were stupider than she imagined—which was saying a lot. They were already chummy enough. She noticed the way the men seemed to relax around her, now that she'd bared her soul for them. She tried not to cringe as she recalled the way she told them she was afraid of dying alone.

"Fine," Killian sighed. "We can head to the barracks. But don't make any trouble," he said as he gave Elyse a stern look.

She shook her head at him. "You realize *I'm* not the one who drinks, gambles, and thieves, right?"

Killian shrugged, as close to an agreement as she would get.

Honestly, what kind of trouble did he think she would make?

The men started to walk off, but Elyse stayed planted.

"Are you planning to walk the whole way back? Or would you like a ride?" she asked, a hint of mockery in her voice.

"Our horses are tied up about a quarter mile east of here," Killian explained. "Where's yours?"

Elyse shook her head. "I didn't bring one. I have something better." She fished through her pocket for a vial.

Both men cocked their heads at her. Elyse reveled in their curiosity, but she didn't bother to explain.

"See you in an hour," she said as she threw the vial to the ground and disappeared in a burst of blue smoke.

She wished she would have been able to see the looks on their faces, but she was gone too quickly.

CHAPTER 15

— : —

ELYSE

An hour later, Elyse leaned against the wall encompassing the palace. She watched as two figures on horseback approached her on the cobblestone street.

"Took you long enough," she drawled once they were within earshot.

Killian wiped sweat from his brow with the back of a filthy hand, but he made no reply. Perhaps he was too tired to jest.

The men dismounted, and the trio walked the last few yards to the gate without speaking, only the *clip clop* of hooves and the sounds of the bustling street to accompany them.

Two guards stood at attention in front of the gate. They gave the lieutenant a warm nod, and although they said nothing about Elyse's presence, she saw the way their eyes narrowed on her, the way their heads tilted curiously.

She knew how people in town looked at her—like she was a criminal, like she was dangerous. It probably had to do with the way she dressed and the way she carried herself. She didn't wear layers of flouncing skirts with matching scarves and hats; instead, she opted for trousers and an oversized tunic, and on the rare occasion that she wasn't barefoot, she wore heavy, knee-high leather boots. She'd never walked with the same light and delicate steps that she saw other women take. She walked with purpose, her eyes set ahead on a predetermined target. Every aspect of her persona was carefully curated, a planned facade to keep anyone from approaching her, or even looking at her for too long.

Elyse held her head high as they strolled through the gates and into the courtyard. A three-tiered fountain greeted them, crystal clear water streaming delicately from one level to the next, but it was the only cheery thing about the place. The spring sun seemed to disappear behind a cloud the moment they stepped through the gates, casting a gloomy air over the whole courtyard. Servants milled about, their shoulders drooped, their faces a mixture of sorrow and apprehension. Even the foliage, which should have been bright and blooming, seemed dull and lifeless.

"Everyone looks so miserable," Elyse said in a low voice that only Killian could hear.

Killian glanced at her but didn't break stride, a slight crease forming between his brows.

"What did you expect? Their king has been murdered, and their queen is grief stricken. King Cyril was beloved. News of his death did not come easily."

Killian handed his horse's reins to a stable boy who met them in the courtyard, and another boy took Manny's black mare. Elyse observed them all with intrigue. The two stable boys looked to be about fourteen or fifteen. They were mostly clean, their hair combed and their clothes fitted to their lanky bodies. They were nothing like the other young boys she'd seen in town, whose faces and hands were filthy with mud, and whose hand-me-down rags were either too large or too small. Killian and Manny both thanked the boys, a genuine acknowledgement of value and respect.

She saw it then—how well the servants must be treated, how much their king must have meant to them, and how bitter his absence must feel. To her, the king's death had just meant another powerful old man in the ground, but to these people, he was someone—someone revered.

Elyse lowered her chin and, no longer concerned with emanating her usual air of confidence, followed the soldiers to a large stone building. A set of wooden double doors welcomed them into a large hall with row after row of long tables. The smell of roasted meats and fresh bread made Elyse's mouth water in a way it hadn't in years, and she tried not to stare at the plates of the dozen-or-so men scattered throughout the hall. When was the last time she'd sat down and enjoyed a proper meal? It had been months, possibly a year, she decided. But what was the point of cooking a whole meal for one measly person when a simple spell could produce a loaf of bread or a kettle of soup that would fill her up just fine?

Elyse's view of the food was cut off as Killian stepped in front of her. With a gentle touch on her elbow, he guided her along the wall, all the while keeping himself between her and the other soldiers. She shot him a glare—she didn't need to be hidden away or protected—but he kept his gaze on the exit at the back of the hall.

When they approached the door, Killian looked both ways before entering the corridor, then darted to the left, pulling Elyse behind him. She had to refrain from rolling her eyes.

"Why are we sneaking around?" she asked, not bothering to lower her voice.

Killian didn't answer right away, so she looked to Manny, who only shrugged. Killian stopped abruptly at a door and pulled a key from his pocket, quickly unlocked the door, and disappeared inside. Elyse and Manny followed at their leisure.

Apparently, Killian felt more comfortable speaking in private, because as soon as he closed the door he said, "We weren't *sneaking*. It's just—the fewer people who see you, the less questions we'll be asked. And the less questions we're asked, the better."

Elyse opened her mouth to say something—perhaps who would be asking questions or why their questions mattered—but for once, she decided not to bother. Instead, she closed her mouth and focused on the room they were in.

It appeared to be an office, and it was neither grandiose nor wanting. The oak furniture was simple yet durable, scrolls of parchment sat in a neat pyramid atop a desk, and a small coat rack stood in the corner with a lone leather jerkin hanging from one of its limbs. Elyse could hardly see the wooden walls beneath the parchment that lined nearly every inch of the room—parchment displaying maps of the city, maps of the kingdom, rules and regulations, shift schedules, and dozens of other memoranda. Every piece of parchment was tacked to the wall with precision, creating an intricate and meticulous mosaic of information.

Manny seated himself in one of the high-backed chairs and propped his boots up on the desk. Killian swatted his friend's boots off the edge before taking his own seat behind the desk. Elyse pondered how either of them could look so relaxed in such a seemingly rigid room as she opted to rest on the arm of the chair, rather than the seat itself.

"Well," Killian said as he laced his fingers in front of him. "I suppose our next step is to find where Bast went. I think the fact that he ran strongly implies that he's guilty."

Elyse snorted. "Guilty of something, yes. But not killing the king necessarily." It was actually laughable to her that these two were pulling at such a weak thread.

"No, but we can't rule him out." Killian's voice was firm, like a teacher speaking to his pupil.

"Do you have any other leads?" Elyse looked with genuine curiosity from Killian to Manny, both of whom avoided her ruthless gaze.

"You're kidding me," she laughed. "Bast is really all you've got?"

Manny smiled, and the shimmer in his green eyes told her he was about to say something flippant. "Well, you were my number-one suspect until an hour ago."

Elyse batted her lashes at him. "I'm flattered."

Since the king's death, she'd wondered if she would be considered a suspect. It hadn't seemed likely, given that she had no obvious motive for killing him, and nothing tying her to the murder. It made her queasy to think they had actually suspected her beyond a mere whim.

With a sigh, she sank down into the seat and leaned toward the desk, resting her elbows on her thighs. If she was going to do this, she would need a plan. She looked Killian square in the eyes as she said, "Tell me everything you know."

Killian hesitated, sending Manny an uncertain look.

Elyse ignored her growing unease, twisting it into frustration. "I've answered your questions, I've gone through my ledger, I saved you in the forest, and I took a damn truth serum. You either trust me or you don't. Which one is it?"

Tension flooded the room. Manny picked at a speck of dirt on his trousers, deferring to Killian. Killian's eyes never left Elyse as he studied her face for several long moments.

And Elyse let him. She had been cooperative. She'd given him every reason to believe she was innocent. Yet something stirred inside her as Killian measured her with his gaze. He stared deep into her eyes, as if he could see the many secrets she held. But she refused to cower. She had no reason to worry.

As he took his time deciding how much he could tell her, the words he'd uttered under the effects of the truth serum echoed in her mind.

People who use magic are selfish and reckless and cannot be trusted.

She'd never cared what anyone thought of her—it was perhaps one of her best qualities. Yet she felt an undeniable need to prove the lieutenant wrong.

Out of spite, she told herself. It was a challenge, and nothing more.

Finally, Killian leaned back in his chair and loosed a quiet breath.

"We've interviewed every guard, every servant, every member of the royal family. No one saw anything out of the ordinary."

He went on to describe the king's final day, up to the point where the guards spotted the blood coming out from under the door and burst into the room. He said the queen was in such a deep sleep, they had to splash water on her to wake her up. Manny was the one to check the chamber for secret passages, and he had determined there were none. The king had only a handful of lords and courtiers that held grudges against him, and each had been interviewed, leaving no reason to suspect them further. No names had come up during their investigation into any magic-wielders who might be connected to the king's murder, except, of course, Bast.

"And the queen," Elyse reminded them. "You're certain it wasn't her?"

The light in Killian's eyes seemed to dim. "It wasn't her," he said in a quiet but firm voice.

"How can you be so sure?" Elyse accused.

Killian didn't meet her gaze, instead staring at his hands. "I interviewed her myself. *No one* can fake that kind of grief."

The tight line of Killian's mouth told her that he knew a good deal about grief, and for a moment, her heart felt a gentle tug. What had this man faced to make him so dejected, so callused to this world? Who was this implacable lieutenant who sat before her?

"What about Prince Maelor? Is he grieving as well?"

"*King* Maelor," Manny corrected, "is not taking his father's death lightly. They were very close, and saw eye to eye on nearly everything. I can't imagine any reason why he would want King Cyril dead—they practically ruled together."

"So where does that leave us?" Elyse asked as she leaned back in her chair.

There was a pause before Killian said, "I think pursuing Bast is the best use of our time."

Elyse could barely suppress her amusement. "If you say so."

Killian's eye twitched ever so slightly—just enough to inform Elyse that she had gotten to him. She wondered when was the last time anyone questioned him. And then she wondered if they would both survive this week together.

With seemingly great effort, Killian continued, choosing his words carefully. "You and I will look into Bast, and Manny will . . . gather information, to see if there are any other leads worth pursuing."

The vague way he'd described Manny's duties made Elyse turn to the man beside her with an arched brow. She studied him, recalling the way he had tricked her, manipulating her emotions as a distraction to lift the truth serum.

"What exactly *is* your job?" she asked him.

Manny just smiled, and Killian said, "That's classified."

Manny's smile grew wider as Elyse continued to scrutinize him. She waited for him to speak—surely he would tell her—but he just kept taunting her with that grin.

Whatever the answer was, she would need to keep an eye on him.

"Fine," she said. "I know of a few places we might find Bast hiding out."

"Great," Killian answered, his voice smug. "We'll leave as soon as I get changed."

CHAPTER 16

— · —

KILLIAN

To say Killian was glad that Elyse had passed the truth serum test and that she was working with them would be an understatement—even if she was still being a pain in his ass. He'd wanted to make it clear to her that *he* was leading the investigation, not her, but he'd decided that might push her over a very steep and dangerous edge. Instead, he opted for feigned cooperation, which seemed to soften Elyse's harsh personality at least somewhat. She'd hardly glared at him when he'd emerged from the barracks, cleaned up and dressed in a plain tunic and trousers instead of his guard's uniform.

The feigned cooperation didn't last long. As they made their way through the courtyard, Killian asked, "Do you ride?"

Elyse grunted a noise of disapproval. "I do, but we won't be needing horses."

She increased the speed of her pace, strolling right past the stables and toward the iron gates.

Killian's nostrils flared but he said nothing. *It's one week*, he told himself. Maybe less if luck was on their side.

They walked through the gates, passing the guards, and Killian noted for the second time the way the guards looked at Elyse—with lustful reproach. Was that how Manny thought Killian saw her? As someone to be fantasized about, a taboo he longed to conquer? If so, Manny was madder than Killian realized.

She was pretty, of course, which was easier for Killian to admit now that he'd confirmed her innocence. And she did hold herself with a sort of haughty grace that was captivating. But she was a witch, and not a very nice one at that. She represented everything that had torn his family apart. Sometimes he would forget what she was, slipping into a sort of comfortable camaraderie, before horrid memories flooded him, and he remembered to keep himself in check.

They were a few blocks away from the palace when Elyse shot him a look that said, "Follow me," and headed down an alley. She stopped abruptly, turning on her heel to face him.

"Hold on tight," she said with a wicked gleam in her eye.

Before Killian could ask, "Hold on to what?" she grabbed his hand, entwining her delicate fingers through his larger ones, and pulled a vial from her pocket. He saw blue liquid shimmer inside the tiny vial for a split second before Elyse threw the vial to the ground, and blue smoke erupted around them.

The ground beneath Killian's feet disappeared, and his body was pulled upward—but downward at the same time. His limbs stretched out like he was on a rack, yet he felt compressed, like his skin was enveloping his body, smothering his organs. The absence of sound was deafening, the darkness blinding. He held tightly to the one thing that kept him tethered to reality—Elyse's fragile hand.

The dirt road returned, along with a row of brick buildings. And the sun—the sun was bright and warm. He could hear again, the sound of his panting breath echoing in his ears.

That wicked gleam was still in Elyse's eyes as she lowered her gaze to her hand, which was still encompassed in his own white-knuckled one.

But Killian's mind was still spinning. He wasn't ready to let go of her hand. What the fuck had just happened? He felt wrong, so, so wrong. Man was not meant to travel in such ways.

"Catch your breath before we go in," Elyse told him. There was a hint of amusement in her voice, but it wasn't unkind, and she made no movement to free her hand from his. She looked as collected as always, not a strand of silvery hair out of place. Her own tranquility mocked his dishevelment.

Killian simply nodded his head when he felt ready, too afraid to open his mouth for fear of vomiting. He released Elyse's hand and took a timid step toward the brick building before him. The street was abandoned, the buildings like ghosts. But Elyse walked surefooted to the bedraggled wooden door. She lifted one slender finger and traced a quick but intricate design on the surface of the door, and Killian heard the lock click open.

Elyse paused as she reached for the handle. "Don't say a word," she ordered.

Killian's irritation returned to him, pushing out all the queasiness of their godforsaken method of traveling. He wanted to grab her by the shoulder and remind her that this was *his* investigation, and that she was assisting *him*, but before he could do so, Elyse turned the knob and strolled into the building.

The moment the door opened, a pungent smell met his nose. It was acrid and rotting and vile.

"What is this place?" Killian growled.

The windows were boarded up, but several small fires smoldered around the room, casting nefarious shadows across the walls. He spotted a handful of figures, their backs stooped as they hovered over what Killian could only assume were cauldrons.

Elyse didn't bother answering him. Her stride was sure and cool as she approached the silhouette of a stocky man in the center of the room. Killian followed. It wasn't until they were standing a few feet away from the man that Killian could make out his features. His stern face was studying a cluttered pile of parchments, and his faded red hair was combed across the top of his head in a poor attempt to hide his pale scalp.

The stocky man looked up and nearly jumped when he spotted Elyse. "To what do I owe the pleasure?" he asked in a gruff voice.

"Hi, Pete. Has Bast been around? I might have a job for him." As Elyse spoke, Killian saw the way she brimmed with authority, and the way Pete seemed to squirm beneath her gaze, sweat glistening on his brow.

But before Pete could answer, one of the other men in the room approached him, flustered.

"Pete, we're out of baby teeth."

Pete rubbed a pudgy hand against the back of his neck. "Just use the adult teeth, 'en. Should work the same."

The man hurried away to the corner of the room, where crates and baskets littered the floor. Killian looked more closely at the cauldrons, which boiled with thick, bubbling liquid. They were making potions, likely for sale. And they weren't even bothering to get the ingredients right. He expected nothing less from mangy, black market warlocks.

Killian took a deep breath, but the putrid stench did nothing to calm him.

"Bast, eh?" Pete said, returning his attention to Elyse. Then his gaze slid slowly to Killian, who instinctively straightened his posture. "Naw, I haven't seen 'im in a few days," Pete continued.

Elyse jerked her chin toward Killian. "He's with me. I vouch for him," she said coolly.

Pete continued to give Killian a wary look but said, "Ye might check Lex's place. 'E's been known to go on a bender there."

A bender. Why wasn't Killian surprised?

Elyse thanked Pete and flipped him a silver piece, which he pocketed greedily.

"What is this place?" Killian asked him.

He didn't have to look at Elyse to feel her hateful gaze incinerating him.

Pete tilted his head and offered a rough, "Wot's it look like?" He turned to mockingly survey the room, holding his hands wide to display the dimly lit operation. His brows knitted together as he spotted something that made him waddle over to the nearest cauldron.

"No, no, no!" he shouted at a boy who couldn't have been older than twelve. "Ye put the doe's blood in *after* the potion stops boilin'."

The boy froze, a large wooden spoon in one hand and a now empty jar in the other, both of which trembled.

Pete snatched the wooden spoon from the boy and gave the mixture a stir. "Won't do no good now. We'll have to sell it at half price," he spat.

Killian tried not to flinch but failed. It was hard enough to listen to Pete berate the boy, but his disregard for following any sort of protocol was just as bad. He looked at Elyse, but her eyes were glued to the ground.

Every fiber of Killian's body screamed at him. The regulations regarding potion-making were in place for a reason. Who knew how many people would be hurt from such negligence? He didn't want any more families to suffer the way his had.

"Get back to work!" Pete barked at the rest of the crew, who all stood staring at the boy.

Killian assessed the room. There were six of them total—Pete, the boy, and four others. He wanted to arrest them, but he knew he couldn't. He was damn good with his knife, but he couldn't take them all on. Who knew what sort of tricks they'd pull? Not to mention, he didn't even know if Elyse would have his back.

"Thanks again," Elyse called to Pete. This time, she grabbed Killian by the wrist and walked steadily toward the door. Killian didn't fight her. He knew what he had to do.

CHAPTER 17

— · —

ELYSE

Elyse was furious. She had given Killian one job—one damn job. To keep his mouth shut. She'd vouched for him, and then he had to go and ask a stupid question. Didn't he know she had a reputation to uphold? She should have gone alone, but Killian's trust in her was already thin enough. He never would have let her go alone.

They were no less than two steps outside the building when Killian demanded, "Take me back to the palace."

Elyse whirled on him, dropping his wrist. Who did he think he was, ordering her around?

"We should go to Lex's now—before Pete tips Bast off that some asshole asking stupid questions is looking for him."

"No," he said, his voice unwavering. "That can wait. I need to get a unit out here to shut this place down."

"Are you out of your mind? Do you know how that will look?" He couldn't be serious. She should magick him straight to Lex's.

But Killian's face was full of grave anger as he took a step back, out of her reach. "They're making illegal potions and selling them. My duty is to uphold the law."

"Forget your duty," she growled. "If you send your men in there, I'll lose all credibility. You think they won't link it back to me? You're a bigger imbecile than I thought."

Killian just shook his head, unfazed by her insult. "Those potions are dangerous. Innocent people could get hurt. And that boy—"

"*That boy*," Elyse interrupted, "probably needs this job. They all do. And the people who buy from Pete are hardly innocent. If they're stupid enough to buy from him, then they deserve whatever fate they meet."

With a deadly speed that was far too quick for someone who never used magic, Killian grabbed Elyse by the front of her tunic and shoved her up against a nearby wall. His left forearm pressed hard against her chest, pinning her to the brick. His right hand held a knife to her throat. With every breath, the cool blade pressed against her skin.

But her hands were still free. She wiggled her fingers, preparing a spell. Killian snarled in her ear. "*Don't.*"

His breath was warm on her skin. She looked into his eyes and saw fury pulsating there—fury that was so far beyond the stoicism he usually bore. Something had triggered him, unleashing a denizen of chaos. Elyse didn't know if it was something he'd seen in Pete's warehouse, or if it was something she'd said. Frankly, she didn't care.

"Do it," she urged him, tilting her head further back against the brick wall and baring her neck for him. His threat hadn't landed the way he'd hoped it would. Being slaughtered here by the lieutenant's knife would only confirm her suspicions–that she wasn't truly worthy of being cured from the widow's decay.

Killian's nostrils flared, but he didn't move. His knife remained steady at her throat, though his ragged breathing betrayed his emotion.

Finally, he released her, and her hands flew to her throat. She expected to feel a trickle of blood, and was surprised when her hands came away clean. She stared daggers at Killian, planning her next move.

In an icy voice, Killian said, "Fine. We'll go to Lex's."

His face was still grave, fuming with ire, but he offered his hand out to her.

She slowly reached her left hand toward him, while her right hand stayed in her pocket, clutching the blue vial, readying herself to haul them out of there before either of them could do anything stupid.

But it was too late for that.

She felt it before she saw it, the cold iron of shackles clamped around her wrist. Still clutching the vial, she freed her right hand from her pocket and made to throw it to the ground—but Killian predicted her move. He gripped her hand tightly, and she could feel the bones pressing against one another in ways they shouldn't, before he shackled that wrist too.

Rage flowed through her as she released an animalistic growl. She flicked her wrists toward him, reveling in the onslaught that would soon rain down on him—

But nothing happened.

Killian grasped the iron chain that bound the two cuffs together, and yanked her in close. Their chests pressed against one another, each breathing at a rapid, frantic pace.

"I thought these might come in handy," he purred in her ear. "These shackles are special. You can't do any magic while you wear them."

When he pulled away, the smirk he bore made Elyse snarl. It was a smirk of victory, well plotted and well earned. She wanted to scratch his eyes out and tear that stupid smile right off his face. Yet in these shackles, she could barely move, and she certainly couldn't take on a lieutenant of the Royal Guard.

She had no choice but to let him drag her all the way back to the palace.

CHAPTER 18

—·—

ELYSE

Elyse sat in Killian's office, her wrists still cuffed. At least he had stowed her away in there instead of an interrogation room or a dungeon cell. Still, the small kindness did little to quell her anger.

It had been an hour since Killian shoved her into his office, ordered two guards to stand watch outside the door, and marched off down the hall. He didn't need to tell her where he was going. It was obvious he was gathering a posse of soldiers to go and arrest Pete and his men, and shut down their entire operation.

What in hell had gotten into him? He'd been so agitated, even more brooding than usual. She'd known he despised magic, but at the tavern he'd at least kept himself in check. Whatever he'd seen at Pete's warehouse made him reckless—reckless enough to go and ruin her reputation. What would happen once word got out that she was going around with a member of the Royal Guard?

Refusing to think on it further, she stood and ambled around the room, taking in the hundreds of items that lined the walls. Among all the parchments, maps, and medals of excellence, there was not one personal memento. Perhaps he kept them in his bedroom or . . .

She slipped over to his desk and began rummaging through the drawers. Most of it was uninteresting. He had more quills and jars of ink than one person could use in a lifetime. She opened another drawer and reached to the very back. Her fingers clutched a familiar vial, and she recognized it to be the one she sold him on the day they met, the one that would prevent any hexes from working on him. How curious that he had kept it.

She didn't have long to reflect on it, though, as the door opened and Killian appeared.

A flicker of annoyance—or perhaps amusement—passed over his face. "I wouldn't have stowed you in here if there was anything worth finding or stealing."

Elyse stood and held the vial so he could see it. "Odd of you to keep this," she said. "What if it came from Pete's crew?"

She'd meant it as a joke, but Killian strode across the room and snatched it from her hands.

"You never know when it'll come in handy," he said as he pocketed the vial.

Elyse just gritted her teeth. She wanted to slip into her usual stance—leaning against a wall with crossed arms—but the shackles made it impossible, so she settled for merely glaring at him.

He didn't seem to care. "I've sent a group of guards to the warehouse. They should be there soon."

Elyse let out a huff and rolled her eyes as a slew of curses ran through her mind.

"How the fuck do you expect me to remain in business after this?" she spat.

Killian barely glanced at her as he sat down at his desk and unraveled one of the scrolls of parchment. "You seem like a smart woman. You'll think of something."

She didn't say anything as her eyes continued to bore into him. He was acting like this was a game, like Pete and the others were pawns to be used to lord his power over her. They were supposed to be *helping* one another, and yet he barely seemed to care about the repercussions of his actions.

Killian looked up at her with a smile and added, "I could throw you in the dungeons with them. They'll think you got duped too."

She shook her head and turned her back on him. Oh, the things she would do to him if her hands weren't magically incapacitated. She'd been a fool to think they could ever cooperate. Slowly rotting away from the widow's decay would surely be better than spending a week with him.

As if summoned by the thought, her rash began to itch. Elyse struggled within the constraints of the shackles to scratch her forearm. As the itch faded, she let out a sigh. She was, of course, being dramatic. She'd seen the toll that widow's decay had taken on her mother, and she spent so much of her time in denial that she would share the same awful fate. Working with Killian for six more days would be worth every moment of frustration if it meant she could be cured.

When she finally glanced over her shoulder at Killian, she was surprised to see him watching her. His posture held none of the swagger he'd carried a moment ago.

"I'm sorry," he murmured, much to Elyse's surprise. Yet she forced her expression to remain cold.

"My intention was not to harm your business or your reputation," he continued, his voice calm and measured. "I only wanted to protect innocent civilians from danger, and I'm sorry for any consequences that may bring. And—" he paused, inhaling slowly as if drawing strength, "I shouldn't have threatened you like that. I'm sorry—truly."

Elyse pursed her lips and blinked a few times. She wasn't sure what to say. Apologies weren't something she heard often, unless they were coerced from thieves. She studied his face and found genuine strife. Maybe he did understand how Pete's arrest would affect her. Maybe, whatever had compelled him to act was just stronger. As much as she hated to admit it, his conviction was somewhat admirable.

"I will take your apology into consideration," she said as she turned back toward the wall.

"Can't you do a memory charm or something?" Killian asked. "Make them forget that you were there?"

Elyse shifted her weight as she considered it. That was a viable solution. No one had seen them come or go from the warehouse, and if they didn't remember her being there then they couldn't connect her to the arrest. But it was beside the point. He had blindsided her, held a knife to her throat, and put her in handcuffs. And Pete's crew were good men. Okay, maybe not *good* men, but they weren't the worst either. And the boy . . .

Killian seemed to read her thoughts because he said, "We won't keep the boy in jail. I'll take him somewhere safe. Somewhere where he can go back to school."

Elyse bit her lip for a moment, thinking. Aside from the blatant disrespect he'd shown her, she supposed no real harm was done that couldn't be salvaged. It wasn't like this was the first time Pete had been arrested, and it likely wouldn't be the last. And Killian was right about the boy. He deserved to be in school with other children his age, not slaving over a cauldron.

Finally, Elyse turned to face Killian, and nodded her head.

Killian let out an exhale, then stood tall and stepped toward her. "If I take these cuffs off, are you going to attack me?"

"I guess you'll just have to see," she purred.

He reached into his pocket and pulled out a tiny brass key. Taking her hand delicately in his, he lifted her wrists and undid the clasp.

Once she was free, Elyse twisted and flexed her wrists, noting the slight bruising. She flicked her hands toward Killian, pretending to cast a spell. To his credit, Killian barely flinched.

"Very funny," he said dryly.

"This doesn't mean I forgive you," she replied.

"I know," Killian said softly. "I wouldn't expect you to. But it still had to be done."

At least he had conviction. That was something she could respect.

"Fine," she hissed. "But I think it goes without saying that if you *ever* hold a knife to my throat again—if you ever put me in shackles—if you so much as *look* at me the wrong way, I will not hesitate to hex your head right up your ass."

Killian brows lifted. "I'd actually like to see that."

"Shut up," she snarled.

"No, seriously," he laughed. "Can you show me on Manny?"

"You're a bastard," Elyse spat, though she had to hide her own amusement.

Killian pursed his lips, trying and failing to stop from smiling. He laid a hand over his heart and said, "I promise, from here on out I will treat you with the utmost respect."

"Good," Elyse snapped, holding her chin high.

They stared at each other, unsure how to move forward. For all their banter, which Elyse was actually starting to enjoy, they were truly from different worlds. They would never be able to see eye to eye.

After a beat, Killian cleared his throat. "I'll walk you out," he said, turning toward the door.

They ambled through the corridors of the building and out to the courtyard where the sun was setting overhead.

"Meet here tomorrow?" Killian said. It wasn't a command but more of a request. "Bring whatever you need for the memory spell, and then we'll go to Lex's and see if we can find Bast—if that works for you?"

Elyse raised an eyebrow curiously. "Are you being polite?"

Killian rubbed the back of his neck and let out a sigh. "It's been a long day. I don't think I have any more fight in me."

Elyse smirked up at him. "Don't worry, I have enough fight for both of us."

She winked, and the corner of Killian's lips tugged ever so slightly.

Without saying goodbye, she strolled through the iron gates. She was still pissy about being cuffed and hauled around like a prisoner, but at least she was one day closer to a cure.

CHAPTER 19

KILLIAN

The next day, Killian's ears rang as blue smoke wafted around him. Elyse had just transported them from the palace to somewhere outside the city limits, wherever this Lex fellow's hideout was. She had been cold and unreadable all morning, even after she'd performed the memory charm to ensure she wouldn't be associated with Pete and his crew's arrest. Not that it surprised him. Witches were probably the type to hold grudges.

He'd be lying if he said he'd lost sleep over her irritation. He knew he'd done the right thing by breaking up that sorry excuse for a business, and if Elyse had to do a little clean up, then so be it. At least now she knew that Killian wasn't someone to be fucked with.

Elyse shucked Killian's hand off her own and trudged toward the house before them. The building was a step up from Bast's place, not that that said much. At least there were painted shutters surrounding the windows, and the smell of stale mead wasn't stinking up the whole grounds.

Elyse didn't even glance at him before she banged on the front door. Killian heard laughter coming from inside. He counted three or four distinct voices, all male.

"Elyse," Killian whispered. "If Bast recognizes me—"

"I've got it covered," she hissed back at him.

He was about to ask what the hell that meant, but the door opened a crack. Elyse didn't bother to greet whoever stood on the other side. She simply shoved her forearm against the door and pushed her way in.

"Lex!" she called out.

Killian stepped cautiously behind her into the house. The room was stifling, the air stagnant despite the mild weather outside. A cask of ale sat in the corner, half drunk, with flies buzzing around it. Killian quickly surveyed the man who opened the door. He was stout, his face bruised, and he held a decent sized knife at his side. The man was sizing him up as well.

"Wot's she on about?" grumbled a man seated at a table. He glared up at them from behind a handful of cards, his buddies on either side of him doing the same. If they had any weapons on them, they weren't currently displayed.

"Lex!" Elyse shouted again, and Killian turned slightly to take in the rest of the room while still keeping an eye on the doorman. In the corner, standing straight as an arrow, his eyes glued to Elyse, was Bast. He either hadn't noticed or hadn't recognized Killian.

"Elyse—" the doorman began, but she shot him a stern look that quickly shut him up.

Footsteps sounded from upstairs, slow and methodical. Killian traced them as they walked down a flight of stairs at the back of the house, then through a hallway. A door at the far end of the room opened, and a man, tall and strong with slicked back hair, stood facing Elyse as if no one else were there. A flicker of amusement danced in his eyes.

"Elyse," he said in a voice so low, so quiet, Killian had to strain his ears to hear it. "What a pleasure."

"Lex," Elyse said, equally low but with none of the quiet patience of the man. "We have a problem."

Lex threw a seductive smile at her as he clasped his hands behind his back, and Killian's stomach roiled.

"And what might that be?"

Killian tried not to gag at Lex's whole demeanor, the haughty tone of his voice.

"Him." Elyse pointed dramatically at Bast, who hadn't moved one inch. Killian wasn't even sure if the man was breathing.

"M-me?" he stammered.

"Yes, you!" Elyse spat as she took a step toward him. "You're putting everyone at risk. You've been going around bragging about killing someone important, one night after the king's murder, and now the guards are coming after all of our asses, looking for *you*."

Bast flinched at each accusation she threw at him, and he seemed to shrink down into his already small frame.

Lex let out a pompous laugh. "You women and your dramatics." He waved his hand, absently dismissing Elyse's words.

Elyse turned toward Killian. "Tell him," she demanded with a jerk of her chin.

That was when Bast noticed Killian for the first time, his face paling. He took two steps to run—and crashed head first into a wall of hard air.

Everyone's hands flinched toward their weapons, but no one made any moves to draw them.

"Fucking idiot," Elyse sneered, and she stalked toward where Bast lay on the ground, cradling his head. She gripped him by his hair, yanking his head up so he was facing Killian.

"Do you recognize this man?" she asked over Bast's whimpers.

"Y-yes!" he shouted. "He's a guard. He was at my house!"

All eyes shifted to Killian, who had no idea what Elyse's plan was. He stood rigid, glaring back at each and every one of them.

"You're damn right he's a guard. And he's on my payroll," Elyse growled at Bast. "So when he comes to me and says that the whole fucking Guard is looking for some loser named Bast, and that they're going to tear apart every known den, warehouse, tavern—anywhere people with magic go—then I believe him."

Each of the men's eyes were still on Killian, but they had shifted slightly. They were no longer sizing him up as a physical opponent, but as a man to be trusted.

"Fucking hell, Bast," one of the card-players murmured.

Elyse released her grip on Bast's hair, and he fell to the ground again, his whimpering resumed.

Lex still stood on the threshold, his face unreadable. He merely said, "Idle threats are all that is."

This time, Elyse didn't turn to Killian. She glared at Lex as she repeated, "Tell him."

Gods, Killian hoped she knew what she was doing. And he hoped he had guessed correctly at what he was supposed to say next.

"Yesterday, a unit arrested a crew running a black market potions trade out of a warehouse in Hunt's Quarter. All six men are currently residing in the dungeon beneath the palace."

Elyse gave Killian a subtle nod, an imperceptible acknowledgement that he had chosen his words correctly.

"Shit, mate. That's Pete's crew," said the stout doorman.

Killian said coolly, "We were informed Bast is a frequent visitor there."

Now all eyes were on Bast, as the crew began piecing together Elyse's carefully woven story, as they realized the danger they were in just being there—another one of Bast's frequent hideaways.

Bast stopped cowering long enough to look around and see the angry faces of his comrades glaring back at him.

Lex was the only one who didn't appear angry. He gazed calmly upon Bast's fetal form.

"So they've made six arrests?" he chided. "And now you want us to just hand Bast over so we can all go about our dark business?" He clicked his tongue. "Please, Elyse. What are you actually getting at?"

"It's more than just that," she snapped back, and Killian heard the tiniest quiver in her voice. "Three other crews too. Magda's out in the eastern district, Paulie's in midtown, and . . . "

Her voice trailed off as Lex's smile grew wide, a wicked, cheshire grin.

"You really do need to get out more, darling," he said in that slick voice. "Magda's been dead nearly a year now."

Fuck.

One glance at Elyse, and Killian knew she realized the gravity of her mistake. She'd played the wrong card.

The stifling air was now churning, billowing in the anticipation of the fight.

Elyse whipped her palm toward Killian, and suddenly he was flying through the air, his back crashing through the door. He slid a good twenty yards out onto the dirt path. The wind was knocked out of him, and it took him a moment before he groaned and slowly got to his feet.

What the fuck had she done that for?

Still rattled from the blast, Killian struggled to get to his feet. From inside the house came the sounds of blades whirring through the air, and the booms and bright flashes of magic.

He drew his short sword and sprinted toward the open doorway. As he crossed the threshold, what he saw made him stop short.

Elyse was taking on all six men at once. Weapons flew like leaves in a breeze, this way and that, and Killian couldn't tell who was controlling what. Elyse sent a burst of green light at Lex, knocking him back against the wall and wiping the smug grin off his face. Not a second later, another man sliced his dagger toward her, but with a flick of her hand she conjured a shield and blocked his blow. A third man charged at her, and she kicked him square in the chest, sending him stumbling back, toppling into the hearth. With a twiddle of her fingers, she set the hearth ablaze. The man screamed and crawled out of the fiery mess, rolling frantically on the ground to smother the flames.

Killian watched in awe as Elyse moved with grace and speed and fatal precision. She seemed to read their minds, predicting their attacks and countering their moves, pushing back on the offensive. She snatched a short sword out of the air and twirled it around as naturally as any guard at the palace might have.

It dawned on Killian that Elyse hadn't been trying to hurt him by blasting him out the door—she'd been trying to save him from a melee that he was drastically unprepared for.

One of the men noticed Killian standing in the doorway, and he barreled toward him. Killian lifted his sword and prepared to swing, but the man sent a whirl of smoke at him, and Killian had to duck and roll away. The man just laughed and raised his hand toward Killian, then slowly curled his fingers into a fist.

Killian's throat closed up, and he dropped his sword. Both of his hands reached for his neck, clawing at the invisible vines that restricted his airway.

Around him the room was entrenched in chaos, but the man walked slowly toward Killian, a wicked smirk on his face.

"You guards are nothing but scum," he growled.

Killian wanted to tell the man he wasn't exactly fond of him either, but panic took hold of him as his lungs burned for air. His lips parted, but no words escaped—only a strangled rasp.

The man stooped over him and reached toward Killian's sword. Killian tried to kick the sword away, then watched, horrified, as the man merely flicked his fingers and levitated the sword into his grasp.

His vision started to darken, his insides burning.

"I've never killed a guard before," his attacker snarled as he weighed the sword in his hand.

Killian looked around frantically, trying to find anything to use as a weapon, or shield, but he could hardly think straight without air.

The man lifted his hand, preparing for the deathblow—but a blue smoke appeared, and suddenly Elyse was standing beside the man, a dagger in her hand. She plunged the dagger into his ribcage, then whirled back toward the others, flinging spells at each of them.

The man collapsed to the ground as blood spilled from his side.

Killian gasped, and air flooded back into his lungs. He scrambled away from the man's twitching body and leapt to his feet, scouring the room for Elyse. She was battling two of them now, quite literally with one hand tied behind her back in some sort of magical green lasso.

Killian nudged the man's body with his foot, making sure there were no signs of life, before he reached across the body to snatch his sword.

By the time Killian looked back at Elyse, she had freed her bound hand and was shooting indigo arrows toward the men, who dodged them with waves of their hands.

Somewhere in the room, Killian heard a whimper.

He followed the sound to the corner of the room. Bast was curled into a ball, trembling with his knees against his chest. An iridescent shimmer of hard air surrounded him—a shield, no doubt. Killian stalked over to him, furiously gripping his sword. Despite the shield, Bast trembled harder.

Standing over the pathetic man, Killian tested the shield with his sword, jabbing at the shimmering barrier. His sword glanced off it with an eerie zapping sound. Again, he tried, but the shield didn't budge. He kicked at it—and immediately regretted the decision as he grimaced in pain.

He turned back to Elyse. She had knocked one of the men unconscious, and now it was just her against Lex. They circled each other, carefully stepping over debris, their eyes dark and narrowed on one another. Killian tried to think of a way to help, to attack Lex, but Elyse had already managed to disarm four men. Would he do more harm than good?

Lex blasted a ball of flames at Elyse, but she doused it with a quick flick of her fingers. She extended her hand, and a dagger flew into her grasp. Lex tried to send another green rope to entangle her, but she was too quick. In a swift motion, she leaped onto the wall and ran across it, her body parallel to the floor. She hurled herself from the wall to a chair, then jumped from the chair onto Lex, knocking him to the ground.

Killian watched, transfixed, as Elyse pinned Lex to the floor and expertly plunged the dagger into his heart.

The room went still. Elyse's panting breath and Lex's choked gasps clamored in Killian's ears. When Elyse finally rose from the ground, dusting off her black tunic and brushing her silvery hair from her face, Killian realized he was still staring at her. What had he just witnessed? Elyse had single-handedly taken down five grown men using a combination of magical and practical combat. She looked disheveled, yes, but her face held a sobriety that made it clear she was well versed in this sort of brawling.

What was it she said back at the Black Cat? *I don't feel like saving your ass.* He'd taken her words as mere hubris, another instance of her arrogance. He'd never considered that she was actually someone to be revered.

Killian shook his head and turned to face Bast. He was still huddled in the corner behind his shield. Together, Killian and Elyse approached him. She stood with one hand on her hip while Killian watched her, waiting for her to speak or move.

Elyse just glared down at Bast. In that moment, she wasn't just a witch who sold wares to the desperate and ignorant. She was a woman, capable and strong. She could do anything. She could burn the whole world down if she wanted to, though Killian suspected she would never dare. He'd seen the good in her, the way she had guided him at the tavern, the way she genuinely cared for the boy who worked for Pete. So why did she hide away in her cottage, selling love potions and cursed objects?

Elyse lifted a hand and aimed it at Bast, and he let out a piteous moan. Elyse just rolled her eyes and demanded, "Lower your shield or I'll burn the whole place down."

"I-I can't," he stammered.

Without breaking eye contact, Elyse moved her hand toward the wall, and the wooden planks ignited.

Bast moaned again.

"I promise you, we'll be much kinder if you just come out from behind that shield."

The flames raged against the wall in a way no normal fire should, spreading upward and outward, blasting heat across Killian's face. The fire glowed in Bast's dark, beady eyes. Finally, he waved his hand and the shield fell.

Elyse, too, waved her hand, and the flames dispersed, leaving the wall unscathed as it had been before.

"He's all yours, Lieutenant," she said with a smirk.

Killian cleared his throat, which still ached from having the breath sucked out of him.

"Hold out your hands," he instructed.

Bast refused for a moment, but all Elyse had to do was lift her finger, and he was holding out his trembling hands obediently.

Killian snapped the shackles around Bast's wrists, the same shackles he used to bind Elyse the day before. Then he stood up straight, towering over Bast's huddled form.

"You were at the Black Cat tavern the other night, flaunting a full purse and bragging about killing someone important," he said in a low but commanding voice.

Bast's throat bobbed as he squeaked out, "Yes, My Lord."

Elyse rolled her eyes.

"I am not a lord," Killian corrected. "I'm a lieutenant in the Royal Guard, and you will tell me who you killed or—"

"No one!" Bast cried. "I swear it!"

Killian squatted low so he was eye level with Bast, who squirmed, trying to press himself further against the wall.

"Elyse," Killian said, extending his hand toward her.

She slipped a hand into her pocket and pulled out a tiny, clear vial.

Bast's eyes were wide, never leaving the vial as Elyse placed it in Killian's open hand.

"W-what is that? What are you going to do to me?" he blubbered.

"Relax," Killian said with little patience. "It's just a little truth serum." He reached his free hand around to the back of Bast's head, grabbed a handful of his hair, and yanked his head back. Bast squirmed, but Elyse said, "Ah, ah, ah!" with a wag of her finger, and Bast went still again.

"Open up," Killian demanded, and Bast meekly obeyed. Killian uncorked the vial and poured half of it down the coward's throat.

He stood again, watching as Bast's eyes glazed over the way Elyse's had, the way his own surely had.

"Where did you get that money?" he asked.

Bast's reply was calm, his expression blank. "A man came to my house. He brought a hundred gold coins with him. Told me it was all mine, all I had to do was go 'round bragging about killing someone—someone important."

Elyse let out a condescending laugh, a laugh that echoed with, "I told you so."

But Killian ignored her. This was still something. Bast might not have killed the king, but someone was trying to throw him off their trail.

"Who was it? Who gave you the money?"

Bast's voice continued evenly, the truth serum still at work. "It was Tanner, Tanner Wills. He probably thought I couldn't see 'cause it was dark, but he wore his master's ring."

"His master?" Killian pressed, but it was Elyse who answered.

"Tanner works for Niall Royce. Everyone knows Royce. He's a collector."

"A collector?" Killian wondered aloud.

Elyse nodded. "He collects expensive magical items. I've never heard of him using them, though."

"Royce," Killian whispered, letting the name sink into his mind. He'd heard of the man before—a wealthy merchant who ran in elite circles. But what motive would he have for killing the king? His name hadn't come up on the short list of the king's enemies, and the man seemed to be doing well for himself. What would he gain from King Cyril's death?

Bast shivered as the serum wore off. His face went pale, his eyes horror stricken.

"W-what have I done?" he stammered. "Royce will have me killed!"

"You probably should have thought of that before you accepted money from a mysterious figure who wanted you to brag about murdering someone important," Elyse snorted. There was no sympathy in her voice.

Not that Killian felt any sympathy either.

"Come on," he said, grabbing Bast by the upper arm and yanking him to his feet. He had to hold the man upright, his knees were shaking so badly.

"Please, please just kill me! Make it quick!" Bast begged.

The fear in Bast's voice at whatever Royce was capable of did not go unnoticed by Killian, but he wouldn't give in to his pleas.

"Don't worry, you'll be safe in the palace dungeon," Killian said with a hint of satisfaction. Still holding on to Bast's arm, he linked his free hand with Elyse's.

She nodded, pulled a little blue vial from her pocket, and the three of them disappeared in a haze of smoke.

CHAPTER 20

— · —

KILLIAN

A drenaline still coursed through Killian's veins, even after they returned to the palace, deposited Bast in the dungeons, and updated the magistrate. With a spring in his step, he hurried back to his office, where Elyse waited for him.

He opened the office door, expecting to find her snooping again. Instead, she sat behind the desk, reclined in the chair with her boots on the desk and her arms crossed.

"I see you made yourself comfortable," he said as he closed the door behind him. He tried to sound annoyed, but he couldn't mask his own happiness.

"I take it that things went well?" she asked in that even voice of hers, the one that never faltered.

Killian just stared at her for a moment before replying. She'd just killed five men—five grown, magic-wielding men—and there was not a hair out of place or a scratch to be seen. The way her eyes met his, with no hint of remorse or self-hatred, told him all he needed to know. She had killed before. Killian didn't know whether to be in awe of her, or terrified. She strolled around the office to the front of the desk, delicately leaning her petite frame against it, and this time he didn't see a woman crossing her arms defiantly. He saw a woman who was raised as a sorceress and a soldier, who had no place in this world of kings and guards—and she knew it.

"Come on," Killian said softly, his smile still on his lips. "Let's take a walk."

Elyse hesitated for a faint moment before putting on that brave face of hers and following him out of the office.

He led her out of the building and into the courtyard, telling her about his conversation with the magistrate as they went. The magistrate, a middle-aged man named Longfellow with a receding hairline and an oversized nose, had insisted on interviewing Bast. Bast vehemently recanted everything he'd told Killian and Elyse, but Killian wasn't bothered by it. He knew in his gut, knew by the goose pimples on his skin and the weightlessness he felt, that they were on to something.

He and Longfellow agreed that they couldn't just go and arrest Wills or Royce. The citizens of Rhodan were watching them carefully, and any slip ups could incite mistrust in the Royal Guard, and in the newly established king. Arresting someone of Royce's public stature would bring no small amount of attention with it, and if they were wrong—or even if they were right but couldn't prove it—the results would be disastrous. So Killian needed to discreetly gather more information on Royce, something concrete, before making an arrest.

But as Killian and Elyse ambled through the winding paths of the courtyard, passing stone buildings and manicured gardens, Killian wasn't worried or anxious or flustered. He was happy. He had a solid lead, and he was alive. Gods above, he'd thought he'd taken his last breath today, before Elyse swooped in and saved him. She'd done it so swiftly, so beautifully.

"How did you learn to do all that?" he asked. The question had been burning in his throat for hours.

She glanced at him, then set her eyes farther down the path. "The same way you learned to use the sword and the dagger . . . Practice."

"No, I mean," he began, fumbling over his thoughts. "Who taught you?"

Elyse tucked a loose strand of her silvery hair behind her ear. "My mother taught me the basics. She wanted us to be able to defend ourselves, since it was just the two of us."

"That was more than just the basics." It had been incredible—artful even.

She smiled up at him. "I know."

Days ago, Killian would have thought her statement arrogant or haughty. Now that he'd seen what she was capable of, though, he understood her confidence.

"There wasn't much else to do after the shoppe closed each night, so I trained a lot," she continued. "I would beg my mother to send spells at me so I could work on shielding, and I would practice hex after hex until I got them down perfectly."

"What did you practice on?" Killian imagined Elyse as a little hellion, terrorizing unsuspecting customers.

"Anything I could get my hands on," she said, a bit of nostalgia in her voice. "Mostly vegetables, though. My mother taught me how to bewitch them so they would float around on their own, and I could use them as moving targets."

Killian shot her an incredulous look. "So you got that good from playing around with vegetables?"

Elyse laughed, her lips spreading into a wide smile. "No, definitely not. For my thirteenth birthday, my mother paid for someone to come train me for a week. I learned everything I could from him, and incorporated his exercises into my own routine. When I got a little older, I started seeking out others to train me. I didn't just want to be good at fighting—I wanted to know everything about it. The theories behind magical combat, the different styles of fighting." She shook her head as she added, "When I was younger, I had a dream of teaching women to defend themselves, but . . ."

She didn't finish her sentence. Killian glanced at her, only to find anguish in her eyes.

Her words struck a chord within him. He, too, had been enthralled by learning to fight—not just the actions, but the techniques and their histories. He'd poured countless hours into training with the sword, the dagger, the bow and arrow, the staff, and today he'd realized that in Elyse's world, his skills meant nothing.

He knew what he was about to say would be difficult, but it had to be done.

"I know I'm not a defenseless woman . . ." he began tentatively.

Elyse raised one eyebrow at him.

". . . but I was thinking you could train me," he finished.

Elyse's other eyebrow lifted to join the first.

It was probably the last thing she ever expected him to say. Truthfully, he couldn't believe he was saying it either. But if he ever found himself in another predicament like today, he wanted to be sure he could get out alive—even if it meant learning some magic.

To his surprise, Elyse didn't tease him. "I could do that," she replied, never breaking her leisurely pace.

Excitement and anxiety mingled in Killian's stomach. He didn't know if he imagined Elyse's slight smile, or if she was actually looking forward to it. Gods, she would probably make his life hell.

"I should get going," she said after a moment. "I've been a terrible shopkeeper the past few days."

"Of course. The gates are this way," he said, steering her down another path.

They continued walking in silence, and Killian noticed the way her eyes roved over every flower, every precisely trimmed shrub, every white oak that towered to the sky.

"You like flowers, don't you?" he asked. When she looked at him curiously, he added, "I noticed the flowers outside your cottage. They're pristine."

"Magic," Elyse replied with both a glimmer of pride and sorrow in her onyx eyes. "Flowers were my mother's thing. She would have loved to walk in this courtyard."

She returned her gaze to the pale pink chrysanthemums that lined the path.

A servant girl was approaching them, her head held low. As she shuffled past, she lifted her eyes and gave them a brief smile—a smile that Elyse meekly returned.

"How are they handling it? The royal family?" Elyse asked when the servant girl was out of earshot.

Killian didn't need to clarify what she meant. She was asking about King Cyril's death. He cleared his throat before saying, "Not well. Andrielle has nightmares. She's been heard screaming in her sleep. It nearly wakes up the whole palace. And Prince Maelor—King Maelor—he blames himself, though there's nothing he could have done to save his father."

Elyse merely nodded as her throat bobbed. She was no doubt thinking of her own mother's death—and perhaps her father's. Her face was grave, paler than usual as she asked, "What do we do next?"

"Well," Killian sighed. "I'll talk with Manny, see what he's found and what he thinks he can gather on Royce. And then I'll let you know what we decide after that."

They meandered their way back toward the iron gates leading out into the city, and occasionally Elyse reached out and brushed her hand along a shrub or a low-hanging branch. What Killian wouldn't give to know what she was thinking, but he knew better than to ask.

When they crossed the threshold, past the guards and into the bustling city, Killian continued to walk with Elyse a few blocks.

"Are you going to escort me all the way home?" she asked wryly, her expression unreadable.

"Well, no. I thought you would magick yourself back," he said, indicating an empty alleyway.

"I can't," she said. "I only brought three vials, and I've used them all."

Killian did the math quickly in his head. One to take them to the hideout. One to take them back to the palace . . . His throat went dry as he realized the third one—the one she'd used to transport herself across the room to save him. And not only had she saved him then, but she had blasted him out of the house at the start of the fight, leaving her alone to handle the band of assailants.

"Elyse," Killian murmured. He gently touched her upper arm, guiding her toward the side of the road and out of traffic. But he didn't know what to say. Her dark eyes peered up at him, her silvery hair shining white against the sunlight, but no words seemed to come to his mind to express how truly grateful he was—for everything.

So they stood there like that, his hand on her arm, their eyes locked, exchanging a look of understanding.

Finally Killian said, "You didn't have to do that. Especially after yesterday . . ." His voice trailed off as his hand slid down her arm, grazing her strong but feminine muscles. He could have sworn she leaned into his touch, just the slightest bit, and without thinking, his feet took a minuscule step toward her.

She still held his gaze, her pale lashes sparkling in the sun.

"Of course. I had to," she said as she finally looked away. "I need that cure."

Something twisted in Killian's stomach.

"Right," he breathed, letting his hand fall to his side. "Of course." It was obvious then, wasn't it? She had merely acted in her own best interests, as she likely always did. He took a step back, and the noise of the crowded street came buzzing back to his ears.

Elyse took a step back as well. "Tomorrow morning," she said. "Early. I'll pick you up at dawn."

"You'll pick me up?" he started to ask, but then realized the implication. She would transport them wherever they were going. "Ah. I'll be ready by the gates."

"Good." She took a step back and gave him a salute. "Lieutenant," she said sternly, before she turned and disappeared into the crowd.

Chapter 21

Elyse

*F*ire *blazed around Elyse. It did not burn her, but she coughed from the haze of smoke. Ear-splitting screams assaulted her ears. They wouldn't stop, no matter how much she begged them to. The flames grew taller as her anguish crescendoed.*

The smoke dissipated, and Elyse could see a form taking shape before her. The familiar black skull, the one whose eyes were alight with fire, whose voice was a cold, nauseating growl. The skull opened its jaw, a toothless but distinct snarl overtaking its features, and—

Elyse sat upright in her bed, panting. It was just a nightmare. No screams met her ears, no flames engulfed her bedroom. She chanced a look at the altar that stood in the corner of the room, the one with a black skull perched in the center, surrounded by crystals and dried flowers. But the skull didn't move. It didn't burst into flames and speak to her. Not today.

The room was still dark as dawn had not yet graced the sky. Elyse exhaled and fell back into her bed—and then she remembered. Dawn. She'd promised Killian she would meet him and train him.

Damn. Why had she agreed to train him, least of all so early? She was not a morning person in the slightest, but she knew she needed to spend the day at the shoppe she'd been neglecting. She grumbled as she rolled out of her small bed and padded downstairs.

With a sleepy wave of her hand, a fire sparked in the hearth, warming the kettle that hung there. Then she set to work grinding citronascia leaves for her tea, as she did every morning.

Stupid, stupid, stupid, she told herself with every mash and twist of the pestle. And not just for agreeing to train him, but for letting him pull her in so deep. She needed to stay far away from him—he was a lieutenant in the Royal Guard for the devil's sake.

She hated the way she was starting to grow comfortable around him. Nausea hit her as she recalled telling him about her childhood, about her mother. He'd listened so intently, curious to know more. What if she told him the truth? That she grew up with no friends, that her mother hid them away out here in the forest so that no one would learn their secret. That she was more dangerous than he understood, and that he would hate her if he knew what she was hiding from him.

Yet here she was, going around with a damn lieutenant and helping him arrest black market mages. Or worse, killing them. Not that she would miss Lex and his crew. They were nothing but lazy scoundrels trying to get rich on half-assed schemes.

The kettle screeched and she levitated it to pour steaming water over her freshly ground leaves. The citronascia tea was pungent, but necessary. She would never be caught dead without the magical protections it offered. Just this week, it had already saved her ass more than once. If it weren't for the tea, she would probably be hiding out in one of the lesser kingdoms right now.

As she sipped her tea, she considered that it wasn't too late to run. The Emporium turned a great profit, and she'd stashed away most of her earnings. She could get a little cottage far, far away. She wouldn't even have to work, just mind her garden and read. But even as she thought of it, she knew she would be dreadfully bored.

Her rash itched, reminding her of another reason she couldn't run away. Even if she managed to leave, she wouldn't last more than a few months without a cure. Killian certainly knew how to play his hand.

Killian. Damn him and his stupid dimples. And damn her for thinking about his dimples. They had entranced her as they stood together on the city streets—along with his kind brown eyes that shone with much more than simple gratitude. For a moment, she'd thought he was going to kiss her. And for a moment, she had wondered what his lips would taste like.

But it had just been the adrenaline from the fight that had her swooning for him. He had fought bravely, if not poorly. She was curious to see how he handled himself with a little training.

But that would be it. She would train him a few times, they would get something on Royce, and they would arrest him. Then she'd get her cure. After that, she'd likely never see Killian again. It would be for the best, that much she was certain of.

She swallowed down the last of the bitter tea before she hurried up the stairs to put on her usual long-sleeved black tunic, tan trousers, and leather boots. Then she stuffed a few vials in her pocket and headed out to the edge of the wards.

CHAPTER 22

— · —

KILLIAN

As Elyse strode down the empty street toward Killian, the rising sun behind her painted a backdrop of hazy orange above the wood and stone buildings. She moved slowly, surreptitiously, like a white-haired cat.

"Good morning," she yawned in greeting.

Killian, on the other hand, was wide awake. He'd been up for an hour already, eating breakfast and looking over documents, both of which failed to distract him. Although he felt this training was necessary, he was dreading it. The thought of actually using magic made him restless. He just wanted to go for a long run through the forest to clear his mind.

But he was a soldier, and he had work to do.

"Not a morning person?" he asked.

Her only response was an indiscernible grumble.

"And yet you wake up early for me?" he said, playfully laying his hand over his heart. "I'm touched."

"We'll see how touched you are after I kick your ass," she mumbled. She slipped her hand into Killian's.

"Here?" he asked, but apparently she couldn't be bothered to pick a more discrete location or even vocalize that to Killian before she threw the blue vial on the ground.

It was much easier to cope with the transportation once he knew what to expect. This time, as they whirled through time and space and landed in the forest, his ears barely rang and he was hardly out of breath. He paused to get his bearings, which was difficult in the unfamiliar woods, but Elyse simply released his hand and marched off in a seemingly arbitrary direction.

"Where are we?" he tried to say through still-numb lips as he stumbled after her.

"My cottage is just up here," she said with a vague gesture. "There are wards preventing anyone from magicking in or out of the property."

She stepped expertly over roots and around trees. Killian had no doubt she could have walked this path blindfolded.

"I talked to Manny," he called out after her. She didn't answer, so he continued. "He's going to look into Royce. I'll let you know what he finds."

Still, she said nothing. Had she heard him? Was she sleepwalking?

He spotted the cottage up ahead, but instead of approaching the front door, Elyse veered toward the back. Killian jogged to catch up. For someone so short, she walked very quickly.

Behind the house was a small vegetable garden, a chicken coop, and even a little pond. But Elyse continued past all of them, marching farther into the woods.

"Where are we going?" Killian asked as he stepped into stride beside her.

This time Elyse turned to look up at him. "You'll see."

They walked for another five minutes or so, Killian's curiosity growing with every step, until they came to a clearing.

His jaw fell open.

Wooden contraptions filled the space, making an obstacle course full of ramps, trapezes, climbing walls, platforms, and so much more. Stuffed burlap mannequins—the same type the Royal Guard used for training—were scattered throughout the course.

Elyse studied Killian's face as he took in the scene. Without taking her eyes off him, she waved a hand toward the obstacles, and the course came to life.

The ledges on the climbing wall started to shift, changing their positions with ease. Logs suspended from a scaffold swung back and forth across the path. Levers worked to raise and lower platforms, and the mannequins seemed to move of their own accord.

Killian felt Elyse's light touch on his chin as she gently pushed his jaw closed.

"Don't worry," she said with a false sweetness. "You won't be attempting any of this today."

With another wave of her hand, all the motions stopped.

Apparently more awake, she moved gracefully through the course. Killian followed closely behind her, marveling at all the gadgets. Elyse stopped when they reached the center, in what appeared to be a large fighting ring.

"Here," she said. She held out a pale pink crystal toward him.

"What's this?" He took the crystal and examined it. He could feel its subtle power radiating through his hand, humming happily, and he didn't know what to make of the sensation. It was both invigorating and foreboding.

"It's a crystal," Elyse said plainly.

Killian shot her a look that said, "Obviously."

Elyse narrowed her eyes. "You really don't know? You need it to do magic."

In truth, he'd never thought about how people did magic, just that they did it and it was reprehensible. He studied the crystal again, weighing it in his hand.

"Why is it pink?"

Elyse shrugged and gave him a half smile. "It suits you."

He huffed his disapproval as he slipped the crystal into his pocket. "How does it work?"

"Everyone has a small amount of innate magic. The crystal just helps to harness it and channel it into something physical," Elyse explained with little enthusiasm.

Killian felt a tiny wave of nausea. He had magic within him? The thought unsettled him.

"So anyone can do magic?" he asked. "Are there limits to what I can do?"

Elyse nodded. "There will be limits. Some people's powers are more inclined to different areas of magic. Take Sera, for example. She comes from a long line of clairvoyant women, so she's predisposed to be a seer. But reading people takes different catalysts, like tarot cards and tea leaves. She's excellent with telling fortunes, but when it comes to physical magic, she's . . . well, unremarkable."

Killian pondered this for a moment. "So I likely won't be able to predict the future?"

The corner of Elyse's mouth turned up slightly. "No, not unless you have a clairvoyant relative you didn't know about. And even then, it tends to be passed down only to women."

A mixture of relief and disappointment swirled in Killian's mind. He'd only just learned he had some innate magic, and yet he simultaneously wished for immense power, and felt disgusted by it.

"What about you? What is your magic inclined for?"

"Physical magic," Elyse replied.

"So you use a crystal?"

She shifted slightly on her feet. "No, I don't need one." Then abruptly, she added. "Shall we get started?"

Why was she changing the subject? It was rare for Elyse to appear rattled, even if only slightly.

"What do you mean you don't need one?" he pressed, enjoying her discomfort.

She shrugged. "I just don't."

"Does that mean you're more powerful?"

"I suppose."

"Are there limits to what you can do?" From what he had seen so far, Killian felt as if Elyse could do anything. "Can you turn invisible? Or travel through time?"

Elyse frowned and crossed her arms over her chest. "So many questions."

Killian only smiled at her. "Consider it part of my training."

She rolled her eyes. "Yes, I'm one of the few people who can turn invisible. No, I cannot travel through time."

Truthfully, Killian was fascinated. He opened his mouth to ask more questions, but Elyse held up a hand.

"No more questions. Take off your shoes," she ordered.

Killian didn't move. Surely she was having a go at him.

"Take. Off. Your. Shoes," she said again, enunciating clearly for him.

But Killian just furrowed his brows and asked, "Why?"

Elyse put a hand on her hip. "Because it will help you feel the earth's energy. And because I said so," she added with extra snark.

He stared at her for a few moments, but she didn't retract the order. So Killian knelt down, unlaced his boots, and removed them.

"Pew," Elyse said, waving her hand in front of her nose.

"Oh please," he said, rolling his eyes, though he smiled.

"Now plant your feet firmly on the ground," she instructed. "And close your eyes."

This was it. He was really going to learn to do magic—the very thing he'd spent so much of his life hating. He told himself it wasn't too late. He could change his mind and head back to the palace right now. But there was something about Elyse's challenging stare that made him want to find out exactly what he was capable of.

He set his feet shoulder width apart, firmly planted on the cold, hard dirt, then closed his eyes and let his hands lay gently by his sides.

"Breathe in," came Elyse's soft voice, "and feel the power coming from the ground, and from the crystal."

She had to be joking, right? He could feel no power coming from the ground, so instead he focused on the crystal vibrating quietly in his pocket.

"Continue to breathe in and out slowly, concentrating on that power."

He did so, and felt the crystal grow a touch warmer—so slight that he might have missed it if he hadn't been focusing so hard on it. Or perhaps it was his imagination.

"Fighting with magic is ninety percent defense, and ten percent finding the perfect moment to strike when your opponent is off balance."

Killian let out a slow exhale through his mouth.

"Luckily, summoning a shield of hard air is one of the easier spells to learn," Elyse continued.

Killian inhaled through his nose, the way he had done in hundreds of sessions of combat training.

"Starting off, you'll want to say the words aloud. It will help you harness the power."

Killian breathed out again through his mouth, and the crystal sang at the word "power."

"Repeat after me," Elyse said. "*Aerodurum.*"

"Aerodurum," Killian repeated. The word felt ridiculous coming off his lips.

"Again," she demanded.

"Aerodurum," he said again, this time with a little more force.

"Good," she commended. "Now feel it. Imagine it. Let your mind and your body tell the world around you what to do."

Killian squeezed his eyes tighter. "Aerodurum," he said, and he was surprised by the way his hand instinctively waved as he spoke the word.

"Like you mean it—like your life depends on it," she growled at him.

"Aerodurum!" he snarled back, flicking his wrist defiantly.

"Open your eyes."

There was a seductive cruelty in her voice that made Killian hesitate, but he blinked a few times and peered at her.

She stood in the center of the ring, one hand holding a half dozen small stones, the other hand tossing a stone menacingly in the air before catching it gracefully, and tossing it again.

"Let's see what you've got," she said with a wicked smile.

She chucked the rock at him with unnatural precision, and his soldier instincts kicked in.

"Aerodurum!" he shouted as he flicked his right hand toward the rock.

It pelted him in the chest and fell to the dirt with an unceremonious *thud*.

Elyse barely waited for it to land before she chucked another one.

"Aerodurum!" Killian said again. This time the stone hit him in the shoulder.

Then another. And another. And another. Elyse seemed to have an endless supply of stones in that tiny, pale hand of hers.

Killian started to move back and forth, zigging and zagging around the ring, but her aim stayed true.

"Aerodurum! Aerodurum! *Aerodurum!*" he spat out time after time, but no shield conjured to protect him.

"I learned this spell when I was three years old," Elyse mocked him.

"Well—aerodurum—isn't that great—aerodurum—for you?" he quipped back. He was breathing heavily and starting to sweat, but he was far too stubborn to quit.

The more he struggled, the more Elyse seemed to enjoy herself. Her body was practically shaking with all her laughter.

"Let go of your inhibitions," she called to him. "I can get you some ale if you'd like."

Killian considered her offer for a moment before trying—and failing—to block another stone.

"Come on," she whined. "It's not even fun anymore."

When had it ever been fun?

"Fight!" she screamed. "If you won't fight for yourself then fight for Manny! Fight for your mother!"

Killian pictured them—Manny and his ridiculous bravado, his mother in her apron, a wooden spoon in her hand. He pictured his men, who he pushed through drills just like this to make them stronger, to give them a chance at survival. To give them a chance to become a part of something bigger than they had ever dreamed of. He pictured his beloved King Cyril, who had been ripped from his family and his kingdom.

Still the stones pelted him, a maelstrom of rocks thudding against his arms, chest, and legs.

No, Killian thought. He knew who he fought for.

"Aerodurum!" he bellowed from somewhere deep in his lungs.

The stone bounced off an iridescent wall and *thunked* to the ground.

Killian was panting, his eyes wide. He'd used magic! He stared at the rock, at the little ripple of dirt around it. He had done that.

Elyse, on the other hand, seemed unimpressed.

"Do it again," she ordered.

It took another ten stones before Killian was able to produce the shield again, but after that he blocked them more often than not. They did this for an hour, circling one another in the ring as the sun rose higher and higher in the sky.

When they stopped, Killian was thoroughly winded, though physically he had barely done anything more than walk around and wave his hands.

Elyse squeezed her hand shut, and the stones she was palming disappeared.

"You're not a natural, but you're getting the hang of it," she commented.

"Thanks, I guess," was Killian's response. He couldn't argue it. Nothing about that had seemed natural, but he was starting to feel less self-conscious about yelling gibberish and waving his hands.

"Come on," she laughed. "I'll make you some tea."

They walked slowly back to the cottage, Killian flexing and stretching his exhausted muscles the whole time. When they reached the shoppe, the familiar scent of incense greeted Killian. He spotted the phoenix, perched in its spot atop a shelf, and the oversized ledger, sprawled across the worktable. The potions and cursed objects didn't set him on edge the way they had the first time he'd been there.

Elyse headed straight to the hearth and grabbed a jar of dried leaves from atop the mantle.

"Adulphia leaves," she said, raising the jar for him to see. "It helps replenish your energy."

"Any . . . side effects?" he asked, not bothering to hide the skepticism in his voice.

"No," Elyse replied curtly as she poured the already steaming kettle over a mug. "Unless you consider hearing voices a 'side effect.'"

Killian sent her a playful glare as he took the mug from her. They were both quiet as he reflected on the training. It hadn't been nearly as bad as he'd imagined. He'd worried that she would make him slice open his hand and give blood to the goddess of war, or something ridiculous like that. Instead, it was very straightforward—surprisingly so. He didn't feel as disgusted with himself as he'd expected.

In truth, he was itching to try the obstacle course out back. Who had designed and built it? Elyse must have devoted countless hours to training if she'd gone through the effort to construct such mechanisms. He wondered how his own men would fare against her.

And even more curiously, she didn't need a crystal to harness magic. Was that common? The way she'd clammed up when he asked her about it made him think it was not.

The tea had cooled to a manageable temperature, and he took a sip. Its warmth spread through his body, immediately revitalizing him.

"So, do I start hearing the voices right away? Or . . ."

Elyse smiled as she peered up at him through her lashes. A different kind of warmth spread through Killian, one he tried to push away.

"I'm starving," he announced, breaking the silence. "I could eat a whole roast."

"I don't have any meat, but I have some bread," Elyse replied. "Maybe some vegetables."

Killian blinked at her a few times. "Some bread and some vegetables? Maybe?" he repeated. "Is that all you eat?"

Elyse just shrugged. "It feels silly to cook a whole meal for one. I usually just use a duplication spell, and it works best on simpler items."

Killian pointedly set his mug on the table and leaned toward her. "Well, I count two of us. I'll cook for you sometime, as a way to say thank you for training me."

He meant it, too. Living in the barracks, he didn't get to cook as often as he would like to, but he enjoyed seasoning and grilling his own meats. His mouth began to salivate as he dreamed of all the dishes he could make.

"You would cook for me?" Elyse asked, clearly skeptical. She looked at him like he was crazy.

"Sure," he shrugged. "You earned it. You're a good teacher, honestly."

Elyse bit her lips and stared down at her tea. "All right," she said finally. "But it better be a damn good filet."

"Great!" Killian clapped his hands together, grinning. "I know the best butcher in Rhodan. My family has been going to his place in the market for as long as I can remember." He smothered his smile as he added, "Well, except for a short period of time when he had to close up shop."

Tilting her head, Elyse asked, "Why'd he close the shop?"

Killian shrugged. "Fell on hard times I guess. But he still sold meat on the side." He shook his head but smirked as he said, "He just couldn't quit cold turkey."

Elyse just stared at him, then her jaw slowly fell open. "Did you just tell a terrible joke?" she asked, aghast.

135

Killian could no longer conceal his pride at his own wit as he burst into a fit laughter, practically doubling over.

Elyse just shook her head as she chuckled at him. "Is it even true? Did he ever close his shop?"

"No," Killian said through his laughter. "No, his shop's been open for twenty years. But you should have seen your face!"

"Get out of here," she said, grinning as she pointed toward the door. She stood and started swatting at him. "I've got a business to run. Go on! Get!"

Her poor attempt at shoving him out of her cottage only made Killian laugh harder, until he was wiping tears from his eyes.

"Okay, okay! I'll go!" he ceded, throwing up his hands in surrender. "But you have to take me back to the palace."

"Oh, I *have* to?" Elyse asked, giving him a stern look.

Killian just pouted his lips—or attempted to. It was difficult not to smile.

"Please?" he asked.

Elyse scoffed as she tried to hide her own smile. "Fine," she grumbled, pushing past him and storming out the door.

For the rest of the day, whenever he had a free moment, Killian practiced his shielding spell.

CHAPTER 23

— : —

ELYSE

What the fuck was she thinking?

Elyse's boots touched down in the forest, just outside the wards, and she had to stop and lean against a nearby tree for a moment. She had just delivered Killian back to the palace, and it was very clear to her that what she felt for him was utterly unacceptable.

Every moment she spent with him, she found herself enjoying his company more and more—to the point where she was disappointed when their time together ended. And when he'd told the joke about the butcher—the stupid, immature, ridiculous joke—her heart had done a tiny somersault, like she was seeing a side of him that most people never had the privilege of seeing.

She couldn't stand it. He was not an option.

Fortunately, she was used to giving off the appearance that she didn't give a damn. She was certain Killian had no idea the way his presence made her soften. She'd been detached as she taught him magic, taunting even—though his determined countenance had made her root for him internally.

Clearly there was something else going on with her. It had been an unspeakable amount of time since she'd been with a man, and her body seemed to be lashing out at her in response, grappling for a warm body with a chiseled jaw and lean muscles.

Stop it, she chastened herself as she forced her feet to carry her back to her cottage. There were plenty of other tall, handsome men who could meet her needs that *weren't* abysmally uptight and oh-so wrong for her.

It was settled then. She'd work a full day at the shoppe, maybe head out to the obstacle course to blow off some steam, and then she'd pop over to Sera's place in the city and talk her into going to a tavern with her.

So that's what she did. A little before sunset, Elyse put on a black corseted dress, donned her long black gloves, and braided her hair back into a messy chignon. She even lined her eyes with kohl and painted her lips a stunning shade of scarlet.

Shortly after sunset, Elyse marched up the twelve flights of stairs to Sera's apartment and parted the sea of beads to let herself in.

"Sera?" she called as she scanned the opulent main room.

Her friend appeared in the bedroom doorway, looking glamorous as always in a flowy, soft green dress. She tucked a lock of her silky black hair behind her ear as she smiled at Elyse.

"We're going out," Elyse told her. "I need to meet a man."

As soon as the words left her lips, she noticed it—another presence in the apartment.

Manny joined Sera in the doorway, standing half a head shorter than her, one hand wrapped comfortably around her waist.

"Hello, Elyse," he said with a grin.

Sera just gave her an apologetic look, though it was Elyse's own damn fault. She should have known better than to blurt out something so ridiculous.

"Don't stop on my account," Manny added. "You were saying?"

Internally, Elyse was screaming, and she was certain her cheeks were bright red. But she said as coolly as she could manage, "Women have needs too."

"I'm aware," Manny replied, and Elyse almost gagged at the look he and Sera exchanged.

She was about to run right out of the building and straight home to gouge her eyes out when Sera said in her usual sweet voice, "Manny and I were going to a tavern tonight. You're more than welcome to join us."

"Oh no, I couldn't possibly intrude on this," Elyse said, making an awkward gesture with her hand. "And also, I don't want to."

"*Please*," Sera begged. She broke away from Manny to step toward her friend, and pouted her lower lip. "I promise it'll be so fun."

Elyse groaned.

"Come on, Elyse. We got off on the wrong foot. Let me make it up to you by picking up your tab tonight," Manny offered.

She glared at him, and then looked back to Sera, who was giving her puppy dog eyes. Dammit, Sera knew she couldn't say no to that face.

"Fine," she growled. "But I'm getting the good stuff."

Sera clapped her hands together happily.

"Great!" Manny said. "We can stop by the palace and see if Killian—"

"No!" Elyse cut him off. She realized too late how loudly she had said it, and based on Manny's wide eyes, he'd noticed it as well. "No," she repeated, quieter. "He's seen enough of me lately. Let's give the guy a break."

Manny opened his mouth like he was about to protest, but he didn't say anything.

A short while later, the three of them were sauntering down the street. Or rather, Manny and Sera were sauntering hand in hand, and Elyse was trudging along beside them, trying not to roll her eyes.

"What tavern?" she asked, interrupting their whispering and giggling.

"Taverne de Lac," Manny answered. "I'm actually meeting someone there to get information on Royce."

"Oh." She'd heard of Taverne de Lac before, and it was certainly not a seedy black magic bar. It was much more high end, frequented by courtiers and wealthy merchants. She was glad she'd dressed to impress tonight.

"Manny tells me you're training Killian in combat magic?" Sera asked. Her dangling gold earrings shimmered in the moonlight, and her thin eyes eagerly awaited a reply.

Elyse let out a small laugh. "I'd hardly call what we did today 'combat,' but yes, I'm training him to defend himself with magic."

"You must have worked him hard. He was sluggish today. Distracted even," Manny added.

"Have you been to Taverne de Lac before?" Elyse asked, abruptly changing the subject. Didn't they understand that Killian was the last person she needed to think about?

"A few times," Manny said with a nod.

Thankfully they didn't ask any more about Killian's training as they strolled the last few blocks to the tavern.

As they approached, two men in black jerkins hauled the double doors open for them, and another man greeted them inside with a warm smile and an offer to relieve them of any coats. Sera was just slipping off the light cloak she donned when Elyse heard a familiar voice call her name.

She turned and scanned the dim and crowded room, letting her eyes adjust to the tea lights that adorned each small table, when she saw a tall man with pale hair and a paler face walking straight toward her. She recognized him immediately. She'd never forget those eyes—clear and blue as the sky. Eyes that she'd spent many nights staring into.

"It is you," he breathed when they were face to face. He stooped to kiss her on both cheeks.

"Jaime," she said as her lips curled into a smile. Something animalistic fluttered in her stomach. "You're back."

He smiled in return and nodded. "And business is well," he said, gesturing to the room, where well-dressed patrons sipped expensive cocktails.

"It must be if you can afford to drink here. Last time I saw you, you barely had two coppers to rub together."

He frowned at her playfully, his full lips forming a seductive pout. "That's a slight exaggeration." His blue eyes, which seemed to light up the dark tavern, never left her face.

"You remember Sera," she said, turning toward her friend.

"Yes! The lovely Madam Sera, how are you?" he greeted her before he planted two kisses on her cheeks as well.

"Quite well, thank you," Sera offered in her ever-polite lilt. "And this is Manfried."

"Manny," he corrected with a smile as he extended a hand toward Jaime.

"Jamie Lindgren," said the blond beauty as he gripped Manny's hand. Then he turned back to Elyse.

"I've just finished up a business meeting. Please, join me for a drink?"

Elyse was about to politely decline when something fluttered again in her stomach. After all, she was out of practice, and who better to reawaken her sexuality than Jaime, whose body and moves she was already so familiar with.

"That'd be lovely," she said, and she let him guide them toward a table in the far corner.

A pianist serenaded them, plinking out a jazzy mid-tempo tune, and a dashing waiter came around to take their drink order. Once everyone settled in, Elyse turned to face Jaime, who sat beside her.

"When did you get back?" she asked. He'd left what seemed ages ago to embark on a trading expedition across several kingdoms. She remembered their last night together, the way their bodies had merged into one as if they never wanted to part. The way he had tasted her late into the night as if his tongue never wanted to forget her.

"Six months," he said easily.

Elyse tried not to flinch, instead giving a cordial smile. Six months he'd been back, and yet this was the first she was seeing of him?

"I've been incredibly busy," he added, probably reading the poorly concealed hurt on her face.

"Haven't we all," Manny added with a chuckle she didn't quite believe.

"What do you do for work?" Jaime asked him.

Elyse angled her head as she sipped water from a pewter cup, curious to hear his answer.

"Banking," Manny replied simply. "At a small firm in the western sector of the city."

A nice touch. The western sector was notoriously wealthy.

Jaime gave a small, impressed smile. "You must be doing well for yourself. I'm sure with your income you frequent Taverne de Lac."

"Actually, I've never been here," Manny lied. "But my partner, Killian, raves about the place, so I thought I'd see it for myself."

Elyse suppressed an eye roll. She understood why he lied about his profession—obviously he was some sort of spy or covert agent for the Royal Guard—but did he have to bring up Killian?

"Sounds like your partner has good taste," Jaime replied. As he spoke, he laid his hand atop Elyse's, stroking her fingers with his thumb. Just the simple touch had Elyse's entire body awake and on edge.

"I think he and you have very similar tastes," Manny said, and Elyse noted the way his eyes flickered to their touching hands as he said it.

The waiter came by and dispersed their drinks, and Elyse freed her hand from Jaime's to accept the chalice of rose-colored wine. She sipped at it and sighed in delight. The wine was sweeter than what she normally opted for, but she'd been craving its sugary taste all day.

They made idle small talk until Sera launched into a story about one of her clients from earlier in the day. As she spoke, Manny listened attentively, his eyes focused on her painted lips, her long lashes. He laughed genuinely as she described the client's misinterpretation of the reading.

Jaime listened well, too, his gaze never trailing down toward Sera's cleavage the way most men's did. He glanced at Elyse occasionally, and each time he did, a familiar warmth spread between her legs. She found herself fantasizing about his touch, the muscles beneath his tunic.

Things had been so easy between them, seeing each other every few nights and going about their own business during the days. But whenever they were together, the weight of her life, the pain of losing her mother, the nightmares of screaming and fire, all that seemed to fade away.

Something caught Manny's eye, and he excused himself from the table. Probably the informant he'd said he'd be meeting with. Sera took the opportunity to produce a compact mirror and check her cosmetics.

Jaime leaned toward Elyse and whispered, "I missed you."

"I missed you, too," she whispered back.

He clasped her hand under the table, and she entwined her fingers with his. His hand was soft, not callused like Killian's, which she'd grown accustomed to holding as she magicked them around. A pang of disappointment tugged at her heart.

But then Jaime smiled, flashing his perfect white teeth at her, and she melted once again, lost in memories of that smile as he thrust himself inside her.

"So, Sera," Jaime began, turning his attention toward the seer as he squeezed Elyse's hand beneath the table. "You and Manny seem to make a good couple. I'm happy for you."

Elyse's own heart echoed the sentiment. Sera had always been easy going, a merry soul, but the way she looked at Manny, the way her face seemed to light up, it was different. She'd never seen her friend so happy before.

"Well, it's a rather new relationship," Sera replied truthfully. "But the heart knows when it's found someone special."

"That it does." Jaime gave Elyse's hand another squeeze, sending another tantric wave of warmth through her.

"Tell us more about your trip," Sera requested, and Jamie released Elyse's hand so he could animatedly describe his expedition.

He'd traveled through six kingdoms, meeting with various mages and sorcerers and black market traders, learning from and bartering with each of them. He'd spent a month apprenticing under a potions master in a city Elyse had never heard of, and he claimed they'd concocted a potion for shapeshifting. He'd also stayed in a monastery where warlocks used silence and celibacy to magnify their powers.

Interesting, Elyse thought. Perhaps her own celibacy explained why her powers were so strong lately. Then again, she remembered the way her energy had coursed through her when Jaime pleasured her for countless hours.

Manny returned to the table as Jaime told a story about a mermaid tribe he'd encountered.

"Mermaids?" Manny repeated as he seated himself. "I bet they were hard to tear yourself away from. A horde of beautiful, topless women and a handsome fellow as yourself? You must have felt like a king."

"Not really," Jaime drawled. He slid his hand onto Elyse's thigh, sending shivers coursing through her. "I prefer my women fully human."

He rubbed her thigh, and she pressed harder into him as his sultry voice rang in her ears.

"So you're in the magic business as well?" Manny asked. "I should have realized that's how you knew these two upstanding citizens," he joked.

But there was no judgment or distaste in his voice the way there was when Killian spoke of magic. Or at least, the way Killian used to speak of magic. He'd seemingly mastered his hatred when they were training.

"That I am," Jaime confirmed. "When you're born into it, it's difficult to get away."

Wasn't that the truth, more so than he even knew.

"Although, the anti-magic movement made everything much harder than it should have been. A bunch of scared little bastards lynching witches, as if half the capital didn't benefit from magic in some way or another."

Elyse shuddered at the memory. A decade ago, there had been a huge push to destroy all things supernatural, sending the capital into a crazed state. Though Elyse and her mother were mostly safe outside the city limits, every month they heard of another friend being burned at the stake or hanged at the gallows. Fortunately, the movement had fizzled out, but magic-users still kept to themselves all these years later.

Manny just nodded. "Though one does wonder if our departed king would still be on his throne if magic had been stamped out," he stated coolly.

Jaime's hand abruptly stopped rubbing Elyse's thigh.

"You think that if the movement succeeded, King Cyril would still be alive? You think that it's even possible to stamp out magic?" His voice had a disdainful edge to it, setting Elyse's nerves on edge.

Manny was the epitome of calm as he took a languid sip of his red wine. "I'm not saying either of those things. I'm simply making a hypothetical statement, a conversation point."

Elyse felt Jaime relax beside her, but it was a moment before he responded.

"Those of us who wish to do magic will always be able to do so. They've tried to stop us before, and failed."

Manny gave a tilt of his head, as if to say, "Fair enough," before he took another sip from his chalice. Elyse and Sera exchanged a look of discomfort.

"This assassination is a curious thing, though," Jaime continued. "From what I hear, it took a powerful sorcerer to enact the spell."

His hand resumed rubbing her leg, inching closer and closer to her hip. She bit her lip at the excitement of things to come after such a long dry spell, remembering the way it felt to be touched by a hand that was not her own.

"From what I hear," Manny articulated carefully, "you know many powerful sorcerers. And you, yourself, are one."

Elyse glared at Manny across the table. This wasn't a fucking interrogation. He ignored her cold stare.

Luckily, Jaime laughed. "You flatter me. I'd hardly call myself powerful. I just know how to grease the right palms."

Manny seemed satisfied with his answer, because he lifted his chalice and said, "I'll drink to that."

Elyse couldn't help but let out a tiny laugh. He played the elitist banker very well.

They ordered another round of drinks, and the conversation took a much more subdued turn. Manny delivered a dreadfully boring but convincing account of the kingdom's current economic state that made Elyse wonder if he had done his research or if he was speaking out of his ass.

Jaime's hand continued to gravitate up her leg, and her skin purred at his touch, like a muscle memory. Oh, how she'd missed this, the anticipation, the way her breath caught when his fingers grazed her inner thigh. Occasionally Manny gave her a strange look, but she shrugged it off. He could mind his own damn business.

Sera yawned and mentioned something about needing to be up early. It was likely a lie. Elyse imagined she and Jaime weren't the only ones fondling each other under the table.

Elyse didn't mind Sera's suggestion to leave, though. After all, she'd accomplished what she'd set out to do: find a man to bed. She turned to Jaime to confirm that he was ready to leave as well, and the hunger she saw in his eyes left her weak.

Manny paid the tab and they meandered toward the exit. A group had gathered to either collect or deposit their cloaks, and the space near the door was crowded.

"We'll wait outside," Jaime said to Sera and Manny as he slipped a hand around Elyse's waist and guided her toward the door.

They stepped outside, and the cool night air kissed Elyse's skin, awakening her from the stupor of wine and lust. She let out a small shiver, and Jaime pulled her up against him. He slid his hands over her bare shoulders in an attempt to warm her.

"I missed you," he breathed, repeating his words from earlier.

Elyse leaned into him, letting her body rest against his lean muscles. She looked up into his blue eyes, her gaze tracing the hard line of his jaw. She was about to say she'd missed him too, but something over his shoulder caught her eye.

A guard was walking down the street, dressed in his black uniform, a short sword at his hip. Elyse immediately wondered if he knew Killian. A smile tugged at her lips. Of course the guard probably knew Killian—he was a lieutenant after all. And not just that, he was the one assigned to investigate King Cyril's murder. He was probably a celebrity among the Guard.

"Elyse?" Jaime asked, breaking her wayward thoughts. He laughed and added, "This is the part where you say you missed me too."

Elyse blinked a few times, then looked up at Jaime. She parted her lips, prepared to tell him she had missed him, when she stopped herself.

Had she though? Maybe after the first few weeks he'd been gone, but truthfully, she hadn't thought of him in a very long time. She would admit she missed his hands, his tongue, his muscled stomach, but did she really miss *him*? And if he'd missed her so much, why hadn't he stopped by?

But the real question was, did any of that matter right now? His body was simply a means to an end, and one night together would be a mutually beneficial endeavor. She tilted her head, still unsure of what to say, when someone cleared their throat.

Still pressed together, Elyse and Jamie both turned their heads toward the sound. Manny and Sera stood holding hands, staring at them. Manny's lips were a thin line.

"Elyse, do you want to walk with us?" Sera asked.

"I'll get her home safe," Jaime said before Elyse could speak.

Elyse just nodded, her mind elsewhere. "Good night," she added as Sera and Manny turned and walked down the street.

"Unless you'd rather come back to my place," Jaime whispered in her ear, his breath tickling her neck.

At that moment, Manny glanced back over his shoulder at them, and in the moonlight, she saw his expression. Was that concern on his face? Poorly hidden disgust?

Elyse looked back to Jaime, his blue eyes penetrating her with a lustful gaze. This time, though, she didn't feel her knees weakening beneath his stare. Instead, she felt something like shame. Jaime didn't look at her with respect or intrigue. He had hardly asked her about herself all night. He was too busy bragging about his adventures. No, he looked at her like a trophy, an item to boast about.

And she had done the same to him. Did that make it wrong? They were two consenting adults. Moments ago, his touch had exhilarated her. Now, in the sobering night air, she felt conflicted.

"I . . . should be getting home. Alone," she added quickly before he could misinterpret her words. "I'm sorry, I just . . . I thought this was what I wanted, but . . ."

But what? She was hurt that he hadn't called on her? She'd barely thought of him over the last year? She spent her days thinking about a dimpled soldier in the Royal Guard?

"You always were one to play hard to get," he murmured against her skin.

Suddenly, his touch felt wrong. No, this wasn't what she wanted at all. She pushed away from him, and he let her go, though his eyes were narrowed, his brows furrowed.

"I'm not feeling well," she lied. "I'll see you around."

Before she could change her mind, she marched off into the night.

CHAPTER 24

— ⁑ —

KILLIAN

S ometime after sunset and before sunrise, Killian heard a soft knock at his chamber door. Unable to sleep, he'd been lying in his simple cot reading an old history book his father had loved. Usually, the dry prose put him right to sleep, but not tonight. Tonight, his head was filled with shielding spells and obstacle courses and wicked smiles.

"Come in," he called, not bothering to get out of his small cot. He assumed it was just Manny stopping by his room—if it had been anyone else on official Guard business, they would have knocked harder and louder.

Sure enough, Manny opened the door and let himself into the chamber. He smiled at Killian, but the smile didn't reach his eyes.

"How'd it go?" Killian asked. He sat up in bed and put the book on the small table next to him, then braced himself for whatever news Manny delivered.

Manny seated himself in one of the wooden chairs. He leaned back and propped his dress boots up on the table. He must have just come back from the tavern, or Sera's apartment. "Good—really good actually," he said. "Royce is definitely into some unsavory business. He's got black market dealers all over the kingdom, so he would have access to the ingredients for the spell. He was also apparently pushing King Cyril to lower the tariffs so he can profit more on his imports, but Cyril wasn't keen on the idea. But you know who is?"

Killian arched a brow at his friend. "Prince Maelor?"

"Exactly." Manny clasped his hands behind his head, looking satisfied with himself.

Killian pulled the covers off himself and joined Manny at the table. He was only wearing undershorts, and Killian caught Manny's eyes flicker toward the scar on his chest. It was a brutal scar, one that he had borne since childhood—since the day magic changed his life forever. His entire left pectoral was covered in puckered, colorless skin. He didn't blame Manny for glancing. It was hard not to look at.

"So, we have an idea of his motive," Killian began, "and we know he's capable of acquiring the ingredients for the spell . . . Do we have anything concrete?"

"Not yet."

"Not yet?" Killian sighed. "Manny, it's the middle of the night. Out with it."

Manny just grinned at Killian, making him wait for a moment, before he said, "Royce is having a party at his townhouse in three nights, and I know two lovely ladies who will be able to get us on the guest list."

Killian furrowed his brows, but then realization dawned on him. "You want us to go to the party—with Elyse and Sera—and what? Snoop through his things?" He couldn't possibly think this was a good idea.

"That's exactly what I'm proposing," Manny said, a wide grin still on his lips. He was far too excited about the whole thing.

"Manny," Killian said as he rubbed his temples. "There are protocols to follow."

"Fuck protocols. No one has ever balked at my methods before. If he's our man, we nail him any way we can."

Killian sat up straight and considered Manny's words. As much as he wanted to close the case quickly, to restore some semblance of respite to the palace and the kingdom, Royce was a man of great means. If they slipped up, and Royce used his money and power to escape—or even to influence the court to believe him innocent—then justice wouldn't be met for King Cyril. And that's *if* he was actually the murderer.

But he had to be. All roads lead to him. They had to be quick and cunning—yet careful—to gather evidence against him. And he could depend on Manny to use his best judgment. He almost never steered him wrong.

"All right," Killian agreed. "We'll go to the party and find out what we can."

Manny let out a long exhale. "Hopefully we find something useful." His face was solemn, and Killian wondered if he, too, was plagued with mental images of the king's bloody, lifeless body, and the queen's catatonic grief.

It was quiet for a moment, a rarity when Manny was involved. Killian was in no rush to get back to his dreadful history book, so he asked, "How was your night with Sera?"

Instead of smiling as Killian expected him to, Manny shifted his weight, setting his feet back on the floor.

"Good," he said, avoiding Killian's gaze.

"What is it?" Killian asked with some amusement. "Problems in the bedroom?"

"No," Manny replied immediately, shooting his friend a terse look. "It's . . . Elyse joined us for drinks."

Of all the things he'd expected Manny to say, that was not one of them. He tried to read him, to discern why he was acting so weird, but he was stumped.

"Did she ruin your romantic evening or something?"

"No," Manny began cautiously. "Nothing like that. But at the tavern she ran into a friend, maybe an old lover, and they went home together."

Killian felt a sudden pang in his chest—perhaps something he ate not sitting well within him. His mouth had gone dry but he managed to ask, "Why are you telling me this?"

Manny seemed to be searching his friend's face, contemplating if he had made a mistake bringing it up. "I thought you liked her. And I thought maybe she felt the same way about you, but—"

Killian snorted rather loudly. "I don't care what she does in her spare time—or who she does for that matter."

But as he said it, her pillowy pink lips flashed in his mind.

Manny just stared at Killian through narrowed eyes. The room seemed to grow warmer as Killian waited for his friend to speak. He refused to say anything else on the matter.

"Okay," Manny said after a beat. "I shouldn't have said anything. I'm sorry."

"No need to be sorry, mate. I know you were just looking out for me," Killian said with a wave of his hand. "Sounds like meeting Sera has turned you into a hopeless romantic, though."

And this time, at the mention of Sera's name, Manny did smile.

CHAPTER 25

— : —

ELYSE

K illian hadn't deflected a single stone all morning.

The sun was still low, its light barely kissing the tops of the trees, but to Elyse it felt like hours had passed.

"Aerodurum! Aerodurum!" he shouted again and again, but the stones just pelted him in his chest, his stomach, his leg.

"Clear your head—focus!" Elyse ordered, but the next rock just thunked him in the arm.

Killian let out a low, angry growl. Elyse sighed and made the stones in her hand disappear.

"Let's take a break."

She walked to the edge of the fighting ring and sat down on the grass, folding her legs in front of her. The grass was still wet with dew, and she huffed, annoyed. Annoyed by the dew, annoyed by being awake at such an ungodly hour, and most of all, annoyed by Killian, who seemed to have taken a massive step backward with the shielding spell.

He'd been especially brooding this morning—which was saying a lot. In as few words as possible, he'd told her about going to the party at Royce's townhome, about the tariffs and suspected motive. When she asked about coordinating their gowns, he didn't quip back with some witty retort, only stared at the ground and continued trudging ahead.

Now he came grumbling over and sat beside her. They sat for a moment, feeding off one another's frustration, until Elyse finally broke the tense silence.

"What's going on with you?"

She let her irritation seep through her tone.

Killian didn't bite back his aggression either. "Nothing."

An obvious lie.

"Everything's great. We have a promising lead," he continued.

Elyse gave him a dry, unsympathetic glare. "Then why can't you do the spell?"

"I don't know, you're the expert."

He didn't shout the words, merely said them in a low voice, saturated with angst.

There was no helping him, so she shifted her body away from him and debated telling him to go home.

But then he cleared his throat and asked, "You went to the tavern last night?"

"Mm-hmm," was Elyse's simple reply. She had zero interest in small talk—especially not so early in the morning.

"How was it?"

"Fine."

Another festering silence.

"Manny said your friend joined."

The pit of her stomach turned to lead as she remembered standing close to Jaime on the street, practically throwing herself at him, and the humiliation of lusting after someone who hadn't bothered to call on her for six months.

"What about it?" she asked dryly.

Out of the corner of her eye she saw him shrug. "Just making conversation."

Elyse didn't deign to reply.

She could hear him, shifting, plucking strands of grass. Then he said, "I suppose you're just grumpy because you didn't get much sleep last night."

She whirled on him, her fingers itching to cast something nasty his way.

"Excuse me?"

But he didn't cower. "What? You took your friend home with you, didn't you?"

One simple flick of her fingers, and she could have his balls in a tourniquet.

"That's none of your business."

Killian scoffed. "Well, if you can't teach me properly because you're too tired, then it is my business."

Unbelievable. Un-fucking-believable.

"We're done here," she snarled, standing up and glaring down at him.

He blinked a few times, shook his head, and then held up his hands toward her.

"I'm just having a go at you, Elyse. This is what we do. You say something snide and then I chaff back."

She didn't say anything, instead letting her smoldering gaze do the talking.

"I'm sorry if I crossed a line," he went on. "It was just a joke."

His voice was softer than before, his eyes searching her face for forgiveness.

Perhaps she was overreacting. There was something about this conversation that had her on edge. She was naturally protective of her personal life. And Killian was right. She had teased him about far worse before.

"It's fine," she said eventually, sitting down beside him again. "But for the record, I got a whole seven hours of sleep last night."

"He's a real minute-man, then," Killian said as he tried to fight back a smile.

At that, Elyse actually laughed. She couldn't help it. "No, you ass. Nothing happened. I came home alone last night."

"Oh." Killian's golden eyes were still on her, still searching for something. "Manny made it sound like—"

"Manny should learn to keep his mouth shut," Elyse interrupted. She would have to teach that man a lesson.

Then she sighed and started to fidget with the grass at her side. "I was going to . . . you know. But something changed. Suddenly it felt . . . wrong."

She wasn't looking at Killian, but she could feel his stare.

"Wrong?"

"I don't know. Jaime and I were close for a while, and it was fun. But I sort of realized that fun isn't what I want."

"Fun's the worst," Killian said, and when she turned to whack him in the arm, he was grinning.

"You know what I mean," she snapped, her own lips mirroring his grin.

He laughed, a soft quiet chuckle, and she marveled at how open she was being with a near stranger. Killian didn't feel like a stranger, though, he felt like a friend or a brother or . . .

"So, what do you want?" he asked, interrupting her thoughts.

She bit her lip, not truly knowing the answer, and decided on, "I want you to master the shielding spell."

"Done," he said, still smiling. He scrambled to his feet and marched toward the center of the fighting ring.

Much more slowly, she got up and followed him.

For the rest of the training, Killian deflected every stone.

CHAPTER 26

—— ❖ ——

ELYSE

Two days later, Killian had sufficiently proven himself with the shielding spell—though Elyse would never boost his self-esteem by showing that she was impressed. She immediately started teaching him a basic stunning spell, drilling him for an hour.

Training had been going more smoothly the past few days. Elyse was able to set aside her unfounded desire for Killian and instead focus on teaching him. To his credit, Killian seemed to thrive under her mentorship. She pushed him hard, but he pushed himself harder, as if he had something to prove. Perhaps it was just an innate desire to master everything he did that drove him, or perhaps it was something else. No matter the case, Killian threw himself into each training session with rigor and determination.

After an hour of practice, Killian begged Elyse to let him try the obstacle course—just once!—and she finally caved.

He looked like a child, giddily making his way toward the climbing wall, and Elyse imagined this was how he acted when he had a stack of paperwork on his desk. Still, his excitement was contagious and she couldn't help smiling at him as she gave him pointers.

"It's not about speed, just keep your eye on what's ahead of you."

He simply brushed her off, dismissing her advice.

"All right then," she shrugged. And with a wave of her hand, the course came to life.

He struggled a bit on the climbing wall, not quite sure which of the ever-changing ledges to grasp on to, but he eventually reached the top. Next came a set of hovering wooden planks that required expert balance to maneuver. Elyse held her breath as he stepped on to the first one, but he managed them easily. His body was fine-tuned, moving fluidly with precision and grace as his muscles rippled beneath his clothes. *A soldier's body*, she reminded herself. An off-limits body.

The whole time Killian was running and jumping and climbing, that silly grin was plastered on his face. Occasionally he looked like he might stumble, but he always managed to right himself. The bastard was good.

He leapt over hurdles and through a spinning wheel, up a ramp that sped downward and down a ramp that sped upward. Even the rope bridge—Elyse's least favorite—didn't slow him down.

He approached the swinging logs, and paused for a moment, watching the pattern of their movements. There were six logs in all, each swinging at their own intervals. Elyse watched him, her heart racing, and then she realized what he was doing.

He was going to try and run straight through.

Elyse knew first hand that it couldn't be done. There was no perfect timing where one could run right through the swinging logs without having to stop and wait for one to pass. He wouldn't make it.

She was about to warn him when he took off.

He was dashing at a mad pace, his face scarlet and drenched in sweat. He made it through the first and second logs, as expected, but the third one nearly took him out. Log number four was another near miss, and Elyse could see the fear in his eyes, but he didn't slow down. He sped up, as did Elyse's heart rate. She realized her fists were clenched tight, her knuckles white.

Killian cleared the fifth log, and Elyse opened her mouth to cheer, disbelief filling her whole body when—WHACK!

The sixth log pummeled Killian, sending him flying toward the woods.

"Killian!" she screamed. She sprinted toward where he lay on the ground. She didn't know what she would do if he was badly injured. Manny would have her head, and the cure–

Please be okay, she thought.

"I'm okay," he rasped, clearly winded.

Elyse knelt down beside him and placed a hand on his shoulder. "Don't move. Are you hurt?"

"I'm okay," he repeated. But there was blood on his tunic.

"You're not okay, you're bleeding!" Elyse tugged at his shirt, trying to determine the source of the blood.

"It's just a scratch," he grumbled, his eyes squeezed tight. She had no doubt he was seeing stars.

"Just let me look," she demanded. She waved her hand and his shirt disappeared.

Her eyes scanned his stomach where she had seen the blood on his shirt. It was just a scratch, a long one, but not very deep. He would be fine.

Then she noticed something else—a scar covering his entire left pectoral. It was as wide as three of her fingers, and it left a gouge in his flesh. The scar was pale, pronounced against his umber skin.

"Am I dying?" Killian wheezed, his eyes still shut tight.

"Yes," she said, a slight smile on her lips. "But only of embarrassment."

Killian laughed, then groaned and hugged his side.

Elyse frowned. She clutched Killian's wrist and magicked them to her bedroom, landing him right on her bed.

Killian's eyes darted around the room, and he tried to sit up. "This is not necessary—"

But Elyse just pushed him back down. "Hush. Just lay here for a minute and let me clean the cut." It certainly wasn't an ideal place to bring him, but it was comfortable and she had everything she needed nearby.

She grabbed a salve from the vanity by the bed then began to work on him. Her fingers, covered in cool ointment, touched his skin, and Killian shivered.

"Sorry," she said, then held her breath as she continued to work, trying to ignore the intimacy of the situation. Yet her fingers seemed to tingle each time they grazed his skin, a sensation she hated that she enjoyed.

Her eyes kept flickering up to the scar on his chest, and he must have noticed because he said, "It's from when I was a kid."

Elyse felt her cheeks warm. "I didn't mean to stare," she said quietly. She knew it was out of character for her to sound apologetic, but she couldn't help herself. Killian was the one who had been injured, but having him in her bed with his bare torso—it felt as if her head was the one spinning.

"It's . . . all right," he said in a voice that told her he was self-conscious of it.

She tried her best not to look at the scar that mangled so much of his exquisite physique, but it was hard not to glance, not to wonder.

"There are ways to get rid of it. I could heal it for you," she offered.

"No," he said firmly, and Elyse jumped. "Sorry, I just . . ."

His words trailed off. Elyse paused, waiting for him to say more, her hand resting against his stomach. It was warm and inviting, the muscles of his abdomen pronounced. She held his gaze, trying her best to stay focused.

"My scar is a reminder," he said finally.

"A reminder of what?"

She resumed cleaning the scratch, but from the corner of her eye, she saw his throat bob.

"When I was seven, my brother brought home a box of firecrackers. He was older than me, twelve at the time, and he was always up to something."

Killian's lips smiled, but his eyes gleamed with pain. Elyse wasn't sure she wanted to hear the rest, but she stayed quiet and listened. She would hear the story, would bear witness to his pain.

"His name was Jonnie, but I called him Joe. That was my first word, and it just stuck. Joe was . . ." His voice caught and he paused for a moment. "Joe always made time for me. He always let me play with him and his friends, even though I was so much younger than them. I'm sure I annoyed the hell out of them," he said with a melancholy laugh.

Elyse kept rubbing the ointment into his wound, letting the touch tether her to reality as she felt the overwhelming inevitably of Killian's next words.

"One day, he brought home that box of firecrackers. He was so happy, and I begged him to shoot them off, but he refused. He was saving them for something special. He said they weren't ordinary firecrackers. They'd been bewitched to take the shape of dragons and tigers and birds that ran and soared around in a stream of light and fire. I wanted to light them so badly, but I never disobeyed Joe, so he set the box in a corner and I tried not to think about it. It was three days later when the box went off, of its own accord."

Elyse went rigid, a chill snaking up her spine. She'd heard of these bewitched firecrackers before, a favorite around festivals, but for them to go off on their own—Joe had gotten a bad batch. Probably a two-bit hack rushing the spell-work to churn out more product. Oh gods, her heart ached for Killian, for his mother.

He kept going, though, his voice a quiet rasp. "I wasn't in the room. I was helping my mother in the kitchen. But something pierced me, some bit of shrapnel that tore my chest open."

A tear slid from Killian's eye, and Elyse instinctively grasped his hand. From the tremor in his voice, she guessed it had been a long time since he'd spoken of these horrors.

"But Joe was in the room, sitting not far from the box. He was—"

Killian gasped, choking on the words that must have made him feel sick. Elyse felt her stomach twist in anticipation, felt herself wishing that if he didn't say the words then it couldn't be true.

But it was so much worse than she thought.

"He was reading to our baby sister," Killian murmured.

All warmth seemed to leave Elyse's body, leaving her cold, weak, defenseless against the images that played again and again in her mind. She squeezed tighter onto his hand, willing the pain to leave him, to leave both of them, but she knew all too well that wasn't how pain worked.

That poor boy. This poor man before her. No wonder he hated everything about magic. It had robbed him of his family. The image of his sibling's lifeless bodies must be stained in his mind— an image that now plagued Elyse's mind, that sent acid to her throat.

She remembered the words she'd said outside Pete's warehouse. No wonder he had snapped. She'd insulted his late brother. *If they're stupid enough to buy from him, then they deserve whatever fate they meet.* The words twisted in her head, mixing with the bloody images.

"I'm sorry," Elyse whispered in the bravest voice she could manage. She laid her head against their entwined hands. "I'm so sorry, Killian."

She wanted to say more, to tell him she understood now, understood so much of the brooding and the hatred. But she couldn't manage the words. So they sat quietly, letting the agony wash over them.

When Killian spoke again, it was not what Elyse expected.

"I owe you an apology too," he said.

She lifted her head and, with furrowed brows, gazed into his golden eyes.

"For what?" she breathed.

She didn't want to hear his apology. Life had been cruel to him, something she understood, as much as she wished she didn't.

He moved to sit up in bed, and Elyse helped him, but she didn't release his hand. She sat on the bed beside him, anxiously waiting for his explanation.

"I'm sorry for not trusting you. For thinking you're all the same." He stared at his lap as he spoke. No doubt apologies didn't come easily to him, just as they didn't come easily to Elyse.

She touched a hand to his chin, and lifted his face to look at her. If he knew the truth, the unspeakable things she'd done in the name of magic, he wouldn't be looking at her with any of the softness that he wore now.

"I see you, Killian," she said firmly. "I see you, and I'm still here."

His eyes gleamed, but he held her gaze. Her hand lingered on his chin. She saw his eyes flicker down to her lips, and she wished he would eliminate the space between them. She prayed that he would lean forward, press his lips to hers, and set her world on fire. And the look in his eyes proclaimed that he was thinking the same thing.

She wasn't sure who leaned in first, who initiated the kiss, but their lips met and she tasted his skin. There was a tenderness to their kiss, one that Elyse never would have expected from him, and the warmth that had been stolen from her before now flooded her body. He lifted one hand and clutched her hair, pulling her face closer to his, and she let him. Her own hand caressed his neck, sliding down to feel the muscles of his shoulders, as his tongue slipped between her lips, sending her heart racing.

He was delicious, a potion that cured her sorrows, and she never wanted to stop. He didn't seem to want to stop either as his lips pressed harder against hers, their lust building as they explored each other's mouths. She leaned in to him, pressing her hand firmly against his chest, seeking more of his touch. Kissing him was easy, comfortable yet extraordinary, just as all their interactions were. She felt vulnerable, and yet she reveled in it, wanting more. But at the same time, she wanted to savor this, to take her time, to—

To what?

What was she doing?

She broke off the kiss, and she tried to hide her disgust—not with Killian, but with herself. When had she become such a sap? A man tells her a sob story, and she throws herself at him? She knew better than to get involved with Killian. If he knew the truth about her, the immense secret she was keeping from him . . . He'd have her beheaded, or worse, burned alive at the stake.

She owed it to him to end things before they got too far.

Killian looked at her, his head slightly tilted, his lips still parted.

"This was a mistake," she whispered, her heart still pounding from his touch. "We shouldn't, we can't—"

Hurt flashed in his eyes for a moment, but it was quickly replaced by understanding. Surely he felt the same way? How could he be okay with kissing a witch after a lifetime of hatred for all those who used magic?

She abruptly shifted away from him, then decided to stand. Her eyes traveled aimlessly around her bedroom, which felt too crowded.

"I should go," Killian murmured.

He hesitated, though, as if waiting for her to change her mind, but she couldn't. She waved her hand, and his shirt, cleaned and pressed, covered his bare chest once again.

They were silent all the way down the stairs, out the shoppe, and past the wards. Killian still moved slowly from his injuries, and she wished he would move faster. She wanted this moment to be over with. Every moment she spent with him, her heart and mind battled within her.

When it came time to link their hands so she could magick him to the capital, neither one of them looked at each other. Their feet landed on cobblestone, and the morning noises of the city greeted them. Before he let go of her hand, Killian said, "For the party tomorrow, we're meeting at Sera's. Around seven."

Elyse nodded and slid her fingers from his. Without a word, she was gone.

CHAPTER 27

— • —

KILLIAN

As the blue smoke cleared, Killian touched two fingers to his lips. He could still taste Elyse there, the sweet hunger she'd gifted him not ten minutes earlier.

This was a mistake, she'd said.

He knew she was right. He didn't hate magic the way he had a week ago, but still. Elyse was a witch. They came from different worlds. What was he going to do, quit the guard and help her run the Emporium? There was no future for them.

But that hadn't made her taste any less delicious—didn't make him desire her any less.

Still standing in the alleyway, Killian took a deep breath. He combed his fingers through his hair, then straightened his tunic.

I am a lieutenant in the Royal Guard. I will not lust after a witch.

He repeated it over and over again as he marched back to the palace, paying no mind to the citizens on the street. But the more he tried not to think about her, the more his mind wandered . . . To her lips, to her touch, to the adorable way her brows furrowed when she cleaned his injury.

Fuck. This wasn't going to work.

He gave the guards outside the gates a curt nod, then stormed straight for the dungeons. He didn't stop until he reached Pete's cell.

The pudgy man sat on the stone floor on the other side of the iron bars. He seemed to be in a daze, barely noticing Killian's presence. Killian cleared his throat, rousing the man. "I need your help."

CHAPTER 28

— ❖ —

ELYSE

The bell to the Emporium chimed, and Elyse looked up from her spell book to see not a tanned young warrior, but a middle-aged woman.

Elyse frowned—not at the woman, though. At herself. She had to stop expecting her lieutenant—no, *the* lieutenant—to come marching in and kiss her.

For the devil's sake, she needed to find a spell that would make tonight's party bearable, but for now, she had a customer to help. The woman, dressed in a simple yet fashionable skirt and blouse, was perusing the crystals. She looked comfortable enough in the shoppe—thank hell. Elyse couldn't deal with a skeptic today.

Or any day for that matter.

"May I help you find anything in particular?" Elyse asked the woman, trying her best to hide her frustration at being interrupted from her search.

The woman smiled—not just a polite, obliging smile, but one with genuine warmth.

"Yes, it's my daughter's birthday next week and I'm looking to get her a crystal—her first one."

Elyse returned the smile as memories of her own mother flooded her. Of course, she hadn't ever needed a crystal for magic, but every year for her birthday, her mother would surprise her with a new spell book, and together they would read it and learn all the hexes, curses, and potions.

"Well, you've come to the right place," Elyse said, striding toward the woman. "I personally guarantee all my crystals. One of these should last her whole life if she cares for it properly."

"Oh, I know." The woman reached down into the neck of her blouse and pulled out a small purple crystal threaded through a chain. "I bought my own here decades ago, when your mother owned the Emporium."

Pride—that was the feeling that warmed Elyse's heart, her very soul, as she gazed upon the purple rock.

"If you'd like, I can string it on a chain for her as well," Elyse offered.

The woman nodded. "That would be lovely."

Her fingers grazed over a few of the crystals, and Elyse knew she was feeling their energy, searching for one that called to her. She settled on a foggy, pale blue crystal, and handed it to Elyse with utter confidence in her decision.

Elyse took the crystal and headed for a chest of drawers that sat near her work table, and gathered the supplies she needed.

"How old will she be?" she asked idly as she began drilling a hole through one end of the rock.

"Fifteen," the woman answered simply.

Elyse froze, her whole body going rigid. Instead of a crystal in her hand, she felt the cool steel of a dagger. Blood trickled between her fingers, the blood of a fifteen-year-old girl.

"Are you all right?" the woman asked, pulling Elyse back to reality. Elyse looked down at her hands and found no blood, no dagger, only a crystal and an awl. Her hands trembled though, and she knew if she looked in a mirror, her face would be pale as parchment.

"I'm fine," she said, shaking her head. "I just—" She lifted her gaze and lied bravely. "Remembering my mother is difficult at times."

The woman nodded, seeming to accept her explanation.

Elyse hurried through the rest of the transaction, sending the woman on her way as quickly as she could. She tried to keep her voice light, her hands steady, but it was an effort not to scream as images of a dying girl plagued her. It had been a long time since she'd allowed herself to think of those horrors, and now they flooded her, threatening to unravel her.

The door was barely shut behind the woman when Elyse collapsed to the floor, sobs rocking her body.

She hated herself.

She could never be with someone as brave and valiant as Killian, not when she had done such awful, unspeakable things. She was a bastard witch at best, spawn of a demon at worst. And though she could no longer deny her feelings for him—the way he made her smile no matter how hard she tried not to—she could never be with him. He could never know her secret. And she would never pull anyone into this life she lived—of lies and death and sacrifice.

The pain ate at her more than she ever would have guessed. A week ago she hadn't even known the man, yet now she was a crying mess on the floor of her shoppe.

But her tears weren't just for the loss of a budding romance. Killian felt like more than that. He had pulled her from a numbness that had enveloped her the last few years. In her attempt to block out her pain, she had eradicated all emotions—good or bad. But Killian had come along and reminded her what it was like to care.

She pulled her knees to her chest and rocked herself back and forth. She wanted so desperately to be a better person, but she was bound to this life of exile, the way her mother had been. She wiped salty tears away with the back of her hand because she knew she wasn't worthy to breathe the same air as Killian, let alone kiss him or be loved by him.

So when her breathing steadied and the self-loathing dissipated, she rose from the floor, dusted herself off, and returned to her spell book, determined more than ever to find some way to make her stop pining after Killian—at least for one night.

CHAPTER 29

— · —

KILLIAN

It had been a long time since Killian wore his stuffy dress clothes, though with the emotion-suppressing potion he'd gotten from Pete, he couldn't really be *annoyed* by the heat that stifled him beneath the thick trousers and dark jacket. He was merely aware of the correlation between his attire and gathering sweat, and accepted it for what it was.

Pete had been skeptical about helping, to say the least.

"What's in it fer me?" he'd grumbled.

So Killian bargained. If Pete could give him a potion to muzzle his emotions, he would talk to the magistrate about lightening his sentence. Killian was sure to add that if anything went wrong, if he ended up harmed in any way, his second was ordered to see Pete executed.

Pete acted tough, but in the end, he'd agreed and sent Killian out to fetch whatever ingredients he needed, telling him where to go for each item.

The concoction tasted foul, but after a moment, Killian was apathetic to the bitterness on his tongue. Before he left the dungeon, Pete gave him two pieces of information.

"The potion will last four and twenty hours. The only thing that can break it early is honeysuckle."

Killian thought that honeysuckle was an odd antidote, but made note of it anyway.

Now he and Manny rode through the streets of the city toward Madam Sera's apartment in a carriage they'd hired for the night. Manny didn't seem to notice any change in Killian. He supposed his naturally stoic nature was to thank.

It was a bright, sunny evening, but the citizens were anything but cheery. Clouds still loomed over them, likely due to the uncertainty of King Cyril's murder, the fate of their kingdom, and their untried new king. But Killian felt no stir of anguish, only cold acknowledgment of their anxiety.

They turned down Sera's block, finding it eerily empty as usual, exited the carriage, and entered her building. Sera had agreed to meet them in the entrance foyer so that the men wouldn't have to climb all those flights of stairs. He noticed Manny practically salivating over her, and Killian assumed it had something to do with the way the pale blue silk of her dress clung to her thin figure—how her breasts threatened to spill over the top of her gown.

Beside Sera stood Elyse, wearing a black high-necked dress with a slit that rose to her thigh. Her moonlight hair was pulled into a low chignon, and long black gloves covered most of her arms.

Killian peered at Elyse's delicately painted face and felt . . .

Nothing.

CHAPTER 30

— · —

ELYSE

To Elyse, Killian looked handsome—but in a way one might admire a painting. As he and Manny entered the foyer of the building, she smiled politely, but not affectionately, at each of them.

Manny immediately approached Sera, kissed her on both cheeks, and muttered something about ravishing her later, making Sera giggle. The two of them turned to face Killian and Elyse, eyes wide, watching them like they were performers at a show. Elyse hadn't told Sera about the kiss—she'd never been one to kiss and tell—but she was sure her friend knew something had happened, either by means of clairvoyance or her uncanny ability to read people. Elyse was also certain, based on the way Manny was watching them carefully, that Killian had told him.

"You look nice," Elyse told Killian. She meant it, too. But as her eyes roved over his torso, taking in the well-fitted black dress shirt that complemented his tan skin, the finely made jacket that accentuated his broad shoulders, and the fashionable trousers that caressed his warrior thighs, she felt no desire to touch him the way she had only the day before.

The spell worked.

"You look nice, too," he returned in an even voice, and Elyse searched his face for something—pain, anger, lust—but found nothing.

Manny and Sera just watched, their expressions a mixture of intrigue and caution, until Manny finally asked, "Shall we?"

He took Sera by the elbow and guided her out the door, ever the gentleman—at least when it came to Sera.

Killian held his elbow out for Elyse to take, but neither warmth nor discomfort shone in his eyes at the gesture. Elyse took his arm, watching him warily to make sure he didn't make any sudden movements. The spell she'd cast on herself, which suppressed all romantic feelings toward Killian, could only be broken one way: skin-to-skin contact with him. She'd carefully designed her outfit to cover her nearly completely from the neck down. Only a sliver of pale skin peeked out between the short sleeves of her gown and the long velvet gloves. If Killian so much as grazed a finger against her upper arm, her feelings for him would no longer be platonic. She would remember just how badly she'd yearned to let her lips wander over his body yesterday, and how she wanted him to do the same to her.

At the moment, though, she could hardly imagine feeling that way. He was handsome and kind and deserved to be touched that way by a beautiful woman—just not her.

They strode out onto the street, and at the sight of the carriage, Elyse grinned. She had never been one for finery, instead opting for subtlety, but if they were headed to a fancy party, they may as well go in style. The wooden frame of the carriage was painted white—no doubt scrubbed clean by servants after every use—and carved with intricate scrolling leaves. Inside was just as grand, with a bench cushioned by silk-covered pillows that looked to be brand new but were as comfortable as an old favorite chair. The curtains were drawn back on the window, letting the low-hanging sun stream into the carriage.

Manny and Sera, of course, sat next to one another, leaving Killian and Elyse to cohabit the bench across from them. Each inevitable bump in the road sent Elyse and Killian's bodies tumbling together, and she kept a sharp eye on his hands to ensure they stayed far away from her skin. She wanted to hug herself and cover her upper arms with her gloved hands, but knew that would be too obvious.

They soon arrived at Royce's townhouse. Elyse was the first one to rush out of the carriage, not daring to let Killian offer to help her out, and she found herself face to face with—

There were no words for the building before her, the elegant people who sauntered through its double doors. A fountain sat in the center of an immaculate courtyard, splashing clear, bright water down three tiers of marble, the trickling liquid sounding like coins jingling in a coin purse. The townhouse itself was made of pristine gray stone, and it stretched three stories high. A dozen windows lined the facade, each one displaying a brightly lit room and finely dressed partygoers traipsing about.

The whole scene made the carriage they'd just arrived in look like a cart pulled by a mule.

The rest of the group joined her in staring at the property. Manny let out a low whistle, Sera a quiet gasp. Killian merely looked bored.

They followed the bustling crowd up the grandiose staircase and slowed their pace as people funneled through the open doors.

Elyse felt a hand at her elbow and flinched, then realized it was only Sera.

"I can't wait to tuck in to the crab cakes. They were imported from the coast just this morning," her friend whispered in her ear.

Elyse didn't bother asking how Sera knew there would be crabs and precisely how fresh they were. She focused instead on the beauty that awaited her just across the threshold—and was not disappointed.

A sweeping entrance hall greeted them with crystal chandeliers, tiled floor, and a high ceiling. Partygoers exchanged niceties all around her, their excited voices nearly drowning out the hum of a string quartet. Everything was white and lavish, curated to perfection—a far reach from the mismatched jumble of Elyse's home.

They settled themselves in an alcove, huddled together awkwardly. Elyse had no doubt the others felt as out of place as she did, like obvious imposters. A waiter came by and offered them sparkling beverages in fluted glassware.

"What is it?" Sera asked as she accepted the glass and peered at the pale bubbling liquid.

"A seasonal delicacy," the waiter obliged her. He handed a glass to Killian. "Sparkling honeysuckle wine."

Killian practically threw his glass back at the waiter, who fumbled to catch it. Elyse gave Killian a perplexed look. Manny and Sera did the same.

Killian just shrugged. "Allergy," was his simple response.

The way Manny furrowed his brows at the explanation did not escape Elyse, but she chalked it up as another of Killian's absurdities and took a sip of the wine—and then another large gulp. Devil's tail, it was delicious.

The waiter carried his tray away, and the foursome huddled their heads together.

"What's the plan?" Elyse whispered. Well, whisper-shouted as the hall was filling with more and more attendees.

Manny looked around casually to make sure no one was listening before he said, "We should make our way to the great hall. There's a set of doors on the back wall, next to a painting of Royce wrestling with a bear. Try and post up near there."

Elyse couldn't help but smile. The man was a scheming bastard, something she could appreciate. At least, when he wasn't stealing from her.

The bedroom eyes Sera was giving him told Elyse that she was not the only one who appreciated his scheming.

Elyse glanced at Killian to see if he had anything else to add, but the lieutenant still wore that bored look on his face. A rumble of annoyance stirred in her chest. Did he have to be so uptight all the time? She gave a quiet hmph and turned toward the grand archway that invited them into the great hall. She wouldn't let Killian's blasé attitude sully her good time. She took a step toward the great hall, toward festive music and lively dancing—and promptly fell flat on her face.

CHAPTER 31

— • —

KILLIAN

One moment Elyse was standing there, huddled together with the rest of their group, and the next she was gone. Her body lay sprawled face down on the hard tile floor, the contents of her little black purse scattered across the foyer. Several of the partygoers gasped.

Killian felt neither alarmed nor embarrassed for her, only a sense of duty to help her up. He and Manny both moved toward her, but a nimble servant swooped in before them.

"My lady, are you all right?" he fussed about her. Then recognition glimmered in his eyes as Elyse lifted her head and pushed herself up to her knees. "Ms. Crenshaw? I don't believe we've had the pleasure of your company at one of our parties before."

He offered her a hand and hoisted her up with an ease that was uncharacteristic of a man so thin. He continued to hold her hand as she steadied herself, and Killian spotted a ring on his right hand. Large, silver, and stamped with the Royce family crest. He was not just any servant. He was Royce's top man, the very same one who had paid Bast for spreading lies. Tanner Wills.

Killian glanced at Manny, who arched a brow at him in return. He'd noticed the ring as well.

"I'm fine," Elyse finally answered as she tucked a loose strand of hair behind her ear. Her cheeks were rosy pink, and her voice wavered a bit, but she appeared unscathed. "I tripped over the hem of my dress. Thank you for helping me—Tanner, I presume?"

Tanner bent and picked up Elyse's clutch, which was nothing but an empty shell, and returned it to her with a slight bow. "Indeed. I apologize, Ms. Crenshaw, for not introducing myself." His professionalism was unrivaled, and Killian noted the fine suit he wore. No doubt he was good at his job, and paid handsomely for it.

"I seem to have lost the contents of my purse," Elyse said, frowning as she held the purse open to reveal its emptiness. She searched the ground, spotted a vial, and stooped to pick it up, and Killian, Sera, Manny and Tanner joined her.

"There, I think that's everything," Elyse said. She latched the little silver clasp on the clutch shut and tucked it under her arm.

Tanner bowed again. "Please let me know if I can be of any assistance to you this evening." With a smile, he turned and disappeared among the crowd.

"Are you sure you're all right?" Sera confirmed with her friend.

Elyse simply nodded and waved a hand nonchalantly. This time she hoisted her skirt up a few inches before sauntering into the hall.

It was loud and crowded and stunning and lively, and the scent of roasted ham drifted to Killian's nose, but he couldn't have cared less about any of it. The beautiful women that batted their lashes at him as he strolled by made him feel nothing at all, and neither did the men who leered at Elyse.

He focused instead on the guards—how many there were and where they were positioned—as Manny guided them to the portrait he'd described. Once they'd claimed a spot along the wall, another waiter brought them new refreshments, and this time Killian had the sense to ask the man to bring him a simple pear wine instead.

"Two guards posted at each of the doors, and three dressed as courtiers out on the dance floor," Manny said in a low voice.

Killian nodded. He'd noticed the same. He glanced at the two guards who flanked the door nearest them—the door that Manny had learned would lead to Royce's study. The guards appeared bored but nevertheless alert.

"Too bad Elyse couldn't have fallen out here. We could use a distraction like that," Manny continued.

Sera gave Manny a playful whack on the arm as the waiter returned with Killian's drink, sparing him from having to feign amusement—or defend Elyse? He wasn't sure what the right call was.

He turned back toward the wall where Elyse and Sera were standing, and saw that Elyse's eyes had darkened.

"Here comes Royce," she said in a low voice as a smile slithered its way onto her lips.

Killian hardly had any time to brace himself before a deep, refined voice called, "Such powerful and beautiful women shouldn't hide themselves away against the wall."

Killian peered over his shoulder, and there he was. Royce stood in a regal purple suit with long coattails, his dress boots as shiny as the tile floor beneath them. Killian spotted no weapons on him, but the man was no doubt a predator. Royce's green eyes danced as they took in both Elyse and Sera, giving Killian the distinct feeling that he was calculating their worth, as if they were prized mares.

"Royce," Elyse drawled back at him. "I'm surprised it took you this long to seek us out. Maybe Tanner isn't as efficient as everyone gives him credit for."

Her tone was dry, but flirtation simmered in her expression. Killian felt Manny glance toward him.

"Oh, Tanner is just as exceptional as people say, if not more. But I expected to find you two on the dance floor, fighting off a horde of suitors," Royce said with a wink toward Manny.

"Your home is exquisite," Sera offered with a wide smile. "I regret not having attended one of your parties sooner."

"Ah, Madam Sera. You live up to your reputation as the Sweet Seer." Royce's stare was hungry as he studied Sera, then took in the long slit of Elyse's dress, the one that ran most of the way up her thigh. "I wonder if I shall say the same for Elyse Crenshaw."

Elyse took a delicate sip from her glass and said, one eyebrow arched, "That depends what you've heard."

Again, Manny glanced toward Killian.

Sera jumped in, indicating Manny with her hand. "This is Manfried. He's a banker in the western sector. And this is his associate, Lou."

Royce shook their hands in turn but didn't look happy to do so. Not that Manny looked any more excited.

Royce immediately turned his attention back to Elyse. "Ms. Crenshaw—"

"Please, call me Elyse," she corrected sweetly.

Royce's smile widened, exposing glistening teeth. "Elyse," he purred, dragging out each syllable. "Would you do me the honor of looking over a few things in my *private* collection?"

Oh, he was certainly a man who knew what he wanted and didn't hesitate to take it—and probably wasn't used to being denied.

Elyse had to go with him. It was an opportunity to get out of this hall and into a room that might hold valuable information. Perhaps she could find a way to distract the guards too.

Elyse sent Royce a wicked smile before saying, "Lead the way."

With graceful, rapacious movements, Royce took Elyse's elbow and nodded to the guards, who opened the doors wide for their master and his guest. Royce jerked his chin, and the two guards followed him and Elyse into the corridor before shutting the doors behind them.

Sera turned to Killian with something like worry in her eyes. "She'll be fine," she told him.

Killian didn't know why she was telling him this. Of course she'd be fine, he'd seen her take down five grown men at once.

But Manny was giving him a peculiar look as well, one that he ignored.

"Wait two minutes and then go," Killian instructed.

Manny nodded and looked away.

Though the room was large, it was nearly filled with wealthy courtiers, merchants, bankers, and the like, all dancing, laughing, or gorging themselves on the feast that took up nearly an entire wall of the great hall. It wouldn't be hard to slip through the doors now that the guards were gone—though they were likely not far away. Manny could handle them.

At the appropriate time, Manny opened the door and disappeared through it, quick and quiet as a cat. Now they just had to wait.

Sera's eyes lingered on the door until she abruptly turned to Killian and said, "Come on, let's dance." She pried the glass from Killian's hand and set both their drinks on a nearby high-top table before taking his hand in hers and leading him out to the middle of the room. They joined the other dancing couples, Killian making sure to maintain a respectable distance from his friend's lover as they moved to the lively music.

"Something's different about you tonight," Sera said. She leaned in and sniffed a few times. "I can smell it on you."

Killian had no idea if she was having a go at him or not, so he simply said, "I have no idea what you're talking about."

Sera narrowed her kohl-lined eyes but didn't say anything. He twirled her around and brought her back to his grasp, letting her long blue dress flow. Others were staring at them, most likely at Sera's beauty and elegance. Or perhaps they had seen her with Manny before and were wondering if she was the sort of woman who entertained more than one man at a time. He was vaguely aware that if it weren't for the potion he would have been irked by their stares, but as it stood, he didn't mind. Let them watch and think what they wanted.

The song changed to something more subdued, and Killian and Sera slowed their movements to match. With her heels on, Sera was just as tall as Killian, and they were eye to eye as they swayed.

"How's your wound healing?" she asked him.

Killian's stomach muscles tightened instinctively as he thought about the cut on his abdomen, the one he had gotten while training with Elyse.

"It's fine," he answered. "It was hardly more than a scratch."

Sera's gaze penetrated him as she said, "That's not the wound I was referring to."

Unsure what to say, Killian pursed his lips. She was being cryptic, but he was certain she meant the emotional wound of losing his brother and sister. Had Elyse told her? Or had Sera learned of it through other means? He supposed Manny could have told her as well.

He reached deep inside him and tried to find the answer, but all that met him was a cold numbness.

"I . . . don't know," he answered truthfully.

Sera just nodded, and they danced to a few more songs in silence. Killian didn't particularly enjoy himself, but he wasn't bothered by the dancing either. Sera seemed to find it a sufficient distraction, so he let her spin and sway around him until she dabbed at nonexistent sweat on her brow and claimed she was parched. It was just as well. He expected Manny to return shortly.

They strode back to the table where Sera had set their drinks, and she picked each of them up and gave Killian his. She lifted her glass in a silent toast, and he clinked his glass against hers before raising it to his lips. He hadn't realized how thirsty he was until the sweet liquid met his mouth, and he gulped the rest of the glass down—then froze.

Pear wine wasn't sweet. It was crisp, tart, and delicious, but not sweet.

Sera stared at him with horror on her face, seeming to realize her mistake. She had given him *her* glass, with the honeysuckle wine, instead of his own.

"I'm so sorry!" she cried. "Are you all right? Do you need a doctor?"

Though he had lied about having an allergy, he did feel a reaction surging through his body. His tongue and extremities tingled, fire and ice battling in his core.

"Killian? Say something. You look pale. Are you going to pass out?" Sera blurted out, her hand gripped tightly around his arm.

Killian thought he might actually pass out. All the emotions he'd suppressed the past hour were rushing his body—tenfold. Gods above, they were in the house of the man who murdered the king, and Killian had let Elyse go alone with the man. He couldn't get the image of Royce practically drooling over Elyse out of his head. Of course Royce was drawn to her—she was the most stunning woman in the room. And she had kissed Killian, tended to his wound, held his hand as he told her about his tragedy.

Yearning wasn't a strong enough word for how he felt. He craved her presence, the way the body craves sustenance or the mind craves stimulation. Air was nothing. Water was nothing. She was everything.

He couldn't think straight—not until he found her, tore her away from Royce, and told her how he felt. Which was how exactly? He didn't know that either. It wasn't love, it was far too soon for that, yet the word still floated through his mind, haunting yet exciting him.

"I have to go," was all Killian managed to tell Sera before he marched to the corridor where Elyse and Royce had gone. He didn't bother to look back.

CHAPTER 32

— · —

ELYSE

Royce was certainly attractive—if you enjoyed men who wore their power as blatantly as a suit of armor—but Elyse didn't think that was what she was looking for. At least, not anymore. A part of her, a younger part that yearned to be seen and loved, reveled in the way Royce undressed her with his eyes, the way he walked, shoulders back, as he paraded her through his private collection of ancient spellbooks and cursed objects. But another larger part of her realized that Royce was doing this because *he* yearned to be seen and loved. He sought her approval, and if he didn't find it, he would discard her and find a more foolish woman to give him that satisfaction.

But she could play along.

She let him ramble on about where he'd gotten each item and how much he'd paid for them, and she raised her eyebrows and feigned being impressed. In truth, he'd been ripped off multiple times. She batted her lashes and asked him to tell her more, hoping to buy time for Manny to quietly disarm the two guards and find whatever he was looking for.

Royce guided Elyse, his hand on the small of her back, to a large knife displayed proudly on the wall.

"And this is the Blade of Hanael," he said, trying to sound casual. "It's the only knife ever forged capable of killing a demon."

Elyse had to fight not to roll her eyes. Knives wouldn't work on something incorporeal such as a demon—she would know.

But instead of saying that, she laid a hand on Royce's chest, feeling the soft fabrics of his jacket, and said with just the right amount of amazement in her voice, "Have you ever used it?"

Royce gave her a slightly condescending smile. "Something as priceless as this is not meant to be *used*."

She wanted to vomit. He was a collector through and through.

"Of course," she laughed. Perhaps it was time to move the conversation elsewhere. She didn't know how many rooms Manny would need to search. "Tell me," she said, entwining her fingers in his, "is there somewhere more romantic we can go? The sun ought to be setting right about now."

Royce leaned in, and Elyse braced herself for the most repugnant kiss of her life, but he simply whispered, "I know just the place."

He guided her toward the exit and let her step through the doorway first, which was a good thing because it gave her the opportunity to glance down the corridor and spy that the guards were missing. Manny must be at work. Before Royce followed her into the hallway, she quickly flicked her fingers and cast an illusion spell. She'd studied the guards' figures enough, just in case, that the illusion was a fairly good likeness. If Royce didn't look at them too long, he'd never know he was looking at magical replicas.

Fortunately, his attention was fully focused on Elyse as he led her the other way down the corridor toward a set of stained-glass doors. She marveled at the lovely glass, probably laying it on too thickly, but Royce devoured her words.

"Beauty recognizes beauty," he said as he opened the door for her, and Elyse hid her gagging by pretending to giggle.

She stepped outside and nearly gasped. All her fake pandering to Royce's ego was worth it to see the courtyard behind the house. Her mother would have adored the hundreds of flowers and various colors that covered the vast space. Roses, tulips, lilies, hydrangea, more flowers than she had ever seen at one time—even inside the palace walls. Candles were lit and scattered throughout the area, combining with the sunset to create a mesmerizing glow. For a moment, she forgot who she was with.

Until Royce's hand slid from her back to her ass.

"What do you think?" he whispered in her ear.

She tried not to cringe as she removed his hand from her backside and laced their fingers together.

"Now, now," she said coyly. "There will be time for that."

Hunger gleamed in his eyes, like a hunter whose game had gotten away, but he smiled and said, "I should have known you wouldn't give in that easily."

Elyse didn't know what to make of the comment, and she hoped Manny was close to finishing up. She didn't know how much longer she could stand this.

"How long have you lived here?" she asked, spewing out the first thing that came to her mind.

But Royce didn't get the chance to answer.

"Elyse!"

Her mouth agape, she turned toward the voice—and saw Killian standing in the threshold.

His hands were balled into fists at his side, and he stared at her hand still holding Royce's, his expression pained. Before she could speak, Killian closed the space between them in three strides and gripped her gloved arm.

"Come with me," he said, more yearning than demanding.

"I—what are you doing?" she shouted back.

But Killian didn't wait for another objection as he stormed off, dragging her behind him.

Just before he pulled her through the door, Elyse flashed a smile at Royce. "Just give us a few minutes," she called over her shoulder, adding a wink for good measure. Royce's shocked expression faded into one of greedy anticipation. Hopefully whatever Killian needed to tell her would be quick, before Royce grew impatient.

"Killian," she growled once they were back in the corridor. "Killian, let go of me!"

He released his grip on her wrist but didn't step away from her, his eyes boring into her with crazed desperation.

"We need to talk," he said in a low voice.

"Right now?" she demanded. She worried that something had happened, that Manny was in danger, or even Sera, but surely Killian would have a more tactful way to handle that than dragging her away from Royce.

Killian merely opened the door closest to them and gestured for her to enter. "Please?"

He looked frazzled, eyes wild and shoulders tense. Elyse sighed. He wouldn't have come and torn her away from Royce without good reason.

She entered the room, which appeared to be some sort of meeting area, and Killian shut the door behind both of them. He stepped close to her, letting the warmth of their bodies mingle. He took a deep breath, seeming to gather some courage. She'd never seen him so unsure of himself.

"What is it?" she asked, all of the anger now gone from her voice, replaced by faint worry.

He half smiled, half grimaced at her. "The other day, when we kissed—"

"Oh, devil's tongue!" Elyse shouted. "That's what this is about?" She took a step back and clenched her gloved hands to keep them from hexing him out of pure frustration. "You have a lot of nerve!"

"I'm sorry! I shouldn't have interrupted like that. I can explain!"

"I don't want to hear it!" Elyse stalked across the room and flung open a different door, not caring where it led. She could hear the party continuing on without them, and she stomped into the empty grand hallway toward what appeared to be the entry hall.

"Stop!" Killian ran after her, and he gripped her upper arm to spin her toward him, his fingers brushing against the sliver of exposed skin.

She knew the spell was broken long before she lifted her eyes to meet his.

CHAPTER 33

— : —

ELYSE

Killian's hand was warm where it gently held her upper arm. Warm and oh so tantalizing. She leaned into his touch, and it felt as if her heart restarted, furiously pumping blood into her face, among other places. Her chest ached as the memory of how much she had dreamed of that touch came surging back to her.

She closed her eyes and let out a soft moan.

Killian immediately released her arm.

"I'm sorry—did I hurt you?"

"No," she murmured, barely audible against the backdrop of music and chatter.

She opened her eyes and saw the confusion on his face. That strong jaw and those dimpled cheeks. The lips that sometimes flashed a smile that sent her heart hammering. The golden eyes that had learned to see her as more than just a witch, at least she hoped.

"Elyse, I . . ." he began tentatively, taking her hand lightly in his, and she felt her heart beating faster, if that was even possible. She was drunk with lust—maybe more.

"I think about you all the time," he went on. His voice was gentle, yet it held undeniable force. "And tonight I realized, I don't want to pretend not to care about you. And I'm sorry for pulling you away from Royce, I know that was stupid, but I just saw you together and—I lost my mind.

I wouldn't have done it if I wasn't fairly certain that, well . . . That you feel the same way about me."

He was rambling. Her calm, cool lieutenant was rambling.

Because he wanted her. He'd been so out of his mind with jealousy that he'd made a fool of both of them. She knew she should be angry about it, that he had possibly jeopardized their mission, but anger was the furthest thing from what she felt. His words had her feeling light, practically hovering off the ground, and she squeezed his hand tighter to keep her tethered to him, to this moment.

Elyse took a step toward Killian, and she swore she could smell his longing for her, taste his desire. She inhaled deeply, letting his passion fill her lungs, before she said, "That *was* stupid of you."

His shoulders fell, but he held her gaze.

She continued, "But I've found I like it when you do stupid things."

She gave him a smile that was wholly her, wicked yet pure, the closest she had let him come to seeing her true self.

Killian closed the already small space between them, pressing her back up against a nearby pillar, never taking his eyes off her face.

"Well, I'm about to do one more stupid thing," he breathed against her mouth.

She clutched his shirt and pulled him closer just as his lips met hers. She didn't know if it was the aftermath of the spell, or if he was just that good, but the languid movements of his tongue made her back arch. Every place their bodies touched—their lips, their torsos, his hand that roved from her shoulder to her breast—seemed to radiate with pleasure. She moved her own hand to grip his usually neat hair, disheveling it as she pulled his face closer.

Behind her, on the other side of the pillar and down the hall, she could hear the party. It felt foreign, so far away, and yet—the thought that someone could catch them entangled like this made him taste all the better.

As if reading her mind, he moved his lips to her ear and whispered, "We should stop."

In response, Elyse gently turned his face back to hers and lightly bit his bottom lip. He groaned, racking her body with shivers.

The look in his eyes told her enough. *Challenge accepted.*

He grabbed her thigh, pulling it free through the long slit and lifting it up to wrap around his hip. She felt him growing hard against her, and she reached her hand down to feel him, but he stopped her, lacing his fingers through hers and pressing the back of her hand against the pillar.

"Oh, no," he purred. "I'm the one who messed up, remember? Now it's time for me to make it right."

Oh, by the devil. He would be the end of her.

With his free hand, he grazed her exposed thigh, slowly, lovingly. Elyse bit her lip, both at the way he touched her and because she knew he was about to discover she wasn't wearing any undergarments. His middle finger found its way under her skirt, tracing its way higher up her leg until—

Only wet, bare skin met his fingers, and he paused, apparently surprised. The heavy rise and fall of his chest declared that he enjoyed what he'd found.

"Elyse." His voice was a deep tremor that licked up her spine, curling her toes.

"Do your worst, Lieutenant," she commanded.

She brought her lips to his again, an invitation to continue. As his tongue drew lazy circles in her mouth, his finger did the same, but much lower. Elyse gasped, and not just because it had been a long time since she'd been touched like this. She pressed herself against his hand, the only hand she ever wanted to touch her, the hand that made her feel safe every time she held it. He answered her by slipping a finger inside, working some sort of magic she never knew existed.

Elyse let out a whimper as her exhilaration grew, and Killian breathed a laugh against her skin. "That's it," he encouraged.

She wasn't used to submitting to a man this way—she was usually the one in control. She fought to stay quiet, but Killian seemed to take pleasure in her struggle, pumping faster and harder with each gasp she let out. He withdrew his finger, focusing again on her most sensitive area, and just as she was about to scream out, to cry his name so loud the whole damn party would hear, he clamped his other hand over her mouth, drowning the sound of her ecstasy.

That didn't stop the euphoria from overtaking her whole body, spilling down her legs while she squeezed as tight as she could onto Killian's shirtfront. Her body trembled, utterly drained, and Killian held her until her breathing finally slowed.

Then he planted one more gentle, lingering kiss on her lips.

She closed her eyes, afraid that this wasn't real, that she'd open them and be all alone. She slid a hand to Killian's face, forcing herself to believe in this moment.

Finally, she opened her eyes to see him smiling sheepishly, like he was proud of his handiwork but too humble to admit it.

"It looks like I've made a mess of you," he chuckled.

Okay, maybe not that humble. She couldn't help but let out a quiet laugh.

"Am I forgiven?" he murmured as he nuzzled his face against her neck.

"Yes," she breathed, her voice serrated. "Yes, definitely."

He pulled back, just slightly, so that their eyes met. "That's a shame," he growled. "I was hoping you would demand more."

Elyse giggled—oh, he made her giggle more than she ever had in her life—and they kissed again, tender and easy.

CHAPTER 34

— · —

KILLIAN

K illian rested his forehead against Elyse's. Her scent of jasmine filled his lungs, like taking a drug after suffering withdrawals. His hands encased her waist, pulling her close. He needed to feel her presence, to make sure he hadn't dreamt everything, to hold on to her and this moment for as long as he could.

Pleasuring her had been all he could think about as he had kissed her. Hearing her gasps, the way she murmured his name . . . There were no sweeter sounds. And now, feeling her nestled against his chest, knowing that she felt the same way about him, he didn't remember the last time he felt this happy. He wanted to disappear somewhere with her. The forest, her little cottage, even a quiet street. Anywhere besides Royce's townhouse.

All at once, the roar of the party came back to him, along with the recollection of why they were there, and he tore his body from her.

"We should go find the others," he said, and watched as that same realization dawned on Elyse, sobering both of them from the high they'd just reveled in. She magicked herself clean—a handy little trick—and they hurried back into the great hall.

All of his lust for Elyse was replaced by concern for Manny. What had he been thinking, leaving him on his own? When he drank the antidote, the rush of emotions made him senseless. He wouldn't forgive himself if something happened to Manny on his watch. Yet the feeling of Elyse's hand in his as they shuffled through the hall gave him a steadiness that he needed.

Killian let out a relieved breath as he spotted Manny safely tucked away in a corner, Sera at his side. The smug look on Manny's face told Killian enough. He'd been successful. And the way Manny's eyes flicked toward Killian's hair—still unkempt from Elyse's pawing—told him enough, too.

"Killian! You're all right," Sera said in her sweet manner, a glimmer of solace in her eyes.

"Yes," he said quietly, giving Elyse's hand a gentle squeeze.

Elyse squeezed it back and asked, her expression eager, "Did you find anything?"

Manny nodded discreetly. "Ready to leave?"

"Yes!" Elyse and Killian both said at the same time. They definitely needed to get out of there before Royce came looking for Elyse again.

Manny and Sera exchanged knowing glances before the group moved out. No one spoke as they left the townhome, sent the valet to retrieve their carriage, and clambered inside. The party was several blocks behind them when Manny pulled a small piece of fabric from his pocket.

Killian's heart hammered as he watched Manny slowly, with great care as if he were sewing up a wound, pull back the folds of the pale fabric to reveal a small, dry, white bone.

It took a moment for realization to hit Killian, but when it did, the racing of his heart doubled. The way Elyse's body went tense beside him, he could tell she knew the significance as well.

"What is it?" Sera asked quietly.

"Well," Manny began in an uncharacteristically serious tone, "according to the label on the jar it was in, it's the ring finger bone of a virgin—one of the ingredients needed for the spell used to kill King Cyril."

"Good work, mate," Killian breathed, letting a smile ease onto his lips. Then he turned to Elyse. "Is there a way to verify? Make sure it's not just some other bone?"

Elyse nodded, her eyes never leaving the tiny, delicate bone. "Yes, I can help you with that."

It wasn't much, but it was a start. Hopefully enough to grant a deeper investigation, even an arrest.

"What about the other ingredients? Did you see any of them?" Killian asked.

Manny grinned. "All of them. This was just the easiest one to take."

Now, Killian grinned. They'd found their man. He caught Elyse's eyes, which were bright with excitement.

"We'll go to the magistrate first thing in the morning. Then we'll make the arrest," Killian said, more to himself than anyone else. He reached for Elyse's hand, his thumb stroking her skin. Gods, they never would have found Royce without her help. He owed her so much—and he would be sure to deliver his gratitude in ways that made her cry out his name, for starters.

It was only a few minutes later that they pulled up before Sera's apartment, and the four of them descended from the carriage. With a wave goodbye and a hug for Elyse, Manny and Sera disappeared into the building, leaving Killian alone with Elyse.

As if pulled by a rope, his feet led him to her, and his hands easily found their way to her waist. Though it was dark save for a flickering lantern poised outside the door to Sera's building, he could see the happiness, the comfort at his touch, that radiated from her face. And he was sure his face matched.

"Tonight was . . ." he began, but then found himself unsure of the remainder of the sentence.

"A whirlwind?" she finished for him. They both laughed, a chummy, contented laugh that had their bodies pressing closer together. He was amazed at how relaxed he felt around her now, how liberating it was to be vulnerable with her, and how very much he enjoyed her vulnerability as well.

Elyse seemed freer too, her movements less inhibited, her expression dazzling. Those dark eyes no longer seemed cold or cruel. Instead, they were alive with affection and desire. He would do anything to keep her this happy.

"I'm sorry for before—" he began again, but Elyse cut him off.

"Don't," she said, letting out a small laugh. "It's sort of irrelevant now anyway."

So he kissed her, long and slow, savoring her lips and taking his time the way he'd been too eager to do before.

When they parted, she said, "I suppose I should let you get some rest, since you have work to do tomorrow."

Killian swallowed down his disappointment. If she wasn't comfortable spending the night together, he wouldn't push her.

But then she said, "Unless . . ."

As a reply to her unspoken question, he kissed her again, this time letting his tongue caress hers. The catch in her breath conveyed her agreement.

"Okay," he murmured against her skin. "But if you get too handsy, I'm remarkably decent at stunning spells."

She laughed, the feeling vibrating his lips and warming his heart—which had been so stony for so long. Elyse took a step back so she could riffle through her purse, but her smile slipped into a frown.

"What is it?"

Her brows were furrowed in the most adorable way that he'd never seen, as anything or anyone rarely seemed to get the best of her.

"I can't find my transportation potion," she said, still fumbling through the contents of her purse. "Devil below, it must have fallen out when I tripped."

Killian glanced at the carriage, where the driver was waiting to see if he needed a ride home, then glanced up at the sky. It was a beautiful, cloudless night, and the waning moon still provided some light to see by. He slipped his arm through hers and said, "It's a nice night for a walk. May I escort you, my lady?"

She looked like she was fighting not to roll her eyes, but she smiled and said, "It's a long walk."

And with a lightness that he hadn't felt in years, Killian said, "Good thing there's nowhere else I'd rather be."

CHAPTER 35

ELYSE

It was well into the night when Killian and Elyse finally arrived at the cottage. She'd removed her shoes only a quarter mile into their trek, and Killian kindly offered to carry them for her the rest of the way. Though it took them hours, she'd wished the walk would never end. They'd talked nonstop, Killian describing his mother, his father who had passed away, and even divulging a little about his deceased siblings. She heard the pain in his voice as he spoke of them, which only made her more grateful for his sharing.

And yet the guilt ate at her. The guilt of who she was, what she had done, and the knowledge that if he had any true notion of the blood that coated the hand he held so delightfully in his own, that he would never be able to forgive her.

Though her skin still tingled from where he had pleasured her earlier, she was glad they had refrained from doing more. The night air helped awaken the logic that escaped her upon the spell's breaking. She let him defile her while courtiers partied mere feet away, her moans echoing through the tiled hall. And as much as her body yearned for him to take her—

She knew she couldn't be with him, not like that. What she felt for him was built on the little bit of trust and respect they'd accrued for each other, and if she joined him in the most intimate of ways . . . She wouldn't let herself go there.

So as they approached the Emporium, dread began to churn her core. Though she was sure Killian would be a proper gentleman, she couldn't help but feel an ounce of guilt at making him walk her all the way home, surely expecting something when they arrived, only to have to tell him that she wasn't ready. She'd refrain from telling him she wasn't sure if she'd ever feel ready. Perhaps one day she'd be able to come clean, and then she could bed him with a free conscience. But as soon as the thought occurred, she knew it would never be.

They entered the shoppe, and Elyse lit the candles with a wave of her hand. "Go on up," she told Killian, pointing toward the back staircase. "I'm just going to wash up."

He kissed her cheek before bounding up the stairs, and Elyse was left standing, marveling at the events of the night.

You're making a mistake, said a voice in the back of her mind. *A very dangerous mistake.*

But she pushed the voice away as she filled a basin of water and splashed some on her face, letting it cleanse the cosmetics and her guilt. Freshly emboldened, she mounted the stairs, ready to explain to Killian that she liked him and she respected him, and therefore she wanted to do this right, to do this slowly, despite what happened earlier that night.

As she reached the top stair and heard the soft, rhythmic breathing that accompanied sleep, she realized that conversation would have to wait. Killian lay sprawled atop the covers, fast asleep, his dress clothes still on. She couldn't help but smile at the peacefulness of the scene, the bliss that filled her at seeing him in her bed, this time without an open wound. She magicked him into something more comfortable, laid a blanket atop him, and curled up beside him to sleep.

CHAPTER 36

— • —

ELYSE

Elyse woke to soft lips on her neck, teeth gently tugging at her ear lobe. The room was still mostly dark, so it couldn't have been long after sunrise, yet she smiled as she rolled over to face Killian.

"I could become a morning person if that's how I wake up every day," she said.

He grinned back at her as his hand rubbed up and down her arm, then around to her back to pull her closer.

"I figured you'd go back to sleep." His voice was soft, like a lullaby, and she nestled deeper into the bed, into him. "I just wanted to say goodbye before I left."

Elyse groaned. She knew he had to leave, had to go arrest Royce, but the thought of his warmth abandoning her made her want to pin him down and force him to stay.

But her groan only made him chuckle. "I'll be back," he said with a kiss on her forehead. And then he added, more seriously, "I want to take you to meet my mum tonight."

Elyse shifted, giving Killian a tentative look. That seemed like a big next step to take, yet the idea stirred a longing she didn't even know she held.

"It's a bit soon," she said with a timid smile, "but I'd love to."

Killian's brows furrowed, then he laughed. "I meant so she can tell you about the cure. But I'm glad you seem invested in . . . whatever this is."

"Oh." Elyse's cheeks warmed at her own stupidity. What on earth had this man done to her senses? She'd forgotten the whole reason she was even working with him, to cure the disease that marred her arm.

"Speaking of 'whatever this is,'" he continued, stirring a bit as he spoke, but never taking his eyes from Elyse's face. "I'm not normally so . . . forward. At least, not with women I really care about."

Elyse smiled, but before she had a chance to begin the speech she'd prepared the night before, Killian went on.

"I took an emotion suppressing potion last night. And when I accidentally drank the antidote, I went a bit mad. I couldn't help myself from finding you, telling you how I felt, and, well . . . You know the rest."

At that, Elyse burst into a fit of laughter. They were so different, and yet the same on so many levels. He looked at her with confusion, so she explained, "I placed a spell on myself to feel nothing but friendship for you. When you touched my bare arm last night, the spell broke."

Now it was his turn to laugh, a rare sound and one that Elyse savored. "I guess the old saying is true. Great minds do think alike." He stroked her hair, which had fallen loose from its chignon during her sleep, and she closed her eyes to focus on his touch.

"I can't say how I normally act when I care for a man," she murmured, her eyes still closed. "I've never wanted to get to know someone before, as I do with you."

And it was true. She'd thought she'd felt affection for Jaime, but she realized now that it was more a relationship of convenience. With Killian though, she was drawn to him, no matter how hard she tried to pull away. Her thoughts were consumed by him, wondering what he was doing, wanting to tell him about something funny that happened to her, or even just wishing he was around to make her feel . . . complete.

He continued stroking her hair as he said, "Then I'll let you set the pace, so you can figure that out for yourself."

She nodded, not trusting her voice, which would surely betray the gratitude she felt at his understanding. Of course he understood. How had she ever thought he would react any differently?

Ironically, his acknowledgement of her feelings only made her want him more, and she was keenly aware of how close they were, how they shared her bed, and how romantic the early dawn light was as it crept through the window.

He seemed to sense it too, because his throat bobbed and he slowly moved out of the bed.

"Where are my clothes?" he asked, as if he'd just noticed that he wore a simple cotton shirt and baggy trousers.

Elyse pointed to the dresser behind him, to where his dress clothes were neatly folded. She couldn't bear to watch him dress, as that meant there would be nothing to keep him from leaving, so she closed her eyes and focused on his oaky scent and the warmth that still lingered on the bed.

When he finished, he stooped over the bed to kiss her. "Meet me at the palace this evening? I'll let the guards know to let you in."

"Fine," she groaned, trying not to think of how slowly the day would go as she yearned to see him again.

But something happened—a shift in the air of the room—and she quickly opened her eyes to see if Killian had noticed the change.

Lazarus was calling.

Killian simply smiled at her a bit sleepily, clearly unaware.

"Get out of here so I can go back to sleep," she told him, hoping she sounded convincingly teasing, and not as worried as she felt.

She held her breath, hoping he would obey, and after one last kiss on her cheek, he strode out of the room.

Elyse waited until she heard him descend the stairs, make his way through the shoppe, and exit through the door before she let herself glance at the altar across the bedroom.

The skull's eyes were glowing.

Chapter 37

Elyse

No, no, no, no, no . . .

Elyse flung the covers off herself and ran to the little altar. Among the rose petals, candles, and crystals sat the human skull, its eyes now smoldering as the flames inside of it grew.

The full moon wasn't for another few weeks. What was Lazarus doing trying to communicate with her now? Her heart raced as she waited—waited for the skull to speak.

Finally, its skeletal jaw opened, and Elyse swore it wore a mocking grin.

"It sounds as if you had an eventful night," crooned the skull in its low, sinister, unnatural voice. The voice of its master, Lazarus.

"What do you want?" Elyse snarled back. She felt violated, as if she'd been spied on. Though she knew the demon whose magic controlled the skull could watch her every move, it felt different when Killian was involved.

Despite its lack of teeth or a tongue, the skull made an undeniably condescending clicking sound. "I'd think after my last task led you to meet the lieutenant, you'd show more gratitude."

The guilt that roiled in her stomach now threatened to make an appearance through her mouth. She hated the sound of those words, and the truth behind them. If Lazarus hadn't sent her to kill the king, she never would have met Killian.

Yet if she'd never killed the king, she wouldn't be feeling like such a conniving, worthless liar, as she felt now.

She refused to show any weakness.

"Is that why you wanted to talk? So you could gloat?"

A wicked chuckle escaped from the skull's mouth. "And here I'd thought you'd come to enjoy our chats."

"Never," she growled. "If you believe that, you must be the biggest idiot in hell."

Another low laugh, one that sent chills coursing through Elyse.

"I'll see you in a few weeks to relay your next task," the skull said coolly. "Don't bother trying to think of a clever way to get out of it. You know it never works."

"Leave," Elyse demanded through gritted teeth.

With one last laugh of victory, the black skull went still, and the flames behind its eyes and mouth flickered and disappeared.

Elyse stood still, trying to steel herself, trying not to think about all the lies she'd told Killian. He'd believed wholeheartedly that she was under the influence of the truth serum. He was so naive about the world of magic, he didn't even consider it a possibility that she knew a workaround. And she used that naivety against him, the man she was falling for against her better judgment.

Unable to smother her guilt any longer, she collapsed onto her bed, pulled the covers over her head, and sobbed.

CHAPTER 38

— • —

KILLIAN

E ven after a bath and a fresh guard's uniform, Killian could still smell Elyse's fragrance on himself. He smiled as recognition took hold. Jasmine, that was her scent, a surprisingly floral choice for someone so . . . prickly. But he supposed Elyse's surprising nature was what he liked so much about her.

Waking up beside her had been just as intoxicating as pressing her up against the pillar at Royce's. He'd watched her sleep for a few minutes, awestruck by her beauty. As breathtaking as she was when she slept, he preferred the fire in her onyx eyes whenever she teased him.

Tearing himself from her side had been nearly impossible—at least, until he remembered that today was the day he would arrest Royce.

Everything was falling into place.

He and Manny walked through the city streets toward the magistrate's home, which was only a few blocks from the palace. It was shaping up to be a dreary morning, but Killian didn't mind at all. Sunshine coursed through his veins each time he remembered kissing Elyse, holding her while she slept, pushing her up against that pillar—

Manny cleared his throat, interrupting Killian's thoughts. "You and Elyse seemed pretty chummy last night," he said quietly.

Killian felt his cheeks heat, despite himself. "Yeah, we sort of . . ." He trailed off, unsure of how to finish. Sort of acted like teenagers? Sort of desecrated a stranger's home?

But Manny didn't seem to need to hear the rest of the sentence to understand. As they approached the magistrate's townhome, he simply said, "Just be careful."

Killian didn't have time to ask what he meant before Manny darted up the few stairs and knocked on the door. The magistrate, Thomas Longfellow, lived in a large but plain townhome with curtains cinched closed in every window.

Finally, a stout housekeeper opened the door, and Manny flashed her a charming grin.

"You must be Mrs. Longfellow," he practically sang.

Right on cue, the woman tittered a laugh. "Oh, no. Mrs. Longfellow left us some time back, gods rest her soul. Master Longfellow is currently getting a massage, but . . . oh, I suppose I can see if he's accepting visitors."

"Thank you, madam," Manny said. "It's a most-urgent business."

The housekeeper ushered them inside and made them wait in the foyer while she hurried up a set of stairs. When Killian was sure she was out of earshot, he hissed at Manny, "What do you mean, 'be careful'?"

Manny gave him an exasperated look, as if he'd opened a door that now wouldn't close.

"I just mean . . . You don't know her very well."

"Oh, and you know Sera so well?"

Manny opened his mouth to retort, but the housekeeper came hobbling halfway down the steps.

"Come, come," she called, waving them up the stairs. "He says you have five minutes."

Wasting no time, both Killian and Manny sped after her. She stopped at the top of the landing and pointed to the first door. "Right through there," she said. Killian swore she winked at Manny.

They entered a bedroom, grandly decorated with a four-poster bed against the far wall. Longfellow was seated on the edge of the bed, wearing a loosely tied robe that revealed the curly hairs of his chest, which was ironic given the poor comb-over he sported atop his head.

"This better be good," he said gruffly, pointing his long nose in the air. "Nina here was just about to get started. And once she does, well . . . Let's just say I'm not in any position to stop."

He flicked his eyes toward a girl who huddled in the corner. Killian hadn't even noticed her in the room. She practically cowered, clutching a robe around herself. She had mousy brown hair that hung limply to her shoulders, no doubt from lack of hygiene, and her face was rather plain. Longfellow's eyes lingered over her body, and Killian couldn't help but shudder.

"Nina, go freshen up in the bathing chamber while the men talk," Longfellow ordered her.

"Yes, Master Longfellow," she said meekly before disappearing through the door beside her.

Killian fought not to cringe—not only at her calling him *Master* Longfellow, but because her teeth were black and nearly ground down to the gums.

Longfellow must have noticed Killian's sour expression because he said, "She's not great to look at, but her lack of teeth is beneficial in . . . other ways."

Killian could not believe that this vile man before him was in a position of such power. If he didn't desperately need the magistrate's cooperation to take down Royce, he would have pried the man's teeth from his mouth right then and there.

"It's Royce," he said, clenching his fists as he restrained himself.

Manny continued. "You might need to cancel your . . . massage. We need you to draw up a warrant."

Longfellow glanced toward the door where Nina had disappeared. "That's a shame," he sighed. "The uglier ones are willing to do the most depraved things."

Killian ignored the nausea roiling in his stomach at those words, and instead focused on why they'd come there. He quickly explained the events of the previous night, leaving out, of course, his excursion with Elyse.

When he finished, Longfellow wore an expression of pure skepticism. "You want me to prepare an arrest warrant based on some ingredients that you stole from a room you weren't even supposed to be in?" he drawled out.

Killian's nostrils flared. Was Longfellow really going to push back on this? "We've arrested on less evidence before," he stated, trying to keep his tone professional.

Longfellow scoffed. "Yes—petty vandals and scam artists. Not powerful merchants with connections."

"So?" Manny interjected. "He's guilty. Who cares if we stole the evidence or if he has connections?"

Longfellow's eyes darkened as he stood from the bed. "You don't understand. A man like him can turn the whole kingdom against us. He'll use any means he can to wiggle himself out of a guilty verdict. If this investigation isn't airtight, it'll just be fuel for his manipulation."

Killian lifted his chin an inch higher and stared down at Longfellow. "So, you would have us do nothing?"

Surely that wasn't what he was saying. The evidence was all there—Royce was their man. One way or another, Killian would see King Cyril's death avenged.

Longfellow moved lazily over to a desk on the side of the bedroom. "I'm just warning you," he said as he picked up a quill. "You're about to make an enemy of one of the most powerful men in Rhodan."

CHAPTER 39

— : —

KILLIAN

With the emotion-suppressing potion, and then the drunken-like stupor he'd been in after, Killian hadn't really appreciated the beauty of Royce's townhome. Yet as he strode through the manicured courtyard with two dozen guards in tow, all he could think was, *Whose blood paid for all this?*

He barged his way through the heavy front doors and past the blubbering doorman. "Split up and find him," he barked to his men. As discussed ahead of time, the guards divided and dispersed themselves throughout the enormous house while Killian waited impatiently, gripping the arrest warrant in his hands.

It wasn't long before Manny himself came swaggering down the corridor, dragging a manacled Royce with him.

"He tried to sneak out the back," Manny explained with a smug grin. Exactly why Killian had ordered Manny and a handful of guards to enter from the rear.

The elegance with which Royce had carried himself the night before had vanished. His white hair hung across his face, which was red and sweaty. But his haughtiness still remained.

"What the fuck is this?" he spat at Killian and the growing crowd of guards.

Killian reveled in the man's confusion as he stepped forward and proudly held the warrant on display.

"Niall Royce, you are under arrest for the murder of King Cyril Vandever III."

Royce's nostrils flared, and he tried to tug himself free of Manny's grip, but Manny held firm.

"You're making a huge mistake," Royce growled, flashing a glimpse of the predator that Killian had sensed the night before.

Killian took another step toward him, but Royce didn't flinch.

"The only mistake I've made," Killian said in a voice drenched with disgust, "is not arresting you sooner."

A guard emerged from the great hall, carrying a handful of items. "We found them, Lieutenant. Just where you said they would be."

Killian's own smile grew feral as he viewed what the guard carried: jars, no doubt labeled and filled with the ingredients used for the spell that killed the king.

Royce was staring with furrowed brows toward the guard and his bounty.

"The evidence is stacking up against you, Royce," Killian declared.

Royce spat at the floor, marring the otherwise pristine marble. "Probably planted by this street rat," he said with a jerk of his chin toward Manny, "while you were fucking that witch."

Despite his best effort, Killian blanched. How had Royce known about him and Elyse? He felt the heat of the other guards as they stared at him, their commander, and he prayed to the gods that they hadn't seen him flinch.

"Your imagination is refreshing, but no amount of creativity will get you out of this," he said coolly.

Royce bared his teeth in a hideous snarl and said, "We'll see about that." Then his lips contorted into a smile. "Send your mother my regards. Is she still on Persimmon Street?"

Killian swallowed as he felt his face drain of color. He tried to keep his expression neutral, but he was rattled. Royce was threatening his mother. How had he even known about her? And her address? Longfellow was right—they needed to be prepared.

He refused to back down, though. He glared back at Royce, fire burning in his veins and ordered, "Take him away!"

"With pleasure." Manny shoved Royce forward, pushing him out the door and toward the armored carriage used to escort prisoners.

Killian just watched. He knew he should feel satisfied. He'd just arrested King Cyril's murderer. So why did he feel like this was far from over?

CHAPTER 40

— · —

ELYSE

Elyse wandered the streets of the city, even as her meeting time with Killian approached. She couldn't do it, couldn't face him—and certainly not his mother. Talking with Lazarus earlier had made it real. Until then, she'd mostly been able to deny her lying and manipulating, pushing it down in some deep, dark corner of her soul. Who was she kidding? After the things she'd done, she no longer had a soul.

She meandered through the streets of happy citizens, barely noticing them. She tried to focus on her breathing instead, keeping it slow and steady, and fighting down her nausea. But it didn't help. Her mind was a frenzy of guilt and self-loathing, going through all the horrid scenarios of what would happen when Killian eventually found out that *she* was the murderer he sought.

Unable to take it anymore, she leaned against the wall of the closest building and closed her eyes. She had to go through with it. And not just for the cure, but because it would be suspicious if she didn't show up. Even as she told herself this, the urge to flee the kingdom overwhelmed her.

That is, until a familiar figure strode in front of her. She saw his umber skin, his perfectly curled hair, and smiled. All worries seemed to vanish as her body moved of its own volition, following him down the street.

Killian's guard instincts must have kicked in, because he turned to see who was following him. When he saw her, his entire expression lit up, and Elyse's knees buckled. Then she noticed what he carried.

Two bouquets: one of salvia and irises, complementing each other beautifully, and the other—

Jasmine flowers. For her.

Killian waited for her to catch up, beaming at her the whole time. Devil below, he was handsome, especially when he smiled. She could barely breathe as she closed the space between them.

"Were you following me?" he teased. He placed a kiss on her cheek, and she leaned into the sensation of his lips on her skin.

"Only for a moment. I was early so I was just sort of wandering."

Killian's smile turned sly as he said, "You're nervous."

Indeed, she was more nervous now than she'd been when she snuck into the palace grounds to kill the king. She didn't respond, though, and Killian moved closer to her.

"Don't be nervous. My mum will love you," he whispered, sending shivers through her body.

"Here," he said, taking a step back and extending the bouquet of jasmine toward her. "These are for you."

"They're lovely," she said breathlessly. She stood on her tiptoes to give him a kiss, one that she hoped truly conveyed her appreciation. No one had ever bought her flowers before, and the small gesture was intoxicating.

"Are you ready?" he asked.

Elyse nodded as she examined the flowers. They were exquisite, all beautifully clean and white, and their scent was divine.

Killian took her hand in his and they walked together down the streets. Elyse was no longer a loner watching the other citizens go about their merry ways; she was one of them. People smiled at them as they passed by, their faces bright. What did they see when they looked at the two of them, strolling through the streets hand in hand, bouquets of fresh flowers in tow? A happy couple, drunk with infatuation? Did they seem carefree and content? Was the charade working?

"How did it go today?" she asked, shoving down her guilt. After all, Killian had arrested the man she actively framed for the murder she committed.

Killian hesitated to reply, and Elyse's stomach churned. *He knows something*, she immediately thought. But he couldn't—he wouldn't be there holding her hand if he did. Would he?

"We arrested Royce," Killian finally answered, but there was doubt in his voice. "He's being processed now, and Longfellow—the magistrate—is conducting his interrogation."

Elyse felt a lump forming in her throat. "So why don't you sound more excited? You still think Royce did it, right?"

"Of course," Killian answered right away.

Elyse relaxed, though Killian's next words were little comfort.

"He made threats, though—A threat toward my mum."

The street no longer seemed like a happy, bustling place as despair overcame Elyse. Royce had threatened his mother? Her vision began to blur. She had incited that, even if it was indirectly. She would never forgive herself if someone else—especially someone so close to Killian—was hurt by her actions.

Her throat was dry, but she managed to croak out, "That's terrible. I'm so sorry."

Killian gave her hand a small squeeze. "It's okay. It's not the first time this has happened. When my father was captain, we were threatened several times. I've arranged for guards to watch over her house." He said it so casually, though the pain in his golden eyes betrayed his true fear.

Before Elyse could think of a reply, Killian's expression turned serious and he uttered, "We can go as slow as you like, Elyse."

Taken aback by his strange change of subject, she laughed and gave him a side glance. "Where is this coming from?"

She felt him go rigid, his hand tensing in hers as they walked, and he lowered his voice. "When I went to the magistrate's earlier, he had a prostitute there." He seemed to struggle to maintain his calm as he recounted the young woman's demeanor and the horrible things the magistrate said about her.

Elyse squeezed his hand. Killian was perhaps the only true gentleman she'd ever known, and that came with burdens. Her heart ached for him almost as much as it did for the young woman—Nina, he'd called her.

She kept her voice light, though, as she said, "So you saw the disgusting way that Longfellow treats women, and now you're worried that I might feel—what, pressured?"

He hesitated. "No." Then after a few steps—"Well, maybe."

She laughed again, and when his brows furrowed, she pulled him to a stop.

"Killian, you are nothing like that man. When a woman is with you, it's because she chooses to be, because she sees all the goodness in you, as I do."

"I just . . ." he began. "I don't want you to feel like you have to do certain things to make me happy."

She freed her hand from his and laid it on his face. "I don't," she whispered. "But I am grateful for the sentiment."

She lowered her hand and said, "Besides, do you really see me doing anything I don't want to?"

At that, he finally smiled, his eyes lingering on her a moment before they resumed walking.

It was another ten minutes or so before they turned down a quiet street filled with quaint little houses. Even if there hadn't been two guards in black uniforms posted outside, Elyse would have known right away which house belonged to Killian's mother. It emanated a peaceful quietude, the same way Killian himself did as she grew to know him better. The house was unremarkable, wooden and simple like the others on the street, save for a rocking chair on the front porch and a few potted plants scattered about the small lawn. Something about the sight of the home made Elyse's heart swell, a tranquility soothing her nerves. She could do this.

Killian stroked his thumb along the back of her hand as he gave her an encouraging smile. Yes, she could do this. Together they walked past the guards and up to the front door.

Killian didn't bother knocking. He strolled through the door with a grin as bright as the flowers he carried.

As soon as they walked in, Mrs. Southwick pounced.

"Oh, honey! I've missed you," she crooned as she pulled Killian into a tight embrace.

"You saw me last week, Mum," he managed to say through her chokehold.

Finally, she released him. "I know, and it was too damn long ago."

Then she turned her attention to Elyse.

Elyse had heard it said many times that men go after women that resemble their mothers, but Mrs. Southwick could not have been more different from Elyse. She was tall with dark skin, and she had more curves than a cauldron. Her round face was warm and loving as she hugged Elyse—who was not usually keen on touching anyone, let alone strangers. But she supposed for the sweet woman who wrapped her sturdy arms around her, she could make an exception.

"That's enough, Mum. Elyse needs to breathe," Killian teased.

Mrs. Southwick shot him a glare but let go of Elyse.

"Are you hungry? I roasted a chicken for the occasion," she said, leading them toward the back of the main room toward a table with mismatched chairs.

Elyse tried not to think about what Killian had told his mother for her to deem this an "occasion," instead focusing on the decor. A homemade afghan lay across a weathered couch, and wooden figurines crowded every table and shelf. Bright, inviting colors were strewn about on the cushions, candles, and paintings.

Killian must have noticed her taking everything in because he said, "It's eclectic—like the Emporium."

Elyse smiled. The home was indeed reminiscent of her shoppe—cozy and colorful, if a bit cluttered. "I love it. I was expecting it to be . . ."

"Like my office?" he finished for her.

Mrs. Southwick threw her head back and laughed, the sound reverberating pleasantly through the room. "Oh no, Killian got that from his pa. He got a lot of things from his pa, like those dimples." She poked his cheek, earning a frown from Killian.

Elyse decided she very much liked this woman.

Mrs. Southwick gestured for them to sit, and she brought a platter of chicken over and set it in the center of the table. Bowls of potatoes and stewed vegetables were already laid out, along with a pitcher of ginger tea.

"Dig in!" she insisted, spooning food onto their plates before helping herself.

"Are the guards sticking to their post?" Killian asked as he cut into his chicken.

"Who, Jari and David? Oh, they're delightful," Mrs. Southwick praised.

Elyse smiled to herself, noting the way Killian's mother referred to them so genially. Killian didn't seem as amused.

"Mum, they're not supposed to be delightful—they're supposed to protect you."

Mrs. Southwick waved his concern off. "You worry too much. How many times was your father threatened, only for nothing to come of it?"

"So, you're not afraid?" Elyse asked, surprising herself with her frankness.

"Not at all," Mrs. Southwick cheerily replied. "I've slept with a dagger under my pillow for thirty years—just let someone come in here and try to harm me and mine."

Her eyes lit up as she spoke, in a way that told Elyse she was deadly serious. Killian glanced at Elyse to make sure she wasn't put off by the comment, and she gave him a smirk.

"Besides, I know Killian will handle everything. He's always been a smart boy," Mrs. Southwick continued. "Did you know he got the top marks out of anyone to ever join the Royal Guard?"

"It was the third best marks, Mum," Killian corrected.

"And he's humble," Elyse said, which earned her another roar of laughter from Mrs. Southwick. Elyse couldn't help but chuckle some herself at the woman's infectious cackle.

"I like her," Mrs. Southwick said, pointing at Elyse with her fork.

"I do, too," Killian replied. "So try not to scare her off."

Mrs. Southwick whacked him in the shoulder with the fork.

Killian shot his mother a glare, though a smile betrayed his amusement. "See? That's what I'm talking about!"

But Mrs. Southwick just gave him an almighty smile and asked him more questions about his work.

Everything about their relationship was so different from how things had been between Elyse and her own mother. They had been close, especially being just the two of them for so long, but close in a cooperative sort of way, or like a comfortable silence. There had rarely been laughter growing up, and even less once her mother grew ill. She envied Killian and his mother, she realized. Perhaps the pain they had suffered together had made their relationship stronger. Or maybe they had to laugh just to stay sane.

When they had each cleared their plates a second time, Mrs. Southwick grabbed a bottle of red wine from a cupboard by the hearth.

"Well, I know you were just coming to ask me about the cure," she said as she uncorked the bottle, "but Killian's never brought a girl home, so I think we should celebrate."

"Never?" Elyse asked as Killian stood to grab three pewter mugs of varying shapes and sizes.

"Never," Mrs. Southwick confirmed. "I thought he was going around with Manny for a while."

"Mum!" Killian looked positively horrified, which only made Elyse giggle.

Mrs. Southwick poured them each a generous helping of wine. "I'm just saying, a handsome man like you, I'd expect women to be all over you!"

Killian's face was nearly as red as the wine.

"Maybe he was just waiting for the right girl," his mother said with a wink at Elyse.

Elyse looked down at her lap as guilt forced its way into her stomach. She twisted her fingers together. How could she be here, eating this food, having a drink with such a delightful woman, when she was lying to her son? She took a deep breath in and lifted her chin, trying to stay brave.

Her expression must have gone sour, though, because Mrs. Southwick whispered sweetly, "I'm just teasing you, honey." Then with a smile she added, "Now why don't you show me your arm."

Elyse forced out a soft laugh and glanced toward Killian, who gave her a nod. She rolled up her left sleeve, expecting Mrs. Southwick to gasp or swear, but the kind woman only took her wrist and gently turned it toward her to see better. The rash covered nearly every inch of Elyse's forearm now, and the growing heat of spring seemed to further agitate it. She tried not to look at it too long, lest she remember the way the sores had covered her mother's chest and back before claiming her altogether.

Mrs. Southwick clicked her tongue. "That's the widow's decay all right. Killian's looked just like it, except his was on his bum."

Killian nearly choked on his wine. "It was not!"

"Was too! I should remember, I'm the one who had to put the cream on it!" she chirped back.

Elyse laughed, and Killian just sighed. "Can you tell her about where you took me, please?" he asked, slightly exasperated.

"Of course, honey." Mrs. Southwick took Elyse's hand in her own, her chubby fingers like little pork links. "I'll never forget the woman who healed my baby boy. Her name is Privya, and she has a clinic of sorts about fifty miles southwest of the city. I'll write out the directions for you." As she spoke, her smile held pain, but also the triumph of living through such anguish.

Elyse's throat was dry, her voice difficult to call upon. "And she can really cure me?" she murmured.

"If anyone can, it's her."

Beneath Elyse's gratitude, she felt a flurry of other emotions: uncertainty about whether or not it would work; anger that she hadn't learned about this healer before her mother had passed; and bitterness that told her she deserved to suffer, not be treated. All the doubt and skepticism felt heavy on her chest, tightening around her lungs and making it difficult to think straight—but she met Killian's eyes and felt a steadiness wash over her. She had survived much, and she would survive this disease, and this guilt, no matter what.

"Thank you," she managed to say.

Mrs. Southwick's returning smile was both a comfort and a stab to the heart.

Elyse sipped at the wine, which turned out to be sweet and summery, and let its crisp flavors warm her from the inside out.

"There's one more thing," Killian began hesitantly.

Elyse froze, unsure where he was headed with this conversation, but Mrs. Southwick just said, "Well, out with it!"

"There's this kid, Georgie. I arrested him this week. He's real polite, well mannered, he just got caught up with some bad influences."

Mrs. Southwick sighed, but when she spoke there was an underlying delight. "You know my home is always open."

Killian smiled and kissed his mother on the cheek. "Thanks, Mum. I'll cover all his expenses, and I'll see about getting him a job."

"No, no," she cut him off with a raised hand. "If he's going to live here, he's going to school."

"Yes, ma'am," he said with a grin.

Elyse's heart swelled as she put the pieces together. Georgie must have been the boy that worked with Pete's crew. She hadn't known his name, and certainly hadn't expected Killian to take the boy under his wing like this. Devil's might, he was so much more caring than she'd ever thought him to be, and it physically pained her. She wanted to throw her mug at the wall and tell Killian and his gracious mother how undeserving the whole world was of their kindness, how undeserving she was, but instead she sat very still, urging her tears to stay confined to her eyes while they sipped their wine in a quiet tranquility.

She set aside her self-hatred and did her best to enjoy herself. It grew easier with each sip of wine, and each time she laughed as Killian grew flustered by his mother. They played games all night, one after another, sitting around the table, sharing stories and jokes and happiness until Elyse could hardly keep her eyes open.

Mrs. Southwick gave her another hug before they departed, and whispered in her ear to come back any time she wanted, with or without Killian. Elyse very much wanted to take her up on the offer, and she told her as much.

She returned home with Killian and fell into an easy sleep with his strong arm draped across her body. No terrors of flames or screams haunted her as she lay beside him.

That was the night Elyse first learned what it was like to feel normal.

CHAPTER 41

— • —

KILLIAN

K illian was getting used to traveling by magic. In fact, it was a more effective way to jolt his body awake than the strongest cup of coffee.

He emerged from an alleyway in the city shortly after sunrise, still intoxicated from another night spent sleeping in Elyse's bed. He could still smell her sweet, floral scent, and he could still picture her sleepy smile as he kissed her awake.

There was no way he could have a bad day after waking up like that, nestled against her. Even as he made his way back to the palace, he toyed with the idea of shirking his responsibilities and going back to her, planting endless kisses on her lips, her neck. After all, the king's murderer was imprisoned. He deserved a day off. But he also knew Elyse was independent and she wouldn't want him lingering around her shoppe all morning. Besides, she needed to get on her way to the healer.

As he strode through the gates and wound his way through the palace courtyard, he took in each passing servant. He expected them to be smiling, less distressed, an ominous cloud of uncertainty no longer hanging over their heads. But each servant kept their gaze low, their shoulders slouched. Perhaps news of Royce's arrest hadn't reached them yet.

He entered the mess hall and found several guards milling about, discussing something in hushed voices, and his euphoria began to dissipate.

He marched directly down to the dungeons, hoping his unease was just in his imagination.

Several other guards glanced at him as he made his way through the dark, stony tunnels of the dungeons, all quickly looking away. *Shit.* Killian picked up his pace, dreading whatever he was about to find.

Just outside the door to the interrogation room, Manny and Longfellow stood talking to one another. They both looked up as Killian approached, Manny giving him a despondent look.

"What is it?" Killian asked. "Has Royce said something?" He glanced through the small window in the door to where Royce sat at a table, arms crossed, a smirk on his face.

Manny shook his head. "No, he hasn't—At least, he hasn't said anything more than demanding to talk to the three of us."

Killian's eyes darted from Manny to Longfellow, and back to Manny again. "Us?"

Longfellow nodded. The torches that lit the dungeon tunnels accentuated the hollows of his eyes, making him look almost sinister. His expression was clear: he had warned them about this.

"Well, we're all here," Killian said, trying to sound unfazed despite the ominous feeling in his gut. "Let's get on with it." Before anyone could object, he yanked open the door to the interrogation room.

Royce perked up his head the moment Killian stepped into the room. Royce looked like hell—his white hair was tangled and greasy, his clothes wrinkled. His green eyes were rimmed with dark circles, but they were alive with malice.

"Oh good, you finally made it," he crooned as Manny and Longfellow filed into the room.

Killian didn't want to hear his bullshit. "You wanted to talk?" he asked. "Talk."

Royce cocked his head, a wicked grin splitting his chapped lips. "I just wanted to give the three of you an opportunity to hear me out. I want you to listen carefully, and take heed of my words."

"Get on with it," Manny sighed, sounding bored, though Killian could see the worry in his eyes.

Royce's grin only widened, and Killian repressed a shudder.

"I am innocent," Royce continued. "Let me go now, and we will forget this whole thing. But—" He paused, looking directly at each of them in the eyes in turn. "—if you continue to hold me here, if you proceed with this trial, you will regret it."

"Oh, please—" Manny began, but Royce spoke over him.

"I have more power and connections than you could dream of. I can have you hunted. I can have your families hunted. I can incite a fucking war if I want to."

Killian refused to show any weakness, even as his chest constricted. He pictured his mother, wielding the dagger she kept beneath her pillow. She hadn't seemed worried, but that didn't keep his own anxiety at bay. Still, he had no choice. He would never let Royce walk.

"Is that all?" he asked.

Royce blanched ever so slightly at Killian's bland tone—then quickly resumed his snarling. "Do we have a deal?"

Killian kept his face neutral as he stepped closer to Royce and squatted down so they were eye-level. With disgust in his eyes, he glanced at the restraints that bound Royce's hands. "If you bring harm on anyone in the Guard, or their families, I will make sure you're executed with the dullest sword in the armory," he growled. He leaned closer, his face mere inches from Royce. "And if you lay one gods-damned finger on my mother, I'll kidnap you myself and take you somewhere no one will hear you scream."

When Killian pulled away, Royce's face was pale and seething. Killian looked to Longfellow to find the magistrate was drenched in sweat, despite the cold air of the dungeon. Manny, at least, gave Killian a firm nod.

"Is that so?" Royce asked through gritted teeth.

Killian gave him one last scathing look before uttering, "We're done here," and storming out of the room.

CHAPTER 42

— · —

ELYSE

Rain started to drizzle as Elyse ducked into the inn where she would find rest for the night. She'd ridden all day and was more than glad to exchange a saddle and canteen for a stool and ale. As she made her entrance into the inn's tavern, all eyes slid to her, then lingered for a moment too long. A small, sleepy town like this likely didn't see many outsiders. In fact, based on the rundown condition of the tavern, Elyse could nearly confirm that.

She padded across the dusty floor, ignoring the stares and murmurs, and settled onto a bench in the corner of the room. Her arm itched like mad, the rash irritated from sweating all day, but she left her long gloves on, reminding herself that by this time tomorrow she would be at the clinic, and hopefully, a cure would be within her grasp.

A barmaid flounced over, a friendly smile on her young face. Smart girl. The patrons of the tavern could mutter and stare all they wanted, but this girl worked on tips. "Safe travels?" she asked by way of greeting.

Elyse ignored the question. "I'll have a pint of whatever ale you've got, and I'll need a room for the night." She was far too tired for niceties, too on edge by the others' curiosity, and too anxious about getting to the clinic. Just before the barmaid walked away, Elyse added, "And something to eat, too—surprise me."

The barmaid sauntered off and disappeared into the kitchen, but not before Elyse caught one of the patrons leering at her. She tried to smother her disgust. The girl's round cheeks and bright eyes suggested she was barely a teenager, but her body, with full breasts and wide hips, said otherwise. Regardless, the grisly man who ogled her was at least twice her age, and there was nothing but heinous intent behind his gaze.

The kitchen door swung open, and the barmaid appeared carrying a tray of pints. She made her way toward the leering man and his group, who sat together playing dice. Elyse watched as, one by one, the girl set a mug down before each of the men. As they thanked her, she noted how the girl nodded at each of them in turn, except for the man who had stared at her. When she set down his mug, her hand trembled slightly, almost imperceptibly, and she didn't make eye contact with him as she had with the others.

Elyse shuddered. The girl was aware of the man's attraction to her—perhaps he had acted on it before. She perked up slightly as the girl made her way toward Elyse's table, a lone mug of ale on her tray.

"Here you are, miss," the girl said sweetly, smiling as she set down the mug. She pulled a key from her apron pocket and set it on the table as well. "Here's the key to your room—upstairs, first door on the right. I'll have your dinner shortly."

"Thank you," Elyse replied with more warmth than she had shown before. "What's your name?"

"Anika," the girl replied with a small curtsy.

"Anika," Elyse repeated. "If I need anything during my stay, should I seek you out? Or is there someone else?" She hoped her question was subtle enough that Anika wouldn't think twice about it, but the leering man made her nervous, and she wondered if there was someone here to look out for Anika.

But Anika didn't even bat an eye. "It's just me—well, my paw is here too, but he's been so sick the last few months he can hardly get out of bed."

Elyse's brows furrowed. "I'm sorry to hear that," she said with genuine sympathy. She refused to let her eyes flicker to the deviant across the tavern.

"That's very kind of you, miss. Can I get you anything else?" Anika asked in her pleasant voice.

Elyse declined and let Anika see to the other patrons. Every time she glanced toward the man across the room, though, his eyes were on Anika, lustful and persistent. She'd seen that look before, but she hadn't understood it until it was almost too late.

Her arm itched maddeningly. She longed to escape upstairs, remove her gloves, and slather herself with salve, but she knew she should stay and watch what was playing out. Resigned to stay in the tavern, she took another sip of ale and tried to ignore the irritating sensation. Perhaps it was some form of penitence. She'd had a penchant for suffering lately. It'd started with this damn disease, which she had accepted as a curse from the gods for all of her wrongdoings. It was fitting that she should have to endure such a nasty, blistering rash with seemingly no cure. Most people would have been terrified, frantically searching for some way to stop their inevitable death. But Elyse knew death wouldn't be the end for her. It never was.

She'd practically embraced the disease, accepting its pain as well-met punishment. Even when Killian offered her information on a cure, she'd wanted to laugh in his face and tell him she deserved every bit of her suffering. She hadn't agreed to help him because of the cure. No, looking back on it, she'd agreed because even then, there was something alluring about him, something that drew her to him.

It had only been a dozen hours since she'd seen him, since he'd kissed her cheek that morning and whispered his goodbye against her skin. Yet she longed for his company. Her rash never seemed as irritating when he was around, and her mind always felt more settled. She yearned for his distraction as, once again, she caught the grisly man leering, and memories came flooding back to her—memories of unspeakable things she'd done for Lazarus.

The full moon ritual, demanded by Lazarus each month, hadn't always been so bad. Growing up, her mother, had even made it seem fun. Each full moon, they did whatever the demon asked of them, and in exchange they were granted innate, powerful magic. As a child, her mother had brought her along a few times on whatever obligation Lazarus just so happened to choose. They were often simple things like digging up a grave and burning the bones of the deceased, or slaughtering a goat.

When Elyse was fourteen years old, her mother went out on her own to perform the ritual. Elyse didn't think much of it when her mother hadn't arrived home by sunup—perhaps the ritual was taking longer than usual. But when her mother still hadn't returned that evening, she began to worry.

For three full days, Elyse ran the Emporium by herself, putting on a brave face for each customer. When they asked after her mother, she told them all her mother was ill with a fever, and they all wished her a speedy recovery. Truthfully, Elyse was frantic. She'd never gone more than a day without her mother, and she had no idea how to search for her. She couldn't go to the Royal Guard—her mother had made it very clear that the Guard was never to be involved in their business. So she paced the narrow aisles of the shoppe, hoping her mother would return.

On the fourth day, her mother soundlessly entered through the door of the shoppe. Elyse ran to her and threw her arms around her mother, who weakly hugged her back.

"Where have you been?" Elyse asked through her tears. She inspected her mother for injuries, but she looked as sound as ever. Her hair was combed, her clothes were clean, and she had no visible wounds.

That's when Elyse noticed it. There was something different about her mother's eyes. Her gray eyes were normally filled with cheer and life, but now they were . . . Hollow. Icy. Crazed.

Her mother grabbed her by both shoulders and shook her slightly. "Promise me, Elyse," she rasped. "Promise me you will never disobey Lazarus."

Elyse was speechless. She'd never seen her mother so unhinged. Where had she been? What had happened to her? And why was she making her promise this?

"Promise me!" her mother practically screamed, digging her fingers into Elyse's shoulders. "Promise me you'll do whatever he asks, or—"

"Okay!" Elyse agreed, wincing at the pain.

Her mother grasped her in a tight hug as together they sobbed.

They never spoke of it again, and Elyse never received any further explanation for her mother's disappearance. Eventually the darkness in her mother's eyes faded, replaced by her usual merriment, but occasionally Elyse would find her staring off at nothing with a haunted expression.

When Elyse grew older, she and her mother took turns performing the ritual, but even then, most things were relatively harmless. One night she'd been tasked with taking down the wards around a stranger's house. With her power, it was an easy enough feat, and she'd done it diligently. The next day, a customer came by and told them about a nearby fire that had burned a house to the ground, killing an elderly woman. As the customer described where the house was located, Elyse realized with horror that it was the same house whose wards she'd removed. Somehow, someone had known the wards were down, and they'd struck. She'd cried herself to sleep that night, and then swore she'd never speak of it or think about it ever again.

After her mother died, the responsibility of performing the full moon ritual fell solely on Elyse. Lazarus didn't wait long to make her bloody her hands.

He ordered Elyse to visit a particularly shady tavern, seek out a man named Devik, and kill him.

At first, Elyse thought she had heard wrong. Surely that wasn't what he'd said.

But the black skull had merely laughed at her, mocking her unease.

"Don't disappoint me, daughter," Lazarus had crooned.

As the skull's fire dwindled, Elyse could only see one thing: her mother's face, all those years ago, her eyes crazed and haunted.

Promise me you'll never disobey Lazarus.

Elyse was nearly sick as she readied herself for the tavern. She sat alone at the bar, quietly sipping her ale, and desperately trying to calm her nerves. When her mother had made her promise, had she known what sort of things Lazarus would demand of her?

Finally, a hideous man with yellow teeth and beady eyes entered the tavern, and his friends called out to him.

"Devik! Come join us!"

Elyse watched them laugh and drink for a few minutes before she paid her tab and slinked out of the tavern. She trembled as she stood in the alleyway beside the tavern, clutching her knife. Hours seemed to pass as she waited, and each minute stoked the flames of anxiety. And when Devik finally appeared, a woman on his arm, instead of attacking, Elyse froze.

It wasn't supposed to be like this. She had assumed he would be alone. What was she to do with the woman? Having a witness seemed like too much of a loose end.

She'd stalked them down the street, using a silencing spell so her feet made no noise on the cobblestone. It wouldn't have mattered anyway. They were both too drunk to notice the hooded stranger that followed them.

When they disappeared down a dark alley, Elyse pinned herself against the wall, listening to them, waiting for an opportunity. At first, they just kissed passionately, and Elyse was forced to listen to their smacking lips and heavy moans. Then she heard the tear of fabric.

"What are you doing?" the woman asked, fear coating her question.

"Turn around," Devik grumbled.

"What? No—not here," came her frantic reply.

"Shut up!" Devik growled, and Elyse heard the sound of a body being shoved against brick.

"Stop!" the woman cried, partially muffled by her struggles.

That was when Elyse moved.

Her body acted on instinct alone as she hurled herself into the alleyway and swiftly plunged the knife into Devik's back.

As Devik fell to the ground, the woman screamed. Without thanking Elyse, she took off down the street, barely managing to pull her skirt back down around herself as she fled.

Elyse had stood over Devik as he bled out, and then remained there for long after. Long after she watched the life drain from his eyes. Long after the smell of his piss filled the alleyway. Long after she ripped the knife from his back and wiped the blood on his shirt.

"Another pint?" Anika asked, breaking Elyse's trance.

Elyse blinked a few times, then smiled up at Anika. "Yes, thank you," she replied quietly.

Anika brought her another mug of ale along with her dinner—a few slices of ham and a buttery roll. The girl was no prize chef, but the food was warm and tasted pleasant enough. While Elyse ate, she observed the other patrons. Most of them were quiet, keeping to themselves or in small, placid groups. By the time Elyse finished her mug, many of them had paid their tabs and exited, until finally it was just Elyse and the group of dice players. The men had grown more rambunctious with each round of ale, though most of them seemed harmless enough. It was only the grisly man with the beady eyes who sent shivers down her spine.

After murdering Devik, Elyse had been forced to kill two more times that year, each man as horrid as the last. She couldn't say it grew easier, though. Despite their wickedness, it felt wrong to take their lives, to play a god. But she feared what Lazarus would do to her if she didn't obey. She feared breaking her promise to her mother.

Then one full moon, Lazarus had ordered her to kill a young girl. She was fifteen and her name was Kelia. Elyse had waited outside the inn where she worked, wondering what this girl had done to deserve the demon's malice. When Kelia finally emerged from the inn, smiling back at somebody wishing her goodnight, Elyse tried to invent some terrible backstory for the girl, some justification.

But Kelia had kind eyes and an aura of innocence. As Elyse followed her home, Kelia stopped to admire the flowers outside the various homes and businesses she passed, even going so far as to pluck one and tuck it behind her ear.

When Kelia finally arrived home, Elyse watched through the window of the house as Kelia's mother greeted her warmly, and the two of them sat down for a late dinner. Even when they'd gone to sleep, and the house was dark and still, Elyse stood outside, watching. It wasn't until the sun kissed the horizon that she allowed herself to go home, forsaking Lazarus's demands.

She'd paced her bedroom, glancing nervously at the skull, waiting for the demon to appear and punish her for disobeying. The waiting was intolerable as she imagined how Lazarus would retaliate. She wasn't sure what he was capable of, being confined to hell, but her imagination ran wild. Would he burn her? Torture her? Summon her to hell?

By nightfall, she couldn't take it anymore. She had taken charge of her own life by defying his orders, and she would take control of her death the same way. She lay down on her bed, took the same knife she'd used to kill Devik and the others, and slit her wrists.

She didn't want to live in a world where she was forced to kill young women. She barely wanted to live in the world as it was. Nothing the demon could give her was worth this terrible existence of murder and lies. So as the blood flowed from her wrists, and the cold of death embraced her, she was at peace.

Until the next morning, when she awoke in her bed. No blood, no cuts. Not even a scar.

For a moment, she'd thought her suicide had been a dream, but it hadn't. She knew it hadn't.

Lazarus still didn't call to her. Her revival was message enough. There was work to be done, and Elyse was to do it.

But she couldn't do it—wouldn't do it. So she tried again, this time with poison, only to wake up again, her skin warm and free of the vomit she so viscerally remembered.

Ten times she tried to kill herself, in ten different ways, each time hoping Lazarus would grow tired of her antics and let her stay dead. But each time she awoke with no traces of harm.

But Lazarus did eventually grow tired. On the eleventh day she awoke in her bed, same as she always had. This time, however, a message had been scrawled across her bedroom mirror—a message written in blood.

DO YOU THINK YOU ARE MY ONLY SERVANT?

The handwriting was haunting and chaotic with splatters of blood trickling down, marring Elyse's reflection. Her own blood felt icy, her breath cold and serrated. Did this mean what she thought it did? If she didn't kill Kelia, would Lazarus send someone else to do it? A part of her felt relieved—she was free from the horrendous task. Yet the menacing nature of the message wasn't intended as a pardon. It was a threat.

Pain shot through her body, racking her mind, and she clutched both hands to her head. She squeezed her eyes tight as she tried to block out the pain, yet she could somehow see clearly. She was inside a house—Kelia's house—as the girl and her mother sat chatting over dinner. Kelia's bright eyes were squinted as she laughed at something her mother said. Then the door burst open, and two masked men invaded the room. Everything happened so fast, and Elyse cried out, begging the men to stop as they grabbed Kelia and her mother and held knives to their throats. But no one could hear her. She could do nothing but watch as the men did vile and atrocious things to Kelia while her mother sobbed and screamed. It seemed to last hours while the men beat and berated both of them, until finally they exited through the door, laughing and leaving the women to succumb to their injuries.

Elyse wanted to go to Kelia, to kneel beside her and whisper something comforting, but she was yanked back to her bedroom. She collapsed to the floor, gasping and retching, unable to breathe or think.

"Please," she had sobbed to no one in particular.

"Please," she begged again and again.

No one deserved to spend their final moments like that, especially not someone whose soul was so beautiful.

When Elyse finally looked up, a new message had been written across her mirror.

GIVE HER MERCY.

She understood then. The vision, all that she had just witnessed, was another threat. Elyse could do nothing, she could continue to kill herself to try and avoid her task, or she could offer the girl a swift, merciful death.

So she'd gone to the inn. Bile burned her throat as she watched Kelia appear in the doorway, and tears clouded her vision. She followed Kelia home. The girl deserved to at least die sleeping in her bed. Finally, when the night was dark and the house was quiet, Elyse crept in and slit Kelia's throat.

That time, she hadn't lingered.

She'd magicked herself back to the outside of her wards right away, then collapsed in a heap in the dark woods. When she saw the blood on her hands, she stripped herself naked and ran to the nearest creek, immersing herself in its cold waters. She shivered there for hours, forcing herself to suffer. It was the least she could do.

That was when Elyse started to distance herself from the world—more so than she already had. She ricocheted between bouts of pessimism and utter numbness. Sera was the only one who seemed to be able to break Elyse from her foul moods.

For the next three years, she did whatever Lazarus asked of her, including sneaking into the castle and killing King Cyril with the most heinous spell she'd ever encountered. The demon had won.

A clatter across the room caught Elyse's attention. The drunken dice players were gathering their shares and donning their cloaks, and one of them had knocked over his chair, inciting a riot of laughter from his friends. One by one they exited the tavern, all except for the grisly man, who requested that Anika bring him a fresh pint.

She did as asked, awkwardly setting the mug on the table. She began gathering up the empty mugs and piling them onto her tray, but the men had enjoyed so many rounds that it would take her several trips just to collect all the glassware.

Elyse moved swiftly, quietly appearing beside the table. "Let me help," she offered.

Anika jumped, startled by Elyse's sudden presence. But she nodded and muttered, "Thank you."

Elyse grabbed two empty mugs in each hand, then let Anika lead the way toward the kitchen, all while the man reclined and slowly sipped his ale. Once in the kitchen, Elyse set the mugs down on some open counter space, then turned to Anika.

"I'll be heading to bed now," she told her.

Anika only nodded again, her throat bobbing. "Please let me know if you need anything," she said shakily.

Elyse offered her a smile, or as much of one as she could, given her own morose state. Then she swept back through the doorway and into the tavern and headed straight for the staircase, without so much as a glance at the man at the table.

She waited at the top of the stairs, holding her breath, listening. There was the distinct sound of a mug being plunked onto the table, followed shortly after by a few shuffling footsteps. Elyse slid her hand into her pocket and wrapped her fingers around a vial. Her other hand clutched at her knife. She took a deep breath, and then flung the vial at the ground.

Blue smoke dissipated around her as she stood inside the kitchen, facing the swinging door. She heard Anika scream, but Elyse didn't turn toward her. Her target would reveal himself momentarily.

The door swung open, and there stood the man, a smug, drunken grin on his face. His expression turned sour, his eyes glazing over as he tried to comprehend why Anika was screaming, and how Elyse had ended up in the kitchen. Before he could move, Elyse's knife was at his throat, and she had pinned him against the wall.

"Stop screaming, Anika," she said calmly.

Anika's screams reduced to whimpers.

Elyse kept her eyes trained on the man as she asked, "Has this man ever hurt you?"

The man's face was red with anger, but he didn't try to fight. Anika's reply was a stammered, "N-n-no!"

A sneer coated the man's features.

"Has he ever tried?" Elyse asked.

Anika's silence was answer enough. The man's eyes widened as Elyse pressed her knife harder, a trickle of blood flowing down his fat neck.

"You will not hurt her—or anyone," Elyse growled at him. "And if I hear about you so much as *looking* at her, I'll slice your dick right down the center."

He jerked his body, perhaps involuntarily, but Elyse held her grip firm. "Do you understand me?" she snarled.

He didn't move. Elyse retracted the knife slightly.

"Nod if you understand."

He nodded, his whole body trembling, and Elyse felt a sense of satisfaction.

"Now get out of here," she ordered, pulling the knife away and shoving him toward the door. The man stumbled, then skittered through the door. She heard him bump into a chair on his way out of the tavern.

Elyse looked over her shoulder to where Anika still stood frozen across the kitchen. Her eyes were wide, her face ashen, but she met Elyse's gaze with unmistakable gratitude. She would be all right.

Without a word, Elyse shoved through the swinging door and padded up to her room. Suddenly exhausted, she sank onto the bed.

She couldn't save Kelia, or King Cyril, but that didn't mean she had to sit and watch the world burn around her.

CHAPTER 43

— · —

ELYSE

The next evening, Elyse arrived at the clinic. It appeared to be an ordinary wooden building, plain in shape and design, yet it was the most daunting building Elyse had ever seen.

She'd had to depart from the main road several miles back and wind her way along a narrow, gravelly path. The sun had fully set, but the clinic was aglow with candlelight brimming from each of its windows and a lantern by the door.

Elyse forced her breathing to remain steady as she dismounted her mare and tied her to a post outside. Her boots crunched on the gravel as she took slow steps to the front door, trying to suppress her hope. Hope was a dangerous thing from her experience. And yet, she wasn't entirely sure what it was she hoped for. A cure? To be turned away? Or for some sort of deeper absolution.

She lifted her hand, about to knock on the door, when she noticed a sign that read "Enter" in neat handwriting. She pushed the door open and was greeted by the sharp scent of patchouli as she stepped into a large room. There were several round tables for dining, a fire despite the warm night, and a few cushiony armchairs scattered about. It appeared more like a cozy inn than a clinic—clean yet inviting.

Perched in an armchair in the corner was a woman with tan skin, and hair as black as the night Elyse had just come from. As Elyse approached the woman, she noticed a few rogue gray hairs intermingled with the black, and crow's feet lining her blue eyes.

"May I help you?" the woman asked, her voice steady and strong.

"I'm looking for Privya," Elyse said politely.

"I am she."

Elyse wasn't sure what to say. She hadn't expected to find Privya right away. She hadn't really expected to see Privya until her actual examination. Yet there she was, face to face with the woman who may hold the key to her salvation.

Elyse nodded, buying herself time to muster her strength. It was rare for her to be intimidated by anyone, yet Privya held herself with such fierce dignity that Elyse found herself seeking the healer's approval. "I was told you could help me. I have widow's decay, and you cured my friend of it many years ago."

Privya held Elyse's gaze. There was no pity in her eyes, no disgust as she smiled and said, "Then you've come to the right place."

Elyse let out a slow exhale as the hope she had kept at bay flooded her core, and she felt her lips tugging at the corners. But with that hope came a pang of guilt.

"Have you eaten?" Privya asked, rising from her chair and smoothing out her white trousers.

"I'm not very hungry," Elyse replied.

"That is not what I asked," Privya said with a stern yet amused look. "Come with me."

She didn't wait for Elyse as she disappeared through a door at the back of the room, and Elyse followed tentatively. The door led her to a kitchen with a massive butcher block counter and an enormous hearth. Just like the previous room, it was decorated in a homey sort of way.

"Sit," Privya ordered, gesturing toward a stool along the counter. Elyse obeyed as Privya went to the hearth and began ladling out some hearty stew. She set the bowl of stew in front of Elyse, then poured her a mug of pungent tea.

"Your body needs strength, even if you are not hungry," she said. "Especially if you are battling disease."

Privya stood across from her, arms crossed, waiting for her to dig in. She looked like someone who was used to giving orders. Elyse's instinct was to disobey—no one ever told her what to do. But again, she found herself wanting to be liked by the woman, so she thanked Privya and blew on the stew to cool it.

"Where do you come from?" the healer asked.

"I stay just northwest of the capital." Elyse brought a spoonful to her lips, and her mouth began to water in anticipation. She gulped it down and moaned. It was divine.

"And you say I healed your friend?"

Elyse nodded as she swallowed another bite of stew. "Yes, but it was almost twenty years ago."

Privya smiled and held her chin high. "I never forget a patient."

Elyse looked at Privya for a long moment, marveling at the wisdom and grace that poured from her. She was everything Elyse wanted, and tried, to be: confident, intelligent, and even a bit reclusive all the way out here. There was a sort of kindness, though—not overly sweet but a kindness nonetheless—that lay beneath her stoic exterior.

"His name is Killian," she said finally. "He would have been ten."

"Killian," Privya breathed, the smile now spreading to her eyes. "Of course I remember him. Such a well-mannered young man, but haunted by such tragedy."

Elyse tilted her head. She wondered if Privya knew of Killian's brother and sister, or if she had merely sensed a struggle within him.

Privya continued. "Healing is as much about caring for the physical as it is the emotional. I was able to help Killian enough to cure the widow's decay, but I fear he is still burdened." She paused and stared intently at Elyse. "We must all face our demons in order to heal."

Elyse shifted in her seat. The word "demon" screamed at her. The phrase was common enough, but Elyse couldn't shake the feeling that Privya seemed to have selected it specifically for her.

Unable to meet Privya's gaze, she turned her attention to the tea. It tasted as awful as it smelled, and Elyse choked on it as it went down.

"Fallowsprig," Privya explained. "It will help you sleep better and revitalize your muscles after such a long ride."

Indeed, Elyse's backside was stiff and aching from having sat in a saddle for so long, and she hoped the tea would do its job.

"Where can I keep my horse? I should go tend to her. I can pay you to stable her," Elyse said.

Privya just waved her hand. "I've no doubt that someone has already cared for the steed and tucked it away in one of our stables. There is no cost for your horse, nor for you."

Elyse hadn't seen or heard another soul on the property, but she didn't bother to ask about it. Now that her belly was full and the tea was starting to take effect, she longed to be horizontal.

Privya seemed to sense this as she said, "I will show you to your room. We'll begin treatment in the morning."

She led Elyse into a hallway with a staircase, then up to the second floor. There was a long corridor with nearly a dozen rooms, and Elyse wondered how many were occupied. A cough as she passed by a door let her know that at least one of the rooms was inhabited.

"Here you are," Privya said as she opened a door on the left. "If you find that you need anything, please let us know. We will do our best to accommodate."

Even if something was missing from the room, Elyse had no plan on asking Privya for anything, not when the nearest village was at least ten miles away.

"Thank you, Privya," she said as she took in the room. It was cozy like her own bedroom, with a full-sized bed, a chest of drawers, and a single curtained window.

"I never asked you your name," Privya seemed to realize.

Elyse turned to the healer who stood in the doorway. "It's Elyse."

Privya studied her face, as if assessing the name and its suitability to its owner. "Well, Elyse," she said. "I hope you find what you're looking for here."

Then she shut the door, leaving Elyse to ponder what exactly she meant.

Chapter 44

Killian

Killian was exhausted, despite the three cups of black angelica tea he'd already drank that day. After yesterday's meeting with Royce, he and Manny worked tirelessly, combing over the details of the investigation. They'd worked late into the night and risen early that morning, jumping back into their notes.

Now they sat in Killian's office, both staring at the stacks of parchment before them, utterly drained of energy. Aside from the jars of evidence they'd seized during Royce's arrest, no additional proof of his guilt had surfaced. On top of that, Tanner Wills was missing, so Killian couldn't even bring him in to testify about the deal he'd wagered between Royce and Bast.

He knew that they had a good case. They had the means, the motive . . . But Killian wanted *more*. He wanted something irrefutable to wipe the smirk off Royce's face.

"I reckon we should take a break—get something to eat," Manny suggested. His blond locks had fallen loose from their bun, making him look even more fatigued as he rubbed his eyes.

Killian yawned, nodding his agreement. "Okay, but then I want to go over the interviews with Royce's staff again."

Manny sighed, and Killian didn't blame him for it. They'd already reviewed the interviews twice.

Both men stood and stretched out their stiff muscles. Killian stepped toward the door, his stomach growling at the thought of getting lunch, when the door suddenly flung open.

Longfellow stood in the threshold, his dark eyes wide. He looked like he'd run straight to Killian's office—he was winded, his thin hair a mess. He carried a large paper box, like the kind that usually held ridiculous hats.

"I'm letting Royce go—immediately," he spouted out.

"What?" Killian and Manny said at the same time. They exchanged disbelieving glances.

"The hell you are," Killian growled. Technically Longfellow did have the power to grant the release of prisoners, but Killian wasn't about to let that happen.

Longfellow stepped into the room and frantically closed the door behind him. He plopped the box down on Killian's desk, and Killian noted the heavy thud it made.

"I wasn't asking your permission," Longfellow spat. "I was letting you know as a courtesy. But Royce isn't spending another second in that dungeon."

Killian blinked a few times, then studied Longfellow. The magistrate was pale, his dark eyes wide with terror. Something had happened.

Killian's eyes flickered toward the box that rested on his desk.

Whatever had happened, it involved that box.

"What's going on?" Manny asked, shaking his head. "Why are you so rattled?"

Longfellow's chest rose and fell repeatedly as he struggled to form words. "I'm not . . . I can't . . ."

"Longfellow," Killian began, his voice quiet. "Is there something in the box?"

Longfellow pressed his pale lips together but nodded his head.

Manny's brows furrowed together. "What is it?"

A chill slithered up Killian's spine. Longfellow opened his mouth, then closed it again, unable to bring himself to speak.

Goose pimples covered Killian's entire body as he reached toward the box. He let out an exhale, steeling himself against what was about to come, as he removed the lid.

The smell was what he noticed first. It was like rotten meat, mingled with a nauseatingly sweet odor.

Then he noticed the skin, pale as parchment with purple veins painting a horrifying mosaic. The tongue was swollen, lolling from the mouth, and the eyes were bulging. Organs dangled from the neck where it had been severed from the body. The features were distorted, but Killian still recognized the face.

This head belonged to Tanner Wills, Royce's right-hand man. Royce must have suspected Wills of betraying him, and he was sending a message—this was how he dealt with his enemies.

"Shit," Manny sighed from where he peered over Killian's shoulder. Then he turned to Longfellow. "Where did this come from?"

The magistrate pressed himself against the door, as if hoping to stay as far away from the head as possible. "It was dropped at my doorstep."

"Shit," Manny repeated.

Longfellow dug his hand into his pocket and fished out a parchment. His hand trembled as he extended it toward Killian. "This was tied to the box," he uttered.

Killian snatched it and read it aloud. *"Your move."*

This was a scare tactic. Royce was flexing his power—and it was working. Killian didn't know how he had managed to have Wills killed, but he would find out. His heart hammered in his chest, but he refused to come undone. Now, more than ever, he needed to stay calm. He needed to talk Longfellow down. If he showed any sign of fear, it would only exacerbate Longfellow's fragile state.

Killian took a deep breath, suppressing a gag as the odor of the rotting head reached his nose.

"Longfellow," he began, but the magistrate just shook his head.

"No—no you can't talk me out of it. It's too dangerous. I'm not—I'm not becoming . . . *that!*" he shouted, pointing at the box.

"You won't, we'll make sure of it," Manny coaxed him.

"You can't protect me!" Longfellow bellowed. "Royce is in a cell, and he still had someone killed and their head delivered to my doorstep—the doorstep of the royal magistrate—in broad daylight!"

"So you're just going to let him go?" Killian snarled. "He killed King Cyril."

"I don't give a fuck!" Longfellow roared. "I'm done with this!"

Killian took a step closer to him. "You think if you just let him free, he won't come after you?"

Longfellow's mouth hung open as he stared at Killian with desperate eyes, as if he hadn't considered the possibility. Then he shook his head, frantically wiping sweat from his brow. "I think he's less likely to kill me if I let him free than if I keep him in the dungeon."

"Longfellow, this is a mistake," Manny tried.

"*Shut the fuck up!*" Longfellow snapped. "I just had a fucking head brought to my house like it was a fucking bouquet of flowers. You don't get to tell me what to do!"

The room was silent for a moment, save for Longfellow's heavy breathing. Tension brewed in the room, until Killian finally scoffed.

"You're a sniveling coward," he breathed.

Longfellow looked at him with wide eyes.

"A sniveling coward who pays women for sex," Manny corrected, his voice cold.

Longfellow's eyes darted between the two soldiers, hate burrowing in his expression. "Go to hell," he said, his voice cracking. He bolted out the door, leaving the severed head behind.

Both Killian and Manny just stood there, too shocked to move. Killian couldn't believe it. Royce was going to walk. What would he do once he was free?

"What now?" Manny asked as Killian replaced the lid on the box.

Killian let out a sigh. He rounded his desk and flopped back into his chair. He no longer had an appetite.

"You're going to put together a detail on Royce," he began. "I want to know where he goes, what he does. I want to know who he talks to. All of it."

"Done."

"And the guards, too. Look into every person who's had contact with Royce since we arrested him. If he was able to have Wills killed, that means he has an accomplice. I want to know who."

"Done," Manny said again.

"And we're going to continue the investigation. Get me an appointment with King Maelor—as soon as he can see me."

"You think he'll reverse Longfellow's decision?" Manny asked, sounding skeptical.

Killian sat up in his chair, leaning his elbows against the desk. "If he's anything like his father, he'll know the right thing to do."

CHAPTER 45

— ◦ —

ELYSE

P rivya had never specified when the treatment would begin, so Elyse stayed in bed long after the sun began to peek through her curtains. She was amazed at how well she'd slept in a bed that wasn't her own, and that her muscles weren't sore despite the long ride. She nestled deeper into the plush mattress and wished Killian were there to hold her, to murmur kisses on her neck. She wondered what he was doing. He'd probably been up for hours and was prancing through the palace, still elated from the arrest—the arrest that she had orchestrated.

She rolled over on the bed, as if she could turn away from the dreadful thought. She wouldn't allow herself to think about it, not today at least.

Elyse finally pulled herself out of bed and changed into a fresh set of clothes, including a short-sleeve tunic. She wrapped herself in a loose sweater to hide her rashy arm—it wasn't exactly appetizing to look at during breakfast. Before she could change her mind, she padded down the stairs and to the main room and found a half dozen women talking at the tables, sipping on tea over cleared plates. To Elyse's surprise, no one so much as batted an eye at her, though a few gave her warm smiles. Her anonymity felt refreshing. She rarely went anywhere in the capital where people didn't whisper about the "notorious witch" and her unrivaled shoppe.

She pushed through the swinging door to the kitchen, which was empty save for one young woman with coppery hair and freckles. The woman glanced up at Elyse from where she stood at the counter, kneading dough.

"Good morning," she practically sang. "You must be our new patient." When she smiled at Elyse, her freckles scrunched up.

"Good morning," Elyse rasped back. "Could I get a mug of hot water?"

"Of course, Miss Elyse—That is your name, right?" the woman asked as she wiped her floury hands on her apron and fetched a kettle from the hearth.

Elyse nodded. "And your name?"

"You can call me Corin." She filled a ceramic mug and passed it to Elyse before adding, "We have all kinds of tea, or I can get you lemons if you'd like. We also have—"

Elyse held up her hand. "Thank you, but I brought my own tea." She pulled out a small linen sack full of citronascia leaves and plunked it into the steaming mug. As she let the leaves steep, she watched Corin return to kneading the dough. Despite her wiry frame, she worked with vigor, humming to herself quietly.

"So you work here?" Elyse asked.

Corin nodded excitedly, her eyes beaming. "Yes, I've been here for about two years. Privya is wonderful. She's done a lot for us."

Elyse lifted the mug to her lips and blew on the scorching liquid. "Us?"

"Me and the other women," Corin said as if it were obvious. "She takes us in, helps us rehabilitate."

"Rehabilitate? Like, you were in an accident?"

Corin reached for a rolling pin and began flattening out the dough in neat, precise movements. "No, not like you're thinking. We all experienced some sort of trauma, and Privya provides us a safe place to mend ourselves, emotionally and spiritually. She just asks that we help out around the clinic."

Elyse swallowed down the bitter tea as she tried not to think about what traumas Corin and the others had faced. "Do you help with the healings?" she wondered aloud.

"Not the actual healings, no. But we assist the patients with other things like escorting them to and from the caves, helping them eat when they're too weak to do so on their own."

Elyse froze with her mug lifted halfway to her mouth. Caves? Mrs. Southwick had made no mention of caves. And why would patients be going into caves, especially if they needed help to do so? Would she be going into the caves? And would she need help with eating?

She suddenly felt the urge to eat a little something, just in case. "I think I missed breakfast . . ." Elyse began, but Corin smiled and lifted a hammered metal cloche, revealing a large plate with eggs, pork, and a biscuit smothered in preserves.

"I saved you something," Corin said brightly.

Elyse thanked her as she slid the plate across the counter. Two more women emerged through the swinging door, carrying stacks of plates and silverware, and Elyse left them to their work while she tucked into the food. She'd been eating better these last few days than she had any time in her recent memory, and she wondered if Privya would be able to tell with her eerie wisdom that most of Elyse's meals consisted of a single piece of buttered bread.

Elyse watched the two other women as she ate, noticing how neither of them seemed to share Corin's cheery demeanor. She wondered what had happened to them to make them shrink in on themselves this way, and she was sure whatever the answer was, it was not pleasant. After cleaning their dishes, they filed out of the room without a word or even a glance in Elyse's direction.

Privya came in after that, her black hair pulled into a long plait that fell to her mid-back. "Good morning, Elyse. Did you find your accommodations suitable?"

"Yes," Elyse said earnestly. "The bed was very comfortable, and the tea you gave me last night worked wonders."

"Good. And breakfast?"

"Delicious."

"Excellent. Are you ready to begin treatment?" she asked with a business-like precision that could rival Killian's.

Elyse took a deep breath. She had made it this far; there was no backing out now.

"Yes, I'm ready," she said quietly.

"Come with me," Privya beckoned before sauntering out of the room.

Elyse tentatively followed her to a smaller room. The walls were lined with shelves filled with tonics and salves and instruments that Elyse didn't recognize—not that she'd spent much time around healers. In the center of the room was a long table with a pillow at one end.

"Take off your sweater and lie down on the table," Privya instructed.

As Elyse removed her sweater and mounted the table, Privya pulled the heavy curtains closed, plunging the room into darkness. Elyse shivered a little, despite the warm day, and took a deep, calming breath.

Through the darkness, Elyse could just make out Privya's form as she moved to stand over Elyse. She hovered her hands over Elyse's arms, her chest and stomach, both of her legs, but she never touched her. A frown pinched her face as she worked.

"What are you doing?" Elyse asked, trying her best to hide her skepticism. Shouldn't Privya be inspecting her arm? In the light?

Privya's voice was low, as if she feared waking something dreadful. "I'm searching for the source of the disease."

Elyse tried to keep her face neutral. "It started on my arm, near the wrist," she said.

"That may be where it manifested, but that is not the source," Privya replied as her hands hovered over Elyse's feet. "What did you have to eat today?"

Elyse arched a brow. "Corin gave me a plate. It had pork, eggs, and a biscuit with preserves—raspberry I think."

"And did you have anything to drink?"

"Yes, ma'am. I had a cup of citronascia tea."

Privya's gaze whipped to Elyse's face, but in the dark her expression was unreadable. "Citronascia has certain suppressive qualities."

"I know," Elyse replied. Those suppressive qualities were precisely why she drank it every morning. Every witch did, lest they leave themselves vulnerable to certain potions, poisons, and hexes.

"Well, you'll have to drink the antidote," Privya said as she turned toward one of the many shelves. She plucked a bottle and poured it into an empty cup, then handed it to Elyse.

Elyse swallowed the lump in her throat. She'd drank citronascia every morning of her life. Being without it would feel like running naked through the streets of the capital.

But with a sigh, she obeyed and drank the whole cup in one swig. It tasted even more foul than the citronascia tea.

Privya yanked the curtains open, and harsh sunlight streamed through the window. "Now," she said, settling herself onto a stool in the corner. "While we wait for the antidote to take effect, why don't you tell me about yourself."

Elyse squirmed. She rubbed awkwardly at her shoulder as she said, "Well, I own a shoppe outside of the city."

Privya nodded, urging Elyse to continue.

"It's just me, but I do well enough on my own. The Emporium is pretty successful."

"And what do you sell?" Privya asked, ignoring Elyse's blatant discomfort at talking about herself.

Elyse shrugged. "Anything magical you can think of. If you name it, I've got it."

No judgment passed over Privya's face. She simply said, "I guessed as much, with your affinity for citronascia." There was a pause, and then Privya added, "I suppose it's a good sign if Killian has befriended a witch."

Elyse cocked her head, unsure how to reply.

"I was able to help him sift through some of his anger toward magic and those who wield it," Privya continued, "but I feared there was too much hatred there that no amount of time could heal. It seems my fears were misguided."

Elyse looked down at her lap as she entwined her fingers together. It hadn't been easy for Killian to come to trust her, yet she spat on that trust with every breath she took.

"Tell me why you're so opposed to being cured," Privya said suddenly.

Elyse gaped up at her. Was she really that easy to read? Or was Privya just that skilled at reading people's internal struggles? Either way, she wasn't going to tell her the truth—at least, not the whole truth.

"I . . ." she began. "My mother died from widow's decay. I suppose I feel guilty about seeking treatment when she was unable to be cured."

"Hmm," was Privya's reply. "I am sorry about your mother, truly, but that is not it. You will need to make strides toward whatever it is that you're combatting before the treatment will work."

Elyse sucked on her teeth. Privya hadn't used a condescending tone, but Elyse still hated being told what to do. She hadn't come here to sort out her problems, she'd come here to treat a rash on her arm—not her torso or her legs or her feet. She debated telling Privya to take that crock of shit and shove it, but she just sat, simmering with anger.

Who was she truly angry with though? Privya? Or herself?

"That should be enough time for the antidote," Privya said. "Lie back down."

Elyse begrudgingly obeyed, and Privya set to work hovering her hands over Elyse's body once more.

"Ahhh, just as I suspected," Privya breathed with far too much satisfaction for Elyse's liking. Her hands floated just above Elyse's abdomen.

"It is indeed guilt that plagues you—" a shift of her hands to the left "—but not because of your mother. Something deeper."

"Can you heal me or not?" Elyse muttered.

Privya didn't deign to answer. Instead, she put her hands on her hips and said, "I think some time in the caves will be good for you."

CHAPTER 46

— · —

ELYSE

Thirty minutes later, Elyse heard a knock at the door to her private room. Corin entered, carrying a basket full of various items.

"Are you ready to go to the cave, Miss Elyse?" she asked.

"Yes," Elyse said with a huff, still bitter from the emotionally invasive examination. "And you can just call me Elyse." She gestured for Corin to lead the way.

Corin gave a sweet, freckled smile before retreating to the hallway. She traipsed through the hall, down the stairs, and out the door, Elyse dragging her feet behind her.

When they rounded the building, Elyse blinked a few times as surprise set in. An enormous cliff towered over the clinic. It had been too dark to see it the night before, but now it seemed ridiculous that she hadn't noticed its existence. In the center of the cliffside was a massive hole that appeared to lead down into a shadowy, black cave.

Corin pulled two tapers from her basket, then fumbled around as she searched for her matches.

"Here," Elyse said. She snapped her fingers and ignited both wicks.

"Thank you," Corin breathed, her eyes wide. She handed one of the tapers to Elyse. As they started to walk again, Corin stole glances at Elyse every few seconds.

"I guess you've never seen magic before?" Elyse asked.

Corin shook her head as they continued toward the gaping mouth of the cave. "Privya uses some magic in her healings, but nothing like that."

"That was nothing," Elyse said lightly. Perhaps a bit giddy by Corin's simple excitement, she added, "Watch this."

She let go of the taper, and the candle floated alongside her as she marched toward the cave.

Corin gasped. "Can you do that with mine too?"

Elyse nodded, and Corin slowly released her grip on the candle, which hovered along beside her. She stared at it with complete awe.

As they entered the dim cave, Elyse made the flames grow brighter to light their way. She stepped carefully over the rocky ground, avoiding the more slippery areas. Down, down, down they went, past the stage where the cool temperature felt refreshing, and on to where it was downright frigid.

"Sorry about the cold," Corin said, shooting Elyse a grimace. "But I promise it's worth it."

No one had told Elyse what was in the caves, and she hadn't bothered to ask. She just wanted this to be over. She wanted to be healed and back to her home—to Killian.

No, *not* to Killian. Or at least, she wouldn't rush pathetically to him, even though she wanted nothing more.

The air grew warm again, and suffocatingly thick. A strange hissing sound could be heard from up ahead. Elyse glanced at Corin, who smiled knowingly, the candlelight playing it up as a wicked grin.

The rocky passageway narrowed, tunneling down into a hole only large enough for one person at a time. The candles' flames seemed unable to penetrate the space, and Elyse quickened her pace to find out just what was on the other side of that opening.

She stepped through the narrow tunnel, but still couldn't see anything. Thick clouds of steam billowed all around her, and she instantly began sweating, drenching her clothes.

A hand gently touched her elbow. "This way," Corin said, guiding Elyse to the right.

She navigated the two of them to an area where the steam wasn't so stifling, and Elyse finally spotted the source. There were three massive pools of water in the cave floor, each emitting copious amounts of hazy vapor. That had been the hissing sound—a billion tiny droplets of water evaporating at once. Elyse sniffed. It was scented too—an odor she didn't recognize, but was subtle and pleasant nonetheless.

"You can undress as much as you want, but most people go completely bare," Corin explained. "I'll be soaking, too, but I'll use a different pool to give you privacy." She set her basket on the ground and began parceling out items. "I have some votives you can set out if you'd like, and Privya made a tonic for you to drink."

With one hand, Elyse floated the tonic into her grasp, and with the other, she magically distributed the votives around the edge of the pool, earning another awestruck gaze from Corin.

"We can share the pool if you want," Elyse said, trying not to sound desperate. "I'd like to hear more about you, if you're up for it." The truth was, she didn't want to be alone with her own thoughts at the moment—not that she would ever tell a stranger that, no matter how kind the stranger was.

"Of course." Corin smiled as if she'd been expecting as much.

The women undressed and slinked into the pool, making sure to give each other ample space. With every inch that Elyse dipped further into the warm water, her body relaxed, all tension evaporating along with the steam. The divine waters caressed her skin, massaging away aches she never knew she had. She let out a soft moan as she settled onto a rock and leaned back on the edge of the pool, which made Corin giggle.

"There's a certain substance in the pool, called trysalin, that can heal all kinds of wounds and diseases. It comes up through the hot springs from deep underground."

Elyse arched a brow. "And it's been known to cure widow's decay?"

"Yes, along with the tonic that Privya made."

Elyse reached for the bottle of tonic that lay by the edge of the pool, uncorked it, and sniffed. It smelled the same as the steamy air.

"It's in here too?" she asked.

Corin nodded. "Combined with a few other ingredients. It helps attack the disease from the inside while the waters go to work on the outside."

Cautiously, Elyse took a sip from the bottle, but it tasted mellow, a little sweet even. She held the bottle above the water and closed her eyes, leaning her head back to rest on the ledge.

Dangerous thoughts of plunging below the steaming waters and never coming back up began to creep into Elyse's mind. Desperate for a distraction, she asked Corin, "So will you stay here for the rest of your life?"

She could hear the smile in Corin's reply. "In this pool? I wish I could stay here forever." She paused, and her voice underscored her excitement. "No, I'm actually leaving next month on a mission for Privya."

Her eyes still closed, Elyse took another swig of tonic. "What sort of mission?"

"Well, to find more of these springs. If we can find more springs with trysalin, we can help heal more people across the kingdom, and maybe even in other kingdoms." Corin's voice was more sobered as she added, "It's difficult for many people to journey to us here."

Elyse opened one eye and peered at Corin. "Do you have an idea where to go?"

"Yes and no," Corin answered. "I've marked out a dozen cave systems that I think are worth exploring, but that's all."

Elyse took another sip of tonic. Then another, and another. She finished off the bottle as she and Corin sat in comfortable silence, then she dipped it into the pool, filling it up with the bubbling waters. She magically corked the bottle then floated it to Corin. "Here."

Corin grasped the bottle from the air, her brows furrowed. But then Elyse waved her hand, and a small object appeared next to Corin on the edge of the pool. Corin twisted excitedly to grab the circular metal object.

"It's a compass," Elyse explained. "But instead of pointing north, it's connected to the bottle. It'll point you toward the nearest pool of trysalin."

Corin's eyes were wide as she watched the needle on the compass whizz around in circles.

"You'll have to get away from here before it will actually work," Elyse laughed. "But it should help."

"This is amazing," Corin breathed. "I—thank you so much."

Corin's sincere gratitude made Elyse squirm. "It's nothing," she played it down.

"It's not nothing," Corin insisted as she set the compass and the bottle on the ledge. "It will save me hundreds, maybe thousands of hours. It could be the difference between helping more people, and not." She paused, biting her lip. With an air of heaviness, she said, "You're a good person, Elyse."

Elyse swallowed the lump in her throat. She had a feeling Corin sensed her self-loathing and had chosen those words for a reason. Could everyone in this damned place read her like a book? Perhaps she was overthinking it.

"Giving you something that costs me nothing doesn't make me a good person," she said in a low voice, unable to meet Corin's eyes.

"Doesn't it, though? Are we not the sum of our kindnesses, our everyday interactions with others?"

Elyse had no words. She wasn't very kind on a day-to-day basis, and certainly not enough to outweigh the murders she'd committed. She said nothing, letting Corin's words hang in the haze between them.

"You said you wanted to know my story," Corin began, her voice strong, as if she had spent the quiet moment mustering up her courage. "I'll share it with you, at least the shorter version."

She took a deep breath before continuing, and Elyse braced herself.

"I did a lot of bad things when I was younger. I stole, I lied, I cheated people. I drank myself senseless, I did any drugs I could get my hands on. I could make excuses and say I did it because I was poor and starving, because I was abused, because I had lost someone I loved, but . . ."

Her words trailed off as she tilted her head down, facing the waters, pouring her sorrows into its healing powers. Elyse waited patiently until Corin gathered her thoughts, anxious to hear more. Corin's voice held so much bitterness, and it resonated deeply with Elyse, more than she was eager to admit.

"I stopped taking care of myself," Corin confessed. "My body started shutting down, too weak to handle the way I mistreated it. I thought the gods had cursed me for stealing, for running away from home. One day I passed out in the market, and they put me in a group home for the dying. I was forced to lay in bed and wait out my days. Privya would come up to the capital sometimes, and she came to the group home to volunteer her services. When she found me, I didn't speak, didn't move. I just wanted her to leave me to die. But she refused. She extended her stay by an extra two weeks, just to sit by my side and wait. I was so irritated. I couldn't believe this old woman was pestering me when she could be helping others. But she waited, and she waited, and finally I spoke."

Elyse could picture Privya silently appraising Corin with that calculating bedside manner, but she couldn't picture Corin. Not this smiley, freckled beauty who sat before her.

"I think I wanted to come clean, like a deathbed confession. I told her everything, every last bit of what I'd done. She listened but never touched me, never consoled me or said a word. When I finally got everything out, she handed me a bottle of tonic. She told me the ingredients, how to make it for myself, and that I should drink it every day for a month, and then once a week after that for the rest of my life. She said to come and find her whenever I was ready. And then she left."

"You drank it? And you came here?" Elyse pressed, desperately wanting to hear the rest of the story. No, not wanting—needing.

Corin nodded, tucking a lock of coppery hair behind her ear. "I did. I don't really know why or what changed my mind. I suppose it was the kind stranger who had sat at my side and listened to my pain. Maybe I felt like I owed it to her to get better. No matter the reason, I did it. And after a month, I felt better, back to myself. So I traveled down here and found Privya.

"When I walked into the clinic, I had one question: why? Why had she taken the time to care for me, a worthless addict? And I asked her as much, after she sat me down for tea and a meal."

Elyse laughed. That seemed to be Privya's signature operation: give people food and tea before giving them any information.

Corin smiled and continued. "I still remember her answer, word for word. She said, 'You did things you are not proud of, and you can't change that. But if you died, you would never get the chance to redeem yourself.' I knew right then that I wanted to stay, that I wanted to be a part of whatever she was doing. I wanted to help people—people who were battling with themselves, who needed a reminder that they could be good."

She didn't look at Elyse as she said those last words, and for that, Elyse was grateful. Her heart ached—for herself, for Corin, and for a future that might promise redemption. Could she ever wash away the horrible things she'd done? Could she ever rid her hands of the blood she had shed? She wasn't sure.

Elyse didn't realize how long they had been sitting in silence, each lost in their own thoughts, until Corin emerged from the water, her healthy body glowing from the effects of the pool. She stepped gracefully onto the ledge and grabbed a towel from the basket. Elyse watched the bubbling surface of the water as Corin toweled herself off.

"I need to get back and start on lunch," Corin explained, "but you can stay as long as you'd like."

Elyse nodded and sank deeper into the water until it tickled her chin. She agreed with Corin's earlier sentiment—she could stay here forever. Here in the pools, she would never have to face her past, or her future. But then again, she would never get the chance to redeem herself, as Corin had.

Corin started to walk toward the narrow exit when Elyse asked, "Was all that true? Your story? Or is it just some fable meant to inspire me?"

Corin had seemed genuinely heartbroken as she told the story, yet Elyse wouldn't put it past Privya to manipulate her with lies. The way Corin's shoulders drooped, though, told Elyse enough.

"It's all true," she said. She lingered for a moment as if the memories of her past kept her rooted to the ground.

"I'm sorry," Elyse said, and she meant it—not just sorry for what Corin had gone through, but sorry for doubting its truth.

Corin turned to face Elyse, a small smile on her face. "It's not too late for you, Elyse," she said, and then she disappeared into the fog.

As much as Elyse wanted to deny it, she couldn't reject the hope that poured into her heart. Perhaps it wasn't too late. Perhaps she could slowly, one day at a time, reverse some of the damage she'd done. Perhaps one day she could do enough good to outweigh all the awful things Lazarus had made her do, and all the things he would inevitably force on her in the future. Perhaps one day she could love herself again.

She wasn't sure if any of it was possible, but she at least knew where to start.

CHAPTER 47

— · —

ELYSE

"Wow, you really are a terrible cook," Corin teased.

She and Elyse were slicing up vegetables for that evening's supper. Elyse glanced from her pile, which consisted of large, uneven chunks of onion, to Corin's which was uniformly sliced into tiny cubes.

"Oh, hush," Elyse quipped back, which only made Corin giggle.

The duo had been getting along well the past four days. Whenever she could, Elyse volunteered to help out around the clinic, assisting Corin with laundry or cooking. Corin reminded her of Sera, with her contagious optimism. Elyse wondered if she spent enough time at the clinic, if she would grow to be an optimist as well.

Each day, Corin and Elyse took a long walk through the woods surrounding the clinic. They talked about whatever came to mind, whether it be simple things like books and food, or deeper things, like their childhoods. They had very little in common, which often resulted in passionate debates over nonsense like which cheese was the best, but they always ended up laughing together by the time they made it back to the clinic.

Elyse had considered telling Corin the truth—about Lazarus and King Cyril. She'd never told anyone about the demon before, not even Sera. She felt like she could trust Corin, though. And she felt that, all the way out here, the world was so disconnected from the capital and the politics of the kingdom. Yet it didn't seem fair to burden Corin with something so heavy, so she'd kept it to herself.

Most of the time, despite Elyse's resistance, Corin made her go outside by herself. Elyse would sit in the sunshine with nothing to do but think. She took off her shoes, letting the grass tickle her toes, and dreading the moment when her self-loathing took over.

But each time, it got a little easier to deal with. She didn't squirm and berate herself the way she used to. She acknowledged her wrongdoings, and though she didn't quite forgive herself, she decided she could at least live with the past. And she could take control of her future.

In the mornings, Privya examined Elyse's rash, measuring it for signs of change. That morning, Elyse awoke to find the rash was completely gone. She couldn't believe it, and she hadn't even waited until her appointment to run and show Privya.

"Very good," Privya remarked. "You've made excellent progress. You may return home tomorrow, if you'd like."

"Will it . . . Will it come back?" Elyse asked, hesitant to voice the question that had been on the tip of her tongue for days.

Privya shook her head. "No, once the body is rid of the disease it cannot come back. But—" she said, leveling that fierce gaze on Elyse. "You will need to continue your inner healing. Emotional turmoil leaves you susceptible to other diseases, which can be just as deadly as the decay."

"Yes, ma'am," Elyse replied, determined to comply. "But . . . I can drink my citronascia tea again when I go back home, right?"

Privya let out a breathy laugh. "Yes, you may drink your tea."

That had been a relief. As Elyse continued chopping up her onion, trying her best to be as precise as possible, she thought of all the things she missed back home. The comfort of the citronascia tea, her own bed, and of course, her lieutenant.

She wondered what Killian had been up to. Had they proceeded with Royce's trial? She wanted to see him the moment she was back in the capital, but she knew he would likely be too busy to meet with her right away.

Elyse slid her gaze toward Corin and asked as casually as she could, "Do you have a quill and parchment?"

"Of course," Corin said. "I can fetch them for you when we're done here."

"Thank you," Elyse replied, grateful that Corin hadn't asked why she wanted the items.

That is, until Corin smirked at her and asked, "Are you writing a love letter?"

"No!" Elyse snapped immediately.

Corin's eyes grew wide with amusement. "I was just kidding around, but that was quite the reaction."

"It's not a love letter," Elyse scoffed, focusing her attention on chopping her onion. "I just wanted to let my . . . *friend* . . . know that I would be returning tomorrow."

Corin made a humming sound as she pursed her lips and glanced sideways at Elyse.

"You keep insisting I'm a good person," Elyse said, twirling the knife in her hand, "but if you don't wipe that look off your face, you'll quickly find out just how wrong you are."

"Do people really fall for that?" Corin asked, a hand on her hip. With one eyebrow raised, she stared skeptically at Elyse, who stuck her tongue out.

Laughing and returning to her vegetables, Corin asked, "So tell me about this *friend*."

Elyse felt her cheeks heat as she picked up a fresh onion. Why did Killian have this effect on her? Jaime had never made her feel so girlish.

"We only just met," she said casually. She wasn't really sure what to say.

"Instant sparks?" Corin asked.

Elyse snorted. "Not exactly." She realized she was smiling to herself, remembering all the horrible assumptions she'd made about Killian.

"So what changed?" Corin pressed.

Elyse paused her chopping, contemplating Corin's question. What had changed? "I'm not sure," she said aloud. Then she turned to face Corin. "Have you ever met someone that's just so . . . driven?"

Corin didn't look up as she continued slicing into a carrot. "Yes—Privya," she chuckled. "But she has the personality of a tree."

Elyse laughed and set her knife on the counter. She couldn't deny that Privya and Killian did share certain qualities. "No, I mean . . . He's ambitious and hardworking and disciplined—like Privya—but when he wants to, he can also be funny and compassionate."

"He sounds pretty great," Corin mused.

"Yeah, he really is," Elyse muttered, more to herself than to her friend.

She quietly returned to chopping, her mind filled with Killian. She had thought about him a lot these past few days, and how he made her feel. He made her want to be a better person. And when she was with him, she felt like it was possible, as if some of his honor was rubbing off on her. He made her care again.

And if that wasn't worth fighting through all the guilt she had accumulated over the last few years, she didn't know what was.

CHAPTER 48

— • —

KILLIAN

I t had been five long days. Killian's meeting with King Maelor hadn't gone as he'd hoped. Maelor hadn't been cowardly like Longfellow, but he had wanted to tread lightly. He'd instructed Killian to dig deeper, finding out exactly who had helped Royce. The king wanted to see Royce hanged, but he wanted to do it with as little havoc as possible.

So Killian had spent five days poring over evidence, notes, and the rotation of the guards who had overseen Royce's imprisonment. The whole time, Wills's distorted face lingered in Killian's mind. His anger brimmed within him, anger not only with himself for being unable to find one damn thing that would send Royce straight to the gallows, but with Longfellow for being such a coward.

The only redeeming part of the past few days was seeing Georgie get settled in at his mother's house. The two of them had gotten along famously, though Killian was hardly surprised by that. His mother had welcomed several misguided youths over the years, and they had all adored her. When Killian had stopped by that morning to check in on Georgie, he'd found him with a belly full of pastries and a grin on his face.

Now Killian sat in his office, barely able to maintain focus on the interviews of everyone who had been on duty the night of King Cyril's murder. The interviews were already ingrained in his mind—he could recite them forward and backward. Once again, he found his mind slipping away, wishing he were going to Elyse's shoppe that night to hold her while they slept. He dreamed of her nightly—her soft, alabaster skin, her sly smile, her sweet scent. It felt as if a lifetime had passed since he'd last kissed her.

A knock at the office door roused him from his fantasies, and he called, "Come in."

A young page came bounding in, sputtering, "A letter came for you, Lieutenant."

"Set it on the desk," Killian drawled as he tried to find the place he'd left off reading.

The page, a gangly boy of twelve or thirteen, awkwardly set the parchment on the desk and asked, "Do you want me to wait so you can write a reply, sir? I'll deliver it to the aerie for you."

Killian let out a quiet chuckle. He hoped he hadn't been nearly as eager to please as this young page, but he knew he'd been far more earnest—a brownnoser even.

"No, thank you. I can handle that myself," he said. The letter was probably just bureaucratic nonsense anyway, nothing that warranted a response.

The page saluted and bustled out of the room, leaving Killian to his ennui. After reading three more statements, none of which brought any new perspectives to the situation, he finally reached for the scroll of parchment the page had delivered. To his surprise, it wasn't addressed to Lieutenant Southwick but to Killian, written in neat calligraphy. A smile slowly spread across his face as he unrolled the parchment, and he read the brief note.

Killian,

Privya has successfully cured me. I can meet you at dusk outside the palace tomorrow and bring you to my house to spend the night. You're overdue for a sunrise training session. Be ready to get your ass kicked (again).

Elyse
(The sassy, silver-haired witch, in case you forgot)

He read the letter again and again, savoring each word, each beautiful loop and swirl of the letters. And just like that, all his frustrations melted away.

CHAPTER 49

— : —

ELYSE

The morning Elyse was set to leave Privya's clinic, she magicked herself home and quickly grabbed a few gifts before whirling herself back to the clinic in a puff of blue smoke.

Corin stood wide-eyed and open-mouthed as Elyse reappeared before them. She and Privya had gathered outside to see Elyse off after breakfast, a gesture that warmed Elyse's heart more than she wanted to admit. Before her emotions got the better of her, Elyse walked to Corin and held up a small burlap bag. She pulled a vial of blue liquid from the sack and showed it to her new friend.

"If you're ever in a bind during your travels, just break this vial and think of someplace safe—somewhere specific, that you've been to before. You'll be transported there immediately." She dropped the vial back inside the bag and pressed it into Corin's hands. "There's five of these vials in there. Just let me know if you need more."

Corin was hardly able to utter her thanks, and Elyse felt a lump forming in her throat. Steeling herself, she turned to Privya and held out a velvet coin purse, heavy with gold pieces.

"This should cover your expenses for a while. If you ever need more, please come find me."

Privya accepted the purse with a nod, and Elyse was grateful for the woman's stoicism. She didn't know how she would handle it if Privya blubbered over her charity.

"I know you don't usually make house calls," Elyse continued, "but there's someone nearby that I think could use your help." She explained about Anika and her bedridden father, and Privya agreed to visit them in the next few days.

"Well," Elyse said, feeling uncharacteristically awkward, "I guess that's it."

Corin rushed in to give Elyse a hug, wrapping her thin, freckled arms around the witch. "You're a good person, Elyse," she breathed in a low voice, though Elyse had no doubt Privya had heard.

Privya stared at Elyse with one brow arched before slowly opening her arms, and Elyse embraced the healer. Privya squeezed back tightly, and everything that had been and was yet to come seemed so much less daunting. When they pulled apart, Elyse clasped Privya's hand.

"If any of the women you take in would like to learn to defend themselves, I'd be honored to teach them," she said.

Privya's crow's feet wrinkled endearingly as she smiled back at Elyse.

With a deep breath, Elyse mounted her mare and began the slow journey home. Before she disappeared around a bend, she glanced back at Corin and Privya, who waved goodbye to her.

Elyse had many miles and many hours until she got back to the city, but she didn't mind. She enjoyed the slow, easy pace and the spring air that hummed with new beginnings. The journey would also give her an opportunity to solidify the plan she'd been developing over the last few days, the plan that would help pave the road to her redemption.

CHAPTER 50

— ◦ —

ELYSE

E lyse leaned against the palace walls near the gate, trying to quiet her fidgeting hands. She was anxious for far too many reasons. She'd only just met Killian, yet spending six days away from him had felt like six years. Her body yearned to be close to his, to banter and laugh together.

But time apart had a funny way of toying with people's emotions. What if Killian hadn't missed her? What if she saw him, and she realized her feelings for him weren't as strong as she remembered? Or worst of all, what if he had found out the truth?

Her heart raced as she considered the possibility, and she reached in her pocket and grasped one of the blue vials—just in case. But surely if Killian had discovered that she was the king's murderer, he wouldn't have waited for her to return to the city. He would have marched a small army down to the clinic and arrested her immediately.

Despite the logic of her thoughts, worry still coursed through her, and she felt like a doe in the middle of an open field, hunted and vulnerable.

That is, until Killian emerged from the palace gates. His eyes lit up upon seeing her, and a smile played at his lips. His smile was sincere, boyish even, not the cunning grin of a predator ensnaring his prey. Elyse relaxed, mirroring his expression as joy overtook her. She desperately wanted to run to him, to hurry and close the short distance between them, but she forced her feet to stay planted.

Still smiling, Killian went to her and pressed a kiss to her lips, and she knew from the hunger behind his touch that he had missed her just as much as she'd missed him.

He immediately took her left hand and studied her arm, turning it slowly and running his fingers along her skin. His smile grew as he took in the healthy glow, the absence of any rash or blisters.

"How do you feel?" he asked with genuine curiosity.

"I feel great," Elyse replied. "Good as new." Both inside and out, though she didn't feel like sharing that much with him. At least, not yet. Not in the city streets.

They walked hand in hand, falling into a leisurely pace, until they ducked down an alleyway and Elyse transported them home.

The transition from the stinking city air to the fresh forest breeze was a moment Elyse cherished. With the spring warmth, the budding flowers, and Killian's hand holding hers, she was in a state of pure bliss. And the sun on her bare arm—that was a sensation she would never tire of, not after nearly a year of hiding her rash beneath long sleeves and gloves. Nothing, not one single thing, could bring her down from this high.

Killian cleared his throat as they stepped through the wards surrounding her house. "We let Royce go."

Elyse stepped on a branch, and the *crack* that rang through the woods was just as harrowing as Killian's words.

"What?" she shouted as panic obliterated her. Her hands clenched into fists as she fought off her terror, hoping Killian wouldn't read too much into her agitation.

But Killian appeared just as livid as she was. He ran a hand through his short hair and said, "I know. Longfellow is a bleeding coward who cares more about his own ass than about putting a corrupt man down." He shook his head as he explained everything that had happened while Elyse was away.

Elyse swallowed down the bile that rose in her throat. This wasn't the plan. The plan was to kill the king to satisfy Lazarus, and then pin the murder on Royce. And then maybe in twenty years, her guilt would finally diminish, and she could even tell Killian all about how she'd framed Royce, and they'd have a good laugh about it.

Don't be fucking ridiculous, she scolded herself, not just for thinking that she could ever tell Killian the truth without him hating her, but because she was already envisioning a future with him. She tried to focus on the trees, the wildflowers, the clouds above, anything to soothe her frantic mind, but Killian's own fury emanated from him like a contagion.

Elyse closed her eyes to shut out the visions of how horribly wrong everything was going, and how much worse it could get. "This is terrible," she mumbled.

"I know," Killian said, placing a hand on Elyse's back. "I'm sorry, tonight isn't supposed to be like this. We're meant to celebrate," he added, sending Elyse a smile that didn't quite reach his eyes.

She moved closer to him, and he wrapped his arm around her waist. "Does a celebration mean wine?" she asked, hoping desperately the answer was yes. She needed something, anything, to take the edge off.

"Of course," he said with a grin.

"And maybe kissing?" Elyse asked, her brow raised suggestively.

"Maybe," Killian said. He stretched his arms over his head and faked a yawn. "I might be too tired."

Elyse pointed her finger and magicked a rock right in front of Killian's foot, and he stubbed his toe on it.

"Ow!" he shouted. "You little—" he cursed her as he hopped on one foot, though his smile and the humor in his eyes gave away his true feelings.

Elyse just shot him a smirk over her shoulder as she kept walking.

Killian hobbled to catch up to her. "Okay, maybe *some* kissing, but we can't stay up too late. I'm ready for another go at the obstacle course tomorrow morning."

Elyse snorted, which only made Killian's grin broaden. "Were you hoping to lose a limb this time?"

"I don't know about a whole limb, but maybe a few fingers." He winked at her, sending her heart aflutter.

How did he always do that—turn her worry into joy? There was something about him, strong yet gentle, that made her feel whole, a way she'd never felt before.

They reached the cottage door and he held it open for her. The lingering smell of incense welcomed her home. As much as she had enjoyed Corin, and eventually learned to enjoy Privya, she was glad to be home. The whole place seemed to hum, her magic mingling with that of the various objects to create a soothing symphony.

As soon as he shut the door, Killian pounced on her. His hand tangled with her hair, and he pulled her against him, sealing her lips with his. The suddenness of it made her gasp in delight. His kiss held all the longing she had felt the past six days, and she grasped his shirtfront as if she'd never let him go.

Elyse's body yearned to remove her clothes, to take him upstairs and shove him onto the bed, but she forced those feelings down, even as Killian's arousal grew against her. She softly bit his lip—one last teasing gesture—and pulled away.

"I missed you," he said as he nuzzled his face against her neck.

Her heart simultaneously leapt and ached.

I will deserve him, she told herself. *I am a good person.*

"I have an idea that I think you'll like," she said aloud.

Killian pulled back and tilted his head, an invitation to continue.

Elyse smiled at him, and then explained her wickedly good plan.

CHAPTER 51

— · —

KILLIAN

Killian sat in a stiff armchair in a townhouse in the southern sector of the city, which served as a safehouse for the Royal Guard. It was used occasionally for protecting witnesses who might be in danger, or conducting secret meetings. Based on the firmness of the cushion beneath him and the dust coating the table beside him, "occasionally" was generous, making it the perfect place to conduct Elyse's plan.

He blocked out the simple, unadorned wood walls of the safehouse and stared straight ahead, going over every detail of the plan in his mind. "Preparation is power," he'd been told many times during training, and had instilled that same lesson in his own soldiers again and again.

Elyse's plan was good. When she'd told him, it was clear how much thought she'd put into it. He'd watched her dark eyes light up as she explained, and he'd felt a tug of something in his heart. Not love—no, he wouldn't let himself consider that so soon into their relationship. But there had been no question that he would help her.

Elyse sat at the table, one of the few pieces of furniture. She appeared bored as she studied her nails, but the slight tightness of her jaw gave away her tension. Killian couldn't tell if it was nerves or excitement. Perhaps both.

The sound of hooves and a carriage rolling over cobblestone reached Killian's ears, and he glanced at Elyse. She immediately ripped back the heavy curtain over the window and peered out with a frown. Her face relaxed after a moment, and she said, "It's not her."

Killian reached for her hand and gently pulled her onto his lap. Obsidian eyes stared back at him, all icy fervor.

"You're antsy," he murmured as he pressed his forehead against hers.

"Am not," she replied, but the way she bit her lip proclaimed her lie.

He ran a hand through her silvery hair, cradling her head in his palm. She leaned into his touch and closed her eyes.

"I've never seen you like this before," he said.

Elyse sighed and nuzzled her head further into his hold. "It just—it has to work. I have to . . ."

She trailed off, and Killian was about to press her to go on when another carriage rolled down the street. Elyse leaned toward the window and peeked behind the curtain. "I think it's her!" she whispered, excitement coating her voice, her sight trained on someone Killian couldn't see.

A knock sounded at the front door a moment later, and both their heads whipped toward the noise. With a devilish grin, Elyse rose from Killian's lap and pulled him to his feet.

He opened the door and found Nina on the steps, looking just as meek as he remembered. Her hands were folded in front of her, her gaze cast at her feet. Pity engulfed him—but also affirmation that they were doing the right thing.

"Come in," he said gently, stepping aside to give her plenty of space. He hated the way her body seemed to tremble in his presence, and he wanted to give her a wide berth, to show her he meant her no harm.

Nina hurriedly entered the foyer, her eyes never leaving the floor. Killian shut the door and gestured into the sitting area, and she obliged. She wrung her hands together as she waited for further instructions.

"My name's Killian," he said quietly, like he was coaxing an animal or small child. Gods above, he wanted to put a hand on her shoulder and tell her it would be all right, but he didn't dare touch her. "And this is Elyse."

Nina spared Elyse a quick glance before dropping her chin again. "If the lady wants to join, it'll be an extra silver," she uttered. Her voice conveyed no emotion, only duty.

Killian and Elyse exchanged glances. A measly silver for such a thing? He held in his shudder.

"No, she won't be joining us. In fact, we will not be in need of your services today," he said.

At that, Nina's gaze flicked up to meet Killian's, her eyes wide, searching for answers.

"Let me explain," Elyse jumped in.

It was probably for the best. Nina's eyes were still locked on Killian as if he were a predator she couldn't afford to look away from, not even for a moment. The thought made his stomach churn.

"We want to help you," Elyse continued. "Do you have anywhere to go?"

Nina's hands moved up her arms, cradling herself. She glanced at Elyse again before her gaze darted back to Killian, and she shook her head.

"That's okay," Elyse said, her voice gentle but reassuring. "I have somewhere for you to go. Somewhere safe where no one will hurt you."

Silence filled the room, and Nina held herself tighter. Killian swallowed down the bile rising in his throat as he watched her delicate fingers grasp the fabrics of her gown.

"I can't leave my madam," Nina finally croaked. "She owns me. She'll find me."

This time when she spoke, Killian could see her missing teeth, could see the distinct way she tried, but failed, to hide her disfigurement. If Elyse noticed, she didn't show it. She took a step toward Nina, who flinched but didn't back away.

"*No one* owns you," Elyse stated. There was no gentleness in her voice now, only disdain and conviction. "No one will ever be able to tell you what to do again."

Nina's chin wobbled as she slowly lifted her head. "But the money, my debt—"

"Fuck the money," Elyse cut her off. "You say the word, and you'll never have to give that bitch another copper."

Killian's heart hammered in his chest, its cadence screaming, *Say yes, say yes, say yes!* Nina's eyes watered, and she closed them for a moment, inhaling deeply. When she opened her eyes, she uttered two small words.

"Why me?"

Elyse pursed her lips for a moment, her face contorting with thought. "Why not you?" she breathed, daring to take another step toward Nina. "If I could, I would free every last one of you, and maybe one day I will. But for now, I'll start with you."

Killian had to stop himself from going to Elyse. She was radiant, strong, and so sure of herself in that moment, and it took everything in him to keep from touching her. Some of her vigor must have permeated Nina's apprehension, because color now bloomed across her features, and she gave a small nod.

Elyse nodded back and took another step toward Nina. "If you'd like, before we take you somewhere safe, I can help with your teeth. You'll be able to talk and eat like normal—if you want."

Nina's lips shut tight, concealing her insecurity. There was a long pause before she asked, "Really?"

"Really," Elyse replied. Now there was only a few feet of space between them. Killian could see the tension in Elyse's hand—that she, too, wanted to reach out and assure the girl. "It'll hurt like hell," she said, "but I can do it."

Nina closed her eyes again. "There is nothing you can do to me that is worse than what I've been through."

Killian's heart shattered, cracks tearing through him. He clenched his hands into fists, grinding his teeth, pushing down the sorrow that consumed him and replacing it with raw fury. He wanted to track down every man that had ever hurt her and destroy them with his bare hands. But for now, he reminded himself, they needed to get Nina to safety, to let her begin to heal.

Elyse closed the space between herself and Nina. "I knew you were a fighter," she whispered, giving Nina a warm smile. She placed a hand on Nina's shoulder and guided her toward a sofa against the wall, and Nina stood a little straighter, as if she wanted to believe Elyse's words.

"Lie down," Elyse told her.

As Nina reclined across the sofa, Killian crossed the room to join them and knelt down beside them.

Elyse stood by the arm of the sofa and leaned over Nina. "May I?" she asked as she reached a hand toward Nina's mouth, and Nina opened her lips, finally revealing the black stumps of her teeth.

But Elyse didn't cringe or wince or bat an eye. She simply studied her mouth the way a healer might study an ailment, then placed her hands on either side of Nina's face.

"Ready?"

Nina nodded, her nostrils flaring as she drew a steadying breath.

Elyse flexed her hands and scrunched up her lips. Killian had never noticed her expression when she was concentrating on her magic—he was usually too busy worrying about conjuring a shield or simply surviving. But as her eyes narrowed and her lips shifted to the side, his heart skipped a beat. She was fierce, yet adorable. And she was his.

He didn't have long to appreciate Elyse's countenance though. A cry erupted from Nina's lips, her body undulating on the sofa, and she reached out a hand to clutch onto something. Killian reached for her, and she wrapped her frail hand around his, squeezing tight as another cry escaped her. Her grip was excruciating. He would certainly have bruises—if not a broken bone. But he didn't dare complain.

"You're doing great," he assured her, though his voice was nearly drowned out by her screams.

For five long, agonizing minutes, she writhed on the sofa, screams ripping through the small room. Every time she opened her mouth to cry out, Killian saw a thin white line protruding from her gums, slowly extending further and further. Elyse's eyes remained fixed on Nina, determination and compassion steeling her expression.

Finally, Elyse lifted her hands from Nina's face. Drenched in sweat, her chest rapidly rising and falling, Nina still clung to Killian's hand. She let out a quiet whimper. Elyse waved her hand, and a flask appeared in her palm.

"Here," she said, thrusting the flask at Nina. "This will help with the pain."

Nina released Killian's hand, her body trembling, but Killian reached for the flask and undid the latch. He helped her sit up and held the flask to her lips, letting a healthy swig flow into her aching mouth.

"You did good," he said, and Elyse confirmed the sentiment by placing a hand on Nina's shoulder.

After another sip, Nina asked in a raspy voice, "What now?"

Killian smiled at the row of perfect alabaster teeth that shone between her lips as she spoke. "Well," he breathed. "Now we take you to that safe place."

Nina glanced between the two of them. "What about my madam?"

Elyse grinned, a hint of her cunning showing through. "We'll take care of her."

Nina's eyes widened. "Are you going to kill her?"

"No," Elyse said quickly. "I'm just going to alter her memory a bit, make sure she doesn't come looking for you."

Nina nodded, seemingly soothed that her madam wouldn't be murdered. Killian envied her benevolence—he didn't think he would feel the same way.

"Where am I going?" she asked, her eyes hopeful but anxious.

Elyse smiled, soft and sincere. "Somewhere with fresh air. Where you can heal, along with other women." With one hand, she interlaced her fingers with Nina's, and with the other she pulled a blue vial from her pocket. "I'm going to use this vial to magically transport us," she explained. "It will feel strange, but it won't hurt you."

Killian laughed, earning a sharp look from Elyse.

"I would have appreciated an explanation like that the first time you magicked me somewhere," he quipped.

Elyse stuck her tongue out at him, then turned back to Nina. "Are you ready?"

Nina gave a small nod, and together Killian and Elyse helped her stand from the sofa. Holding Nina's other hand, Killian gave Elyse a look that confirmed he was ready too.

Elyse smashed the vial on the dusty wood floor, and the darkness swirled in. He felt Nina go rigid against him, and had the distinct feeling that she was screaming, though he heard nothing at all. Then his boots touched gravel and the scent of open air filled his lungs. As he looked around, nostalgia overwhelmed him.

The clinic had seemed larger in his memory, but he saw now that it was a simple two-story structure, smaller than most apartment buildings in the city. Behind it was the enormous ridge, and though he couldn't see it, he could still picture the large cave opening. He could feel the warmth of the steaming waters deep inside the cave, could smell their healing power.

Being here felt right.

Nina wore a look of apprehension, but Elyse caught her eye and gave her an encouraging smile. Killian dropped Nina's hand, but Elyse remained holding her other one as she stepped toward the building, pulling Nina with her.

An older woman came sauntering out of the clinic, and no amount of time would allow Killian to forget her countenance. She looked the same as he remembered, just with more gray hair peppered through her jet-black plait. A young woman, whom Killian did not recognize, followed behind her. She smiled broadly at Elyse, her freckled cheeks crinkling.

"Privya, Corin," Elyse breathed, a warmth in her tone that Killian rarely heard. "This is Nina." She released Nina's hand and patted her shoulder reassuringly.

Privya, just as reserved as Killian remembered, gave a simple nod. But the other girl rushed forward to greet Nina.

"I'm Corin," she said sweetly as she took Nina's hand in both of hers. Nina flinched but then relaxed as Corin said, "You're safe here."

"Corin has been here for a few years," Elyse explained. "She'll help you get adjusted."

Corin nodded eagerly, but Nina asked, "What is this place?"

"It's a clinic. Privya here is the best healer in the kingdom," Elyse said, gesturing toward the stony-faced woman. "She takes in women who need help, and just asks that you contribute around the clinic."

Nina viewed Privya with some skepticism, but she nodded.

"Come on, I'll show you around," Corin offered, tugging Nina's hand.

Nina followed, but just as they reached the doorstep, she stopped short and turned around. There was a pause as she looked to Elyse, then Killian, and said, "Thank you." She beamed at them, her new white teeth gleaming in the sunlight.

"You're very welcome," Killian said, though it was a struggle to keep his voice steady. He hadn't realized how emotional this would be—seeing Nina's resilience, watching her strength as she endured the pain of growing new teeth, and now visiting Privya's clinic. His chest felt tight, as if Nina had wrapped him in a bear hug.

Nina and Corin disappeared into the building, and Killian turned to see Privya's gaze set on him. Her eyes were fierce, but the ghost of a smile played on her lips.

"Killian," she said in that low, commanding voice. "You look well."

Killian grinned. "Privya, was that an actual compliment?"

Elyse snorted a laugh, and the corner of Privya's mouth tugged up ever so slightly. Both actions made Killian's heart sing.

Elyse twisted her wrist, and a hefty velvet coin purse appeared in her hand. She held it with ease and grace, as she did everything.

"This should cover Nina's expenses," she said as she hoisted the bag toward Privya, who accepted the purse with her two withered hands.

"Thank you," she said in a flat voice, though a small glimmer in her eyes revealed a deeper gratitude. "And Corin has expressed interest in taking you up on your offer to train in defense. I suspect Nina might be interested as well."

Killian tilted his head as he regarded Elyse. She hadn't told him about any offer to train the women here—though he wasn't surprised. It made sense that she would want to empower them, and also that she would keep that from him. As vulnerable as they'd been together, he knew there were parts of her that she wanted to keep to herself.

She seemed to sense his gaze upon her, because she glanced at him side-eyed and her cheeks flushed. "I can come back in a few days for our first lesson," she told Privya.

"I'd like to join," Killian chimed in. "If the women are comfortable with that."

Now Privya and Elyse regarded him, both sporting an expression of appreciation.

"It would be good for them to practice with someone who knows how to attack without hurting them. And then, Elyse, you can watch and instruct," he added. "Plus, I can get more practice on magical combat."

They had been practicing every morning out on the obstacle course, after waking up in Elyse's bed. He improved every day, but it was never enough. He hadn't experienced a challenge like this in nearly a decade, and he craved more practice, more difficult spells.

Elyse smiled at him, dropping her facade, and Privya said, "That sounds like an acceptable suggestion."

Elyse walked the few steps toward Killian and slid her hand into his, a sensation he never grew tired of. "We should be going," she said to Privya. After a pause, she added, "Thank you. Sincerely."

Killian studied Elyse's expression and saw soft eyes saturated with gratitude, and he squeezed her hand. He sensed that Privya had done more for her, had healed something internally for Elyse, or at least had begun to, the same way she had tried encouraging his own journey of healing, one that he hadn't been ready to embark on.

No, it would take a feisty, silver-haired witch to help heal those wounds.

Privya gave one last nod before Elyse whisked them away.

CHAPTER 52

— : —

KILLIAN

The next day, marching through the palace halls with Elyse in tow, Killian was still riding the high of setting Nina free. Nina's timid smile, the flash of her new teeth, played endlessly in his mind. And Privya . . . He hadn't realized the surge of emotions that would come along with seeing her. Being in her presence again had felt renewing—healing, even, he noted, the irony not escaping him.

Elyse seemed rejuvenated as well. She walked beside him, a slight spring in her step, even after their particularly grueling training session that morning. And they'd hardly gotten any sleep last night as their lips had roved over each other's bodies, their hands eager to caress and explore as the excitement of the day lingered in their veins. Elyse hadn't invited him to fully consummate their feelings yet, and, true to his word, Killian hadn't pushed her. He would let her take whatever time she needed to move to that next stage—though, gods help him, his years of training had done nothing to prepare him for the amount of sheer willpower it took to control himself around her. Especially sharing a bed with her every night, with nothing but a thin, cotton shift covering her skin . . .

Killian blinked a few times to clear the thought from his mind. He would need to keep his wits about him during this meeting, and maintain a professional air.

Yet one glance at Elyse, her dark eyes mirroring his own mischief, and he knew that professionalism would be a far reach for both of them.

They rounded a corner, their footsteps silent on the plush carpets lining the stone corridors of the palace, and stopped before an oak door. Killian took a deep breath, steeling himself and drawing upon the lingering bliss from yesterday's adventure, and pushed open the door without bothering to knock.

The office was four times as large as Killian's, a grand oak desk in the center with several tufted armchairs about. Manny leaned against the wall, arms crossed, his expression conveying his unchecked annoyance. Seated behind the desk in a gaudy, high-backed chair was the denizen of the office himself—Longfellow.

Killian drew upon his prevailing satisfaction as he beheld Longfellow's miserable face. The magistrate had requested an audience with Elyse to go over more details about Royce's arrest, a request that Killian and Manny had both protested. During the last week, it had seemed more like Longfellow was looking for ways to acquit Royce rather than condemn him. The fucking coward. Killian wanted to hold his dagger to Longfellow's throat and force him to write out a new arrest warrant. If this interview with Elyse went poorly, he might do just that.

Longfellow nodded toward Killian, who didn't return the gesture, instead keeping his expression stoic. He noted the way the magistrate's attention roamed to Elyse, lust and distaste mingling in his gaze as he looked her up and down.

"Good," Manny said, arms still crossed as he swaggered to a chair and plopped himself into it. "Now we can get this over with."

Killian gestured for Elyse to take a seat in front of the desk, and seated himself beside her. Instinctually, he reached a hand toward hers, his fingers eager to unite with hers as they so often did, but he remembered his whereabouts and folded his hands in his lap instead.

The movement, however small, did not go unnoticed by Longfellow. The corner of his lips twitched as he said, "We'll be going over the events of the night you procured the evidence from Royce's estate, just to make sure there are no . . . snags."

Elyse didn't miss a beat. "No, thank *you* for having me here today," she said, her voice sugary sweet with sarcasm. "I am at the crown's disposal."

Longfellow's lip curled in the other direction, toward a snarl, and pride welled up inside of Killian. His snarky little witch.

Longfellow swallowed pointedly, as if choking on his own incivility, and continued, "Please go over the events of the evening, in your own words."

The faux pleasantries dissipated from Elyse's voice as she began recounting the night of the party in such militaristic precision that Killian could barely contain the desire burning within him. Bless his soul, either he really needed to release some pent-up sexual energy, or he was incredibly aroused by Elyse's neurotic attention to detail. Perhaps both.

Killian forced his breathing to stay neutral as Elyse explained how Royce had sought her out at the party. Her voice never faltered as she conjured a lie that Killian had feared for her safety and escorted her back to the grand hall, skipping over any mention of their mischief.

Longfellow scribbled down notes as Elyse spoke, his face unreadable. Surprisingly, he didn't interrupt her, but waited until she had finished completely before leaning forward to rest his elbows on his desk, his forefingers pressed against his chin.

"I need to be entirely certain," he began, his eyes narrowing on Elyse, "that you did not plant this evidence in Royce's home."

Killian had to fight from rolling his eyes, and though he couldn't see Manny, he knew he was doing the same. "We've been over this," Killian grumbled. "We have no reason to frame him." It was forbidden to use magic like truth serums in a court of law, and for decades Killian had been grateful for that sort of legislation. It had always seemed barbaric and unreliable. These days, however, he found himself wishing—just this once—that they could bend the rules.

"If that's the case, then everything you say will be airtight," Longfellow parried.

Killian glanced at Elyse, who gave him a subtle but purposeful blink. *I'm fine*, she seemed to convey. *Let's just get on with it.* He relaxed ever so slightly in his chair and gestured for Longfellow to continue.

"What were you wearing?" the magistrate asked flatly.

Elyse didn't blanch. "An evening gown, of course."

"Describe it," he demanded. "Long? Short? Revealing? Tight or loose?"

Killian scoffed—loudly. "You're kidding, right?"

Longfellow looked at him with calm accented by amusement. "Not at all. If she did smuggle in the ingredients, her dress would be the most likely place to hide such things."

"You didn't ask us what we were wearing," Killian retorted, not bothering to mask his disgust. He had no doubt that Longfellow's questions were more for his own perverse curiosity than for any investigative purposes.

"You are esteemed members of the Royal Guard, and therefore above planting evidence," Longfellow said. "*She*," he continued with a sneer, "is an occultist."

Killian was about to protest further when Elyse laid a soothing hand on his arm. She stared Longfellow dead in the eyes as she said, "I wore a floor-length gown, tight through the bodice but loose below the knees. Short sleeves with elbow-length gloves. I wore no undergarments. Oh, and I carried a small clutch."

Killian nearly choked on his own spit at Elyse's taunting words, and Longfellow's hand faltered as it scrambled to take notes. Killian didn't dare glance at Manny and risk seeing his curious expression at whether or not Elyse's description was indeed true.

Longfellow cleared his throat. "The contents of the clutch?"

Elyse recited the cosmetics she had carried with her, along with the small amount of coin, then added, "I did trip and lose the contents of the purse, but everything was recovered except for a small vial of transportation potion."

"How big was the purse?"

Elyse held out her hands to display the rough size of the bag. Longfellow studied it.

"Too small to hold the ingredients," Manny chimed in from the corner.

Longfellow glared at Manny as he said, "Was this clutch magically enhanced? Either able to contain more than it appears to, or perhaps a sort of . . . portal that allows you to store things elsewhere?"

Heaven save him. Normally Killian would appreciate such thorough questioning, but the accusatory way that Longfellow spat each word at Elyse had his blood simmering.

"No," Elyse stated, apparently unfazed. "I can produce it for you if you like."

Longfellow simply nodded before diving into his next line of questioning. Elyse answered each of his inquiries without batting an eye, no matter how demeaning. Yet each thinly veiled insult Longfellow hurled at her made Killian want to ring the magistrate's neck. Instead, he smoldered in his seat, fists clenched in his lap.

"How do we know that the ingredients you obtained are what you say they are?" Longfellow sneered.

"They were labeled as such," Manny answered with a sigh. "I swore to it in my report."

"Yes, but labels can be manipulated," the magistrate retorted.

Killian swallowed his anger.

"I can feel it," Elyse explained calmly. "It's sort of intrinsic. I can tell an item's veracity from the power it emits. But there are spells to confirm the authenticity of an ingredient. I can perform them for you."

"No," Longfellow said with a cold, leering gaze. "We will have someone *else* perform the spell. You are already too close to this investigation as it is." His narrowed eyes shifted toward Killian and then back to Elyse.

"Is there something you want to say?" Killian growled, carefully punctuating each syllable.

Longfellow smiled, slow and cruel, the same smile he'd plastered on his face when regarding Nina. He met Killian's glare and spoke of Elyse as if she weren't sitting three feet before him. "It is odd that she has gotten so involved in this case, is it not?"

Killian felt his nostrils flare the tiniest bit—the only hint of his irritation that he would relinquish. "Not at all. We collaborate with civilians all the time."

"That is true," Longfellow said as he smugly reclined in his oversized chair. "But these civilians are usually upstanding citizens, not witchlings."

To her credit, Elyse showed only mere boredom, no signs of outrage or offense.

"She is an expert in her field, much like other experts we've called upon, and her assistance has been invaluable," Killian replied coolly.

"Yes, an expert in her field," Longfellow said, savoring each word. "And one of the few powerful enough to cast the spell used to assassinate the king, and with access to the ingredients."

Professionalism be damned. Killian shot out of his chair and reached for his dagger, but a hand yanked him back down—a delicate hand that held more power than it appeared to. Killian looked toward his arm to find Elyse's pale fingers wrapped around his sleeve. He glanced at her face, and her dark eyes met his.

Don't, she seemed to say. Not a command, but a reminder. *Do not stoop to his level.*

Killian took a deep breath, then another as he regarded Longfellow and the amusement glimmering in his eyes. Another time, he'd make the bastard pay.

With renewed calm, Killian said, "She swore to her innocence under the effects of truth serum."

"Aye," Manny confirmed. "I witnessed it as well."

292

Longfellow merely arched a brow and glanced between Elyse and Killian. "Then perhaps something else motivates her to see Royce hanged. Perhaps she wants to see her lover successful, renowned even. The lieutenant who caught the king's assassin." With a wicked snarl he added, "Witches can be greedy like that."

In a flash, Killian's dagger went from being sheathed at his hip to being planted in Longfellow's desk. The whole room was tense, still, except for Longfellow's trembling hand, which rested a mere half-inch from the dagger's point.

Still seated but leaning toward the magistrate, Killian seethed, "We're done here. Arrest Royce—again."

Then he stood, yanked his dagger from the desk, offered a hand to Elyse, and guided her out the door. He didn't look back at Longfellow, lest he lose his temper further.

Manny followed them out to the corridor and shut the door behind him. Killian had no words, so he simply nodded goodbye toward his friend. Manny's gaze lingered on Elyse for a moment too long.

Just . . . be careful, Manny's warning echoed in his mind.

It was all Killian could do to grab Elyse's hand and march her out of the palace.

CHAPTER 53

— : —

ELYSE

E lyse stared down at the lunar calendar that lay open on the massive worktable.

Three days. Three days until the full moon.

Where had the time gone?

She knew exactly where the time had gone. She'd trained every morning with Killian on the obstacle course, and she'd met with Corin and a handful of other girls for training a few times now. She'd also gone with Killian to have dinner with his mother and Georgie, and had enjoyed going to the market with Killian on sunny mornings.

And perhaps she'd been in denial too, content to pretend that time wasn't dwindling away. Accepting the inevitability of the full moon meant facing the truth. The truth that she was the assassin Killian sought—the bold yet accurate claim Longfellow had made days earlier.

And beyond that, it meant accepting what she was. A witch and a murderer. Unworthy of her courageous, upstanding lieutenant.

No, she told herself. *Not unworthy. I don't have a choice in what Lazarus makes me do, but I do have a choice in other matters. And I choose to do good.*

I choose to do good. That had been her mantra ever since leaving Privya's clinic, what had driven her to free Nina, to teach Corin and the others, to help Killian look after his mother and Georgie.

But with the full moon only three days away, it felt like an eternity of good deeds would never outweigh her crimes.

The door to the Emporium opened and Elyse looked up. A smile spread across her face as Killian entered the shoppe.

"I thought I'd come say hello," he called to her, his expression mirroring hers.

"You certainly are taking advantage of those transportation potions I gave you," she replied with a smirk.

Killian only shrugged innocently. So far—he had come so far from the man who hated everything magical, all because of the trust they'd built together.

The trust she abused.

She must have made a face, because Killian's brows furrowed. "What is it?" he asked.

"Oh nothing," Elyse said, waving her hand. "I'm just tired. Someone's been keeping me up all night." She closed the space between them and wrapped her arms around his waist, savoring the muscles beneath his black uniform.

Killian bent down to kiss her. His lips were gentle, but his hands slid to her backside, squeezing and pulling her against him.

Elyse giggled against his skin. Devil's horns, when was the last time she'd giggled before meeting Killian?

"You're in a good mood," she muttered.

She could feel his lips curling into a smile against hers.

"I keep thinking about you calmly telling Longfellow that you weren't wearing any undergarments," he said, a guttural hunger to his voice that made Elyse's toes clench inside her boots.

She had very much enjoyed staying cool under Longfellow's penetrating gaze, never rising to give him the reaction he yearned for. She had also very much enjoyed the flash of danger that burned in Killian's eyes as he stabbed his knife into the desk a finger's width away from Longfellow's hand.

She leaned in closer to Killian, treasuring the way his hard body felt against hers, the muscles that could cause damage in her name.

"I thought you might have enjoyed that," she murmured against his ear. His ensuing shudder made her chest constrict as happiness surged through her, and she kissed him, wholeheartedly.

But the moment was short lived.

"Before I forget," Killian began, breaking away from her.

Elyse groaned.

"Was that a groan from my cold-hearted witch?" he asked with far too much amusement in his deep voice.

Elyse leveled a glare at him. "Maybe."

"I'll be quick then, so we can get back to kissing," he whispered in her ear. "Longfellow wants to re-interview everyone at the palace," he continued. "He told me to pick a day to conduct the majority of them. It will probably go late into the evening, so Manny suggested three days from now, as that's the full moon and you and Sera will be out doing your ritual anyway."

Elyse's body went rigid. She swallowed down the bile-tasting guilt that coated her throat. "Okay," was all she managed to say.

"Although, Manny first suggested that we find out where you hold this secret-naked-dance-ritual, and spy on you. But don't worry—I set him straight."

Killian's smile, delightfully mischievous as it was, could not quell Elyse's overwhelming contrition.

It was bad enough, terrible really, that she was lying to Killian. But she had forgotten that Sera was her alibi. The guilt was leaden, pressing her down into the old wooden planks of the shoppe's floor, as she thought about the implications of having involved Sera in her lies. Was Sera feeling a similar guilt? Would her actions cause a rift between her friend and her new lover? Did Sera suspect the truth—that Elyse was, in fact, the king's murderer?

Elyse was spared from her rumination as the door to the Emporium opened again, and an elderly man hobbled across the threshold.

"Mr. Grayson," Elyse called to him as she took a step back from Killian, breaking their embrace.

Mr. Grayson's eyes twinkled as he took in Killian, then Elyse, who refused to blush.

"Hello, my dear Miss Crenshaw," the old man crooned, and Elyse smiled. He was the only one who could call her "Miss Crenshaw" without boiling her blood. Perhaps it was because he was just too damn old to be corrected—or because he tipped generously.

"And who is your friend?" Mr. Grayson asked expectantly, the way that older people always seemed to do. Gods forbid they *weren't* introduced to someone.

Elyse cleared her throat and said proudly, taking Killian's hand in her own, "This is Lieutenant Killian Southwick of the Royal Guard."

Mr. Grayson stood upright—as much as his ancient, crooked back would allow—and saluted Killian. Graceful as ever, Killian nodded his head in supplication.

"I think he's the first man I've ever seen in here—besides myself, of course," Mr. Grayson said with a wink toward Killian.

Elyse just rolled her eyes, though she smiled. "You talk too much, old man."

"Some might say you don't talk enough," Mr. Grayson replied, pointing a wrinkled finger at her.

She simply waved him off. "Do you want your supplies or not?"

"Yes, yes," Mr. Grayson grumbled, though he smiled as well. "I need them if I'm to live to see my 154th birthday, don't I?"

Elyse snapped her fingers, and a large basket appeared on the worktable, stuffed with various items.

Killian hardly glanced at the basket, his attention trained on Mr. Grayson. "I'm sorry, did you say your 154th birthday?"

Mr. Grayson only looked to Elyse as he gestured his thumb toward Killian. "I'm the old one, but he's hard of hearing, eh?"

"Yes, but he's handsome," Elyse replied, shooting Killian a sensual look. "It makes up for it."

Killian just glanced between them and smiled.

Mr. Grayson took a few labored steps toward the worktable and the basket. "It's all there?" he asked. "One pint of liquid gold, four black cat skulls, half a pound of stardust—"

"Three viper fangs, two everroot bulbs, and a gallon of blood," Elyse continued for him. "It's the same every month, old man. It's all here."

"Some things never change, my dear," Mr. Grayson replied. Then he gave Killian an impish smile. "And some things do."

The innuendo did not go unnoticed by Elyse, and this time she could not stave off the heat that warmed her face.

"Let's get you out of here," she told Mr. Grayson. Just as she was about to beckon toward the basket and magick it outside to Mr. Grayson's wagon, where it was no doubt parked in the same place it was every month, Killian swooped in and lifted the basket like it merely held pillows.

"You don't need to do that," Elyse began to chide him, but his charming smile melted the words from her tongue.

"What's wrong with the old-fashioned way?" he asked, then gestured his chin toward the door. "After you, Mr. Grayson."

Elyse's knees practically buckled at Killian's unwavering chivalry.

Mr. Grayson took his time hobbling toward the exit, but Killian didn't seem bothered, even though Elyse knew the basket was heavy. A gallon of blood alone was not fun to carry.

Finally, the three of them made it outside, and Killian loaded the basket into the wagon with ease.

"If I don't see you again, have a wonderful 154th birthday, Mr. Grayson," Killian said as he extended his hand toward the old man.

"Thank you," Mr. Grayson replied warmly as he took Killian's hand in both of his. "Hopefully this will be the year my experimentation pays off!"

Killian glanced toward Elyse, and she shot him a look that said, "Don't ask," but he pressed anyway.

"What experimentation would that be?"

Mr. Grayson's face lit up—making him look more like a man of only a hundred years. "Necromancy!" he proclaimed with vigor.

Killian furrowed his brows and tilted his head, which Mr. Grayson apparently found funny.

"Explain it to him, will ya?" he hollered to Elyse before climbing up into his wagon.

"Of course, Mr. Grayson," Elyse said, waving goodbye. "I'll see you next month."

When he had disappeared down the road behind a cloud of dust, Killian asked, "Necromancy?"

Elyse took his hand and led him back toward the shoppe. "Raising the dead," she explained. "His wife passed away when they were young. He's been trying to bring her back ever since."

Killian was quiet for a moment as he pondered, then said, "That's sweet. Eerie, but sweet."

Elyse nodded. She'd always considered Mr. Grayson a sap and a hopeless romantic, someone to be pitied. That was before she'd met Killian.

She drew close to Killian again, wishing to draw strength from him. She knew she needed to tell him the truth. And she knew he would probably hate her for it. But until she found the right moment to tell him, she would savor every moment with him, her charming lieutenant.

She pressed her lips to his, reveling in the sweetness of his kiss, the power he held in every muscle of his body. Her tongue slid against the seam of his lips, and he welcomed her in, pulling her closer to him. Unable to stop herself, Elyse roved her hand down his firm chest, across his chiseled stomach, and finally down to his trousers.

When they eventually broke away, he smirked. "What's gotten into you? You're supposed to be working. Don't you need to—I don't know—sweep?" he teased. "Take inventory? Write down the sale in the ledger?"

Elyse shook her head, then took him by the hand and guided him toward the worktable where the ledger was splayed open. "No, the book is enchanted to do all that on its own," she explained. She slid her forefinger down the page, stopping at the final entry. "See?" She pointed to the scrambled letters that she could easily read, knowing that Killian would see it as an entirely foreign language. "'One pint of liquid gold, four black cat skulls, half a pound of stardust,'" she recited.

Killian stood behind her, hands wrapped around her waist, peering over her shoulder. He growled in her ear. "Your exquisite organization turns me on," he purred, and she laughed, though she knew he meant it.

"Wait until you see this," she said in her most seductive voice as she thumbed to the back of the book. "It takes inventory too."

"You drive me wild," he groaned.

She laughed again and turned around to face him, their chests pressing hard against one another. Killian's full lips were spread in an immense grin, a wicked gleam in his brown eyes.

Yes, she would savor every moment she had left with her lieutenant.

He lifted her up onto the worktable and kissed her deeply. A gasp escaped Elyse as Killian's lips roamed across her cheek, down to her neck. He flicked his tongue across her skin, sending shivers through her entire body.

Without even realizing what she was doing, her hands made their way to the waist of his trousers. Her fingers grazed the skin of his abdomen, itching to reach further south. Killian's heavy breaths let her know that he wanted the same thing.

He returned his lips to hers, and Elyse nibbled at his bottom lip as she threaded her hands through his hair. Killian let out a soft growl as he lifted a hand and cupped her breast. It wasn't enough, though. As their kissing intensified, Elyse wanted more. She lifted her chest higher, a silent plea, and Killian obeyed as he slipped his hand inside her tunic. His thumb caressed her nipple in slow, tantalizing circles, coaxing a moan from Elyse.

She knew she should stop before things went any further. The longer she kissed him, the more she endured his seductive touch, the harder it was for her to stop. She wasn't ready to cross that bridge with him yet. Not as long as the truth was a barrier between them.

Despite all that, she scooted to the edge of the work table, wrapping her legs around him and pulling him closer. She could feel his desire pressing against her, hard and throbbing. Maybe she could touch it—just this once. What was the harm in that?

She slid her hands from his hair and down his neck, pausing to appreciate his sculpted shoulders. Killian's free hand moved to her waist as the other continued to caress her nipple. Elyse's hands slowly moved down his back, inching their way closer to his hips, toward the muscles just above the band of his trousers—

The bell to the shoppe rang out.

"Ms. Crenshaw, I—oh my . . ."

Elyse immediately broke away, dropping her hands to her side. It took Killian a moment longer to snap out of his ardor as he let out a shuddering breath. But Elyse was already shoving him away.

Mr. Grayson stood just inside the doorway, a rogue grin on his face. "Sorry to interrupt, my dear."

Elyse cleared her throat, forbidding herself from acting embarrassed. "Was there something else you needed?" she asked, trying her best to keep her voice even.

Killian stood awkwardly beside the worktable, his hands folded in front of his pants—no doubt hiding the evidence of their frivolity.

Mr. Grayson's eyes seemed to sparkle with amusement at their predicament. "Yes, it seems I was distracted by your charming lieutenant, as were you," he said, reaching for his coin purse. "I forgot to pay you."

"Oh," Elyse said as blood rushed to her cheeks. How could she have been so foolish to forget something so important? She hurried to Mr. Grayson and took the coin purse he offered. "Thank you."

"You're very welcome, deary," he said with a wink. As he turned to leave, he added, "And might I suggest locking the door next time?"

Again, Elyse cleared her throat. "I'll be sure to do that," she said clumsily. "Take care now."

Mr. Grayson just waved a hand before disappearing out the door.

Elyse turned to Killian, her eyes wide, disbelief and embarrassment pouring from her. Killian returned the look.

Then they both burst into laughter.

"It could have been worse," Killian chuckled, adjusting his trousers. "At least he seemed understanding."

Elyse smiled and crossed the shoppe to lean against the worktable. Yes, it could have been much worse. It could have been someone else. Or Mr. Grayson might not have shown up at all, and Elyse would have made an irreversible decision. She had been careening toward doing something regrettable with Killian, something she knew she shouldn't.

But the moment was past, and now she could think clearly again. She needed to avoid going down that path with him—it was obviously too difficult to stop herself.

Killian rubbed his hand on the back of his neck, looking down at Elyse through his dark lashes. "I should be getting back to the palace anyway," he said sheepishly.

"Okay," Elyse said, planting a kiss on his cheek. As much as she wanted him to stay and keep her company, she was also grateful that he hadn't wanted to resume what they had started. "I'll see you tonight?"

Killian touched a hand to her cheek, taking a moment to stare into her eyes. "I'll see you tonight," he whispered back, before he turned and left the shoppe.

CHAPTER 54

—— : ——

ELYSE

The setting sun draped the city in rosy pinks, delicate lavender, and simmering oranges as Killian and Elyse walked hand in hand through its streets. Though the sun had not yet tucked itself beyond the horizon, Elyse could still spot the moon overhead. Not quite full—only the thinnest sliver was missing. But tomorrow night, then it would be whole.

She had resolved to end things with Killian tonight. After all, there was no future for them. She couldn't tell him she had killed King Cyril, or else she'd be captured and executed, and she couldn't continue seeing him with this lie hanging over her head.

Her every nerve was on edge, her stomach churning. She wondered if Killian noticed just how clammy her hands were, despite the refreshing evening breeze. She couldn't even bring herself to glance at him.

She'd recited hundreds of ways to break things off, none of which seemed right. Should she tell him she didn't have feelings for him? Tell him she was moving away? Should she actually move away? The rabbit hole of her mind was endless and frazzled, one gut-wrenching idea after another.

"Ah-choo!" Killian doubled over as a violent sneeze tore out of him.

Elyse couldn't help but stare wide-eyed as the lieutenant batted his hazy eyes and sniffled. "That was quite the production," she mused, forcing herself to sound more lighthearted than she felt.

Killian didn't release her hand as he pulled a handkerchief from his trousers and wiped his nose. "Ungh—it's been like this all day." He sniffled a few more times, enough that Elyse actually felt bad for him. "It's allergies. The pollen is horrible."

Indeed, over the past few days the trees had dusted the entire city with a smattering of pale yellow pollen. Elyse had always found it somewhat entrancing, the same way a layer of snow appears lovely and mystical across the city. To Killian, though, it apparently meant sneezing and watery eyes.

"Well, let's get you indoors right away," she said as she led him down an alleyway. It was probably for the best anyway. The sooner she got him inside, the sooner she could end things.

Mere moments later they were poised just outside the wards surrounding her cottage. Killian continued to sneeze and wheeze all the way through the woods while Elyse steeled herself for what was to come.

"It's no better in the palace," Killian explained. "Guards and servants track in pollen all day. I may as well have my office in the middle of the—*ah-choo!*—forest."

Elyse could now see the cottage up ahead, the small building looming over her, every step bringing her closer to the end. She tried reminding herself that she was doing the right thing, that this was for the best, but the impending heartbreak made it hard to breathe.

She cleared her throat. "Sera has allergies too," she said, trying to sound unnerved. "She grows a special herb herself that she adds to tea. You might see about getting some from her."

Killian just sniffled and nodded his head.

Despite his evident distress, he hurried ahead to hold open the door for Elyse as they entered the cottage. She would miss these little acts of chivalry.

Killian plopped himself into one of the arm chairs in the shoppe and rubbed his temples, and Elyse busied herself with tidying up. She had never had a difficult conversation like this before. Should she just come out and say it? Was there some way to segue into the discussion? She wiped her sweaty palms on her leggings, and tried to still her fidgeting.

Eventually Killian leaned back, a clarity returning to his eyes. "How was your day?" he asked.

"Busy," Elyse sighed. "Everyone comes in for last minute supplies before the full moon."

"Let me help you then," Killian insisted as he stood from the chair.

Elyse just waved her hand. "No, you're not feeling well. Besides, if I really wanted to, I'd just enchant the place to clean itself."

She snapped her fingers, and the broom twitched upright from where it leaned against the wall in the corner of the shop. It began swishing back and forth, coaxing the dust on the floor toward the door.

Killian watched the enchanted broom for a few moments with an amused smile. Then he shifted his attention to Elyse, tilting his head with curiosity in his gaze. "So why didn't you just make the place magically clean itself?"

Elyse couldn't bring herself to look him in the eyes—those golden, riveting eyes. "I don't know," she said with a shrug. "Sometimes doing things like sweeping and tidying up makes me feel more . . . normal."

She could feel his eyes on her, studying her. Did he, too, wish to feel normal sometimes?

He stood from the chair, and Elyse finally looked toward him as he closed the space between them. She knew she should pull away, that she shouldn't let him touch her, but she couldn't bring herself to move. She could feel his warm breath against her skin, could see the flutter of his heartbeat in his throat. He touched one hand to her upper arm, caressing it with smooth strokes. Then he gripped it gently and pulled her closer so their chests were touching. His head was still tilted, his lips the perfect angle for kissing. Memories of their antics a few days ago surged through

Elyse, warming her core. A glimmer in Killian's eyes told her he was thinking the same thing.

She needed to remember her plan. It was now or never. Yet it was hard to think with Killian's lips so close to her own, that strong jawline and the dimpled cheeks that drove her wild.

"There's . . . something I've been wanting to tell you," she breathed, forcing herself to stay grounded. It was like removing a splinter. It would hurt, but it was best to just do it.

Killian stilled, though he didn't back away. His eyes softened as he said, "You can tell me anything."

Oh, if only that were true.

Say it. Say it! she commanded herself, though no words came forth.

When she didn't speak, Killian lifted a hand to her face and stroked his thumb along her jaw, as if coaxing the words out.

"What is it?" he asked.

But Elyse didn't hear him. All she knew was the feeling of his thumb caressing her cheek, his other fingers firmly pressed against her face. Those same deft fingers that had been her undoing twice now. It had taken everything in her the other day to refrain from telling him to remove his trousers, to demand that he claim her, body and soul. But she knew that could never be. If they let themselves cross that line, let themselves experience that together, she knew it would only make the betrayal worse.

She had to tell him—now.

Killian's eyes were dark and liquid as he peered down at her, silently encouraging her to speak.

She couldn't do this. Couldn't lose him.

"I . . ." she began. But she didn't know what to say. She shook her head as she tried to turn away, but Killian held her arm firm.

"Elyse," he pleaded. "Just tell me."

All she could do was keep shaking her head as a lump formed in her throat.

Killian released her arm, and gently touched his fingers to her chin. He lifted her face to his, and she gazed up at him through her lashes.

"Then let me say something," he said, his voice soft but powerful.

Elyse knew whatever he was about to say, it would destroy her entire plan. Yet she was helpless to do anything but stare up at him, eagerly awaiting his words.

"You are the strongest, most fierce woman I have ever met," he began. "I need you to know that you take my breath away every moment of every day. My heart is completely yours."

Elyse's chest tightened as she leaned in closer to him, entranced by his confession. Her eyes searched his, and she found nothing but sincerity.

"I know that you're broken," he continued. "I see the pain in your eyes when you think no one's looking. But I'm always looking at you, Elyse. I know that you don't need a man's help, or anyone's help for that matter, but please—let me heal you. Whatever you need, let me be that for you, the way you have for me."

She couldn't breathe. No one had ever spoken to her like that before. And to hear it from Killian? Her heart seized, begging her to reach out for him, to kiss him, to give him everything.

"I'm falling in love with you."

The words escaped before she even realized she'd said them. She'd never even confessed that to herself, but as she spoke them aloud, she knew it to be true—knew in her heart what this feeling was.

Killian's reply was a song that filled her soul, a smile that melted her core. "I'm falling in love with you too."

She had failed. She had failed and yet those words were the sweetest victory, an unleashing of a part of herself she hadn't known was confined. Her lips joined his, hungry and desperate, and her fingers wound their way into his magnificent curly hair.

He met her with equal enthusiasm, devouring her with his lips and hands, their bodies writhing against one another. His tongue moved against hers, delicious and seductive, and she moaned, soft and yearning.

Apparently the small sound was too much for Killian, as she felt him grow hard against her. He lifted her into his arms, and she wrapped her legs around his waist. Their kiss deepened as they pressed themselves against one another, desperate to eliminate all space between them.

Elyse pulled her lips away and stared into Killian's eyes, which were dark with desire. She knew somewhere in her core that it wasn't too late. She could still end things; she could still let him walk away. Yet the way that he looked at her, as if she were everything he had ever needed to mend his broken self, as if he wanted to spend the rest of his life making her feel like she was worthy of love—she could never let go of that.

An unspoken message passed between them, a silent entreaty for more. Killian moved slowly, carrying her through the shoppe with leisurely steps. He was taunting her. Teasing her. She dug her nails into his shoulders, a plea for him to move faster, but he only smiled at her, never breaking eye contact.

As he ascended the stairs, their quivering breaths melted together into a melody of anticipation. Every step had Elyse's nerves dancing on edge, screaming for Killian's touch.

Finally, they reached the bedroom, and he lay her down on the bed. Their clothes—they were too much. Elyse was about to wave her hand to magick them bare, but Killian caught her wrist and gave her a pointed look.

Slowly—so damned slowly—he began to unbutton her tunic, savoring every inch of freed skin with a languid kiss. This mixture of cool air and warm breath on her skin was intoxicating as he moved from her collar bone, between her breasts, down to her navel.

When the last button was undone, Elyse shirked off her tunic, but Killian took his time. First with his eyes, lustful as they took her in. Then with his hands, warm against her breasts. Then with his tongue, his teeth, teasing her nipples. Elyse arched her back, her body pleading with him to keep going.

So he did, lazily tracing the waist of her leggings, then dipping one finger beneath the band and drawing tantalizing lines across her lower abdomen. He lowered himself over her and planted his lips on hers, making her breath catch. She could feel him getting harder with every flick of her tongue against his.

Killian dragged his lips across her cheek, up to her ear. "Say it," he murmured, his voice drenched in demand. "Tell me what you want."

Elyse's hand tightened where it gripped his shirt. If there had been any doubt in her mind about what she wanted from him, it vanished as soon as she heard the guttural command in his voice. "I want you," she rasped. "I want all of you."

Killian grazed her earlobe with his teeth.

Elyse stifled her gasp. "I want to give you all of me," she moaned.

And she meant it, every word. She wanted to irreversibly entwine their souls, to cross that threshold, together as one. She wanted to feel him inside her, the greatest pleasure that she could imagine, and know that he, too, received his pleasure from her, and her alone.

Killian kissed her once more, this time on the lips, then lifted his head. "I want that too," he murmured, a clarity in his eyes that enlivened Elyse.

With both hands on his shoulders, she pulled him closer, her body aching to feel his. Killian no longer bothered with teasing. He tore off his own tunic, and heat rippled through Elyse as she took in the body that never ceased to awe her. Her hands roved over his pectorals, his chiseled stomach, even the gnarled scar, as their lips crashed against one another's.

"Do it," Killian growled, barely taking his lips away from hers.

Elyse needed no further instruction. She snapped her fingers, and their clothes disappeared from their bodies. His member pressed against her thigh, solid and massive, and she let out a purely wicked gasp as she imagined it plunging inside of her.

Killian's hand found its way to her hip, then between her legs, which she eagerly spread for him. He groaned as he explored her with his fingers, and he lowered his head to her neck.

"Fuck," he rumbled, and Elyse knew why. She could feel the moisture collecting between her legs, the physical embodiment of how badly she needed him.

His finger surged in deeper, and he added another one. Devil's tongue, he knew how to work her. Elyse writhed on the bed, toes curling, as Killian's fingers moved faster and faster. His other hand reached for her hair, gripping tight and pulling her closer to him. *Fuck*, every movement was hypnotic.

She braced a hand on his hip. "Please," she sighed, barely able to convey her request. She couldn't wait one moment longer to have him. She wanted him now and forever, all the time. She wanted to lose herself in him completely, to be reborn as someone new, someone worthy of this mighty man atop her.

Killian removed his fingers, and Elyse immediately hated the absence of him inside her. But he positioned himself between her legs and cupped her neck in one hand.

Slowly, he worked his way inside her, each thrust deeper and more pleasurable than the last. Their bodies moved together, as if anticipating each other's needs. He pounded inside her, faster and harder, desire alive in his eyes. Elyse could barely contain her own desire. Her heart thundered in her chest with lust, with adoration, with fulfillment. She cried out again and again, which only seemed to stoke Killian's passion. He grasped onto her shoulder, and his hips smacked against her thighs as every inch of him made its way inside her.

Elyse could feel her release building. Her gaze moved down, and she watched him entering her over and over, the sight making her shudder with delight.

Killian raised one of her knees up closer to her shoulder, and Elyse let out a fierce cry as the new angle brought her climax within reach. She found Killian's hand and entwined their fingers. He gripped her hand firmly in his as he thrusted relentlessly, until pleasure raked through her body.

The utter bliss seemed like it would never end as Killian kept moving inside her. Shudders continued to wrack her body, and Killian's eyes darkened as he watched her writhe beneath him. Elyse clutched onto his shoulders, grasping for reality, her nails digging deep into his skin.

With one final surge, Killian met his release, and Elyse went over that edge one last time as she felt his warmth inside her.

Still entwined and breathing heavily, Killian rested his forehead against hers. Their gazes remained locked on one another as they reveled in their shared euphoria.

"That was . . ." Killian began, his breathing still heavy. But he never finished the sentence, and Elyse understood why. There were no words to describe what they had just felt.

"I know," Elyse agreed in a trembling voice. She kissed him, wholly giving herself over to the satisfaction she felt. She was determined to never feel anything else. With smooth deliberation, she climbed on top of him, her legs straddling his hips. Killian's hands gripped her backside, and he let out a shaky exhale that made Elyse smile wickedly. It was her turn to taunt him.

She moved slowly against him, rocking her hips back and forth as she kissed him. With each gyration she felt him growing harder against her, and he gripped her tighter, coaxing her hips to move faster.

"Again?" he asked. His tone was mocking, but the gleam in his eyes was roguish. He wanted it too.

"Again," Elyse confirmed as she slid him inside herself. If she was going to go down this path, she would at least enjoy every second of it.

CHAPTER 55

— · —

KILLIAN

When Killian awoke, naked and beside Elyse, one arm draped around her bare torso, he smiled. As he recalled their lovemaking the prior night, his smile widened. Being with her had been more exhilarating than he could have imagined. A tension had eased in his stomach—a tension he'd felt for two decades. Perhaps a small part of him, a part that had been torn away along with his brother and sister, was beginning to heal.

His smile remained as Elyse stirred, and she rolled over and kissed him. It remained as they snuggled together well into the morning, their hearts beating in unison. It remained when they finally meandered out of bed, donned their clothes, and headed downstairs. It even remained as Elyse poured herself a mug of that putrid-smelling tea, the one she drank every morning. The playful smile stayed there on his lips as he and Elyse walked hand in hand through the forest toward the edge of the wards until—

Ah-choo!

It didn't take long for his allergies to start acting up again. He pulled the handkerchief from his pocket and wiped his nose.

"You should really stop by Sera's apartment and ask her for some of that herb," Elyse said. She paused while Killian blew forcefully into the handkerchief. "Especially if it's so bad inside the palace. You have all those interviews today."

Killian nodded, and then resumed smirking at Elyse. "Look at you, caring about me. If I didn't know any better, I'd say the wicked witch has a heart."

Elyse quickly looked away, training her focus on something in the distance. Killian squeezed her hand. He probably shouldn't have teased her, not after the courage it had clearly taken her to profess her feelings last night. He was glad that she'd said it, though, that she was falling in love with him. When she'd spoken the words, it felt as if some barrier between them had collapsed, and now they could be wholly themselves together.

But apparently Elyse wasn't ready to be so vulnerable together, and that was fine. He would give her all the time she needed. As he glanced at her, taking in her still-sleepy eyes and her silvery hair, he realized there was almost nothing he wouldn't do for her.

They continued their way to the edge of the wards in silence, with only the chirping of birds to accompany them. Each step away from the cottage had reality swooping down on him. Today would be a long day, full of tedious interviews and note-taking. He doubted that anything productive would come of these interviews. They'd already questioned everyone twice, some individuals even three times. It was just Longfellow's way of trying to avoid facing the inevitable—that Royce needed to face trial.

Yet if Killian wanted to get through the day without headaches and sneezing and sniffling, then Elyse was right. He should stop by Sera's apartment and see about those herbs.

They reached the edge of the wards and stopped, but Elyse still wouldn't meet his gaze. He touched her chin and lifted it, and she finally looked up at him, dark eyes peering through dark lashes. Admiration danced in those obsidian eyes, but also something else. Uncertainty, maybe—or fear.

He wanted to ask what was wrong, to assure her he would do whatever it took to wipe away any unease she felt, but the tightness of her lips told him she didn't want to talk about whatever it was. So instead, he said, "I'll come by tomorrow."

Elyse nodded. She didn't let go of his hand. Killian hesitated for a moment, then leaned down to kiss her lips.

To his relief, she kissed him back. She even stepped closer and placed a hand on his cheek. Their kiss deepened, and there was a longing in her lips that he'd never tasted before, as if she never wanted the kiss to end.

Finally, they both pulled away, and Elyse released his hand. He gave her one last smile, which she tentatively returned, before he pulled out a vial of transportation potion and smashed it onto the ground.

When the smoke cleared, he stood in the street just outside the door to Sera's building. Up and up he went, pacing himself as he ascended the twelve flights of stairs. He reached her apartment with the iridescent beads dangling in the doorway, and knocked on the frame of the door.

Sera popped her head through the cascade of beads a moment later. "Oh, Killian," she said, her voice sweet and lively. "Manny's already left . . ."

"I'm not here for Manny," Killian explained. "Elyse said that you grow a special herb for allergies, and—"

Sera held up a pale, manicured hand. "Say no more." She waved him in and gestured for him to sit at the large, round table.

How long had it been since he'd entered this very apartment to confirm Elyse's alibi? It felt like a lifetime ago, though it had truly been just under a month. He recalled his skepticism as he'd sat at the oversized table, in the same tufted chair where he sat now, and how irritated he'd been with the seer and her eccentrically decorated apartment. He'd thought himself exceedingly better than her, yet here he was, entreating her for a favor. She had never been anything but gracious to him, and to Manny. Guilt knotted his chest as he thought of how cold he had been toward her. He didn't want to be that contemptuous person anymore, who judged others and grumbled his way through each day.

Sera was busy with one of the potted plants on the windowsill, but she suddenly looked over her shoulder at him. "It's okay," she called, her purple eyes shining.

Killian stiffened, and then let out a laugh. She had known an apology was on the tip of his tongue. He shook his head and smiled at her.

"Thank you," he replied.

She turned back to the windowsill and plucked another leaf. "None of us have life figured out, not even seers," she said.

Then she crossed to the cupboard and pulled out a small burlap bag. She dumped a handful of leaves into the little sack, cinched it closed, and handed it to Killian.

"It's called yojabe. I've been growing it for years," she said. "I used to have to stay inside all spring, but this keeps the headaches at bay."

"And the sneezing?" Killian asked.

"And the sneezing," she happily confirmed. "I just add a leaf to my citronascia tea every morning, and the pollen doesn't bother me."

Killian wrinkled his nose. "You drink that awful tea, too?" Its stench still lingered in his nostrils from the mug Elyse had brewed that morning.

Sera laughed. "Of course I do. Everyone does—or at least everyone in the magic community does."

Killian shuddered at the thought. "*Why?* It smells terrible."

"It's an acquired taste," Sera said with a shrug. "But the benefits are worth it. It enhances your magical abilities and provides certain protections against basic hexes, truth serums, things like that."

Killian nodded—and then stopped. He stared straight ahead, unable to move, unable to breathe or think.

Truth serums. Elyse drank a tea every morning that protected her against truth serums.

It didn't matter—it shouldn't matter. Elyse was innocent, truth serum or not. Royce was the assassin responsible for the king's murder. Right?

Gods help him. What did this mean? His reality was shattering around him. Had his entire investigation—their entire relationship—been built on a lie?

Sera must have sensed something was wrong because she asked, "Are you all right?"

"Yeah," he said, shaking his head, though he was far from all right. Despite the open window, the apartment felt stifling, and his mind was frantic. "It's just a headache from the allergies."

"I can steep you a cup now, if you—" Sera began, but Killian cut her off.

"No," he declared as he stood. "Thank you, you've done enough." He needed to digest this new information, and Sera's apartment was not the place to do so. His feet were dragging him toward the door, and he could feel sweat gathering on his brow. "I need to get going, we have those interviews."

He reached the door but willed himself to turn toward Sera, to smile and seem normal, but he had no idea how to do that. His tongue was heavy, his throat dry, but he croaked out, "I'll see you."

He barely caught Sera's puzzled look before he bolted out the door and down all twelve flights of stairs.

CHAPTER 56

— · —

ELYSE

E lyse thought she was going to be ill.

Guilt clouded her vision, her heart and mind racing as she stormed back to the cottage on muscle memory alone.

She was so fucking stupid.

Stupid for not ending things with Killian.

Stupid for crossing that line with him.

Stupid for confessing she was falling in love.

Yet she didn't want to take any of it back.

She didn't want to go back to a time when she hadn't heard Killian say those words. To a time when she didn't know what it felt like to lie beneath him, to have him inside of her. To lose those precious minutes of being at peace.

The bright sky overhead, the chirping birds, they were all a mockery of her desperation. Elyse reached the Emporium and flung the door open, then slammed it behind her. With a sharp flick of both wrists, she forced the curtains shut, blocking out the sun's cheery light. She didn't deserve it.

The shoppe was still. Quiet. Suffocatingly so. The calm weighed down on her, pressing against her temples, her lungs. She reached for something—anything—and her fingers clasped around a mug, tea leaves wet and clumped together in its base. She hurled the mug against the wall, and the resulting *crack* as it shattered only made her feel worse.

She paced and paced, her hands wringing together or tugging at her hair. She couldn't think about any of this now. It was the day of the full moon, and she had bigger concerns. The apprehension at what Lazarus would make her do gnawed at her, but she forced herself to calm down. Breathe in, breathe out. For all she knew, it could be something simple. Maybe she would just have to desecrate a grave. Or summon a spirit. As long as she didn't have to kill anyone. She didn't know what she would do if the demon demanded a life.

But there was no point in worrying over it. She would know soon enough. She took three more deep breaths, in and out, and then slowly made her way to the staircase. One stair at a time, she ascended to the bedroom.

The bedsheets were still tousled from where she and Killian had lain, and latent desire still lingered in the air. Images of their lovemaking, of Killian atop her, thrusting and sweating, filled her mind, and she pushed away the memories. She sat at the foot of the bed, her attention trained on the altar before her. There was no hum of magic from the crystals, no glow of fire in the black skull. Only hollow eyes that stared back at her.

So she waited.

It was midday before the energy in the room stirred, alighting an ember inside the skull. Its eyes grew a smoldering orange, then blazed into a burning yellow, illuminating the dried flower petals that lay scattered across the altar.

"Daughter," the skull called in that deep, otherworldly voice. Elyse shuddered. She hated when he called her that. She didn't want to think about whether there was any truth in the word.

"Just get on with it," Elyse snarled, and the flames inside the skull grew taller, hotter.

"You have been so ill-mannered toward me of late, while I have been nothing but gracious to you," the skull, or rather Lazarus, chastised. "Need I remind you that you serve at my will?"

Heat seared Elyse's neck as a phantom flame licked at her skin. She pressed her hand to her throat, expecting to feel her flesh burning away, yet her skin was smooth and intact.

The pain vanished as suddenly as it had come on. Over her heavy breathing and pounding heart, she heard the skull laugh, low and sinister.

"Who do you serve?" it demanded.

Elyse's voice was ragged. "I serve you, Lazarus." The words tasted filthy on her tongue.

But the skull pressed its lipless jaws together in a caricature of a smile. "Good," it crooned. "I can be quite benevolent to those who serve me diligently. In fact, I would offer you a choice tonight."

Elyse's heartbeat hastened. A choice? She forced her voice to stay neutral as she asked, "What choice?" It had to be some sort of trick.

The skull seemed to relish every word as it said, "There is a townhouse in the city. You are to go to it, visit its master, and decide if he lives or dies."

Elyse sucked in a breath. Easy. Her mind was already made up. There would be no murder tonight.

"I'm done killing for you," she spat.

"We'll see about that," the skull simpered. Then it rattled off the address, which Elyse noted.

"See you in a month, daughter," the skull taunted. The blaze behind its eyes sputtered and died out, taking with it the unsettling power that had filled the room.

Elyse stared at the twin smoke tendrils that flowed from the skull's eye sockets, but she didn't truly see them. A choice. A chance to prove herself. She wouldn't have to kill anyone.

She closed her eyes and drew strength in the form of a long, slow inhale. The worst was over.

CHAPTER 57

— · —

KILLIAN

K illian sat behind his desk, elbows on the hardwood, head cradled in his hands. His eyes were closed as he tried to block out all noise and steady his flurrying thoughts.

Beside him, Manny sat on the edge of a chair, hurling terse statements across the desk. Longfellow sat on the other side, fingers pressed together, a glower on his face. "And what of the cook? The waitstaff?" he pressed.

"Nothing, not a damn thing!" Manny shouted. "We could interview the whole fucking kingdom and we wouldn't find whatever evidence you want to get Royce off your pathetic back."

His head still in his hands, Killian let out a quiet sigh. He hadn't been able to bring himself to tell Manny about Elyse, about how she was immune to truth serum—not until he could sort out his own thoughts about it. He'd been reinvigorated during the interviews, though, demanding every detail, something—anything—that might point to Royce, or at least proclaim Elyse's innocence.

But nothing had come up, not in her favor nor to her detriment.

His head ached. Not from allergies, for the yojabe had actually done the trick, but from racking his brain of every facet of the murder, every conversation he'd had with Elyse. His stomach had been in tight, unrelenting knots all day, but he refused to believe that she might actually be involved.

He knew her. She was good beneath her tough facade. She was loving and caring, and he had held her, seen her at her most vulnerable. He had witnessed her soul, had melded his own with it. She couldn't be the king's killer.

Yes, she could, chimed the voice in the back of his mind. *You have been falling in love with the very killer you seek.*

"You're not asking the right questions," Longfellow posited, a slight desperation in his voice.

"We're asking all the questions you gave us, and more!" Manny pushed back. "We can't make evidence appear out of thin air." He leaned back in his chair and crossed his arms over his chest, apparently fed up with Longfellow's demands.

Both Longfellow and Manny stared at Killian, waiting for his input. He sighed more audibly this time. Normally he would have to side with Manny. Longfellow was expecting them to extract information that might not even exist, all to save his own cowardly ass. But Killian understood the man's desperation, just for different reasons. He needed answers like he needed air.

"Let's just finish this last interview and get some sleep," he said finally. "We can go over the information in the morning with fresh eyes."

Neither Longfellow nor Manny seemed wholly satisfied with that response, but they both nodded, even as they continued to glare at one another across the desk.

"I'll be heading home then," Longfellow said as he stood from his chair. "Report to me in the morning."

Killian wanted to remind Longfellow that he didn't report to anyone except King Maelor, but he was too tired to care. "Send in the last interview," was all he said.

Longfellow made a show of donning his cloak, though it was no doubt a warm night this late into spring. Killian heard him grumble something in the hallway, and then a solemn-faced guard appeared in the threshold.

"Lieutenant," the guard greeted Killian with a straight back and respectful bow of his head.

"Have a seat, Andrew," Killian said, gesturing to the chair Longfellow had vacated. "And thank you for meeting with us."

"Anything to help," Andrew answered a bit shakily as he took his seat.

Killian knew that, as one of the guards posted outside King Cyril's chamber the night he was murdered, Andrew blamed himself. In their previous interviews, Killian assured Andrew that the king's assassination was not his fault, that he and his colleague had done everything according to protocol. Today, though, Killian was in no such mood to comfort anyone. It was an effort to keep his head from exploding, exhaustion and confusion weighing heavily on him.

"Start from the beginning," he instructed. "And spare no details."

Killian grabbed a quill and parchment to take notes while Andrew took a deep breath and began reciting the events of the night of the king's murder. None of it was new to Killian. He had heard Andrew's recollection twice now, and it never changed, never offered any information that could lead them to the killer.

Andrew had taken up his post outside the royal bedchamber at around eight in the evening. No one had entered or exited the chamber until close to midnight, when the king and queen finally retired for the night. One lady-in-waiting had helped the queen ready herself for bed, which took ten minutes, maybe fifteen. When the lady left, Andrew could hear the king snoring, so he had still been alive. No one had even come down the corridor between the time the king and queen went to bed and the time when Andrew noticed the blood seeping out from under the door.

No, no one had lit a fire for the king and queen. Andrielle always said King Cyril slept hot enough to keep her warm without a fire.

No, King Cyril had not seemed odd. He was his usual jovial self, and had bade Andrew and his comrade good night as he always did.

No, he hadn't heard anything inside the bedchamber other than faint snoring.

Manny sighed, and Killian's eyes raced over his notes. There had to be something. *Had* to. Andrew had been just on the other side of the wall while the king was murdered. He had to be the key to Elyse's salvation—or damnation.

He studied Andrew, sitting across the desk from him, his shoulders back but rigid. Tense. No doubt he had already racked his own mind, searching for some piece of information that might assist in the investigation. The young guard's eyes were hollow, as if he'd lost a sense of purpose.

"Andrew," Killian said, soft yet commanding. He set down his quill and leaned forward a bit. "Is there anything you haven't already told us? Anything at all, no matter how trivial it might seem?"

Andrew held Killian's gaze, then looked down at his hands.

Manny stirred. "What is it?"

"I . . . don't see how it would be important," Andrew stammered. "But . . ."

Killian's heart was pounding, his head slightly clearer. His palms were sweaty, and he didn't know if it was with dread or excitement.

"It might be nothing," Killian coaxed, "or it might be the precise thing we need to put the killer away."

Andrew's lips parted, but he didn't speak, and Killian gave him a small nod.

"It's probably nothing, but . . ." Andrew began. "When Queen Andrielle came to bed, I think she was wearing a different perfume."

Killian's heart sank. This was nothing, of no use to him. But he forced his face to remain neutral and let Andrew continue.

"See, my uncle owns a perfume shop in the western sector, and I used to go there all the time after school. He said I'm real good with scents." Andrew was now jabbering on, each word a stab in Killian's gut. "Normally Queen Andrielle smells like citrus—you know, like an orange or something. But that night she smelled different—sweeter. I remember thinking it smelled just like this perfume my uncle carries—a jasmine-scented one."

Manny had slouched in his chair, dejection written on his face, but Killian froze. His throat was completely dry, his lungs empty, like the air had been compressed from him.

Jasmine. He knew someone else that smelled of jasmine.

Andrew glanced between Killian and Manny, then started rambling again. "Like I said, it's probably nothing. But maybe it's a clue? You could ask her ladies if she changed her perfume? Because if she didn't, then what smelled like jasmine? Maybe it was an ingredient in the spell? Or—or maybe . . ."

Killian hardly heard Andrew's words before he trailed off. He could hardly hear his own thoughts over the pounding of his heart.

It couldn't be a coincidence. And yet it had to be. Elyse couldn't be involved. Hundreds—perhaps thousands—of people wore jasmine-scented perfume.

And yet thousands of people didn't have access to the ingredients used in the spell to kill the king. Thousands of people didn't wield that kind of power. Thousands of people hadn't lied and pretended to swear their innocence with truth serum.

"You're right," Manny said, startling Killian from his racing thoughts. "It is nothing."

Killian forced himself to nod, to pretend to agree with Manny. He would have to sort this out on his own—at least for now.

Andrew dropped his gaze to his lap again, shame reddening his features. "I'm sorry for wasting your time," he said, defeated.

"Not at all," Killian replied, his voice ragged. He cleared his throat and then added, "Thank you for sharing that with us. You never know what detail will be the tipping point." He tried to smile at Andrew, but his muscles refused to listen.

Andrew gave a weak nod, and Manny dismissed him. Killian simply stared straight ahead.

When the door to the office shut behind Andrew, Manny blew out a long breath and ran his hands through his hair. "What a waste of a day," he sighed. "I'm starved. Want me to have a servant bring—"

"Ask the queen's ladies if she changed her perfume," Killian demanded, cutting Manny off.

Manny froze, one hand still tangled in his blond hair. "You're joking, right?"

Killian didn't look at his friend as he stood, gathered up his notes, and shoved them into a satchel. "Just do it," he barked. He strode past Manny and toward the door, then yanked it open.

"Where are you going?" Manny called after him.

But Killian had already stormed into the corridor, his feet dragging him toward the answers he sought.

CHAPTER 58

—·—

ELYSE

Elyse sat perched on the roof of a three-story building, watching the townhouse across the street—the townhouse that bore the address the demon had given her, where she was to either kill the man who resided there, or let him live.

It was an easy choice. She would never kill again if she could manage it—if it would help redeem her soul. As she sat beneath the sunset, she longed for peace. For simplicity. For happiness that didn't come with a high price.

Tonight would be the first step in that direction.

Across the street, on the short stairs leading up to the front door of the townhome, a guard in all black shifted his feet. It was the only movement he'd made in the last hour—a mere shuffling. Otherwise, he'd stood his post silently, still as a statue.

Elyse again considered whose residence she watched. Whoever it was must have been someone important, to have a guard posted outside their home, even in daylight. She didn't dare approach the home until she had a better idea of what, or who, awaited her.

Though she tried to focus on her task, her mind kept wandering back to Killian. She wondered how his interviews were going. Had he found something to help pin the blame on Royce? Or worse, had he discovered something that would implicate her?

No, he couldn't have. She had executed her plan with utter perfection, leaving no trace behind, no evidence that could link her to the king's murder.

But that didn't abate the worry that congealed in her stomach.

She should have told him. It would be best if he heard it from her, instead of somehow finding out on his own.

Or she could live the rest of her life with this terrible secret gnawing away at her.

Later, she told herself. *I'll worry about this later.*

For a carriage had just rolled up the street and slowed before the townhouse. Elyse held her breath as the carriage came to a stop. She heard the door open, and a few words exchanged, but she couldn't see anyone yet. Her fingers trembled slightly, anticipating a potential foe. She balled them into fists to steady herself.

Finally, the carriage drove off. A figure ascended the stairs to the townhome, a cloak billowing around them in a cloud of arrogance. In the fading light of dusk, Elyse could make out the guard's slight nod, and then he stepped aside to allow the figure—a man—to enter the home. Elyse narrowed her eyes—and then gasped.

The man who arrived in the carriage, the one who now entered the townhome, had a receding hairline combed sloppily across his head, and a large beak of a nose. She would never forget those horrid features, nor the face that had sneered at her from across a gaudy, oversized desk.

This was Longfellow's home.

Dumbfounded, Elyse continued to stare at the residence. The guard made no motion to leave. Candlelight flickered in a room on the bottom floor of the townhome—perhaps a study or a sitting room. Elyse couldn't make out any features of the room, or see who took their leisure there.

She realized, then, that her heart was pounding ceaselessly. Her magic writhed within her, yearning to dole itself out on such a disgusting excuse of man.

This changes nothing, Elyse reminded herself. She was not going to spill any blood tonight.

And yet a satisfying image of her strangling the life out of Longfellow slipped into her mind, inspiring her magic.

The door to the townhome opened, and a portly woman waddled out of the house. She bid the guard goodnight and then sidled off down the street.

Probably the housekeeper.

Was Longfellow married? Elyse racked her brain for anything Killian had told her about the magistrate. His wife had passed, she recalled, and his housekeeper seemed ignorant to Longfellow's heinous pastimes. Or perhaps she turned a blind eye.

So Longfellow was likely home alone. The idea excited her as she raced through the possibilities of how she could make him pay for his treatment of Nina, and likely many others.

No—no she couldn't do anything of the sort. Besides, the guard posted outside would complicate things if she wanted to punish Longfellow. She would simply knock on the door, chat for a bit, and then leave. And that would be it—ritual over.

She made her way down the stairs of the building and then across the street. The guard tracked her every movement as she stepped closer and closer to the townhome. She forced herself to smile—to appear nonthreatening.

"Hello," she called to the guard in the most even and polite voice she could muster. "I'm here to speak to the magistrate, please."

The guard barely looked her over, then resumed staring straight ahead. "No visitors," he grumbled.

"Please," Elyse entreated, placing a hand on her chest. "It's very important. It's about—"

But she didn't get a chance to complete whatever lie was surely about to roll off her tongue, for the front door opened, and Longfellow stood across the threshold.

Elyse wanted to hiss at him, but she schooled her disgust into an expression of concern.

"Hello, Ms. Crenshaw," he purred as he stared down at her. He arched one brow, as if daring her to squirm, to retort, to do something that would challenge him.

"Longfellow—Magistrate," she stammered, and she didn't have to fake her breathlessness. Seeing him so close, that nasty sneer on his face, she was drunk with bloodlust. "Can I speak with you for a moment?"

A slight twitch of his eye was the only indication of Longfellow's surprise. Then he nodded to the guard and beckoned Elyse inside.

In and out. No blood, she reminded herself as she mounted the stairs and crossed the threshold. *In and out. No blood.*

Longfellow closed the door behind her, enclosing them together in the foyer. He slid a hand along Elyse's lower back as he maneuvered past her. Elyse had to tell herself why she shouldn't chop off his hand.

You're not that person anymore.

How would you explain it to Killian?

It is not your job to punish the unjust.

"To what do I owe the pleasure, Ms. Crenshaw?"

Longfellow stepped in closer—too close—as he crooned his question. He smelled of alcohol and sweat.

"I . . . I wanted to know how the interviews went," she quickly lied. "And to let you know that—if there's anything I can do to help, I'm happy to do so."

Longfellow didn't say anything, but his eyes raked over her for a long, uncomfortable moment. Elyse forced herself to remain still, to keep her head high. Just a few more minutes, and then she could be out of here.

Then Longfellow stepped away and opened a door off the foyer. "There is actually something that you, as a witch, could help me with," he said as he held the door open for her.

"Oh," she breathed, then quickly nodded. "Okay."

She took a few hesitant steps toward the room and peered inside. Several candles were lit, illuminating an ordinary study, yet her body was screaming at her to run—to leave *now*. She told herself she was just on edge, eager to be done with this whole night. All she had to do was help Longfellow with whatever he needed—five minutes, tops—and then she could go. She loosed a breath and took another step, entering the room.

At the other end of the large room was a desk and an old, well-worn chair. Disheveled books lined shelves along the wall, and papers littered the desk and even the floor. As she moved to the center of the room, a plush rug cushioning her steps, she couldn't help but think of how much Killian would detest this slovenly space.

"What is it you need help with?" she asked, her anxiety somewhat dissipated. Nothing seemed amiss.

Longfellow shut the door and then picked up a glass that still had a healthy pour of amber liquid inside. He swished it in lazy circles. "I've been looking into defense mechanisms, particularly against magic wielders, should Royce decide to attack."

"Okay," Elyse said, nodding as she thought. "I can help with that. I can train you on making shields, maybe give you some potions for protection—"

"No," Longfellow cut her off. He walked along the perimeter of the room, those hungry eyes never leaving Elyse. "I've been looking into other methods. Traps, if you will."

Dread seeped into Elyse's veins as a chill ran down her back.

"How can I help?" she asked, trying to sound braver than she felt.

Longfellow merely smirked and drained the rest of his glass. When he finished, he wiped his mouth with the back of his hand and leveled his gaze on Elyse. "You already have."

CHAPTER 59

—·—

ELYSE

Everything seemed to stop.

Time.

The air in the room.

The blood in Elyse's veins.

Longfellow continued to smirk at her, his pallid face triumphant. He was a glutton, devouring her confusion like a saccharine dessert.

"What do you mean?" she finally managed to say.

Slowly Longfellow lowered his gaze from her face to the rug on which she stood. He knelt down and carefully lifted a corner of the rug, peeling it back to reveal the edge of a circle drawn in chalk along the wood floor. Elyse recognized symbols that bordered the circle, magical symbols of entrapment and incapacitation.

No, no, no.

She took a step back, then another. As she lifted her foot to step back again, it stopped. It wouldn't move any farther. She felt no wall, saw no barrier, yet her body refused to move backward.

She couldn't be trapped here, not with this sadist. Sweat gathered on her brow, and her hand shot to her cloak pocket, fumbling around for a transportation potion. She gripped it, and in one smooth motion freed it from her pocket and threw it to the ground.

The glass shattered, but no blue smoke erupted. No darkness encompassed her.

She was still in the study.

Longfellow barked a laugh, the sound cruel. "Oh Elyse," he taunted. "Can't you feel it? As long as you stand in that circle, your magic is depleted."

That's when she felt it—a numbness that began at her fingertips and was now traveling its way up her arms, through her core. It wasn't the same as when she had been put in those shackles. Then, she had felt a mere absence of her powers. Now it felt as though her magic was a poison, infecting her body. She was dizzy, the room spinning about her, and her limbs felt heavy.

Longfellow laughed again. "You're bound to the circle, powerless, until I release you."

Her breathing was quick and erratic. "Help!" she screamed. "Help me!" Surely the guard posted outside would hear her cries and come free her.

"Stupid whore," Longfellow growled with satisfaction. "You think I wouldn't ensure that this room is soundproof? No one can hear you scream."

He was lying, he had to be. Her eyes darted to the window, to the door, praying that the guard outside would appear and save her. But there was no movement on the other side of the window. No noise in the foyer. No one was coming for her.

Focus, she had to focus. But her mind was fuzzy, and she struggled to control her muscles.

A knife. She had a knife in her boot. She stooped down to pull the knife free, blood rushing to her head. She stumbled a step, then inhaled deeply as she righted herself and stood, knife in hand, poised to attack.

Longfellow smiled—the smile of a predator who enjoyed watching his prey fight back. He circled around her, and Elyse tracked every movement, pivoting with him, her arm shaking as it held the knife out before her. Her eyelids felt heavy, and she shook her head, trying to clear her mind.

Longfellow used the moment to lunge. Elyse swiped with the blade, but the movement was slow and desperate, and Longfellow caught her wrist easily. He twisted his grip, and pain exploded through her arm as he squeezed tight. She cried out, releasing her hold on the knife. It clattered to the floor, landing on the bare wood just outside the rug.

"That was too easy," Longfellow snarled as he, too, looked at the knife that lay out of her reach.

But *he* was still standing on the rug.

Elyse kicked with all her might, her foot finding its mark between the magistrate's legs. He doubled over and stepped back, exiting the circle. He groaned and cursed, and Elyse tried swiping at him, punching him, kicking him, but he was out of reach.

Still bent over, Longfellow looked at her with dark, ominous eyes. "You've been a bad girl."

Faster than Elyse could comprehend in her fragile state, Longfellow entered the circle and backhanded her across the face. She spun and fell to the floor, landing on her hip with a shattering *crunch*. Something sharp dug into her side, and she realized she had landed on the spare transportation potion that remained in her pocket, where it was now broken into a hundred tiny pieces.

Her face felt hot, and raw. It throbbed as she glared up at Longfellow. But he wasted no time making his next move.

With sickening lust in his eyes, he stepped over her and grasped her hair, pulling hard. Elyse screamed. She clawed at his hands as he pulled her to her feet, her fingernails tearing away skin until his arms were scraped and bleeding. She flailed her arms wildly, kicking her feet, hoping to inflict any sort of damage. She must have hit something, for Longfellow buckled and grunted.

With fumbling movements, Elyse maneuvered herself behind him and hooked the crook of her elbow under his chin. They collapsed together to the floor, but Elyse held her grip, her arm tight around his throat.

Longfellow scratched frantically at her arm, trying to free his airway. His mouth opened and closed but only a choking, rattling sound escaped.

With her free hand, Elyse reached into her pocket and grabbed a handful of broken glass—the tiny pieces from the crushed vial. She shoved the glass into his mouth and then forced his jaw shut.

Longfellow bucked his head, jerking his whole body. Elyse tried to keep her hold, but he bucked his head again, the back of his skull making contact with her forehead.

Pain multiplied exponentially as she released him and clutched her hand to her face. Vomit threatened its way up her throat as anguish and dizziness took hold. The room was a blur, Longfellow a mere fuzzy shape. Every muscle ached, longing to rest, to just lay still, forever. Even thinking was too much effort.

She was vaguely aware of Longfellow edging closer to her, until his body hovered above hers. He took her wrist in one hand and pinned it to the floor above her head. She tried to resist, but it felt as if the air was heavy, weighing her down. Longfellow grabbed her other wrist and brought it up above her head, pinning both arms in one hand. He lowered his face, pressing his cheek against hers, and whispered in a raspy voice, "I like it when they struggle." Blood and spittle sprayed from his mouth, and Elyse cringed away from him.

She felt Longfellow press his hardness against her, confirming his words to be true.

Fight! Don't give up! her mind urged her. She tried. She tried wriggling her wrists free of his grasp, tried turning her body away from him, but nothing worked. Longfellow nuzzled his face against her neck, and he pressed his lips to her skin. She gagged. This couldn't be happening. She just needed to do *something*.

Her teeth found his ear, and she bit down—hard. His flesh tore open, his warm blood spilling into her mouth.

Longfellow screamed and relinquished his hold. He was on his feet in a flash, cursing and fleeing the circle. His hand was pressed to his ear, and blood poured down his neck onto his white shirt.

Elyse spat out the piece of ear she had bitten clean off, and then slowly rose to her feet. This was it. She'd gotten him off her. She couldn't let him pin her again. With a deep breath, she steadied herself, but the dizziness only abated slightly.

Longfellow glared at her, red faced and seething. "You fucking bitch!" he roared. He reached for a glass bottle, gripped the neck, and broke it against a bookshelf. Amber liquid splashed onto the floor. "I'll cut your fucking throat," he promised as he held the sharp, jagged edge of the broken bottle toward her.

Think, Elyse demanded of herself. This might be her last shot. She needed a weapon. Her eyes searched frantically, to the knife discarded just outside the rug, to the spilled liquid creeping its way across the floor.

That. That was the key.

She watched as the liquid inched closer to the rug. She needed to stall.

"Why do you hate me?" she blurted out, the only thing her feeble mind could come up with at the moment.

Longfellow spat on the ground as blood continued to trickle down his neck. "Because you think you're better than me."

Elyse shook her head, trying to comprehend. "I don't—"

"You all do!" Longfellow shouted. "My wife—my mother! All you whores are the same."

Elyse didn't have the energy to pity him. She glanced quickly down at the liquid that had finally reached the rug and was now slowly seeping its way into the fabric. If she could just keep him talking a little longer, the liquid might erase some of the chalk outline—just enough to get her powers back. She prayed to any god that would listen that her plan would work.

"I don't think I'm better than you," she breathed, trying to focus. "You're a very powerful, important man."

"Don't mock me!" Longfellow snarled, stepping closer and shoving the broken bottle forward.

Elyse held up her hands defensively. "I'm not! I swear. I—"

She felt it then. A tiny pinprick in her fingertip. The circle was beginning to dissolve. Her magic was returning, ever so slowly.

"Don't you see it?" she asked desperately. "Don't you feel what's between us?"

She took a pleading step forward as more magic returned to her body. Longfellow glared at her skeptically.

"I came here tonight to see you," she lied. "Not because of Royce or the case."

Longfellow cocked his head to the side and lowered his weapon an inch. "Really?" he asked in a raspy voice.

Elyse held his gaze. Her hand was now tingling, alive with magic and power, as Longfellow stared at her, anxiously awaiting her answer.

"No," she said flatly. She flexed her fingers, and her knife flew to her hand. Before Longfellow could react, before he could even realize what was happening, she stepped forward, out of the circle, and stabbed the knife into his fleshy throat.

Longfellow dropped the broken bottle to the floor as both hands clutched at his neck. He sank against the wall, gasping and gurgling as he took his last choking breaths.

"*All* women are better than you," Elyse spat as she towered over him, watching him struggle.

The light faded from his eyes, and his hands fell to his sides, limp.

Her task was complete.

Chapter 60

Elyse

Elyse's body still ached, even as she felt her magic slowly returning. The moment Longfellow had gone still, she collapsed to the floor, her breathing ragged. She clutched her still-pounding head in both hands, hands that were covered with blood. Blood she had spilled.

But she couldn't think of that now. She had to gather enough magic to cover up what she'd done, and then she had to get the hell away.

For ten minutes, or perhaps ten hours, she lay on the floor, the hardwood pressing against her aching body. She finally forced herself to stir, and dragged herself from the study, through the foyer, and out the front door.

The guard immediately turned to her, and his eyes widened, no doubt at the sight of so much blood. Before he could even place a hand on the pommel of his short sword, Elyse had lifted her own hand, emitting a faint, shimmering light.

"You will not remember seeing me," she commanded in a tired voice.

The guard's eyes glazed over, and then he nodded absentmindedly and returned to his post, facing straight ahead toward the street.

The memory charm had demanded every bit of Elyse's returned powers, and she swayed before steadying herself and trudging down the stairs. She had no transportation potions left; she would have to walk home. At least darkness had settled over the city, making her bloodstained hands and clothes less noticeable.

She stuck to the shadows as she wended her way through the streets, carefully selecting paths that would be less occupied at this time of night. It was all she could do to put one foot in front of the other, to focus on remaining undetected. A blessing, really, that she could keep her mind occupied instead of despairing over what had just taken place.

The bustling quieted and the reek of the city dissipated as Elyse made her way toward the dirt road leading north through the forest. Yet as the city lights faded from sight, the full moon hung overhead, taunting her, a hideous reminder of who she was, and who she belonged to.

After an hour of walking, her magic had restored itself almost entirely, and she allowed herself to wander off the path and through the forest. The thick trees blocked the view of the moon, but Elyse still felt its dreadful presence weighing down on her.

The trickle of a stream echoed in her ears, and she realized she had led herself to the creek—the very same creek where she had gone after killing Keliah. Like a sailor drawn to a siren, Elyse made her way to its running waters and, without removing her boots, stepped into the stream.

Just as the water flowed over her feet, anger and hopelessness flowed from her chest, down her arms, her legs, up into the furthest reaches of her mind. Lazarus had played her. He had known everything—that she didn't want to kill, that she would go into Longfellow's home determined to let him live, and that she would fail.

She was a prisoner, destined to live the rest of her life doing whatever the demon demanded of her. And no matter what, no matter how much she wanted to pretend like she didn't have a choice, the blood was still on *her* hands.

She looked down at her hands then, coated red, cut from when she had clutched the broken glass. She touched a hand to her face, her skin hot and swollen from where Longfellow had slapped her.

She felt the first tear as it spilled.

She didn't use her magic to remove her clothes. With aching muscles, she discarded her cloak then peeled off her tunic. Her leggings and boots followed, and then her undergarments. She sank, completely bare, into the creek's waters. She let her tears become one with the creek, let its cold waters numb her.

She was vaguely aware, through the magic of her wards, that there was a presence in her cottage. Killian, she realized, as she felt the familiarity of his presence. He must be waiting for her to return from her ritual, a ritual he didn't truly grasp.

She couldn't face him, not yet. So she stayed in the water, her hair flowing around her shoulders, until the first rays of morning light touched the horizon.

Finally, Elyse roused herself from the creek bed, and with pruny fingers, she used her replenished magic to dry herself. With another wave of her hand, she burned the clothes she'd been wearing and replaced them with a simple, clean tunic and leggings. She left her feet bare, and she didn't dare heal the cuts on her hands or the bruise forming on her face. They would serve as reminders of her actions.

The earth was warm beneath her feet as she padded toward the cottage. She longed for a mug of tea, and then to curl into bed for days. Perhaps Killian would stay and sleep beside her for a few hours. The thought was both comforting and a sting to her treacherous heart.

As she entered the cottage, she spotted Killian sitting at the enormous workbench. His head snapped up to look at her, and exhaustion marred his face. Had he stayed up all night waiting for her?

"Hi," she croaked as she closed the door.

Killian smiled and stood. "Hi," he replied, his voice sounding as tired as she felt.

"Have you been here all night?"

Killian nodded, then met her halfway across the shoppe.

Elyse moved to embrace him, to steady herself against his solid frame, but she took in his face, noting the grave look in his eyes. Something was wrong.

"What is it?" she pressed.

Killian shook his head, but the solemnity in his eyes didn't falter. "Just tired," he said casually. He lifted a hand and gently touched her bruising cheek, his brows creasing.

"It's nothing," Elyse quickly lied. "I'll explain later." Though, she didn't know how she would actually explain it.

Killian nodded and let his hand fall. "I got you something," he said, his voice breaking slightly. "Close your eyes."

Elyse obeyed, if only for the brief comfort of closing her tired eyes, even just for a moment. Her heart raced as she wondered about what was plaguing him, and what he had in store for her.

She felt him take her hand, running his thumb over the back of it, and then she felt the cool kiss of metal on her wrist.

And then on the other wrist.

"Elyse Crenshaw," Killian stated as she opened her eyes. "You are under arrest for the murder of King Cyril."

Chapter 61

Elyse

"Killian," Elyse breathed. It was all she could do. She couldn't move, couldn't think. The shackles had bound her magic, leaving her utterly helpless. But worst of all was the pain in Killian's expression, the tremor of his hands that held fast to her chains. He patted her down for weapons or potions, like he would any other criminal.

"Killian," she said again, more pleading this time.

"Don't," he warned. He closed his eyes for a moment, and when he opened them again, rage had replaced all anguish. "You can't even deny it, can you?"

She couldn't—wouldn't lie to him, not in this moment. She owed him the truth, should have told him long ago. "I can explain—" she began, but his vicious inhale cut her off. He didn't speak, instead merely stared at her with utter hatred, shaking his head.

Her heart broke completely.

Tears spilled down her cheeks, but she did not wipe them away. Her chest heaved with every painful breath, as if even the air punished her for her betrayal. How many more breaths would she take? Surely she would be executed within the week—perhaps even within the day.

And what would happen then? Would Lazarus bring her back? Or would he finally allow her to be at peace? She didn't know whether to be terrified or relieved.

Yet as she looked at Killian, tears brimming in his golden eyes, she felt regret, pure and simple. Regret that they had not met in another life, where they were free to be together, to be happy. They stood so close together, his hands still gripping her shackles, yet he had never been farther from her reach.

When Killian finally spoke, his voice was shaky. "You were in the room the whole time, weren't you?"

Elyse didn't reply, her throat too dry for words.

"I stayed up all night," he went on. "I reviewed the ledger," he said, glancing at the leather-bound ledger that always lay on the worktable.

"But," Elyse started to say. How could he review the ledger? The entire thing was coded.

Killian let out a dry, melancholy laugh. "You basically handed me the key. Mr. Grayson buys the same thing every month. It wasn't hard to decipher the code from his regular order, and then find last month's. And what would you know, the same ingredients used for the spell that killed King Cyril were taken from your inventory on the day of the full moon."

Elyse closed her eyes. She wanted to put her shackled hands over her ears. She couldn't bear to hear the pain in his voice.

"But the ingredients weren't sold to anyone," he said, his tone deadly serious. "They were merely written off as a loss."

Her chin wobbled as grief, fear, and self-loathing threatened to overtake her.

"You made yourself invisible, didn't you?" he went on, louder this time. "You followed the king and queen into the bedchamber, waited for them to fall asleep, and then cast the spell. And then you waited until the guards sounded the alarm, and you slipped out unseen in all the chaos."

Elyse looked away, unable to respond. Her vision blurred as more tears flooded her eyes.

Killian sighed. "And the ingredients? How did they end up at Royce's estate?"

Elyse swallowed and did her best to choke out an answer. "I brought them. I gave them to Tanner—when I tripped."

The words were acrid on her tongue. She thought confessing would be cathartic, that a weight would be lifted from her, but there was nothing worse than this.

"Dammit, Elyse!" Killian shouted. He let go of her shackles as he spun around and punched the nearest object—a tall wooden bookcase. She shuddered at the sound of his bones slamming against the hardwood, and Killian leaned his head against the bookshelf, grimacing from the pain.

She longed for her magic, just to heal him, to ease this moment for him in any way. Her eyes darted around the tables and shelves around her, searching for something that she could offer him to heal in lieu of her magic, but her gaze settled on one thing.

Transportation potions. A whole shelf of them.

If she could grab one, maybe she could use it later, once she'd freed herself of these shackles.

She glanced at Killian, who was flexing and tightening his hand, his knuckles bloodied and swollen. He wasn't looking at her.

Silently, she slipped a potion off the shelf and tucked it into her waistband.

Killian whirled, and for a moment she thought he'd seen her or heard her, but his mouth hung ajar, like he was mustering up the courage to say something.

"Please, Killian," she said before he could speak. "Please, just listen—I'll tell you everything."

He moved in close, grabbed her chain, and stooped down so they were eye level. "Don't bother," he snarled. "I won't believe a fucking word you say."

Then he spun her around toward the door and pulled her toward it.

No, she needed more time. She needed to explain, to make him listen to her. If he just heard her side of things, he would understand, and they could figure something out. She tried to resist, to make her feet heavier, but Killian was so much stronger than her.

He shoved her out the door and into the soft sunlight. Was it truly still morning? Had it not been a lifetime ago that she had returned to the cottage, weary from her task?

Was this not just a terrible nightmare?

She glanced back at Killian, who had one hand on her shoulder, pushing her forward down the dirt path. His jaw was set, his eyes narrowed and furious.

No, this was no nightmare. And he would not believe her, even if she told him the entire truth.

He kept pushing her further down the dirt path, and then veered east into the woods. Elyse didn't speak, instead focusing all her energy on developing a plan. But without her magic, she was impotent. Killian could physically overpower her, especially as exhausted as she was. She needed a weapon and the element of surprise.

But she couldn't summon a weapon without her magic, and Killian was unarmed. His usual short sword didn't hang at his hip, and his dagger was missing as well.

But a knife? Hadn't he confessed that he always concealed a knife in his boot?

Her mind was racing now, frantically grasping at ways to procure the knife, when she saw something up ahead in the trees.

A lot of something.

Two, maybe three dozen men, a hundred yards ahead, many with arrows trained in their direction. Killian had called in a small army to bring her in, and he had set them up just outside the wards, where they would remain undetected.

She stopped short, and Killian nearly ran into her.

"Move," he growled.

But she was frozen. She couldn't take another step toward them. From this far out, with the trees between them, none of the archers would have a clean shot at her. Whatever she was going to do, she had to do it now.

Killian pushed her shoulder hard, and Elyse let the force knock her to the ground. Her palms and knees stung as they landed on thorny brush, and she let out a whimper.

"Please," she sobbed, still on her hands and knees.

"Get up," Killian snapped, nudging her leg with his boot.

She heard the men mumbling to each other in the distance. "Hold your fire!" someone shouted.

"*Please*," she gasped. "I can't."

"Get *up*," Killian demanded. He moved to nudge her again, harder this time, but Elyse was ready.

She caught his ankle with one hand, while she plunged her other hand down into his boot. Her fingers felt the cool touch of metal, and she could have screamed with joy, but she had to move quickly. She pulled the knife free from his boot as Killian stooped down to grab at her. He managed to get a handful of her hair, but his grip wasn't tight enough, and she slammed her forehead against his face.

Killian released her immediately as his body went stumbling backward. Elyse barely caught sight of the blood gushing from his nose before she bolted.

She was exhausted and shackled and frenzied, but she knew this forest better than anyone. And, if she was lucky, Killian would be disoriented enough to buy her some time.

Her feet, though bare, moved efficiently over tree roots and fallen branches. She heard shouting far behind her, but didn't hear anyone pursuing her. Not yet.

But she would have to get these shackles off to get away.

There was a bank to the south, an old, dried-up creek bed where she could hide for a short time. She sped toward it, running faster than she ever knew she could. Then again, her freedom, her life, had never depended on it before.

Finally, she reached the bank and ducked down, hiding behind its ledge. Her breathing was frantic, ragged, but she had no time to calm down.

It would be okay. It wouldn't hurt for long. She had done this before—sort of.

Elyse rolled up the left sleeve of her tunic. She clutched the knife in her right hand, forcing it to remain steady, and then she pressed it to her left wrist—and sliced.

Chapter 62

Killian

Killian couldn't see anything. First because of the dizzying blackness that overtook him as Elyse's forehead collided with his nose. Then because his eyes were watering so badly, his vision was completely blurred. His nose was surely broken, and blood poured from both nostrils, flowing into his mouth and down his chin and neck.

He could barely hear shouting and footsteps over the pounding of his head. His mind was swimming as Manny and two other guards approached, weapons drawn.

"Which way did she go, Lieutenant?" one of them asked.

Killian grimaced at the question. He didn't know. By the time he'd somewhat collected himself, she was out of sight.

He glanced up at Manny, hating the pity in his friend's eyes. Manny extended a hand to him, but Killian ignored it, standing on his own.

"Give me that," he demanded, grabbing a bow and quiver of arrows from one of his men. "Spread out!" he roared. "Track her! She's still shackled—she can't get far."

"Aye, Lieutenant," the men replied. They ran off to relay the order to the rest of the guards.

Manny looked as if he was about to say something, but Killian didn't give him the chance.

His head still reeling and his vision still blurred, he ran back the way he'd brought Elyse. He kept an eye on the grass, looking for signs of disturbance to see where she might have gone, but his nose was still bleeding, making it hard to breathe. Running was difficult enough—running and tracking was nearly impossible.

But he had to be the one to find her. He had to be the one to bring her in. She'd made a damn fool of him, getting close to him to manipulate the investigation, winning his heart. He would never forgive himself for the rest of his life, but if he could catch her, if he could ensure she got what she deserved, then he could at least find some solace in that.

So he ran, bow at the ready, through the forest.

He heard her before he saw her.

Muffled screams came from somewhere up ahead. Whatever was happening, it was torture—pure agony. He slowed his pace and pulled an arrow from the quiver, and took a deep breath as he approached what looked like a dry creek bed. He moved to the side, searching for an angle where he could sneak up on her undetected, but there was nothing. She let out another roar of anguish, and he hoped that whatever she was doing would keep her distracted. He peered over the ledge of the bank.

Nothing would ever have prepared him for what he saw.

Blood—more blood than he'd seen in all his training. It covered Elyse's entire left side of her body. She gripped her left hand, breathing hard through clenched teeth. And her skin . . .

It was melding itself back together—where the shackle should have been on her wrist.

Killian spotted that shackle, dangling freely from her right wrist.

Gods above. She'd cut off her hand to rid herself of the chain, and was now reattaching it—with her liberated magic.

His stomach churned, imagining the pain she had endured, the amount of desperation she must have felt. The whole scene was so horrific, so shocking—

He'd wasted enough time.

"Stop!" he shouted.

Elyse snapped her bloodied face up to him, her eyes wide. Killian knocked the arrow into the groove, but Elyse, in her wild desperation, moved faster. She screamed—either in pain or terror—as she flung both hands toward him, and a gust of wind sent him staggering back.

Killian quickly righted himself, but Elyse ran, her hair billowing after her. An iridescent shield formed around her, shimmering where the light reached between the trees. Killian stayed atop the bank, tracking her in his sights, his arrow trained on her.

"Over here!" he bellowed, calling his men to him. He heard them shouting, running toward him.

Elyse didn't make it far before her shield started to falter. It disappeared and reappeared, too quickly for Killian to take his shot.

"Over here!" he called again. Sweat ran down his brow to his cheek, mixing with the blood coating his chin.

He wouldn't let her get away. Wouldn't take an eye off of her. She had nowhere to go, not all the way out here.

The shield faded again, and Killian pulled back his string, but the iridescence returned, protecting her.

She was fidgeting with something, reaching for something at her hip. He saw her hand clasped around a small, blue object as the chain swung wildly from her wrist.

No. No, no, *no*.

How had she gotten a transportation potion? She was running toward the edge of the wards.

Killian swore and took off after her, sprinting across the creek bed and darting between trees. Her shield flickered and disappeared, but not for long enough.

"Stop!" he cried out.

Elyse was weak, drained of blood, and he was gaining on her. But there was no marker to indicate the edge of the wards. It could be anywhere.

"Stop!" he screamed again as he halted in his tracks. She was now only fifty yards ahead. If he was going to stop her, he was going to have to take a shot.

He steadied the arrow, ready for the next time the shield dropped.

He didn't have to wait long.

The shield fell, and Killian loosed the arrow.

But Elyse's hand was already in motion, hurling the vial at the ground.

Blue smoke erupted, blanketing the crowded space between the trees. Killian held his breath as he waited, watching and listening for any sign of Elyse.

But as the smoke cleared, there was no sign of her, nor the arrow.

Epilogue

The citizens of Rhodan amassed for the funeral—so many that the cathedral was filled to capacity, and hundreds were left to stand in the streets outside, paying tribute to the deceased. The morning was chilly, and people huddled together, dressed in their finest blacks.

Killian stood among them, though he didn't mourn. The world would undoubtedly be a better place without Longfellow—but that didn't mean the magistrate should have been murdered in his own home, left to bleed out like an animal.

His housekeeper had found him the morning after the full moon, his body cold, his throat stabbed. The guard posted outside Longfellow's townhome hadn't seen or heard anything suspicious, which was all the evidence Killian needed. Elyse was responsible for the magistrate's death; there was no doubt in his mind. She hadn't spent the full moon doing a ridiculous dancing ritual with Sera, she had spent the night murdering Longfellow.

Killian turned up the collar of his jerkin against the brisk wind as he looked at the people around him. The courtiers were allowed entry into the cathedral, so it was mostly common folk who had gathered in the streets. Bakers, butchers, small merchants—people who had likely never met Longfellow but had been told that he was an important figure, a loss to be mourned.

Killian sneered. He should have been inside the cathedral, sitting in the front row with the esteemed members of the Royal Guard. Instead he had been banished to stand outside, a dishonored soldier.

He couldn't think about that now though. He kept his eyes peeled, watching, waiting for her. No one had seen or heard from Elyse since she escaped him that day on her property, but Killian knew that killers had a habit of attending the funerals of their victims, and a killer she was. He scanned the faces of the crowd, searching for dark, cunning eyes and silvery blonde hair. If she was there, he didn't see her.

It was possible, of course, that she had been mortally wounded by his arrow. She could have bled out days ago, wherever it was that she had magicked herself. Killian didn't think so though.

He abandoned his position, wading his way through the crowd of mourners.

No, Elyse was alive and in hiding, and he would find her. It may not be today, it may not be tomorrow, but he would find her, whatever the cost.

Ready for More?

Follow the QR code below to access my LinkTree, where you can join my newsletter, follow me on social media, and find out more about the next book!

If you enjoyed this book, please leave a review on Amazon and/or Goodreads.

ACKNOWLEDGMENTS

First and foremost, I would like to thank Linda Mueller, Jade Austin, Zian Schafer, and Lorna House. These four have held my hand through so much - guiding me, letting me vent, and inspiring me.

To my amazing beta readers - Karina Mancillas, Hannah Combs, Jacki, Brittanie Wing, Ruby Rivera, Gracie C., Shannon Maillet, Ashlee Lynch, Holly LeBeau, Sam, Hayley W., and Bri Kirk. Not only did your feedback make the book so much better, but you gave me the first taste of joy as an author, fueling me forward. I am forever grateful.

Special thanks to Cedric Daniel A. Vitangcol (Instagram: @designs by.ced) for the beautiful cover. Fun fact - I actually fell in love with the cover before I even had the idea for the story! I bought the whole triology, and the rest was history. Thank you, Ced.

Evie, you did an amazing job bringing my map to life. I'm so blessed to have you. (Instagram: @thebakingbooklover_)

Also, thank you again to Shannon Maillet and Emerald Frost Design (Instagram: @emeraldfrostdesign) for making me a stunning trailer!

Printed in Great Britain
by Amazon

36027910R00209